The Pig And I

Erica Adams

First printed January 1998
Reprinted October 1998

Little Crow Publishing
32 Molyneux Park Road
Tunbridge Wells
Kent TN4 8DY

A CIP Catalogue Record for this book is available from the British Library.

Printed and bound in Great Britain.

ISBN 0 9532239 0 6

THE PIG AND I is a crackling funny book with plenty of sauce (and we don't mean apple).

Do not lend it to a friend. It'll be a boar when it isn't returned and you want to get your head down in the trough to re-read it.

Instead, trotter down to your local bookshop and buy another and make two people exsowdingly, exporkingly, exFredaingly happy. (Your friend and the author, snort, snort!)

SPECIAL THANKS TO

KEN PHILLIPS, an old friend from Bushey, for his invaluable help in explaining Planning Application Procedures - and things that could possibly go wrong.

AL ZUCKERMAN, author of Writing the Blockbuster Novel, for his constructive advice and encouragement.

THE TUNBRIDGE WELLS WRITERS, for all their help and for being so good at laughing.

LISA AND PETER MARTIN, for being kind enough to read it in its draft form. And for Peter's thoughtfulness in giving me Al Zuckerman's book, so starting the train of events that led to this novel.

JANICE MOFFITT, my daughter, for her patience, time and input in designing the cover, and for spurring me on.

DAVID ADAMS, my son, for his helpful suggestions, unflagging interest, and business advice.

MAURICE, my husband, for the five o'clock aperitifs and the cooking of truly delicious meals, allowing me time to pound at the keys. And for his constant, loving encouragement in whatever I do.

LARGE WHITE PIGS OF THE WORLD, for living.

One

My stodginess has gradually crept up, unnoticed by me until today, my fiftieth birthday, when the realisation has struck with all the brutal clarity of a close-up flash photo. I have become fat, faded, timid and dreary. I am stuck in a humdrum routine with my husband and my pet pig and I realise it is fucking boring.

That is the first time I have ever even *thought* that word and I have shocked myself. But the worm has twisted. It marks the start. From this day on I shall aspire to become slim, sexy, assertive and daring. And to make money, BIG money, because I am totally sick of being hard up, and winter is upon us so the pig needs extra warmth and, on top of everything, the roof of our lovely old cottage needs repairing.

I wish I'd taken up Bernard's suggestion that we invite friends round for a 'half-century bash' tonight, but, No thank you, I had replied, being fifty's bad enough without advertising it. This evening as I sat watching my Large White pig I rather regretted the hasty decision. Then I realised how boringly true to form I was being, sitting as usual, feasting my eyes on my porky girl, so I put on a record and hauled Bernard up to dance. His eyes registered bewilderment, if not fear, but nevertheless he twirled and feathered up and down the room, pandering to my birthday whim to the tune of 'In the Mood'. Hermione obviously thought Joe Loss a Dead Loss and scrambled up onto the sofa, her snout wrinkled in disdain and glumness all over her face.

We puffed upstairs at ten thirty and I noticed Bernard keep eyeing me as we prepared for bed. Just you wait Bernard Field I thought gleefully, I shall transform myself and amaze you, and this is merely the start.

'How d'ya fancy making love to a fifty-year-old then?' I asked as I jumped on him in bed.

Another full-time teaching day. Another day of hell. Working in a school run by Norah Harker-Balls is like being an Animal Rights Campaigner working in an abattoir. Today she terrorised the children mercilessly. I am adding to my list of ambitions the saving of the poor down-trodden pupils from their despot Head. I'd tell her what I thought of her if I didn't need my pay cheque so much. But I'll probably be given the sack anyway after next week's nativity performance. Today's rehearsal was shambolic. They've left the whole production to me. The grand end-of-term extravaganza involving all four classes. And Muggins the only part-timer there. This is the last time I'll let myself be put upon I swear it.

Measured myself. Hips 42", waist 33", bust 40". When I told Bernard, he made derisive remarks about the bits in between, then tried to pacify me by quickly adding that being on the large size meant there was all the more to love. All the more to love like trying to come to grips with a giant blancmange I inwardly railed, unpacified by the well meant P.S.

I went upstairs and weighed myself. Eleven stone. I shall *not* divulge this to Bernard, he'd only make more funny cracks and then try to make out he enjoyed sleeping with a giant pudding. Back downstairs I scrutinised myself in the mirror. My eyes reflected back like lustrous green jewels set in a plumped up duvet. My hair, once the colour of a fiery sunset, was now faded like an evening sky awaiting the greyness of night. I exuded a long noisy sigh.

Bernard called over, 'You're not looking in that mirror *again* are you Freda.' And then he gave a peculiar sort of laugh.

You wait, I thought grimly. You won't think I'm so funny when my body's deflated back to its pre-marital size.

Spent most of the next day preparing for the advent of mother and father. I am really trying to slim but the worry of their impending stay with us for the so-called festive season has made me stuff myself silly.

Have spent literally hours, and suffered nervous bowel syndrome, trying to decide what to buy my mother for Christmas, but there's about as much chance of her liking the gold-flecked black chiffon stole I finally bought, as there is of Jesus Christ having been born in our mobile home pigsty. More actually! She's never liked a present I've bought since I was fifteen.

Sunday was spent preparing for Christmas and rowing with Bernard. That made me eat wildly again. I've decided to put all my resolutions on hold for the duration.

Bernard went off to do a big shop. The whole lot to be paid for by credit card of course and I don't know where the money's coming from because Bernard's one man driving school has practically disappeared up its own exhaust pipe.

Monday. Laundry day. The predictable dull routine. But, as the pile of dirty washing won't miraculously sort itself, load itself into the machine, then dry and iron itself, I am stuck with it. CD ROMs and the Internet are all very well, brilliant at some things, but not laundry.

Hermione kept getting under my feet throughout the day. Sometimes I wish I hadn't made the pig flap in the kitchen door. She's always barging in and out, snorting and snuffling for food. Bernard is as bad. Even though I made pointed remarks about his paunch and the price of chocolate biscuits, he still devoured three after lunch. He gave Hermione one and she gobbled it up making fewer crumbs than he did. It paid to train her when she was a piglet but, unfortunately, I wasn't around during his formative years.

I ate one when he wasn't looking and then felt guilty. Slimming, I'm discovering, is even harder than I'd thought.

The portrait session down at the Old Bakery Art Club each Tuesday is the highlight of my week, a routine I do not want to change. I walked there this morning. The sky was blue, and sparkling frost mantled fields hedges and trees. In Bramble Lane I gave a cheery wave to the shadowy figure of old Mrs Smith standing in her bungalow doorway. I caught up with my friend Cynthia, who also paints each Tuesday and we linked arms and practically skipped there. I felt on top of the world.

The model was inspirational too, with her jade green beret set at a jaunty angle on her black bobbed hair. She sat still as a statue and I piled the paint on my board and really captured her.

On the walk back home, I was filled with the satisfying contentment of success. People I met in the village all happily laughed and smiled as we exchanged greetings, from nervous Mrs Mole posting a letter, to Mrs Trugshawe coming out of the corner shop. Even Mr and Mrs Bambridge beamed and waved at me from inside their blue Bentley as they cruised by. My heart swelled at the sharing of such a glorious day with friends and neighbours.

It was only when I arrived home that I saw I sported a stupid jade green oil paint moustache and had been a laughing stock. Life isn't clear blue skies and sparkle for very long I find.

After lunch I tackled the cleaning as per usual. As soon as I hauled out the Hoover, Bernie-baby started on his predictable moan that it wasn't necessary to do the cottage from top to bottom every Tuesday afternoon.

'Excuse me,' I replied, as I always do. 'It *is* necessary. You'd soon notice if I missed a week, we'd be knee-deep in germs.'

He always shrugs his shoulders and rolls his eyes in an aggravating way. This week he got a surprise though. 'You've got nothing to do' I said, 'so cop hold of this and dust the sitting room.'

He peered at the yellow duster in his hand, then held it out by two corners as if trying to work out which was the right way round.

Norah Harker-Balls has asked me to work extra this week because of the nativity play, so I'm going in tomorrow morning instead of the afternoon. When she'd first thrust the whole responsibility onto my unwilling shoulders, she stated that this annual event was put on to demonstrate the discipline and high standards of excellence of her private school. Not a word about love, enjoyment and the birth of the son of God. I hope that He realises that I need my salary and if it all goes wrong on the day it's my job that's on the line.

My journey to school was a nightmare. The snow fell so thickly that my windscreen wipers couldn't cope, and I skidded at every corner. Finally I made it, veering into the school driveway and slithering up the slope. The Dambusters' March played gloriously in my head. I had arrived. I was alive. And I was only two minutes late.

Norah Harker-Balls pointedly stared at her watch as I entered, then gave me one of her looks. No wonder the children are petrified of her. Those colourless flat fish eyes magnified by thick spectacle lenses are terrifying in their power. Spiky black lashes jut forward and, within them, the black outline of each iris seems to hold clear water tinged with murk. Hairy black eyebrows were lowered menacingly at me and I wanted to say: My narrow lane wasn't salted or gritted as your wide road no doubt was. My journey was terrifying. I am in need of hot sweet tea and congratulations. Instead I remained mute, turned away and scurried off to my classroom. As I chalked the date on the board I vowed that after Christmas I would stand up to her, I really really would.

By home time I was feeling more relaxed about tomorrow's performance because the dress rehearsal went so well. The mothers have made colourful costumes and the children all know their lines. Even the baby donkey, foisted on me by the woman from Rugged Farm, was docile and well-behaved. And my brainwave of combining Religious Education with Science has given the show pizzazz.

Bernard had dug up last year's Christmas tree from the front garden while I was at school, replanted it in our old barrel, and positioned it in the corner by the french windows. It looked ri-dic-ulous. It must have grown at least a foot during the year and was all bent over against the low beamed ceiling. Ignoring the absurdity of the horizontal fairy squashed flat against the ceiling, he was proceeding to cover the tree with glass balls.

He's like a kid at Christmas, all excited and full of false hope. How I *wish* we'd been able to have children. Then it would be a real Christmas. Hermione's a blessing of course, but a pig isn't quite the same.

No sooner had he finished festooning the sitting room with decorations than my parents arrived. They squabbled their way into the cottage and continued arguing loudly about the way father had driven 'the hellish route' from Peckham to Wood Hill. Hermione immediately bolted out to her mobile home pig sty in its walled yard out the back. When I went to check on her she was already asleep, bathed in the warm glow of her automatic heat-lamp. She sighed contentedly as she nestled into the straw. Lucky pig I thought enviously. It was so peaceful out here compared with indoors. But then so was the Second World War.

As we ate the lamb chops, mashed potatoes and carrots that I'd rushed home and prepared, my mother told me she was gob-smacked at the size of me. And there she was, thin as a rake, shovelling the food in with an arm like a mechanical grab.

I explained to her that I only had to sniff food to put on pounds, but she just snorted like a pig. Well, actually, more like a pig than *the* pig.

Surreptitiously I studied her. Her long blonde hair suited her, even at sixty-nine, especially all swathed up on top to hide the roots. There's only nineteen years between us, but I know it looks much less. She makes me feel dowdy. I often wish I'd been born with a sensible fat mum, instead of zany thin her.

It's a miracle I grew up normal. The things she told me. You trust your mother when you're young. I honestly believed that my private parts were called Beatrice. I did. I had no reason not to and when I tackled her about it when I was eighteen - having had a humiliating conversation with a boyfriend - she just said that she thought the name Fanny too frivolous for such an important part. No apologies for making such an idiot of me.

And she had me calling my periods my 'oh be joyfuls'. That was until I heard the other girls in my form sniggering behind my back. Oh, she had said, some females call it the curse, but the only time I've called it that was the month when it *didn't* come. It didn't need the sidelong glance to tell me that she was referring to my sordid beginning.

I cleared the dishes and all thoughts of my mother vanished as the terror of tomorrow's nativity performance took hold of my inside.

Two

Mother came down wearing her scarlet cat suit. She made jeering reference to the dullness of my brown tweed skirt. 'Mother, I do happen to teach in a private school you know,' I said, forced into irrationality by her attack. Then father appeared and they rowed incessantly over breakfast. I drove to school and my head was pounding. When the time came for the show, it was as if invisible fingers were poking at my temples from inside.

The children were being organised backstage by teachers and helpers. I peeped round the curtain watching the parents vying with each other for best seats. In the front row sat Sidney Slocumb, Great Piddlehurst and District's newly elected mayor, his face as proudly gleaming as the grand chain draped round his neck. Beside him sat Cynthia, all togged up with a lesser chain, looking different being mayoress to being my painter friend down at the Club.

Quietly taking back seats, were Mr and Mrs Bambridge, Wood Hill's wealthiest pair. I wondered what they were doing here. I was sure they only had one daughter who was grown up and living away.

To my absolute horror I spied my own parents sitting three rows from the front. As I stared, my father's jug ears suddenly flared up fiery red, lit up from behind by a low ray of winter sun. I knew then that was a portent of disaster, an ominous sign, like a red sky in the morning being a shepherd's warning.

Mother was now wearing her purple velour track suit and a yellow scarf which she swung in wide circles as she chatted to Mrs Trugshawe who ducked and weaved like a boxer to avoid the flailing bobbled tail. I wondered what indiscretions the rapidly moving scarlet lips of my mother were divulging. I looked at my watch and felt my heart lurch. It was time!

The audience clapped the scenery with enthusiasm as the curtains jerked back. Silence settled, then Mary and Joseph shuffled onto the stage with Daisy, the baby donkey, walking sedately alongside. A ripple of applause and whispers of 'Ahh, it's real' spread around the hall. Cameras flashed. Daisy stopped dead, eyes wild with fear. Mary pulled on the rope but the obdurate creature leaned back taking the strain like the anchor man in a tug of war. Panic rose up in me. If the stupid ass wouldn't move, the show was finished. A two minute nativity play and early retirement for me. I hadn't a clue what to do.

More flashes of brilliant light flared out and the animal threw back its great head and brayed with unearthly stutterings of terror. The audience brayed back and I was still trying to work out what to do when Joseph took the initiative and slapped the demented animal on its backside. The tormented cries abruptly stopped. Joseph smiled out at the howling mob, gave a flourishing little bow, then grabbed Mary's hand to continue their weary walk towards the Inn. I gave a premature sigh of relief.

Mary tugged at the rope but Daisy still wouldn't shift. Joseph, smiling, clearly enjoying taking command, announced, 'The donkey is too tired to continue the journey so we will leave it here.'

Loud clapping greeted this enterprising ad-lib and Norah Harker-Balls called out 'THAT'S WHAT MY SCHOOL TRAINS YOUR CHILDREN FOR, TO BECOME LEADERS, TO TAKE INITIATIVES - YOU WOULDN'T GET THAT IN A STATE SCHOOL.'

Whispered comments from impressed fee-paying parents slowly died away.

Mary and Joseph reached the Inn where Toby Mole, the Innkeeper, threw open the imaginary door. He stood rubbing his hands and grinning and I felt proud. Here was a rebellious eight-year-old who hated school and, because of me, because of my faith in giving him a leading role against everybody's dire warnings, was being co-operative, and loving every moment of the experience. I felt fulfilled. It had been worth all the hassle and effort just for this one precious moment.

Joseph said: 'We have walked for miles over hills and dusty roads, my wife is about to give birth to a baby. Please can we have a room for the night?'

And the Innkeeper, grinning slyly, opened his arms saying, 'Certainly Mr Joseph, why don't you come on in!'

It was as much as I could do not to march onto that stage and cuff that Judas round the ear. This was his revenge on the school he loathed. Then Norah Harker-Balls saved the day by bursting into peels of laughter, and all the rest of the lemmings followed suit.

When the hilarity had died down, Joseph turned to Mary and decreed: 'There is NO room at the Inn!' The rabble exploded into tumult again but Joseph, undeterred by the mass hysteria in the hall, took Mary's arm and dragged her past the immobile donkey. 'We must stay in this stable for the night' he loudly proclaimed.

This was the cue for Johnny Brown to press the switch connected to the large star pinned to the black velvet drape behind the stable. There was a sudden flare, followed by a bang and a puff of smoke. Once more the audience fell about.

'Oh deary me,' Joseph said, 'a cloud has drifted over, hiding the light of the star.' It was then that I remembered his report sealed away in an envelope waiting to be handed out as the parents and children left. *He works conscientiously but lacks initiative* I had written. Suddenly it occurred to me that I had no idea how to set about signing on the dole.

Across the other side, three shepherds were filing onto the stage. The first one pointed up to where the star *should* have shone and said: 'Lo, look yonder at that blaze of light.' And the other two lifted their hands to their eyes to shield them from the glare, saying in unison: 'It is a wondrous bright star.'

More titters broke out from the mob.

Flurries of infant angels tiptoed onto the stage and a burst of rapturous applause greeted them. Haloes of small white light bulbs shone above golden heads. Cries of 'Bravo' came from the hall. It was a magical sight. The tension in my body released like melting snow. Perhaps this was the turning point.

The bevy of angels began to sing and as the words 'While shepherds watch'd their flocks by night' rang out, Sarah, the Angel of the Lord, prepared for her ascent. She walked onto the stage and stood on her allotted spot. The strongest two boys in the school waited in the wings opposite, ready to winch her up by strong fine wires attached to crisscross strapping hidden under her pearly top. She stretched out her arms and the ascent began. There was loud applause as she slowly rose diagonally upwards, coming to a halt feet dangling close above Joseph's head.

'The Angel of the Lord came down and glory shone around,' the angels sang, and suddenly I wondered if I should have changed the words to 'the Angel of the Lord went up,' but it was too late now.

Joseph squinted upwards and loudly whispered, 'I can see her knickers.'

Sarah collapsed. She crossed her legs and clasped them to her chest. Her chin quivered and she gave a sobbing groan.

'Fear not said He for mighty dread had seized their troubled minds,' the angels gustily continued.

A mighty dread had seized my troubled mind. The dread that any minute Norah Harker-Balls would appear beside me and garrotte me. Powerless, I watched the boys on the winch become hysterical and lose control causing the Angel to plummet, landing heavily in a heap of white net skirt on the boards. Screeching loudly she scrambled up and hobbled off the stage. A deathly hush descended as I watched a helper in the wings unhook the wire and lead her away. I took hold of the cord ready to close the curtains on this debacle of a show. But the angels commenced singing again, their sweet voices ringing out, 'Glad tiding of great joy I bring to you and all mankind.' Somehow the show was carrying on. I let go the cord.

Mary walked over and sat beside the manger and Joseph stood behind her. The baby Jesus doll was propped up on the wedge-shaped wooden mattress made by Susie Addams in a woodwork period. Hay cushioned the baby and hid the wedge from sight. Mary looked down tenderly at her baby son and began vigorously picking her nose. The three shepherds approached, then filed past her, bowing low to their Saviour. Mary continued to busy herself with the contents of her nostrils. As the last shepherd bowed he loudly let off wind, creating hysterics in the auditorium and much hand waving of infant angels. I peered round the curtain and saw hankies dabbing at crying eyes. I wished I could run far far away and hide for ever.

The three wise men stood by my side ready to go on stage. They looked magnificent, gold crowns glinting with encrusted jewels, rich velvet cloaks adorning their tiny shoulders. Gifts were held in cupped hands ready to be held high.

As the angels burst into 'We three Kings of Orient are,' haloes began to flicker and die, and I realised we must have worn out the batteries during rehearsals. 'Myrrh is mine, its bitter perfume, breathes a life of gathering gloom,' the distressed angels quavered. I reflected on the gathering gloom of my life as the bitter perfume of the infant fart reached me.

As the singing continued and the three kings were about to walk out into the spot light, the forgotten donkey ambled into view from behind the stable. It made its way to the low manger and sniffed at the hay, then began to eat it! The singing stopped and silence settled once more. The wise men stood stationary beside me. The animal munched on, then slowly it turned itself round to face the dim hall. Spikes of hay poked from its gyrating mouth as it backed and sat down. The creature's bum now completely covered the infant Saviour of the World. Galvanised into action, the smirking three wise men processed onto the stage and lined up to offer their gifts of gold, frankincense and myrrh to the chomping donkey. As they walked off the other side, the animal stood and followed them, lured by a carrot being dangled by its owner: that woman from Rugged Farm. She who had thrust her baby donkey at me, promising it knew how to behave. She who I shall hold responsible for my dismissal.

Mary and Joseph prepared themselves for the grand finale. They stood, held hands and took a pace forward, ready to take their bows. Astonishingly, baby Jesus suddenly catapulted out of his crib into the air, hurtling across the stage. A quick-thinking shepherd threw himself out sideways and made a magnificent catch. As he crashed down to the boards, new born king clasped to his chest, his father in the audience leapt up and yelled: 'How zat! A few people clapped, sounding like the genteel applause heard from a cricket pavilion on a summer afternoon.

There was a tap on my arm. Suzie Addams was looking up at me with worried eyes. 'I didn't really think it would work Miss,' she whispered. 'The release of the spring ...' She foundered. 'The electromagnet ... you know, you taught us in Science ...'

As she sloped off, I realised that I must be brilliant at teaching Science and fucking useless at R E. (That is the second time I've used that word and this time I couldn't care less.)

The shepherd had scrambled to his feet and was checking himself from hurling the baby full pelt at Joseph who stood, bright eyed, arms open ready for the catch. Sedately the shepherd crossed the stage to Mary and placed the baby doll reverently in her arms. A mighty cheer rose up. The whole cast joined hands in two semicircles. They stepped forward and bowed and the applause was deafening. Feet stamped and people stood. I listened in amazement. It seemed as if the clapping would never end.

Norah Harker-Balls floundered up the steps beside me, then dragged me with her out onto the open stage. Applause welled up again. When the clapping had subsided she said, 'I should like to thank Mrs Field for organising a most memorable performance. She never fails to amaze us here at the Harker-Balls' School.'

I could see Mr and Mrs Bambridge, both smiling broadly, slipping out at the back. I could see my mother's yellow scarf twirling as Mayor Slocumb called out 'Hip hip ...' and the crowd yelled back 'HOORAY!' It appeared I still had a job, but, never again would I produce a nativity play, never ever again. Or so I thought.

Children, parents, reports, cars, noise, had all disappeared. I tidied up the classroom, gathered my stuff, then sped home. Despite the cheering of the audience that echoed around my head, I knew it had been a disaster. I pushed open the cottage door and hung the school keys on the hook just inside. Thank God I wouldn't be needing them for two whole weeks. I saw mother watching me from the kitchen doorway.

'What did you think of it?' I asked, dreading the derision to come.

'Think of what!' she snapped.

I hid myself up in my bedroom sorting out Christmas presents. The rumble of their argument percolated through the ceiling, swelling and dying, slowing and quickening, like a Wagner opera, awesome in its power. I draped the present for my mother around my shoulders. The gold-flecked black chiffon mantle weighed heavily like a dark harbinger of doom.

Three

Last night I had a dreadful nightmare that Hermione had disappeared. The picture of her curly tail hurtling away from me, flying off into eternity to her maker in the great pig sky, kept looping round my brain. Awake, the fear became that she'd been stolen and was flying off into eternity to the maker of a great pork pie!

At half past six I could stand the worry no longer and crept downstairs, letting myself out into the icy darkness and heading straight for my girl. As I rushed towards the dim light shining from the shadowy bulk of the mobile home pig sty I prayed to God to make her be there, and to make her be there intact. I dashed through the ever open gate of the walled yard, and up the ramp, all the time calming myself with the knowledge that pig rustling was, generally speaking, not yet part of the British way of life. Heart thumping, I pushed through the swing door at the top. And there she was in her bedroom opposite, snoring contentedly in the warmth of the lamp. She opened one eye and smiled at me, then was back into instant sleep. That's what I should be doing I thought, incensed by her carefree comfort and my stupidity.

I drew my dressing gown collar up against the biting wind and hurried away. But still the premonition of danger clung to me. I knew as sure as my mother would not like my Christmas present, that harm would come to that poor creature today. The grotesque vision of her skewered on a spit over fierce barbecue flames flashed before my eyes. I was getting paranoid I knew, but I truly adore my pig. Warm air rushed at me as I opened the kitchen door.

I had hoped to read the paper in peace before the Enemies arose, but mother was already at the kitchen table, finger tips drumming on the ancient pine filling the atmosphere with staccato bursts of agitation. Father's heavy footfalls sounded overhead.

She looked up at the ceiling. 'Here comes the sex maniac,' she called loudly.

There was the clumping of feet on the stairs then the 'sex maniac' appeared, his maroon Paisley dressing gown matching his maroon Paisley face. I asked him what he'd like for breakfast, hoping to postpone a row.

'Well, what he *wouldn't* like is Mars bars, he's had his fill of them!'

'Quiet Maeve!' he roared and suddenly I was curious about what these two old age pensioners got up to in the privacy of night.

'That would suit you, you perv, for me to keep quiet.'

Father buzzed ominously through clenched teeth. He grabbed hold of the still-furled 'Times' and banged it several times into the palm of his hand, each thwack producing a crescendo of buzzing like a chain saw biting into wood inside his throat.

Rashly ignoring the obvious, she began, 'At our age ...'

He lashed out with the speed of a striking cobra, the heavy roll of paper making contact with the side of her head. Her hair flared out into untidy straw tufts. She screeched. She turned to me wild-eyed, patting one hand at the disorder.

'You saw that daughter. He *clouted* me.'

Privately I thought I'd throttle her if she divulged my sexual perversions - if I had any, which I haven't.

Her mocking blue eyes bore into mine. 'He *knows* I can't stand it in a foreign bed,' she complained, theatrically.

As I wondered what 'it' was, she giggled, and he lashed out again, but this time she threw herself onto the floor and quickly crawled under the table.

I was beginning to wish I was back at school where I had a modicum of control.

Bernard entered the kitchen with the automatic genuflexion perfected to avoid contact with the oak lintel of the doorway. I was surprised. Instead of the usual pyjamas and dressing gown he was fully clothed in his red and grey check lumber-jack shirt and blue jeans. His usually candid eyes stared at me. They held a devious look. He rubbed his clean jaw and sniffed the air as if picking up its vibrations.

'Mother's under the table,' I whispered, rolling my eyes.

His eyes darted to the large bare table. 'Just going out to give a lesson,' he said, batting his thick curling black lashes, flapping his hands vaguely at the freedom to be seen through the window outside.

Lucky devil, I thought as he kissed me goodbye. Even if his excuse were genuine, it must be more relaxing being driven by a learner driver on the treacherous icy lanes of Wood Hill than being trapped at home with my parents.

I threw a red and white gingham cloth over the table and set it for three. I placed the bread in the toaster. Mother stayed put.

Father and I ate without speaking. I lifted the cloth and offered buttered toast to the figure at the far end, crouching in the gloom. An arm shot out and the whole plateful was snatched. Pig-like snuffles quickly emanated from beneath the table.

'Come out you stupid bitch!' father ordered, bending his thick-set body to peer under at his wife.

There was no reply. I fervently wished we'd had enough money to get the leaking patch of roof repaired. Last year I'd been able to escape to my 'studio' up in the attic where there had been a comfy chair as well as a table and my art stuff. This year the room was devoid of anything but buckets set out to catch the rain.

'Leave the silly bitch there,' father said as he helped me clear the table, 'she'll have to come out some time, and, if she doesn't, all the better for us.'

'How about us going out for a spin in the car?' I suggested, knowing she wouldn't stay in her dim under-world if we weren't there.

The trip with father was less dangerous than I'd expected in every way. The lanes had been salted and he didn't buzz once. He even said he liked the glorious countryside, conceding it might even be more picturesque than Tooting Bec Common.

'Even the Hampshire air seems clearer than ours in London,' he stated in a rare fit of generosity.

I began to warm to him. After all, he had a lot to put up with, living with my mother. I tried to picture him fifty years and nine months ago. A carroty-haired fiery soldier on leave from the war, grasping at a bit of romance with a flighty eighteen year old blonde. I wondered how he'd felt when she told him she was pregnant. She'd once told me that she hadn't wanted to marry him. But had he wanted to live the rest of his life with her? I felt guilty. He had done the 'right thing' and married the mother of his child, but somehow he had finished up being the bastard.

'That paint work needs doing,' he observed as Wisteria Cottage came into view.

'Yes, and the back of the roof needs mending too.' Then my heart sank as I saw that some of the tiles at the front had also slipped into haphazard lines. Not long before the whole lot would be letting in rain.

'Your Bernard's too old and out of condition to attempt that,' he succinctly replied. Then, as if something might be expected of him, he added, 'and I've got my hip.'

We entered the cottage. Silence reigned. 'Maeve!' he bellowed. Nothing moved. I went to the table and peered underneath. The space was vacant except for the empty plate.

'Where's the stupid bitch got to', he yelled. He limped up the stairs, shrieking 'Maeve Salmon come on out!' He came down. 'There's no sign of her, put the kettle on, make the most of it!'

Bernard came home looking pale. He tottered out to the garden, then came back. 'Where's Hermione?' he asked, 'she's nowhere to be seen.'

A black fear gripped me. Was my premonition to come true? The boundary of our land had been pig-proofed. There was no way she could escape. I rushed outside in blind panic, haring across the vast expanse of our back garden calling her name. It wasn't until I'd puffed my way all round and back again that it dawned on me to connect mother's disappearance with that of the pig. Hadn't it been obvious all along!

I tossed and turned all night long wondering where they could be. Every time I closed my eyes I saw the vivid picture of her defenceless tail fading away into the valley of the shadow of death. And I heard the unforgivable reaction of the duty policeman on the phone yesterday: 'Your elderly mother and a pet *PIG!*' And then he'd *laughed*. 'If I'd have said my elderly mother and my pet labrador, you wouldn't have thought it so funny,' I retorted.

'Why has that gone missing too' he had sniggered. Then, 'Sorry Mrs Field, can I have their details, starting with name, age, nationality and colour.' He sounded as if he was reading from a form. As an afterthought he added, 'In the pig's case nationality is replaced by breed.'

I took a deep breath. 'Mother - Maeve Salmon, nearly seventy, English, white. Pig - Hermione Field, nearly five, Large White, pink.' I could hear him trying to keep a straight face as he wrote it down. 'How large is a Large White?' he asked.

And suddenly I realised how she sounded just like a loaf of bread. 'For a Large White, she's quite small,' I replied, thinking, just let the insensitive clod dare ask if she's sliced or whole.

At five a.m. I looked out the bedroom window. The darkness glowed with fluorescent rime. Terror gripped me. My pig would die out there.

A sudden thought hit me. Stupidly, I hadn't searched the other rooms of the mobile home. I flung on my track suit and, taking up the torch, ran outside. I headed round the back of the garage to the immobile misnomer shored up on brick piers in the centre of the yard. If my girl had been on her palliasse, the low-slung heat lamp would have been switched on by weight sensors, but all was dark. I opened the door and walked into the silence.

Her room opposite was devoid of pig but, to the left, at the end of the short passage, the door to the garden storage room was ajar. Maybe she was trapped, or unconscious inside. Heart fluttering with hope, I switched on the light and entered, but no mound of pink flesh met my eyes.

I shifted the pitchfork and the wheelbarrow used for moving her old straw. Maybe we should never ever have need of them again I thought sadly. I stared into the large wooden barrow. It would just take a recumbent pig. I pictured wheeling her dead body to the bottom of the garden. Imagined digging her vast burial hole. The vision was so real that my back began to ache to match my heart.

I lifted a tangle of black ridged hose pipe and peered at the pigless floor. I threaded between terra-cotta pots of dry geraniums, kicked at a watering can, moved two buckets, some boxes, a spade and fork, all the time knowing it was a futile search. But that's what love does for you, makes you soft in the head. I knew I'd do the same for Bernard, if ever he were lost.

I went back out along the passageway, past her empty bedroom to the bathroom beyond. The deep tub overflowed with bales of new straw. In a stupid act of arthritic martyrdom, I lugged them all out to the floor. And, for a heart-stopping moment, I thought I spied her curly tail twisted round the cross-bar of the plug hole. I peered down, aiming my torch, but saw that it was just a coil of white binding cord. How stupid could one get.

I glanced in the unused kitchen as I passed but it was bare. I pushed through the swing door and slithered down the frosty ramp. My pig, alive or dead, was not in there. And then I saw it. In the narrow beam of torch light a familiar mound lay inert on the ridged concrete. 'Oh Hermione my baby,' I whispered to the pile of shit that such a short time ago she had gently dropped.

I forced myself to search the back garden again. As I hurried across the crisp white grass, snow flakes began to swirl. Fear clutched my heart in a vice grip. If they'd stayed out all night they'd both be gonners. A hot tear meandered down my cold cheek. I would miss her so. I looked back at the dark cottage where my father slumbered without a thought for his dying wife. I gulped. In spite of her irritations, I'd miss my poor mother too. As I went back indoors, the phone began ringing. I grabbed it, hope flaring.

'P.C. Compton here,' a slow Hampshire voice announced, 'Oi'm the new duty officer. Sorry to ring you so early, no doubt getting you out of your warm bed, but I am just checking that your mother and the, ahem, pet pig have turned up all roight.'

'NO! No they haven't' I cried.

'Out all noight,' he repeated, 'it'sa bit cold for that.'

Rasping sobbing noises broke out from my throat and wouldn't stop.

'Oi'll organise the local radio station to ask for volunteers,' he said, suddenly active. 'They can meet at midday in Tinkers Field ... oi've been studying the map.' He said it with pride, like a child hoping for a gold star. 'It's the field across the lane from your Cottage.' He made the statement as if I didn't know. 'And we'll scour the meadows and woods. You just stay by the phone and wait for news, and don't you worry, we'll foind 'em, alive or dead.'

The tears that had been abating burst out uncontrollably again.

Suddenly my father was beside me. 'You be careful with that phone, it's a delicate instrument and it's getting wet,' he chided detaching it gently from my hand.

'But it's dark out there,' I sobbed.

'Well, the sun hasn't risen so it tends to be like that,' he replied.

Bernard went over to Tinkers Field at midday to join the searchers. Father lounged in the chair reading the papers.

'Make the most of it Freda,' he advised for the hundredth time, 'these opportunities are rare.'

I glared at him mustering hate in my eyes.

'Don't worry about her, she'll be warm and comfortable somewhere and, although she's a selfish bitch, she's generally kind to animals. *They'll* be all right. Believe me.'

But I didn't believe him. Mother didn't know the area. She could be lost. They'd both be cold and tired and maybe injured, close to death. Or already gone. Disappeared into the nightmare black hole from which there was no return. I longed to throw my arms around her and kiss that dear snuffly snout. Where *are* you? I silently cried.

Four
Intrusion 1

Sidney turns on the radio then stands on tip-toe, straining the calf muscles of his stubby legs as he leans across the basin toward the mirror. *Must keep this 'tash well trimmed now I'm Worshipful Mayor of Great Piddlehurst*, he tells himself, raising the scissors, re-living the triumph of his inauguration four days ago. *Twenty-seven years it's taken for the toffee-nosed lot to bestow the honour on a mere northener. But he had ...*

A radio announcement cuts into his thoughts: 'Here is an urgent message for Wood Hill residents. Will those who are able to join in a life-or-death search gather in Tinkers Field, Nuthatch Lane, at midday today.'

Sidney snaps the blades together, hacking a diagonal step into the bristly grey hair. He gives a grunt of annoyance. *He* was the Mayor of Great Piddlehurst and *District*, and that included Wood Hill where he lives. *What* life-or-death search? He's been told nowt.

The announcer continues: 'A pet pig and mother of Mrs Freda Field ...' She splutters then gives an embarrassed cough. 'The pet pig and mother of Freda Field ... the pet pig and mother ... are not one and the same ... they are two separate creatures.'

Sidney frowns. 'Appen this unprofessional woman is ad-libbing on *his* local station. He'd have a word about that.

'Anyway, the mother and the pig have gone ...' She explodes into hysterics which gradually peter out. There is silence. Then she gabbles erratically, 'Wellanyway they've gonemissing and their owner is distraught.' She slows down. 'So if any volunteers ...'

There is fear in that voice Sidney thinks, *fear of losing her cushy job*. Viciously he attacks his moustache, composing his letter of complaint to Southern Radio as he wields the twin blades.

Doggedly the voice continues: '... can spare the time please go along to Tink ... ' A choir singing 'We wish you a merry Christmas' abruptly cuts her short.

Sidney decides that he must join 'his people' in their hour of need. He remembers the dopey school teacher. The one who organised the nativity play which accidentally turned out to be so hilariously entertaining. He wasn't surprised to learn she kept a pet pig, nor that it had gone missing.

'Not that I could give a stuff for Freda Field's mam or the pig,' he informs Cynthia, 'I'd mooch prefer to stay at 'ome in the warm on Christmas Eve.' Cynthia's expression registers that he hasn't said 'he'd mooch prefer to stay at 'ome with her.'

At a quarter to twelve he thrusts his arms into his beige three-quarter length jacket and his feet into black welly boots. Carefully, he arranges the heavy mayoral chain around his neck. 'They look oop t'me as mayor' he says as he opens his new royal blue Georgian PVC front door. He ignores Cynthia's derisive comments about his stature as he steps outside and struts to his garage with its up and over door. *I've made it* he thinks. *Some of them snobby folk have done their best to stop me, but I've got influence, I've got me loyal mates, and now I'm the most important person in Great Piddlehurst and District.* He readjusts the long strands of hair that sweep over his bald pate using both hands as if repositioning a crown.

He looks around at the other four houses identical to his own. *'Appen we are squashed in together, but we're detached. Aye, and double glazed with stone cladding, the lot. Me new house in this most sought-after village in Hampshire.* He frowns as his eye takes in the thatched cottage across the lawn. *All that flaking paint lets this prestigious development down. Now the old feller has had his brass from selling off most of his cherished garden, he could afford replacement plastic windows. I'll go and put it to him tomorrow. Me neighbours'll be grateful and Jake Glazier'll give me commission for getting him the job.* He smiles as he climbs into his Mini. *The next pile I make on a planning scam will finance the Jag.*

He drives to Nuthatch Lane but the usually empty road is lined with vehicles parked nose to tail. As he crouches over the wheel, crawling along the line of sleek BMWs and Rovers to find a space, he wishes he were lounging back in a chauffeur-driven stretch limmo with a triangular flag fluttering at its prow. *Stingy tin-pot council, out-voting him.*

He parks, trudges back beside the high hedge that hides Tinkers Field from the lane. He hears strange gabbling noises from the other side. He turns at the open five bar gate then stops dead. Tinkers Field was milling with chattering people, and a policeman was standing looking stupefied, a loud hailer drooping in his hand. It was like a grand pre-Christmas jamboree, an enormous outdoor party.

The confused-looking copper looks beseechingly at him. 'Oi thought oi'd organise an orderly line of beaters for a start, but just look at this lot! There's hardly a blade of grass t'be seen. No pig or mother could hoid in there, not even pygmies.

Sidney makes a mental note to contact the Constabulary Training School and ask them what the hell they were playing at, sending idiots like this out to police the great British public.

Yet more people were crowding into the field, pushing and shoving past him with no respect for who he was. He stands his ground, trying to draw attention by lifting and stroking the heavy ornate links of his magnificent gold chain. Everyone ignores him. Friends were greeting each other, forming groups, joking and catching up on family news. *It only needs a hot-dog stand for this to turn into a bigger event than the village annual Summer Fete!* No sooner has the thought flashed through his mind than Peter Turner, the local butcher, appears, chubby face glowing, black hair awry. Round his neck hangs a tray heavy with pork pies, sausage rolls, packets of crisps and cans of coke.

A woman rushes up and buys six sausage rolls. She jokes about the pork sausages. 'You haven't slaughtered Mrs Field's porker?' she screams, and everyone within earshot joins in the laugh. In two minutes the tray is empty and Peter Turner is joyously hot-footing it back through the gate.

Sidney grabs the bobby's arm. 'Do something you silly bugger. Take control!'

P.C. Compton's eyes show the fear of a man out of his depth. He holds the loud hailer to his mouth and says 'Please ev -er -y -body, can oi have some soilence.'

Even the people standing nearby merely turn to glance at him, not halting in their chatter.

Sidney decides that as their elected leader he must act. He snatches the loud hailer and bellows, 'SILENCE FOR THE MAYOR OF GREAT PIDDLEHURST AND DISTRICT.' The conversations nearby cease, but in the distance they rumble on. He shouts louder: 'THE MAYOR OF GREAT PIDDLEHURST DOESN'T *REQUEST* YOUR IMMEDIATE ATTENTION, NAY, HE *COMM-ANDS* IT!'

In the silence that follows Sidney hears a man with precise diction say, 'What an awfully stupid little fart.'

Crushed, he hands the loud hailer back to the constable dithering by his side.

'Oi'd loik you all to organoize yourselves into groups of twenty, please, and then set off in all directions, please, to hunt for the elderly lady and the small Large White pink pig ... please.'

Sidney groans, wishing he hadn't capitulated. Anyone who'd ever been a leader knew that more concise directions were needed than that pathetic request. He watches squabbling groups form and re-form. He hears grown adults whining like children: 'I wanted to be in *his* group.' He hears angry shouting and sees scowling faces.

He sees Mrs Harker-Balls, the headmistress who'd phoned him out of the blue last week, inviting him to her school's nativity play 'to impress the parents'. She'd appreciate the honour of his presence in her gang. He swaggers over and pushes himself in.

'We already have our quota of twenty,' a sour faced woman snaps.

'I'm fraightfully sorry,' Mrs Harker-Balls responds, 'you'll have to join another battalion. Look, there's an awfully nice group over there.'

Sidney sees with satisfaction that she addresses the sour faced woman not him.

'Come along mayor.' She pats her huge flank, enticing him to her side.

As they leave the field Mrs Harker-Balls waves towards Wisteria Cottage opposite. He sees the ghostly white face of Freda Field looking out from a first-floor window.

'If it's the pig or your mother, who shall we save?' a wag calls up to her and Mrs Harker-Balls bellows, 'IF THAT TACTLESS MAN WERE IN MY SCHOOL HE'D BE PUNISHED!'

Sidney decides he rather likes this bossy woman whose neatly ordered head seems so out of place on her rolly polly body. Her raven black hair with its central strip of startling white is scragged back into a bun. Behind her large red-framed spectacles amazing eyes gleam And behind her leather jacket a huge bosom heaves. Aye, this hoity toity southern bint were a bit of all right!

'I'm so fraightfully pleased to have the privilege of our mayor in our team,' she says, pulling back pink lips to reveal pearly white even teeth.

Sidney lifts his sternum and puffs out his chest. At last a female who appreciates him. And 'er with the biggest tits in town!

He has stuck by her side like a siamese twin as the rest of the group split up, fanning out to search copses and meadows, beating the undergrowth with sticks and calling out Maeve Salmon's name. They have stayed together as they search barns and outbuildings. They even join hands as they run shrieking, chased by a bull. As they approach the scout hut in Bramble Lane, the scout leader runs out.

'I've been waiting to join you,' the gangling man calls out. 'I thought that might be useful.' He points to a high two-wheeled scout cart.

They halt and stragglers catch up looking weary as they emerge through the dusk. The scout master runs over to the vehicle and grabs up the T-bar, leaning into it, trundling the heavy cart toward them.

'It might be handy if the pig is dead,' he beams. 'Or the woman.' He pauses. 'Or both of course - dib dib dib!'

Sidney, grateful for the brief respite during which he retrieves his breath, says, 'Come and join us lad, 'tis a grand idea.' He doesn't add that already he is scheming that soon he and Norah Harker-Balls will be up there in it, pulled along by the gang. *I'm knackered*, he thinks, *but I'll not let it show joost yet*.

He is knackered but happy, bursting with excitement and hope. He thinks back to a conversation early on the trek. 'Sidders,' she had said, 'one does so *fraightfully* admire your honest north country way of putting things. It's so refreshing.'

He smiles as he re-plays his quick-witted reply in his head: *And I admire the way you talk too Norah, the Queen 'erself could take a lesson from thee!* Secretly he knows it's her big boobs he admires not her affected manner of speech.

As they walk along close together, each rhythmic brushing contact sends glorious sensations speeding to his power house, oiling his rusty tackle. *I haven't felt this randy for years*, he thinks, as his ramrod shifts into gear. He slows down and she calls over her shoulder 'Are you coming Sidders?'

I hope not! he silently groans. He hurries to catch up with her and, with relief, feels the icy coldness of descending night decommission his lust. He looks up into the strange colourless eyes that coyly stare down at him. *Next time I'll make sure we're in private when those magnificent thighs play 'avoc with me willy*, he vows.

All conversations have ceased and footsteps flag. The scout master trundles the cart along, aided by three others. *Soon I'll pretend to rick my ankle*, Sidney decides.

'That is the perimeter of my private school,' Norah announces, pointing to a high brick wall ahead.

'It'll take ages to search in there and I feel dead,' whines a wraith-like man.

'No need. Pass by. Pass by,' Norah trills. 'Only I and my totally trustworthy staff have keys, No pig or mother could break into there.'

A young man called Bobbie May has trudged along all day with a trumpet hanging round his neck. Now he lifts it to his lips and hot jazz pierces the freezing air. Footsteps quicken to the beat. Voices loudly sing: '... the saints, go marching in ...' Some of them break into dance. They pass the school's padlocked wrought iron gates, skirt along the wall then joyously turn for home.

An elderly woman wearing a knitted hat runs up from behind and mingles with them.

'Ow! my ankle,' Sidney shrieks, stopping dead. People gather round. 'It's nay use, I've twisted it. I'll never walk on this.' He groans and clutches hold of Norah's hammy arm.

'Help him up into the cart,' the scout master orders, his Adam's apple bouncing wildly in his tall skinny neck. He holds up two fingers, 'Dib dib dib, a scout is always prepared,' he proclaims proudly.

Many hands help man-handle 'poor Sidders' up into the high cart. He sits on the plank-seat, organising his face into agony.

He bends forward to gently clasp his ankle in both hands. As he goes through the charade, his heavy chain swings out then crashes back onto his hand. He screams.

'Oh Sidders, you're in absolute agony,' Norah cries.

'Aye, I am,' he says, eyes watering, 'I need you up here to help me.' He clutches his hand, then remembers it is meant to be his ankle that hurts. Quickly he bends down and, once again, his chain swings out and this time lams into his knee. 'Oooo, oooo,' he shrieks again.

'LIFT ME UP!' commands Norah, and suddenly he sees a trainer-clad foot on the end of a tree trunk leg appearing over the edge, and then she crashes down beside him.

'One, two, three, heave!' shouts the scoutmaster and their chariot slowly begins to roll. They sit thigh to thigh, and very soon, once again, his equipment is twitching with excitement. *At least I know it's in working order*, he thinks, trying not to smirk. His brain is working overtime on forward planning. She wouldn't need much luring to his home when Cynthia was out.

He reaches out and takes her gloved hand. He watches the shadowy figures of the group who half-heartedly peer behind hedges as they traipse back to the start. As he strokes the leather, a man shouts, 'I bet the pig and her mother are tucked up safe in front of a blazing fire and us silly sods is wasting our time.' Bleatings of discontent reverberate around the flock.

Norah turns and gives Sidney a fluttering flirty look. *Not a complete waste of time*! he thinks.

To his annoyance, he hears the scout master call over to the elderly woman in the knitted hat and invite her to ride up in the cart too. He unlatches his hand from Norah's as the woman's skinny leg cocks over the side and she collapses down at their feet. Who is she, he wonders as she plonks herself on the plank at the opposite end, staring across at them with gimlet eyes.

With heavy heart he recognises the dark shape of Wisteria Cottage at the end of the lane. They are back to the beginning. This beautiful joy ride is coming to an end. He hears the sudden blare of music from Bobbie's horn and sees the dragging feet of the relieved searchers begin to prance to the rhythm.

Through the gloom, he sees Freda open her gate, then lumber down the lane towards them. The voices joyously reach the climax of their tactless song: 'After she's gone A - WAY!'

Aggravatingly, the woman in with them had shot up at the opening trumpet blast. She gyrates to the beat, waggling her narrow hips, arms raised high. He sees her throw her head back and spin wildly, crashing out of control into the low side of the cart. She screams, grabbing out at thin air, making contact with his chain.

As she topples over the edge, she hangs on and he is hauled up, flying in a great arc in her wake. In a terrifying blur he sees her hat fly off before she releases him. His body twists in the air, descends, crashes through spiky branches then slams down onto frost hard earth. He lies face down unable to scream because all the air has shot out from his lungs.

Through the red speckled mist in front of his eyes he can see the woman sprawled out on the tarmac. She lies in a pool of light thrown down by a lone street lamp. He sees that her hair, released from its woolly cover, is long and fair. He sees her open her eyes. He hears her moan 'Oh shit!'

He hears Freda shriek, 'MOTHER!' Then, lowly agressive, 'Where is my pig?!'

'So you didn't actually *find* her' Cynthia says. 'She just happened to be sitting opposite you under your big hooter.' Her buck-teeth burgeon into a smirky grin, her mockery unconcealed.

That's typical of her. More concerned with a cheap gibe than with me injuries. I'm in blewdy agony. He peers past his wife to the dressing table mirror. *What a sight! As if me nose weren't big enough already! And with those black eyes I look like a poxy panda.* Slowly and painfully he strips down to his underpants and vest. He sits on the side of the bed and, with hands criss-crossed with scratches, gently strokes his red swollen knees.

As he watches his mayoress wife rub cream on her homely face he gives a little bounce and, despite the shooting pains, he manages a grin. *I'll get buxom Norah bouncing on this bed with me before very long.*

'When are you going to visit your sister?' he asks Cynthia with feigned innocence as they lay in bed.

Five

I had a vivid dream last night. Not a nightmare like last time, but a real fairy-tale dream. Mother was flying across the sky, snowy white shoulders veiled in the gold flecked stole. Its ends drifted like gossamer wings as she looped the loop high in the dark heavens twinkling with a million stars. She pirouetted, a vision of happiness and joy. She held the black chiffon as if she loved it. But, even before I woke, I knew it had to be a dream because it was more believable that the pig would fly than my mother would like my gift.

Christmas day again. They say that as you get older time passes faster. And it does. It only seems like yesterday that we were going through this hell. As I turned the bend in the stairs the Enemies' barrage below peppered the air with pellets of sound pollution.

'Two days with the pig was great. She was much better company than you,' mother was shrieking as I entered the kitchen. She stood glaring at him, hands on hips, mouth in jeering mode.

A low buzz crept from his lips then faded. 'Well,' he snarled, 'Freda was much better company than you too.'

'Happy Christmas', I sang out trying to sound jolly.

'See!' he said, throwing out an expansive hand in my direction and flashing a look at her. 'See. She's much more pleasant than you.'

I went to the sink and thought wicked thoughts about cutting out both their tongues. My mind was still haunted by yesterday's events. The cold dead flesh I'd pictured lying in some far off foreign field, a brave trotter lying protectively across my mother's body. And then, when I'd poured out my fears to my father, his cruel joke of 'Hold the turkey, there'll by plenty of pork.' And then to learn that all the time my darling mother had been sitting in the warm comfort of the school staff room, having stolen my set of keys.

Bernard's knackered too, mentally and physically. Mentally from the presence of my parents, and physically from the effort of prizing Hermione out of the staff room and then having to push her, struggling and squealing, up the ramp into the horse box. The horse box borrowed from that woman at Rugged Farm. I agreed with her. To lend it to us was the least she could do to make up for her donkey that nearly got me the sack. She said she was risking being thrown into jail over Christmas because, by rights, pigs needed a special licence to move them around. I privately thought it would be a good way to ensure she was with her family.

'Out the way girl.'

I had jumped at the sudden sound of father's voice.

'Move out the way, I want to get to the tap.'

He elbowed me.

'Must get some water to swallow my blood pressure pill.' He sounded almost proud, proclaiming, 'The doc says I must carry on taking them for the rest of my life.'

'How many did he prescribe?' piped up mother, cracking up at her own warped wit.

Hermione bashed her way through the pig flap into the kitchen, her high-heeled trotters clacking on the quarry tiles. 'Come to mummy,' I cried. 'Come to me my lovely girl. I really missed you.' She nuzzled my legs with her damp snout and I knelt and put my arms around her. 'My booful girl,' I whispered. 'My booful booful girl is safe.'

'Chocolate!' father bellowed and my booful booful, *fickle*, girl tore herself from my loving arms and scampered snorting to him. Slowly and seductively he unwrapped a Mars bar, holding it teasingly just out of reach. My mother's slitted eyes watched, a crooked smile raked across her face. She looked sideways at me as if trying to convey a deep message.

I cooked a fry-up breakfast and then afterwards we had the traditional 'exchange of presents ceremony' around the tree. If you could call it a ceremony. There were only eight packages to hand out and two of those were for the pig.

Bernard had forked out three pounds for a sign to attach to the wall of Hermione's compound. He said it was to warn off intruders. The notice said, 'BEWARE! THIS PIG BITES'. He showed it to the pig in question, the one who never bites, and she did. Obviously thinking it was a biscuit, she bit hard into the oval metal then glared up at him with reproachful short-sighted eyes. Instantly, mother snatched father's reading glasses off his nose and organised them on the pig's snout, which set up such a buzzing vibration from father's throat that I looked round, for an instant truly thinking an angry bee had somehow flown into the room!

My present to my mother lay on her lap ignored.

Bernard unwrapped the pair of thermal socks and book of driving instructor cartoons I'd bought him. I wished so much that it could have been the sheepskin jacket he wanted.

Inside his carefully wrapped parcel to me was a water colour pad and a size three sable brush. 'Next year it'll be tickets for a luxury cruise,' he said smiling, but I noticed his eyes had turned sad.

'More chance of going to the moon,' mother sniffed.

And my heart ached for him.

Mother gave me a jar of enriching night cream, saying, 'It might help your skin.' Then she peered closely at me in a meaningful way that said more than a hundred words. She gave Bernard a bottle of Scotch 'to help his shattered nerves!'

She should have given it to me in that case, because my nerves were being shattered to smithereens waiting for her to unwrap the parcel in her lap.

They gave a gaily wrapped present to Hermione and I stupidly allowed her to sniff at it first which resulted in her squealing and cavorting, tail twirling umpteen to the dozen, while I tore the paper apart. When the bag of mini chocolate flakes was exposed she went even more berserk and tried to grab the lot with unusually gnashing teeth. I gave her just one and placed the rest on the top shelf of the book case. She scuttled to its base and sat unmoving, staring up with hungry piggy eyes.

Father thanked us politely for the ten Hamlet cigars we'd given him. But mother's present still lay untouched. Open it, *open* it, I willed her. Father placed the shallow Hamlet tin on the table then drew a fat metal tube from his top pocket. He extracted a long thick Havana cigar and proceeded to cut through one end with a blade, preparing the extravagant monster for his mouth. I blanked my mind to his insensitivity. *Why doesn't she open it*, I inwardly screamed.

Father clicked a flame to his lighter and, as if that were the signal, mother's red-painted talons began to pick at the sticky tape binding the parcel up tight.

I could hear father's lips tightening and slackening in rhythmic pops, could smell the pungent aroma evocative of Christmas since childhood. My eyes refused to leave her. My lungs refused to breathe. This too was part of family tradition. The tension of wondering how my mother would react.

At last the gold-flecked black chiffon scarf was hoisted into view. There was silence. No-one moved. Then, amazingly, dove-like murmurs emanated from her throat. I couldn't believe it. She even smiled. Reverently she clutched the stole to her chest, squeezing it there in both hands, eyes closed, a look of ecstasy on her face. Was she winding me up? She must be!

She stood and spun around, wafting it in the air. I cast a glance at Bernard and he winked back, raising his thumb. Mother held the edge seductively above the tip of her nose, swivelling her eyes and hips from side to side. Suddenly she whisked it dramatically sideways, shaking it like a matador tempting a bull. She laughed out loud then wrapped it around her scrawny neck and scurried to the mirror at the far end of the room. The two ends drifted behind her like gossamer wings. I expected to see her float up to the star-studded heaven of my dream. She *liked* it! She really seemed to like it. Or did she. Wasn't her reaction a bit OTT?

With tiny twinkling steps she ran to me, placed her hands on my shoulders and kissed me on each cheek. '*Thank* you,' she said, 'you have surpassed yourself!' Then she went to Bernard and skittishly flicked a chiffon end in his face. She kissed him too. 'And thank *you* son-in-law,' she gushed.

I felt bewildered. It was as if Norah Harker-Balls had spoken kindly to a child.

Later, as Bernard and I prepared the Christmas dinner, she coo'd and hummed, whistled and sang, the mantle at various times wrapped around her shoulders, her hips and her head. It was tied and untied, looked through and looked around. Each new idea checked in front of the mirror.

I smiled at Bernard. 'She *does* like it,' I whispered, now almost fully convinced.

Then for a while the stole was forgotten and all activities stopped for Her Majesty's Christmas Day television message to the nation.

'What do you know,' anti-royalist mother barracked, 'never lived in a council house in yer life ... talk to your petunias Queenie like yer son does ... a petunia's got more sense than most of your subjects ... can't see one of them kotowing to another because it happened to be fertilised in the right bed ... ha ha ha.'

Mother's cracks and cackles aggravatingly drowned out most of what our Queen was saying, but I managed to pick up the gist.

'Happy Christmas to you too Liz,' mother yelled as the speech wound down.

And the Queen smiled regally into our sitting room and nodded as if she had heard. 'And a prosperous New Year,' her majesty added, staring directly at me. *It was as if she knew I was out to make money and was egging me on*!

'Now you're paying your taxes we might stand a chance of a bit of prosperity,' mother jeered, concluding, 'what's yer tax code Mrs Windsor!' Elated by her witty badinage with the Queen of England, mother grabbed up her glass of sparkling wine and raised it. 'Good luck and prosperity,' she cried.

'Good luck and prosperity,' we all repeated. And as the bubbles fizzed down my throat I thought, *and it* will *be a prosperous New Year. I don't know how it will happen, but I am strangely sure for today our monarch has confirmed it.*

All through dinner mother chattered. Bernard and I had wasted our time slaving in the kitchen. Roast turkey, chestnut stuffing, curls of bacon, tiny sausages, roast potatoes, roast parsnips, brussel sprouts and perfect gravy were all golloped down while she rabbited on.

'Did I ever tell you what happened during the war?' she had started. *Did you ever not*! I thought. 'About how my grandmother sheltered from the Jerry bombs under her table in her house round the corner from where I lived.'

'Yes mother, you've told us - what do you think of the turkey?'

'Turkey!' she screeched, shoving a forkful in her gob, 'there wasn't any turkey. You had to queue for oranges and we never saw a banana let alone turkey. No, my grandmother, your so-called *kind, gentle* great-grandmother, prayed to God as the evil bastard Krauts released their infernal agents of death upon us. She pleaded with Him that she wouldn't be killed and I watched a glinting hell bomb that was destined for her house suddenly veer off and screech its fearsome path smack into the middle of our roof.'

'You stupid bitch,' bellowed father, 'you didn't look up and see that bomb change direction, you were safely packed away on a shelf in your Anderson shelter.'

'Oh yes I *did* see it,' mother persisted, looking defiant. She had told this tale so many times that she now believed it.

'And I looked beyond ...' *Oh dear, she's in one of her creative moods*! '... I looked beyond that black canister of death hurtling towards me and saw his piercing red eyes, fearsomely staring at me ...'

'Whose eyes, the pilot's or the bomb-dropper's?' I asked, mystified by this new addition.

'*GOD'S*' she shrieked, '*GOD'S* eyes. You wouldn't think He'd be so petty would you, re-directing bombs at me because I hadn't had the presence of mind to pray for my salvation as my grandmother had.'

Only the sound of eating could be heard as we all digested this new idea.

'You stupid bitch,' father reiterated. He looked put out and I knew it was because he liked to tell his wartime stories at Christmas, and she'd got in first.

Mother's narrow snout sniffed at a roast parsnip dangling on the prongs of her fork. 'Think you can fob 'em off as potatoes don't you, but I can smell 'em a mile off,' she said, poking it with her finger onto the side of her plate.

I wondered whether, if you did kill such a mother, a jury of twelve intelligent, sensitive citizens, would let you off. I thought they would. Justifiable matricide they could call it.

After the meal was over we all went and relaxed in front of the log fire in the other room. Father wriggled, re-positioning himself in Bernard's chair. He undid the top button of his beige cardi then cleared his throat. We all knew what was to come.

'Did I ever tell you about when I was evacuated at the beginning of the war,' he began. 'I was sixteen, but still bundled off with hoards of kids, a label round me neck and a bar of chocolate in me hand.'

Hermione hove into view, abandoning her position by the book case. She sat straight and alert in front of him, eyes gleaming. *She's recognised the word chocolate again*, I realised, impressed by her porcine intelligence. Her pale amber eyes never wavered from his animated face as he re-lived his year with Welsh bullies and his journey to Aldershot to join the army. As the oft-told stories continued mother wrapped the stole twice round her head, binding her ears tightly down. Her chin drooped onto her chest and she fell into instant sleep. Continuing family tradition, Bernard and I quickly followed suit.

As I dozed I had a feeling of contentment. The day had started off fractious and I'd been taut with anxiety, but it wasn't turning out so badly.

I opened one eye. The pig still sat bolt upright, wide awake, alert, listening, waiting for the promised chocolate to appear. I shut my eyes, giving in to sleep. At least father had one listener. Good old pig.

We set up the card table. Mother insisted on wearing the stole to play bridge in and kept stroking it in an ostentatious way. Doubts again resurfaced. Did she really hate it? Was she winding me up?

When I was dummy I studied her face. She still had the high cheekbones and hollow cheeks I'd always envied. I imagined painting her. The thin nose with its narrow nostrils. The two downward curving lines grooving into the rounded flesh each side of her wide mouth. The finely etched tributaries that branched off willy-nilly that I'd never noticed before. The pelmet of skin above her top lip drawn into neat pencil pleats.

Suddenly her face lit up. 'Having no spades,' she shrieked, banging a card down, ruffing Bernard's ace. She grinned impishly at me, her sparkling blue eyes mischievous like a child's, and suddenly I understood why people thought she was younger than her years. It was her vivacity that blinded them.

'You're two off,' she whooped, face radiant, and I was disconcerted to find I was wishing I could be more like her.

But the game of bridge quickly became a noisy battle ground and Bernard and I sat silent in the cross-fire of their spite. Father called her a silly bitch for the fifth time and I thought *this is enough, I am fifty and I have promised myself to be assertive and daring. Let this be the start.*

'Father,' I said, feeling my heart slip its moorings and flounder in the heavy seas inside my chest. 'Father. Stop being so rude!'

For a few seconds the only sound was the slow tick tock of the grandfather clock and I feared my ticker had stopped altogether.

At last he gathered his wits and roared, 'But she *is* a silly bitch, she should have ruffed.'

I willed myself not to avert my gaze from his outraged eyes. 'That is true, she should have ruffed,' I began. (With relief I felt my heart kick-start into erratic beating.) 'But you could have told her in a more polite way.'

Mother's amazed-looking eyes swivelled round at me. 'Is that you Freda?' she said.

Father glared at me. 'A more polite way! Don't be so stupid Freda, it's your mother we're talking about, not the flipping Queen.'

Across the table, Bernard smiled his encouragement and nodded his head as if I should carry on, but I knew that I was finished. I'd lost the will to fight, the will to play bridge and nearly the will to live.

At bedtime I plastered my face in mother's enriching night cream and fell into instant sleep.

I woke early because my neck and face were driving me mad with irritation. Half asleep, I dragged myself to the mirror. It was not a pretty sight. My eyes were puffy and my face and neck were covered in a blotchy rash.

Downstairs, mother drifted over to stare at me. 'What's the matter with your dial?' she asked.

I peered at her through marshmallow lids. I was astounded. Even though my eyes were mere slits, I could clearly see that she wore the chiffon stole round her shoulders and, inexplicably, a crazy black-sequinned skull cap on her head, from the centre of which sprouted a clump of tall feathers that quivered noisily as she moved.

Her face loomed close, eyes squinting, head dipping and rising as her nose traced out the contours of my face. She drew back, plumes dancing. 'It must be that cream I gave you. Your Aunt Olivia's phizog came up just the same,' she pronounced.

Evil thoughts again pervaded my mind.

During breakfast she announced that they had decided to go back home to 'good old Tooting'. Choirs of angels burst into sweet song in my head.

After we'd eaten, the pig went outside and father went upstairs to pack. Mother, still in her absurd head gear, said, 'I'm just going out to say goodbye to Hermione. Who knows, she might be dead by the time we come again.'

'Or you might be,' Bernard muttered, putting my thoughts into words. (Afterwards I realised it was one of the few times he'd spoken this Christmas.)

As mother struggled into her purple anorak, the feathers on her hat rippled and swayed as if in a gale. 'Don't frighten the pig,' I ventured as she ducked through the low doorway, snapping a plume as she went.

Father limped down carrying their suitcase. He plonked it down. 'What's the time? he asked, flinging his arm out prior to folding it back to view his watch. His speeding fist collided with mother's quills just as she ducked back inside.

'If I hadn't bent my knees when I came through that door you'd have punched me right on the nose,' she complained.

'Pity,' he growled back.

She went to the mirror, crouching to view her crest. Two more broken feathers dangled, but nine or ten others still stood erect. 'I'll have to cellotape them up,' she muttered, and I wondered when and where she intended to wear it again!

Outside, mother bounded eagerly to their car parked on our gravel drive. I watched in disbelief as she manoeuvred herself into it like a limbo dancer, knees bent, arms stuck out straight, head tilted back, feathers diagonal. Father entered the other side. Doors slammed, the engine revved. I held the gate open, and they were away, mother's arm waving from the open window as she steadfastly gazed up at the roof. They disappeared round the corner and suddenly there was blissful silence. I knew that within half a mile she'd remove her hat. It was all done for effect.

'Well, at least they don't hang around once they've made up their minds,' Bernard observed.

'This Christmas was even worse than usual,' I wailed. 'Father still bullies me and mother takes everything we do for granted.'

'But she liked your present,' Bernard reminded me, 'for the first time ever, so it wasn't all bad.'

Yes she did. She really did. She liked my present!

Hand in hand we wandered round the side of the cottage to the pig's quarters. Hermione was sitting stiffly in the doorway at the top of the ramp. Eyes gleaming, she peered haughtily at us down the length of her snout. Tied loosely round her neck was the gold-flecked black chiffon stole!

I could have cried.

Six
Intrusion 2

Was I glad to get back to Tooting and a bit of civilisation. I bore Freda in the maternity ward, but now she sure as hell bores me. Every Christmas is a bore. Staying in their cottage in the dreary countryside's a bore. Bernard's nice but a bore. Bore bore bore. Pity the pig's a sow not a boar! Maeve grins at her own private joke.

'What's happened to your mouth?' Hector enquires.

'I'm smiling.'

'Good.'

'Why good?'

'I thought you'd had a stroke.'

'*Very* funny.'

'It wasn't meant to be funny. It gave me a shock to see your lips all twisted up at the ends like that.'

Pretend to read the paper again. It's only five past two and I've given myself till four without getting involved in a row.

She steals a look at him sitting opposite in his special chair with its long legs, long like his, though his are crossed at the knee with one spasmodically bouncing. Bad for his hip but she doesn't say so, two hours will be hard enough without looking for a row. She stares down at her paper and drifts back to her thoughts.

All that deadly Wood Hill rustic peace and quiet. I wouldn't swap it for the rumble of London traffic and the wail of sirens. Not for anything. At least you know someone's alive out there. Unless of course the wail's an ambulance going to someone dead.

'Your mouth's gone funny again.'

He has to bloody well comment on me all the time. It drives me mad. Needle needle needle. She doesn't look up. *I don't know about me having a stroke, Freda nearly gave me a heart attack the way she stood up to him when we were playing bridge. She never usually says boo to a goose. She reminds me of a limp lettuce leaf - but not so colourful. Not like she used to be: a wondrous butterfly spreading beauty as she flitted through my life. But a butterfly was meant to emerge from its dull grey chrysalis, not skulk back into it!* She gives a wry smile.

'You're at it again,' his aggravating voice pipes up.

Ignore him. Don't rise to his bait. Whatever you do don't get involved. She thinks back to before she had Freda. To when she was eighteen and heady with the excitement of having boobs and pubic hair. A saucy minx always ready for a lark, flirting with the Yanks who told her she was pretty and gave out nylons and spearmint gum. *But I'd hung on to my virginity until that evening.*

Their fourth date, when she'd guzzled down the unaccustomed alcohol then closed her eyes and opened her legs. Not to a dashing G.I. but to Lance Corporal Hector Salmon, home on leave from the war. Seven months after reluctantly tying the knot with him, one was being tied round her baby's umbilical cord. How she regretted it. The thought of what might have been was always there, like a dull ache lurking at the back of her mind. *Why hadn't I heeded my grandmother's dire warning about drink making good girls do things that, when sober, they hardly dared dream of. Why!*

'That's more normal,' he says, Your lips can shrink quicker than a prick in a snowstorm.'

Ignore him again. Riling me is his entertainment. If I can stick out two hours I've promised myself a bar of marzipan chocolate as my reward. Fifty years I've had of it. People think I'm eccentric but I didn't start out that way. I've had to force myself to extremes, like a space rocket thrusting away from his gravity. My wearing that showgirl headgear was my way of saying I am ME - take it or lump it. My way of avoiding being sucked into their mediocrity. Freda's presents are always so naff. I made a special effort this year to be kind, feigned delight at that dreadful scarf. When does she think I'll ever wear such a thing - down at the Bridge Club on a Wednesday afternoon?! But when she couldn't even disguise how pleased she was that we were going home, something snapped and that's when I went outside and tied it round Hermione's neck. I regret it now in a way. She hasn't mentioned it but it must have upset her. Anyway the pig seemed to like it so that should please my daughter, she's besotted with that swine.

Maeve turns a page of the paper, stares at it with vacant eyes.

How could I have been so weak as to allow him to force his choice of name on my babe. My baby was Trixie. But he, dictatorial Hector Salmon, home on compassionate leave to see his two day old little girl, had decreed that Trixie was only fit for a floozy and that Freda was to be her name. If I hadn't been only nineteen and scared of my new husband, I wouldn't have given in.

Maeve closes her eyes seeing disconnected snapshots of the past. Her dear father, going out on his old bike all hours to dig up roads for the Gas Light and Coke Company. It was he who recognised that she had brains and who insisted she stayed on at school. School, but not university. Working class parent didn't know about university. Working class girls didn't know they were allowed to go to university. Working class girls were stupid. Well she'd proved it hadn't she. Proved what people thought. Working class girls were only good for a good lay and getting put up the spout.

Even now I feel the shame of letting my dear dad down. He had trusted me, encouraged me to have ambition, although a secretarial course was as high as he dared dream.

'Are you asleep?'

It's him. The source of all that went wrong. Hector Salmon. She sees a clear picture of the whiskery old man who was her boss at BHS, Marylebone Road. Hears him say, 'I've called you into my office to inform you that you have been made redundant.' Then he had sweetly smiled and she had the notion that he was telling her of something to her advantage, maybe promotion. It was the smile that had confused her. The smile together with the unknown word. *It's hard to realise that in 1944 'redundant' was a little used word that was incomprehensible to me and thousands of others too. And that being pregnant resulted in getting the push.*

She visualises the naive contentment of her mother. Sees her plump outstretched arms as she takes hold of her new grandchild.

'Take no notice of what people think,' she had said, making no judgement on my morals, 'this baby can only bring love.'

And it had been true. I adored my darling daughter and we lived in happiness in Bethnal Green. But five months after her birth the harmony was destroyed by peace.

She looks over to him, thinks of how he was back in 1945: tall and good looking, fiery red hair with a fiery temper to match it. A man she hardly knew.

When the fighting stopped in Europe, war started in my rented flat. He moved in and hung his demob suit in my wardrobe. Not used to having a yowling baby. Not used to having a wife. Not used to his new safe job as a bank clerk. Maybe he was as unhappy as me. Maybe I shouldn't have let him see my resentment that he was there. Maybe I shouldn't have riled him. Maybe it was inevitable that he should lash out and black my eye. Just the once and it scared him as much as it scared me. Months later I dared to call him Sockeye. Sockeye Salmon. He's never accepted the joke.

I didn't know him then but I know him now all right. Look at him. Mouth set tight. A smattering of greyish amber hair on his white speckled bonce. Half-moon glasses like delicate gold edged panniers perched on an elephant! Snake green eyes hiding under drooping eyelids, always secretly watching. Drooping shoulders too, as if taut wires holding him together were stretching and about to give way.

She accidentally catches his eye and hastily looks back down to the paper. *I wish I'd been born later. Nowadays if you were stupid enough to let a sperm-spewing rocket inside you, you weren't expected to marry the careless prick. But, back then it was expected.* She remembers howling her eyes out to her grandmother, saying she didn't want to marry the soldier called Lance Corporal Hector Salmon. *Even now I can recite her exact reply: 'Duckie, when you're bloody stupid enough to have a bun in the oven you marry the bleedin' baker. That's if he'll have you.'*

She thinks of the quick registry office wedding. The fifteenth of May 1944. Barely nineteen, she had dripped tears onto the bunch of red roses clutched in her hands. *What a complete tragedy it had seemed. Complete until Trixie-Freda was born. She'd been such a joy, brightening the austere post-war years with laughter and love. My living doll.*

Maeve jumps up and walks to the window, stares out at the slow moving traffic on the road beyond their low hedge. A little Asian girl wearing a turquoise jacket, its hood edged with emerald green fur, holds her mother's hand as she walks past. *I remember cutting up old dresses and making Freda bright pretty clothes. She always looked a picture. And I would twist her flaming red hair up in rags at night then, next morning, brush the tresses round my finger into bouncing corkscrew curls.*

Maeve smiles to herself then hastily looks over to see if her lip movement has been observed. But he is staring into space, looking thoughtful.

When Freda was eight and I was twenty-seven, I dyed my hair auburn to try to look as if I was her sister, but it turned out too brassy and so I went back to my natural bottle blonde! But we enjoyed each other like sisters all the same. Oh Trixie, where have you gone?

She hears his feet shuffle on the carpet. He was being unnaturally silent. This bet with herself was proving a doddle. She can almost taste the sweet chocolate marzipan in her mouth. She walks back to her chair, picks up the paper and pretends to read again as she tries to remember when the trouble with Freda began.

It was when she left school. That was it. That was the beginning. Not for my Freda the glamour of a modelling career, nor a course at art college to exploit her talent and love of art. For once she was adamant about something. She would go to training college and become a school teacher - to exploit her love of children. I couldn't believe it. All my ambitions for my daughter's fame and fortune dashed, just because she adored noisy brats. How it must have upset her not to have any of her own. Years ago she confided that she stood on her head for three minutes after each sexual encounter, trying to juggle Bernard's sperms into her dodgy tubes.

Maeve tries to imagine her stodgy daughter doing it, but cannot. Not nowadays at any rate.

If they weren't past it they could do the whole thing in a test tube now. It seems so cold, but perhaps not quite as cold as the damp grass in the park where my only conception took place!

Maeve readjusts the combs holding up her hair, poking at the long wispy strands that have escaped. Hector clears his throat and she stiffens, waiting for his remarks, but silence settles again. It's almost spooky.

Being childless should have made her more with-it, less set in her ways, but it seems to have done the opposite. All my friends say that their children are their best pals. I'm not sure I even like mine any more. A Trixie would have been full of adventure and fun, the opposite of my lumpy frumpy Freda.

Hector raises his eyes. 'You look miserable. How about a cup of tea?'

'I'd love one,' she replies knowing full well he isn't offering.

'Stupid bitch! You know I don't make the tea.'

No, all you do is make me tense, she thinks marching out to the kitchen reigning herself in from a row.

As she waits for the kettle to boil she thinks of Christmas again, and her brief escape from boredom and from HIM. *I enjoyed the walk with Hermione along the track hidden by the high hedge. As I whacked the pig along with a branch I'd felt free. Free I think for the first time in my life.*

'Buck up with that tea Maeve,' Sockeye's voice rasps.

She puts down the teapot she'd just lifted and perches herself on the edge of the stool. Let him wait! She gazes out to their small back garden with vacant eyes. She remembers snatching the set of keys labelled SCHOOL off the hook in the hall, then, when she and the pig had arrived there, trying each one in the padlock securing the strong chunky chain. When one had fitted she'd pushed open the heavy wrought iron gate, shoving Hermione in front of her before locking up behind.

Inside the school there'd been no one to tell her what to do or say. No one to comment on her every move. Nothing she had to do. Only Hermione to let out when she signalled the call of nature by giving her three special short honks. *If Freda's as good at teaching kids as she is at training pigs she must be brilliant!*

I sat in the staff room reading magazines, drinking instant coffee and eating biscuits. When night fell I curled up in the lumpy arm chair in front of the two-bar fire and Hermione stretched herself out at my feet. It had been murder. By morning the joy of being away from HIM had been overtaken by stiff joints and boredom. When the pig came in from doing her business I shared a chocolate flake with her - one that I'd taken along. By evening I was wondering why no-one had bothered to find us and how I could get back in time for Christmas without losing face. Then I heard the carnival procession and couldn't resist tagging along. And then to discover they were searching for me! That was a laugh.

'WHAT'S HAPPENED TO THE TEA?' the voice of doom booms.

It's stewing. It's waiting in readiness to be poured down your lazy throat. Or poured down the inside of your trousers. If it scalded your thingy off it'd make no difference to me. Maeve purses her lips, not giving in to the urge to bawl back a reply. She picks up the pot and slowly pours.

It'd been fun getting him going with the 'sex maniac' gibes. He hasn't a clue on sex maniacking, but it was such sweet revenge for all the times he's shown me up in public. It made Freda curious too. I saw the look in her eyes. Although even my vivid imagination can't picture her and Bernard getting devious in bed.

'COME ON - I'M PARCHED!' the voice of King Hector roars.

She carries the tray out of the peaceful kitchen into the trench that leads to the war zone. She hands Herr Capitaine his tea and he looks up with a smile.

'I quite enjoyed this Christmas, did you?' he says.

She feels as shocked as if he's chucked the whole steaming mugful over her head, then machine gunned her to shreds. He had smiled. He had been pleasant. And he had made the kind of statement that proved he must be totally out of his mind.

'Marginally better than being run over by a double-decker bus,' she snaps.

It was nearly quarter past three and the row began.

Seven

The only good thing about Christmas is you get two weeks off school, so when the relations have gone there's still time to enjoy yourself.

When I woke up this morning, I decided to try out my ambition to be sexy (and a bit daring). I snuggled close to Bernie and was just trying to rake up courage to stick my tongue in his ear - a thing I've never done but have read about - when he leapt up saying he had to go and muck out the pig.

I got up and dressed, feeling somewhat dejected. But then I rallied my thoughts. This is part of the test, I told myself. True ambitions are not achieved easily. To transform yourself you must stick with it.

When Bernard came back in he moaned that it had been hard smelly work dumping the old straw in the ditch and he was going up to soak in a bath. Here was my chance.

I gave him five minutes, then crept up after him. I could hear him splashing and singing happily. Hastily I undressed and slunk into the bathroom. Abruptly, his 'Merry merry pipes of Pan' stopped dead. Half closing my eyes, I slowly lifted one foot onto the edge of the bath. He made a peculiar sound as if being strangled and shot his knees up under his chin. I began my slow sexy entry into the swirling space, grateful the bathtub was long.

'KEEP OUT FREED!' he shrieked, 'with the size of you, there'll be a friggin' flood!'

But I did not falter. This was the new me. Deftly, I hoiked out the plug and continued my descent.

'What do you think you're doing!'

'I'm being sexy and daring,' I crooned.

Then, suddenly, my feet slipped, slamming me backwards into the taps and sending a tidal wave of water slapping up to the low ceiling and cascading back down. I shook drips off my deluged head then peered over anxiously at the puddled cork tiles. Forget it, I cautioned myself. Forget the mopping up. Just remember the new sexy you. I forced myself back into the dagger taps and slowly winked at my man. He stared back with a look of total bewilderment. Silently we sat lodged together in the swirling water that gradually seeped out down the plug hole positioned beneath my rear. Our pale bodies seemed to ooze out like wet cement filling the emptying space. He cleared his throat. Yes oh yes I inwardly implored him.

'I am worried,' he stated.

I could feel my breasts gently swaying in the eddies of sinking water and wondered if he might be worried about having an erection brought on by the display.

'Honey,' I said (and that was the first time I'd ever called him that). 'Honey, don't be worried. If you've got a hard-on we could try doing it in here.' As soon as I'd uttered those careless words I became worried. Worried that if either of us moved, let alone writhed, we could crash through the old timber floor, riding the short void in our kamikaze bathtub to a humiliating death pitched into our kitchen floor.

Underneath me, the gurgle of escaping water had changed to the sound of jelly being slowly released from a mould. The titillating currents were playing havoc with my nether outlets. *Soon, make it soon*, I mentally pleaded, my Beatrice in turmoil, my anus sparking sensations I'd never known before.

'I'm not worried about an *erection*!' he said scornfully. 'What I'm worried about is the starter motor of my car. It's unreliable. Especially this weather.'

I hauled myself up feeling gross and ugly. I floundered out, clumsily skidding on the pool patched floor. The last dregs of water whooshed away and he stretched his long legs and sighed. I snatched up a towel and fled.

'It's your fault if my armpits stink. There's no water left and I hadn't even washed!' he shouted after me.

Bernard is full of remorse. He knows he hurt my feelings yesterday. It was a horrible humiliation for me, but it must have awakened his dormant yearnings because he keeps on about having an early night and is for ever putting his arms round me.

'Too late, missed your chance,' I said. 'I've started my period.'
(Doubtless brought on four days early by yesterday's shock.)

Fifty years old and not a sign of the menopause. Not even one hot flush. The monthly paraphernalia costs a packet. It'd be just my luck to be so old when I do stop that all financial gain will have to be spent on hearing aid batteries.

It is the penultimate day of the year and depression has settled heavily upon me. I cannot change. Whatever made me think I could. I have given up trying to be sexy and daring. How can I? I'm all the F words rolled into one. Freda, fat, frumpy, fearful and foolish - fuck it! It could become a habit to think that word: I find it satisfying.

Now it is New Year's Eve and I am waiting until midnight to decide whether to keep to my ambitions or give up and continue in the old dull, yet contented, routine. To give up would be easiest. After all, why change? Not many women are lucky enough to share their lives with a loving husband and an adorable pig, neither of whom seem to give a toss that I'm overweight and boring.

I rang father to wish him a happy seventy-first birthday. Mother came on the line, supposedly to wish us a happy New Year, but really wanting a long-distance referee for their latest spat.

'He's so indecisive. Other people are going to pyjama parties or to Trafalgar Square or to New Year's Eve dinners and he can't even make up his mind about going to the British Legion dance and I've bought him a new tie.'

At least you're contemplating doing *something*, I thought. What are we doing tonight. Nothing except watching other people enjoy themselves on the box. Is this the way to live? I *will* change. I have decided.

At midnight we kissed and drank a toast in Babycham. Bernard went up to bed and I decided to write down my ambitions as New Year Resolutions so I can re-read them whenever I weaken or lose direction. I found my Pig Lovers Diary given by Bernard last Christmas. It was full of blank pages, but on the last page I wrote:-

Nothing worth reporting has happened all year. The fabric of my life has become threadbare like an ancient tapestry, but

I vow to weave it back to its former glory. I therefore make the following New Year Resolutions.

1. I will lose weight.
2. I will speak my mind.
3. I will make money, hopefully BIG.
4. I will be more sexy and try to surprise Bernie in bed.
5. I will do a daring activity.
6. I will save the pupils from their tyrannical Head.
7. If I make enough to afford it, I'll get my girl mated, and rear a family of grandchildren piglets.

As I slipped under the duvet next to Bernie, I quivered with anticipation. Would I really be strong enough to make the big transformation? I lay on my back repeating the seven great aims in my head, like a mantra. A soporific mantra ... the seven wonders ... yawn ... that would change ... my ...

Eight

I chucked out yet another bucket of water but, this time, hysterical squealing joined the sharp slap of water as it landed far below. From the attic room window I could see Hermione careering down the garden, water spraying off her as she bucked like some crazy pink dolphin. Bernard must have seen what happened too because I heard him pound up the stairs then pound down again. I watched him chase after her, his long legs leaping puddles, our best eau-de-Nil bath towel trailing the ground. I hurried down and met him as he puffed back. Gathered up in his hands was the sodden towel covered in filth. He explained that the pig would have caught pneumonia if he hadn't rubbed her down and, once again, pronounced he'd saved her bacon.

'Excuse me,' I said, 'but bath towels don't grow on trees. That was our very expensive best eau-de-Nil.'

'Oh, really,' he replied, holding it up to his nose, 'it now seems to be our very expensive best eau-de-pig! Get it?' He dug me in the ribs. 'Odour pig. Pig pong.'

I wished he was as keen on making money as he was at making jokes.

Later I toiled up to the attic again and stood listening to the soft plips and plops of gently leaking rain. Calming, disarming, like piped music at the dentist's that lulled the gullible but never ever fooled me.

Today has been the start of a new year and, supposedly, a new me, but instead of feeling full of hope and ambition I just feel dejected and old.

Another Monday. Another laundry day. Another rain day. Another day of worry re lack of money.

Bernard went up to empty the buckets in the 'shower room' as he so humorously puts it, before going off to teach. When he came back we were to have a brain storming session on money making ideas. But when he did come back his face was florid as if he was on the verge of a brain storming stroke. He shouted that his stupid learner woman had turned right at a roundabout, *literally*, nearly killing him. I reckon he's been nearly killed more times than James Bond. And on top of that, the flashing wind screen wipers had set off one of his heads.

'*I've* got a headache as well,' I retorted nastily, thumping the iron down on his shirt, 'a headache from worrying about you only nearly getting killed on the road once a day. *One* lesson doesn't even bring in enough to run your car.'

He looked miserable and defeated as he took the Paracetamols and, full of remorse for my unkindness, I unplugged the iron and gently kissed him on the back of his neck. But my tenderness didn't register because he just swatted where my lips had brushed as if I'd been a fly.

There is not even a portrait session down at the Art Club this Tuesday because of the Christmas holiday. Just when everybody needs something cheery to take their minds off things. In my case, things like the memory of my pig sporting the black chiffon stole, plus our tile-dropping roof.

A raindrop spiked my reflected upturned face, exploding my forehead into rippling fragments. I bent down lower, dipped my finger in. There was no doubt. The bucket that had been emptied late last night was already practically full and it was only seven a.m. Forget the sexy daring and all the rest of the resolutions, the only ambition that mattered now was the making of enough money to fix the roof. A pellet stung the back of my head and icy wetness oozed across my scalp. I straightened and surveyed the desolate unfurnished room that, until a few months ago, had been my cosy hide-away. Three buckets, two large plastic cartons and an old Victorian chamber pot were strategically placed under the trickles. But, by the sound of the pounding rain, the trickles would soon become cascades. We are reaching crisis point and I am scared.

Bernard decided on, what he called, a working breakfast, during which we were meant to throw ideas at each other, but, except for the crunching of toast and some 'ums' it was an unusually silent meal, broken eventually by the rattle of the letter box and the sound of a newspaper flopping down onto the mat. Bernard pronounced the meeting over and went to pick up the freebie local paper, bringing it back to the table. An advert on the front page zinged out in big bold letters: *MAKE MONEY FROM YOUR GARDEN! Is your garden too big for you? Could you do with instant cash? If so, contact The Squeezamin Property Development Company who require building plots in your area. Ring Orlford 4568.*

I looked through the french windows to our vast garden sloping down to the wooded valley and far-off misty hills. We'd bought the cottage because of that view nineteen long years ago. I remembered myself aged thirty-one. *If we move here*, I had thought, *children must surely come.* I had dreamed of a son climbing the apple tree and a daughter leaping the shallow rivulets that meandered down from the spring. *It had only slowly dawned on me that I was never to conceive. And it was only today that I realised that I didn't even want to any more and that the ache that shadowed my heart was for the grandchildren imprisoned, unknown and unloved, in our genes.*

I walked out into the drizzle that cried down from the sky. Was the selling of part of this child-free garden the answer? If the garage were demolished and the pig's mobile home relocated, there'd be space for a driveway leading down to a house. Tears spilled, joining soft raindrops trickling down my face. Perhaps it would be easier to sell the cottage and move, but I couldn't see my pig in a normal sized garden. And I couldn't see normal neighbours putting up with her.

'Are you okay?' Bernard asked as I blundered back indoors.

'Perfectly,' I lied, rushing to the cupboard, hauling out dusters, polish and the vacuum cleaner to begin the weekly clean. Vigorously, I laboured at furniture, ornaments and floors, but, no matter how hard I scrubbed, the black cloud that had settled over everything would not shift. I thought things couldn't possibly get any worse but, just as I'd got stuck into the lavatory, the phone rang and Bernard called up: 'It's your mother wanting a word.'

My mother's 'a word' was more like a full length novel and, even though now it's the next day, I'm still smarting from her comments that I was too set in my ways. '*Somebody's* got to do the chores on a regular basis,' I had snapped (completely forgetting at that moment my stated desire to get out of my rut) to which she replied, 'Why?' I find there's no answer to replies like that.

And it is still pelting with rain and my back aches from lugging buckets and tubs to the window. We've had to put even more 'catchers' down too, so saucepans now litter the floor and when the last one gets used I won't even be able to boil a potato. Action has to be taken, and now. Slowly, I forced myself to the hall phone. Shakily, I tapped out the number.

'Squeezamin Property here ...' an oily voice replied.

One hour later, a flashy red sports car pulled up outside and a stick insect unfolded itself onto the lane. It wore a dark suit, red tie and long black wellington boots. A comb was flicked through black slicked back hair before the gate was unlatched and he bounded down our puddled driveway, hateful eagerness in each splashing stride. I opened the door to stare straight into a close-set pair of khaki eyes. Two long narrow incisors shot into a rodent grin and his paw was thrust out to pump my hand in avaricious greeting. The insect, I realised, had turned out to be more of a rat.

'William Boggins,' he announced, 'better known as Bill. Come ta take a gander at yer plot.'

My legs felt heavy as I led him round to the back garden. An ache filled my chest, like when my grandmother died. We squelched to the apple tree. He looked around, hands gyrating together in a sensual twisting dance. I heard myself ask how much the land would be worth.

'Well, it'd obvoosely be worf more if we could git more'n one dwellin' on it,' he replied.

More'n one dwellin' on it! I felt myself sinking into the pig-rooted mire unable to move.

'It's a bit boggy, must be all this pissin' rain,' he brilliantly observed.

All this pissin' rain that's pissin' through my pissin' roof, I thought angrily as I fought to move against the suction of the boggy trap.

'Don't count yer chickens will yer,' he advised, casting me a crafty look. 'Although I do have inflooonce on the council, it's not a cert that I can git plannin' permission.'

It's not a cert that I can git plannin' permission! Maybe it wouldn't happen. With a sudden squelch I was free.

I related the visit of Bill Boggins to Bernard. 'I wonder what makes you take an instant dislike to someone,' I brooded.

'I suppose it saves time,' he replied.

Dear Bernard. Still joking, but sadness clouded his eyes.

We agreed to hang on till Saturday. Just three days to dream up a better idea. If inspiration failed, we'd offer the plot for the dwelling that would block off our wonderful view but give us back a cottage that was rain-proof. And how I was longing to turn the attic back into my studio. The carpet had been too sodden to keep, but the comfy old arm chair, and table and stool, were stored ready in the back of the garage. And all my art paraphernalia was crammed into the cupboard under the stairs just waiting for release. I stared out across the diamond frosted lawn to the silver grey hills beyond. Just three days to think up another solution before it disappeared. But my mind was a blank.

Tomorrow is the start of the new term. I nurture the crazy hope that the festive season will have mellowed Norah Harker-Balls. But I know it's a crazy idea.

Nine

Reluctantly, I pushed open the staff room door. Sylvie Shepherd was inside flapping her hand around. When she saw me she dragged air in noisily through nostrils that flared with accusation.

'What's up?' I asked, perturbed.

The disgusting stink of your pig, that's what's up,' she grumbled, waving her hand about even more vigorously and wrinkling up her nose. 'I met that woman from Rugged Farm, and she told me your pet pig had stayed here in this staff room with your mother when they went AWOL at Christmas.'

'Excuse me,' I retorted, 'the females *don't* smell. Like human beings, it's the males that make all the pong.' But I was mystified, for now I was right inside the room I could smell a vague niff in the air.

Then Norah Harker-Balls marched in and the 'vague niff' became an all-out gas attack. She bore down on me, actually smiling, and I shrank back against the wall, unnerved by the twin assault on my senses.

'Do you like my new perfume?' she trilled clanking her multi-braceletted wrist under my nose.

My head jerked back with whiplash speed more violent than any car crash. Not waiting for a reply, she sailed past into her adjoining office and I rushed out to the fresh air of my class room.

'Does anyone know why Jimmie isn't at school today?' I asked, looking up from the register.

Gary raised his hand. 'I played with him yesterday and he said he was going to jump out of his bedroom window because he didn't want to have to see Mrs Harker-Balls any more.'

'He said that when I was with him too,' agreed Annabel.

Is his bedroom on the ground floor?' I asked without much hope.

'Nope, it's upstairs,' Gary beamed.

A worm of unease slithered around my head. They were all terrified of her. Would Jimmie really do it? Would he deliberately break a leg or even kill himself? Was he that scared?

Suddenly the door flung open and the boy himself burst in and twenty voices groaned their disappointment.

'I told Miss you were going to jump out your window,' Gary complained.

Jimmie snatched off his cap. 'Changed me mind didn't I!'

They settled down to writing about Christmas and I began to hear the slow ones read. As each struggled to make sense of the hieroglyphics on the page I concluded that English spelling made about as much sense as my life.

Next day, Norah H-B, hair pulled back into an elegant pleat instead of her usual scragged-back bun, volunteered to do the lunch-time playground duty. I nearly fainted. She was the one who was 'always too busy with paperwork' to risk getting chilblains outside in the cold. She disappeared and, for the first time I can remember, we four teachers had the chance to talk about her as we ate our packed lunches.

Sylvie Shepherd unwrapped a smelly sardine sandwich and I flapped my hand in retaliation for the slur on my pig, but she was staring at the contents of her lunch box and didn't see my belated riposte. But it was the start of my new assertiveness and it pleased me. Sylvie's eyes darted towards the closed door. In a low, sardine scented voice she said, 'Mrs Harker-Balls came into my classroom yesterday and the only words she uttered were GOOD MORNING CLASS ONE and three of my tiny tots burst into tears!'

Brenda Wilson nodded. 'Toby Mole sobbed his heart out this morning after our dear Head had bawled him out. He was inconsolable.' Brenda lifted a small blood orange out of a plastic bag. 'Of all the children in my class, Toby's the kid she always picks on, and it's so unfair.' Brutally, she she tore the peel back and viciously stabbed a knife into the plump mottled flesh, so like our Head Mistress's chest.

I remembered the rebellious innkeeper in the nativity play and, despite the humiliation he'd inflicted on me, I hoped his fighting spirit would survive his encounters with the She Devil.

'I pray to God each night that He will save my children,' said Elizabeth Blessing, hands held flat together as if in the act right now. 'But as most of them have spent their entire school lives in this establishment, they're either stressed-out prima donnas or aggressive war mongers, and that's so hard to deal with in a loving Christian way.' She twisted a paper tissue as if to throttle it, then aimed it into the bin. 'Something must be done about her,' she concluded, and we all agreed.

'But I need my monthly pay cheque and daren't risk getting the sack,' muttered Sylvie. Again we all agreed.

Then I thought of my resolutions. I *would* be strong.

'*I* have decided to talk to her,' I rashly proclaimed.

'But this is her school, she owns it. She'd get rid of you like she did Miss Brown, and there aren't any other teaching posts around,' Sylvie warned.

I stood up on legs that suddenly seemed to have become filleted. 'I'll go out right now and see what she's up to,' I stated, annoyed that my voice was even wobblier than my pins.

Outside, children were shrieking and running around quite freely. I'd expected to see Dame Harker-Balls striding around menacing silent cowering groups. Where was she? She was meant to supervise them, make sure that they were safe.

I traversed the building, sorting out scuffles, straightening blue uniform ties, saving their untidy wearers from her harsh displeasure. Where *was* she? And then I glanced down the driveway to the road and spied her by the gate, hand on sexily jutting hip, chatting to the mayor.

Furious at her irresponsibility, I strode down towards them. 'Mrs Harker-*Balls*,' I called out, 'your duty is to look after the children and you cannot do that from there!'

She turned, eyes glinting. 'Mind your own business Mrs Field,' she snarled, 'and just get back into my school.' She flung out her podgy hand and pointed to the building where I reflected angrily that I was paid to be a warder, not an inmate.

As I turned away, defeated, I heard her whisper, 'Come up to the staff room next Friday after lunch Sidders, during lesson time.'

I stored the careless words away in the empty barrel of my revenge .

I woke next day to the sound of gently falling rain that gave no hint of its destructive power. We ate breakfast in silence. Today was the day we must inform Bill Boggins that he could buy our precious land and I felt sick. Suddenly the phone rang and Bernard leapt up to get it, almost as if he'd been expecting a call. I heard him give annoying Yes/No answers that gave no clue to what it was about. Finally, I heard him say, 'I look forward to it,' and then he bounded back and threw his arms around me. 'We don't have to sell off our land. It's confirmed!' He was grinning from ear to ear.

'What do you mean, it's confirmed? *What* is? Where do we get the money to repair the roof?'

His eyes sparkled. He sat back down at the table, his face radiating success. 'Yesterday, while you were at school, I rang about an advert asking for people to take mature foreign students into their homes to teach them English ...'

'But I'm out working two and a half days a week,' I cut in, 'and I have my routine. I couldn't ...'

'Not you,' he said, stretching across, taking hold of my hands. 'Not you. Me!'

He couldn't be serious. 'Why are you doing that?' I asked, looking down.

'To earn money.'

'No not *that*. I meant, why are you holding my hands?'

'Because I love you,' he replied, slowly releasing them.

'I wiped the transferred marmalade onto the side of my plate. 'But you can't teach English. You don't know about verbs and tenses and adverbs and ...'

'But I speak it and that's all they want. We take on a mature foreign student. We feed it. We do its laundry and give it a bed and I speak to it. That's all. And the organisation gives us two hundred and fifty pounds a week, paid in advance!'

I went to the window and stared out at the distant rain-veiled hills. 'I suppose we could give it a try,' I conceded.

'Jolly good. She's coming in three days time!'

'SHE! Three days time!'

'Yes, Rosita Vilaplana. She's staying with us for three weeks. The phone call confirmed it.'

My brain whirled. We'd have a foreign intruder but we could keep our garden, our privacy and our view, and the garage could stay un-demolished and the pig's home could stay where it was in the middle of the untampered-with walled concrete yard.

Bernard joined me, staring out at our view. 'I'll ring Gor-Blimey Boggins and tell him to bog off,' he said softly.

My darling man. I threw my arms around his neck and kissed him, and our lips stayed together for longer than they have done for years. I felt surprisingly aroused.

I stared up into his eyes and saw the glint of desire.

'This Rosita Thingummyjig. What's she like?' I asked, not able to hold his gaze.

'Haven't a clue,' he said softly, nibbling at my ear.

I pictured the flaming flamenco dancer who was going to clutter up the place: the slim black haired senorita who was to share his life for three whole weeks while I was out at school. As he led me up to the bedroom, I wondered how much weight I could possibly lose in three short days.

Ten

All night long my poor defenceless pig was being chased around a bullring by a lady Matador with swirling ink-black hair. The crowd roared 'Olay Rosita!' each time she lunged her lance at my girl. Even as I tossed and turned, I knew this nightmare came through worrying that Senorita Vilaplana would turn her nose up at my slimming food. Well, now I'm fully conscious, I don't care. I'm determined to lose weight so she'll have a healthy diet and like it. And it won't include pork.

I searched through my cookery books and worked out the menu for next week. It took ages. Bernie came in and I began reading it out to him: 'Monday grilled fish and steamed vegetables, followed by an orange or an apple. Tuesday broccoli quiche ...'

'Hang on,' he interrupted, 'Rosita Vilaplana might have something to say about what she wants to eat.'

'Excuse me. She won't have anything to say because she can't speak English, so hard cheese on the faddy Spaniard,' I snapped. I'm resenting her presence already and she isn't even here.

He grabbed up my shopping list and charged off to the supermarket and while he was away I had a good think. Dear Bernard was doing his best. He knew it was the Spanish invasion or selling off the land. I must co-operate. I decided to be extra kind to my darling when he came back.

He staggered in and I took the shopping bags from him. 'You leave the unpacking to me,' I instructed, 'and go and relax with the paper in the other room.'

'*Stop* telling me what to do all the time!' he blared, stomping off.

How come kindness such as mine is flung back like a well-aimed cow pat in the mush. 'Do what you flaming-well like,' I yelled at his back.

I started unpacking and there, amongst the skimmed milk, crisp bread and broccoli, was a packet of chocolate digestives. *That* hadn't been on my list. I hid it at the back of the larder but there's so little stock that it stood out like a sore finger.

Next day I caught Bernard standing looking thoughtful by his open wardrobe. He held a navy sweater up against his paunch, one he hasn't worn for years, doubtless thinking that its polo neck would hide his fifty-one year old head-body connection from the senorita's torrid eyes. He looked up and started when he saw me and I knew I'd hit the bull with the lance.

Today's the day the Spaniard arrives, but not till later, so I went to the art club as per usual and became so absorbed in executing the bald man who sat for us that, for those two hours, thoughts of Rosita Vilaplana vanished from my mind.

I dashed straight home, hoping to run the Hoover round before she arrived, but when I pushed open the door she was there. At least someone was there. Not a swarthy beauty, but a fair-haired plump woman of about forty who was looking at me with dark uncertain eyes.

Bernard galloped down the stairs, grinning like a Hampshire cat. 'I've just taken her luggage up to her bedroom,' he said, pointing up the stairs as if I didn't know we had another floor.

The woman stepped forward and shook my hand. 'My name is Rosita Vilaplana,' she said, smiling shyly, 'I think you Bernard's wife.'

Christian names already I thought huffily, but I let it pass and ushered her into the sitting room, directing her to Bernard's chair. Then I went out to the kitchen to make some tea.

When I went back in with the tray, they were chatting away and I was amazed. Her English was fluent. She must have pesetas to burn.

'Rip-off,' Bernard was saying. 'You've been ripped-off by the taxi driver who brought you here.'

'Ah, rip-off,' she repeated, 'these is what I wish to learn -the colloquialisms - next time the taxi driver overcharge I say, don't rip-off me you bastard.

Bernard laughed merrily. 'Jolly good,' he said, 'or you could say, come off it, I wasn't born yesterday.'

'Oh yes, yes, that sound good,' she giggled. 'Come off it, I was not born yesterday you bastard.'

They both shrieked as I poured the tea. He's going to have fun earning his two hundred and fifty pounds a week I thought morosely, resentment stirring in my bosom like thick porridge. Then I remembered the promise to myself to co-operate and I opened my mouth and laughed loud and long.

She turned to me with eyes that shone with friendship. 'I am very pleased you have the sense of humour. I was frighten where I would be, but I see I will be happy here. You both nice people. Thank you for sharing your home.'

'Have a biscuit,' I cried, leaping up and rushing out to the larder.

Hermione bashed her way in through the pig flap and followed me back, sniffing the chocolate scented air with snuffling snorts.

Rosita squealed. 'Look out, a pig, it behind you!'

'It's okay,' I assured her, patting our girl's long back. 'This is Hermione ... more of a daughter than a pet pig.'

As we sipped our tea, I saw Rosita surreptitiously remove a small English/Spanish dictionary from her bag and riffle through its pages. She looked impishly at Bernard and said, 'If Hermione your daughter, you a swine!'

His face was a study and I decided it just might be fun having her with us after all.

In bed, Bernard put his arm round me. 'I've rung the roofing contractor,' he said, 'and they're coming on Thursday to mend the patch.' I sighed and snuggled in. Things were at last coming good.

As I prepared for school I heard Bernard explaining about the slimming diet. He read out the week's menu, explaining words, explaining dishes as he went.

'I like food,' Rosita said, 'but it is good idea. I same as you, too fat!' She traced an arc in the air over her stomach, then pointed to his.

I saw him holding his breath in, in a vain attempt to flatten his paunch. It was a struggle for me to keep a straight face as I went over and kissed him goodbye.

Norah Harker-Balls read out a bit from the Bible to the whole assembled school. It was about the wrath of God, but His wrath was nothing compared to hers. She was at her most wrathful. 'COME HERE YOU SNIVELLING BOY,' she had commanded Toby Mole, who shuffled out and was lambasted in front of everybody for not having wiped his nose.

There was much aggression at play time and I didn't think it a coincidence that it was Toby Mole who'd turned extra violent and was beating up tiny Paul.

I came face to face with her soon after and, screwing up my courage to the sticking end, I said, 'Mrs Harker-Balls, you're too harsh with the children.'

'I WANT TO TALK TO YOU ABOUT LAST FRIDAY!' she bellowed, completely ignoring what I'd said. 'WHEN I TALK TO THE MAYOR OR ANYONE ELSE AT THE GATES OF MY SCHOOL, I DO NOT EXPECT A MEMBER OF MY STAFF TO INTERFERE. UNDERSTOOD?'

Justifying words sprang into my head but refused to emerge from my mouth. I turned away, feeling shaken up inside by her harshness and my spineless retreat.

Back home, Rosita said, 'You look tired, I prepare food tonight.'

She must have noticed my wary look because she added, 'Do not worry Freda. I keep to menu. It good for this.' She tapped her ample tum and I felt blissfully content.

Norah Harker-Balls was even worse than usual. Schools should echo to the sound of children's laughter, not their terrified wails. But I couldn't work out what to do about it and could hardly wait to get out of there and back to the peace of my home.

Rosita ran out of the cottage before I'd even alighted from the car. 'Come round and see,' she called, beckoning me from the side path. 'They fix the bloody roof.'

I followed her to the back garden and looked up. And what I witnessed enveloped me in a warm glow as if a thermal blanket had been wrapped around me. The broken tiles had all been replaced and the whole wayward patch had been organised into straight neat lines.

Rosita's eyes flickered uncertainly at me. 'The builders say they mend that bit but rest of roof is bloody disaster waiting to happen,' she revealed.

And, with those doom-laded words, the comforting blanket was whipped away leaving me shivering in the cold. How would we manage to pay I wondered, when the rest of the tiles pegged out? Before getting into bed, I climbed up to the attic and emptied the last remaining rain water from all the containers. But, superstitiously, put each and every one back in its place .

As I sat at my desk marking books and eating a wholemeal lettuce sandwich at lunch time, Mrs Harker-Balls came in and complained that the children in the class we share learnt more in their half week with her than they did in their half week with me. It was so *unfair*. Wednesday afternoons were always spent calming the children down after their terrifying two and a half days with her.

When I looked at the exercise books they used with her, none of the work had been marked so the children wouldn't have gained a thing. My brain went round in circles trying to devise a plan to help the children, or at least get some kind of revenge. Then I suddenly remembered Norah Harker-Ball's whispered: *Come up to the staff room next Friday after lunch Sidders, we'll be more private there*. That was today!

I set the children work then slunk out, tiptoeing the short distance to the staff room, where, unusually, the door was shut fast. I hovered outside, heart hammering. The mayor's muffled voice could be heard, then her laughter, although not her normal thunder clap, more the tinkling of a fragile glass bell. My innards rumbled in a turmoil of nervous emotion. *I'll get her* I thought. *Somehow*. But I didn't because I had to hasten back to my classroom to quell the burgeoning noise.

On Saturday, while Bernard was out giving a driving lesson, Rosita and I had a chat over a cup of tea and a raw carrot. She told me she came from Catalonia where the people were often fair. 'Your hair, it once was the colour called titian? she asked, peering at my head.

'Yes, like my father's,' I affirmed, 'but its vivid red is gradually fading.'

'The hair shop - they put the colour back for you. When I your age that what I do if my hair go dead.'

When I your age! How old did she think I was! And *had* my hair gone dead? It's colour had faded, I knew, but DEAD? I decided that, whether there was any of her home tutoring money left or not, I was going to get my hair coloured and re-styled. I am sick of being sensible. Sod everything.

We all went to Orlford and looked at the shops then walked along a footpath that skirted an old mill, a waterfall, trout streams and water-cress beds. I wondered why we didn't do it when there were just the two of us. It was exhilarating.

In the evening I marked books, at the same time half listening to Bernard teaching Rosita to play crib.

Gary had written: 'Dick Turpin was chased and then caught by the hangers.' I smirked to myself. Poor Dick, I thought.

'Fifteen two, fifteen four and one for his knob,' Rosita said, and I smirked to myself again.

'Is there anywhere you particularly want to visit while you're in England?' I heard him ask, the game apparently over.

And, without hesitation, she replied, 'Yes, Beachy Head where the people all jump off the cliff.'

Next day Bernard suggested we all get in his Metro and drive to Beachy Head. 'It will take nearly two hours to get there if we take the pretty route, but we can teach Rosita as we go along.'

'Oh yes, I like that,' Rosita said, clapping her hands.'

But it's Monday I agonised, thinking of the pile of washing waiting to be done. Then I remembered my resolutions and mother's gibe about me being set in my ways. Ignoring the perfect drying weather, I said, 'Why not, it's windy but not raining. It would be nice.'

I detected Bernard's sharp glance of surprise in my direction. It would be the first Monday laundry session I'd missed in the whole of our married life except for holidays, and we'd not been away for five years.

I sat in the back to give her the best views. She was like an excited school girl, praising the buildings, the scenery and the sky. Her words were punctuated with yelps as the clutch pedal of the dual control came down whenever Bernard changed gear. But quickly she learnt to tuck her feet back out of danger. I relaxed, listening to their conversation about teaching learner drivers, about the countryside, about the history we passed through. I looked out at the racing clouds and regretted the missed opportunity. All that dirty washing waiting piled up at home could by now be flapping out on the line.

Under two hours later we were walking across the wide expanse of grass towards the cliff edge. A fresh wind buffeted my face and, for a fleeting moment I visualised a billowing flannelette sheet, then I thought: *Bugger it, mother is right, household chores can always wait*. It was as if I had released myself from a strait-jacket and was suddenly liberated. I took off, running, arms outstretched, feet pounding the springy turf.

Rosita caught up with me, and then Bernard puffed up too. We were like three wild elephants galloping free. As we neared the edge, we slowed, then stopped. Then linking arms we shuffled forward and looked down. Far far below at the base of the sheer vertical cliff stood the red and white striped lighthouse, like a toy recklessly placed in the heaving, fuming sea. As I stared down, excitement welled up. Something was going to happen soon and I would plummet or fly!

Rosita squeezed my arm. 'Thank you both of you,' she said, 'this one of the happiest days of my life.'

'Mine too,' I replied, with true feeling.

'This very dangerous place for sport,' she observed. 'Why do people jump off cliff here, it is so high?'

'To be dashed on the rocks,' Bernard said solemnly, 'It's not a place for sport. It's a place for suicide!'

She looked horrified. 'You mean they jump off purposely to die?'

Or they think they can fly I thought, edging nearer, at that moment feeling that if I stretched out my arms and stepped off I would glide on currents of air, swooping and soaring at will.

'Oh! Not too near Freda,' Rosita gasped, pulling on my arm. 'When I read about this place it in English - I obviously no understand, I think it was crazy British sport.'

In silence we turned away. As we walked back to the car I was filled with gloriously strange anticipation and excitement. Something was about to happen soon. Although I didn't yet know what.

Eleven

'YOU PEA-BRAINED DOLT!' Norah Harker-Balls screamed, 'GET OUT!' A deathly silence filled the hall as Toby Mole, white faced, head hanging, made his long walk to the door. At that moment I could have killed her.

Next day I caught Sidney Slocumb skulking around the school and when I asked him what he wanted he looked all shifty and said, 'Joost a word with the Head Mistress.' More like joost a word with your *Bed* mistress I thought, judging by the look in his eyes.

Later, I chalked ten sums up on the board, then crept out to the staff room door which again was shut fast. Scarcely daring to breathe, I leant my ear against the thick wood. Faintly, the muffled voices and giggles of Sidney Slocumb and Norah filtered through. Fearful that the door would suddenly burst open, I stood there, nerves taut, ears straining, but, as before, the racket from my classroom soon forced my return.

At lunch-time she looked radiant, wiggling her arse and running her hands down her hips like an overstuffed Marilyn Monroe. She patted Emily Green on the head and smiled. As is usual on these rare occasions, the child was so flummoxed she burst into tears and fled.

I crept out of my classroom once more. Today, a slit of light pierced the passageway gloom. Rustling sounds came from within the staff room and, heart pounding erratically, I pushed gently at the door. Slowly and silently, the narrow gap widened, and there they were. Norah Harker-Balls and Sydney Slocumb in an embrace. I froze. His back was towards me, arms at full stretch to encompass her bulk. Her head was flung back, eyes tightly closed, upturned face radiating pure rapture up to the ceiling as his face nuzzled her neck. Her eyes began to flicker and hastily I stepped back.

'Norah my love, why not come to my 'ouse when the old woman is out,' I heard him suggest.

And she, MRS Harker-Balls-with-one-grown-up-son-who-had-left-home-to-live-in-a-commune, replied, 'Oh yes, yes, Sidders, absolutely YES!'

'The old trout will be out all day at 'er sister's on twenty-eighth, so how about coming then?'

And, without a moment's hesitation, she replied, 'I'll be there promptly at two.' Then she giggled girlishly, saying, 'Oh Sidney, it's so wicked. I really shouldn't, but I find you fascinating. You're so ...' There was a long pause. 'So different from other men I have known. So ...' The statement hung in the air as I tip-toed back to the rumpus of my classroom, armed with the inside information that spelt power - and revenge!

After school, I sped home and jabbed out Cynthia's number to spill the milk, but it was Sidney's answer machine voice that replied. Unprepared, I obeyed the instruction to leave my message after the tone. 'Cynthia,' I said, 'will you please ring Freda Field ... it is about (oh why did I have to carry on, I didn't have to say) ... it is about ... something I have to tell you ... about a meeting ... the ... (I floundered, wishing it were possible to suck words back out of the machine before they settled onto the tape.) 'The portrait group needs a sitter,' I ended lamely, 'so please ring me back.'

I was in a state of high tension all evening waiting for her call, but the phone remained mute.

I could hardly sleep all night agonising over whether it was right to risk hurting Cynthia by informing her of her husband's philandering ways and his secret meeting with Norah H-B. Was my need to punish that devil woman for all the pain she's inflicted on the children worth upsetting a friend?

I dived at the ringing phone but it wasn't Cynthia returning my call, it was my mother. She stated that she and father would drive down tomorrow to see us, but I knew for absolute certain that for my mother to undertake what she always called 'that boring long journey out into the country' was to take a nosy look at Rosita and not to see me at all.

As I prepared the evening meal, Rosita joined me.

'May I practise what I learn from Bernard?' she asked.

'Certainly,' I replied, curious to know what topics he had tackled.

'Oh *jolly* good,' she said, and no-one who knew Bernard would have wondered who her teacher had been. 'I help you *lay the table*,' she said, obviously savouring a newly learnt phrase. Then she flapped the broad-striped blue and white tablecloth over it, saying, 'This the same colours as Queens Park Rangers Football Club. COME ON YOU R's!'

She chanted the QPR slogan in a sing-song voice like a true football fan and I was astounded. This Spanish woman was speaking pure Bernard-ese!

Sunday. I dialled the Slocumb number again, not quite sure what I was going to say, but it had scarcely started ringing when the sound of wheels crunching on gravel grated the peace and heralded the Enemies' arrival. I replaced the phone and looked out to see the familiar red Skoda pulling up, father at the wheel. Mother was kicking the gate closed with a brown ankle-booted foot. Her slim legs were clad in black leggings and I noted with alarm that there was no vestige of a skirt, just a scarlet cowl-neck jumper that finished mid-thigh. I was shocked. She was togged up like a teenager, but somehow looked good. Reluctantly, I opened the door.

'Typical Wood Hill Conservative frock that,' she called over before I'd even had a chance to say Hello.

I looked down at myself. What did she mean, talking about my best dress with such derision? It had been very expensive eight years ago. Admittedly its colour could be called Conservative blue, but what was typical Wood Hill about it and why should that be an insult anyway? I made towards the car, swirling pleats flacking at my legs as if trying to hold me back. Father stiffly hauled himself out.

'Get the kettle on Freed where's the pig?' he said, all in one breath.

'Quite close to me,' I muttered, pecking him on the snout.

Rosita appeared. 'Good morning Mrs Salmon. Good morning Mr Salmon.' She almost curtsied! 'Freda has told me about you.'

I stared, amazed. I'd purposely said nothing about them, not wishing to frighten her into a premature flight back to Spain.

Mother planted a scarlet kiss on Rosita's cheek. 'She's told you about us. Well I'll tell you about her,' she said ominously, taking Rosita's arm. 'By the way, I like your dress,' she added, leading the Spanish liar indoors.

I watched them walk away. I suppose that bright green woollen affair with the long straight skirt and the pouched top did suit our visiting traitor.

I made straight for the kitchen to make the tea. As I lifted the heavy kettle off the Aga, I could hear mother, even from the distance of the sitting room. She was shouting at Rosita as if she were stone deaf or barmy.

'FREDA USED TO BE SO BEAUTIFUL WHEN SHE LIVED AT HOME WITH FATHER AND ME. SHE WAS SO VIV-A-CIOUS, YOU COMPRENDO VIVACIOUS? HARD TO BELIEVE ISN'T IT? BUT SHE WAS. HER HAIR WAS ...'

Grim faced I rushed the tea tray in.

Rosita, turned to me, sympathy brimming in her dark luminous eyes. 'But your daughter is lovely Mrs Salmon, so warm-hearted. As soon as I arrive I think how like my grandmother she is.'

Her *grandmother*! I banged the pot down, and marched straight on out. Let one of them sort out the cups and saucers I thought bitterly as I clumped up the stairs. I sat on the bed wishing I'd poured a cup for myself, then, for want of something better to do, I dialled Cynthia's number on the bedside phone. And this time she answered. 'Is Sidney about?' I whispered and, when she replied that he wasn't, I tentatively began. 'I've been reading a book about a husband who was planning to be unfaithful to his wife and I wondered, how would you feel if that happened to you?'

'Oh Freda, I am sorry ...'

'No, not my husband, not one husband in particular, *any* woman's,' I floundered.

'Well if it was mine, I'd celebrate with champagne,' she replied cheerfully.

And so I told her.

'Thank you, thank you,' she cried. 'I can't stand the bumptious little creep. I only married him because I was lonely after my first darling husband died and I didn't realise until later that he'd pretended to love me because I owned a house - the mortgage paid off of course with Graham's Life Assurance.' She gave a sharp dry laugh. 'Knowing about the little squirt's secret meeting at MY house with that fat tart of a Headmistress will let me get revenge on him at last.'

There was a lot of revenge in the Wood Hill air I thought, breathing in deeply as I replaced the phone.

I couldn't help it, I felt cool towards Rosita today. I thought we were soul mates and all the time she was comparing me with her grandmother. And mother's critical words about my appearance kept bugging me. I rang up Raymond's, the most expensive salon in Great Piddlehurst, and booked to have my hair coloured, permed and re-styled next Saturday. Damn the expense and fuck the laundry. Let someone else tackle it for a change. (That word, I find, is gloriously liberating to think, but I'd never dare say it out loud.)

Tuesday, my favourite day. I positioned my easel close to Cynthia's. 'Have you come up with a plan yet?' I said softly.

She rammed a thick hog-hair brush loaded with a pukish green onto her canvas. 'Yes,' she hissed,'I'll pretend to go to my sister as arranged, but I'll hide somewhere in the house, catch them at it, tell him I want a divorce.'

'What will you do about *her*?'

'She'll be punished enough if he has his evil way with her. One, two, three and it'll be over and she'll be left stranded like a beached whale gasping for the satisfaction of rolling caressing waves, but they'll never come.' There was bitterness in her voice.

Could it be that Norah Harker-Balls was going to get off scot-free except for the fright of being pounced on in mid-copulation by her lover's wife? I couldn't believe it. As I painted, my mind whirled. I could tell everything I knew to Mr Harker-Balls: the man who Norah bragged was related to royalty. The man who Norah bragged held a top job in the civil service advising ministers what to do. Wasn't the Prime Minister trying to stop sleaze? Wouldn't such a scandal threaten his job? I couldn't really do it I knew, but the threat would frighten his wife, and that would be some retribution.

The face that I was working on was emerging as Norah Harker-Ball's, nothing like the sitter on the platform. On impulse I slit her throat with a straight slash of carmine red, then in case anyone had been looking, scrubbed the paint over the whole face. I turned and saw the quizzical eyes of the elderly man sitting on his donkey stool behind me. 'An experiment,' I lamely explained.

On Thursday, I eye-balled Norah so intently that eventually she was forced to avert her gaze. Her face reddened and she looked perplexed. Little does the floozy know what's coming! I inwardly crowed. Rosita and Bernard had washed, dried and ironed the laundry that I'd deliberately neglected doing, and they'd even prepared the meal by the time I arrived home. She kept on about how nice her grandmother was, how modern, up-to-date and beautiful. Yes, and eighty or ninety years old I thought, still unappeased. Weighed myself. I've now lost half a stone since my birthday and definitely look slimmer despite being at the fat time of the month.

'Stop picking on Toby,' I had said sternly, and Norah's eyes flickered with uncertainty. I put my arm round the sobbing boy and he leaned heavily into me as if trying to become absorbed in my body.

'I'VE TOLD YOU BEFORE. MIND YOUR OWN BUSINESS MRS FIELD!'

'Protecting children *is* my business,' I rashly answered back.

Norah looked nonplussed. 'What's got into you! You used to be so co-operative.'

'*You've* got into me,' I said hotly, without a second thought for my job. 'You've got ...' Then I remembered my pay cheque and shut up. I turned away, ushering the quivering boy back to his classroom.

By home time I felt the familiar stickiness between my legs and knew my oh be joyful had arrived. But the despair that had always accompanied it every month for a quarter of a century didn't surface. Was I at last really free?

Friday, and things are back to normal in the house. Or maybe it's just my PMT that has vanished. I realise that Rosita meant only good when she compared me with her grandmother.

Norah H-B had an air of suppressed excitement and outward joy about her. 'What's the matter darling?' she said to Jimmie, the one who'd planned to jump out of his window because he didn't want to meet her again. Mood swings such as this disturb the pupils more than constant cruelty. The usually voluble Jimmie opened his mouth but no words came. Just you wait Norah *darling*, just you wait, I thought. Tomorrow you might learn what it feels like to be on the receiving end.

I went to Raymond's this afternoon to get my hair done. It looks superb and I keep catching Bernie staring at me with awe-struck eyes.

As I had sat under the hair-dryer drinking coffee and staring absently at a magazine, I'd been trying to picture what was going on inside the Slocumb house. Would Sidney and Norah Harker-Balls really have it off? Would Cynthia loom out of the shadows at the climax of their passion? I wished I could be a fly on their wallpaper to see.

Twelve
Intrusion 3

Two o'clock. Saturday. And the doorbell has chimed out the glad tidings that his hoped-to-be lover has arrived.

Sidney flings the door open and catches his breath at the magical sight of her standing on his doorstep, dark silhouette outlined mystically in dazzling sunlight. He bares his newly whitened dentures in, he hopes, an enticing smile and stretches his arms out in welcome. 'Come in Norah love, come in.'

But her feet remain rooted to the astro mat. He smiles again and beckons with seductive flaps of his hand, but she stands fast, letting out the nervous trill of a mottled grasshopper warbler. (He is proud of his knowledge of birds.) He is nonplussed and smiles and beckons once more and, at last, she deigns to step forward.

'Alone at last,' he whispers, pulling her into his arms. He quivers with randy excitement and kisses her hard but, two seconds into the smackeroo, she pushes him away.

'Sorry Sidders - your bristly moustache.' She looks apologetic, pats her lips. 'I should be used to it by now - it was only a little prick.'

The murky thought sullies his mind that soon it won't be just that little prick she'll be used to, it'll be a bloody great big one!

'Come in petal. Come into our love nest,' he encourages, guiding her down the hall.

'Oh Sidders, this is such an adventure, I've never been inside a house on an estate before.'

'Nay lass, not an estate,' he protests, mightily offended, 'an exclusive development of detached houses built all the same.' He thinks of the council estate on the outskirts of Manchester where he lived as a kid. If she could have seen the ugly buildings, the graffiti, the rubbish blowing around, she'd know how far removed his house was from an estate.

He motions her to the low settee at the back end of his through lounge and rushes to the bamboo and formica bar in the corner. As he clasps a bottle and rams the corkscrew home their eyes lock, sparking messages of lust. She smiles seductively, holding his gaze as she begins her descent to the seat. Abruptly the cry of a frightened macaw explodes from her as she plummets, off balance, legs flailing, blue skirt flying adrift. He averts his gaze but, from the corner of his eye, sees her inelegant scrabble to get vertical, and the hasty rearrangement of stout limbs. He finds the display arousing and uncorks a second bottle with trembling hands. At last her adjustments are over and she sits back, knees in neat formation, arms folded tidily upon her jutting chest.

He pours Liebfraumilch into crystal goblets, knowing Cynthia would have a fit if she could see, for those are her family heirlooms, for display only, never ever to be used. He rushes the two opened bottles over and places them on the floor beside the settee, then carefully transfers the brimming tall-stemmed goblets to the coffee table in front of Norah. He slides down beside her and tentatively lays a hand on her knee.

'Oh Sidders,' she whispers, 'this is so thrilling, just the two of us, alone at last.'

Hold back Sidders, he tells himself, *women expect a touch of romance*. With a delicate, yet hopefully masculine movement, he tilts her face towards him. He closes his eyes, giving himself entirely to the execution of a gentle scratchless kiss. Suddenly, a sharp clicking sound penetrates his consciousness and he pulls his lips away. *Cynthia? Could it be Cynthia?* More clicks rip through his brain, shredding his nerves to pulp and slowly he turns, but sees only Rover, their tabby cat, prowling along the sill. He whistles softly with relief.

Norah lifts her wine to him, then greedily guzzles it down. Promptly he refills the glass. Her pale eyes swivel to him flashing magnified promise behind thick lenses and her fingers caress the long shaft of her glass with tantalising strokes. His pulse quickens and he hooks his arm over her shoulders, letting his hand dangle down to her chest, unsure how fast he should go. But she leaves no doubt.

'Here, let me assist you,' she cries, scrabbling with the top buttons of her sea green blouse.

Immediately her rippling white bosom surges out, each billowing white breaker tumbling over the scant restraint of a hammock bra. She delves both hands in and hauls out an entire rolling breast.

Overcome by its enormity, he touches it with the timidity of a child stroking a large unknown dog. Gradually, he gathers confidence, letting his hand wander over the enormous boob, but soon the intense physical excitement brings on the reflex action he's been dreading. Absurdly, his ears begin to twitch, slowly gathering pace until they are waggling in rhythmic lunges fore and aft. She mustn't see this he thinks wildly, breathing hot mist onto her specs. Inwardly he curses the school friend who'd informed him that to master the art of ear waggling prevented deafness in old age. And he, young and gullible, had believed him and practised every day until he had mastered it. But now in times of passion it mastered him! Norah gives a sigh and he breathes on her glasses again. Then, abruptly, his flailing ear lobes grind to a halt.

'Oh Sidders,' Norah sighs, 'I feel so hot, even my spectacles have steamed up.'

He relaxes, grateful in the knowledge that his spent ears always took hours to re-charge with their wilful reflex power. Carefully, he lifts and releases the mountain of quivering flesh cupped in his hand as if trying to gauge its great weight. The low coo of a pigeon gently vibrates her throat and he knows that, in more ways than one, he has her in the palm of his hand. Soon he plans to invite her upstairs to the prepared bedroom but, suddenly, he hears another sound of movement, this time close by. He freezes, full ripe rippling fruit balanced. He turns, but only the grave green eyes of Rover stare back at him. He breathes a thankful sigh.

'My little turtledove,' he whispers, 'how about a drop more wine - start the next bottle off.'

She nods and he notices the time delay in the focusing of her eyes. *Can't have an 'alf empty bottle around when Cynthia gets back home* he thinks. *Besides, a tipsy woman is more easily satisfied.* He refills her glass and, as if dying of thirst, she knocks it back in one swig. *That should prime her working parts all right.* His inner voice purrs like the cat.

'How about coming upstairs, petal,' he suggests, 'I've got something to show you up there!' He laughs suggestively and her responding cackle reminds him of a kookaburra. *Soon he'd be down under like that bird*! He enjoys the lewd thoughts in his mind.

'Oh Sidders, you're so bold,' she says, giggling as she begins to push herself up off the seat.

Sidney sits back watching her clumsy movements. Her free breast dangles, her dimpled knees poke up beside each ear like a gross grasshopper. She rises then teeters, on the verge of falling back, so he gives her a helping shove.

With a squawk she shoots forward slamming full tilt into the table, and, like a rabbit mesmerized by the lights of an oncoming car, he watches the two precious glasses shoot into the air. Time changes to slow motion as the glinting goblets reach their zenith then pitch back down again. The tinkling of their smash landing on the table deafens him and he clutches his ears.

'Awfully shorry Shidders, but it was your fault, you shouldn't have manhandled me like that.'

Ignore the smashed-up glasses fer time being, don't let 'er off the boil. 'Come on Norah,' he says, firmly clasping her elbow, leading her out of the room and up the heaven-bent stairs. He guides her into the bedroom where he's already drawn the front curtains so nosy neighbours can't spy in, and takes her to the bed at the other end. He notes that the king size love chariot is bathed in sunlight to transport him to eye-popping delights. He quivers with pent-up lust, sits down on the flowery duvet, and pats at the space by his side. 'Come on sweetheart, come and sit beside me. See how springy the bed is.' He bounces up and down to demonstrate, but she holds back.

What's the matter with the woman, she's drunk a bottle of his wine and she were panting fer sex not long back. He smiles encouragement and, reluctantly, she perches herself on the edge. He pulls her to him, draping his arm around her shoulder, letting his hand drop to the still unfettered breast. She groans and peers round at him with drink sozzled eyes. He hears a click from the dark end of the room, has vague thoughts that it must be the cat.

She pulls back and sits stiffly at a weird angle away from him as if about to fall. Surely she wasn't shy! Not after her bold performance downstairs. He hears the cat behind the curtain click its claws on the window pane again. He looks over but sees only the slight movement of the floor-length curtains as Rover, he presumes, prowls behind them.

Norah pushes herself up from the bed. 'I must go to the bathroom,' she croaks, tottering to the door.

'Be quick then petal, turn left and 'tis door at the end.'

Impatiently he waits, fully aroused. He calls out, 'Sidders is waiting sweetpea, waiting to have some fun.'

Unpleasant sounds come from the bathroom.

He busies himself plumping up pillows, his erect trodger straining against his flies. *Supposing he couldn't release it when it were time.* He gives a furtive look round then has a trial run, pulling his zip quickly down. His manhood springs out like a rapier and he stares down, appalled. Blewdy hell! Veins like cables entwine the mottled puce shaft and its knob gleams malevolently in bright rays of sunlight. He grabs the metal tab and yanks it upwards, then screams as his tender flesh enmeshes in the fine teeth of the zip. In a frenzy of panic and pain, he tugs the tab down but it doesn't budge.

He hears the lavatory flush and looks wildly around, catching sight of himself in the wardrobe mirror. His manhood juts out like a signpost. He looks disgusting. He looks absurd. *And him the most worshipful mayor of Great Piddlehurst*! Frantically, he tugs down again and this time it shifts a few teeth, but the gap is too small to re-pack his equipment away. The sound of the bathroom door bolt being pulled back galvanises him and, brutally, he tries to fold his pulsating organ in half, handling it with the strength of a blacksmith bending iron. But the pain overwhelms him and he gives up, releasing it to spring back out like a sizzling sausage.

From the other end of the room he hears a muffled sound that he perceives as the cat having some kind of a fit.

He hears the bathroom door open and, frantically tugging, he prays, 'God, please help me.' And God very kindly obliges. As Norah's shuffling footsteps sound in the passageway, Sidney's ramrod collapses and, as she pushes the door open, his flaccid humiliation is prodded away and re-sealed by the now unimpeded zip. She totters to him and he is devastated. He's never achieved two erections in twenty-four hours, let alone in two seconds flat! But God intervenes yet again.

'Shidders,' Norah slurs, clutching his arm, 'would you mind very much if we go downshtairs again, I'm not really up to thish now.'

In a voice he hopes sounds considerate and disappointed rather than blessedly relieved, he says, 'Of course not petal, I don't mind.'

His mind is racing as he manoeuvres her to the top of the stairs. *Can't very well choock 'er out straight away. Besides, that bottle still needs emptying before hiding it deep in the dustbin away from Cynthia's beady eyes.* 'Let's relax and finish the wine off before you go,' he suggests.

'You're a gentleman Mr Mayor shir,' she hiccups, staggering as linked together they descend the stairs.

Back in the lounge Sidney faces the temporarily forgotten tragedy again. All that splintered glass strewn over the coffee table and carpet! But he'd already invented an excuse. He pictures his humble face: *I wanted to please you Cyn, so I took them out to polish them and the stupid cat knocked two of them over.* Recklessly he takes two more of the crystal goblets from the four remaining in the display cabinet. Gingerly he sets them out amid the shiny fragments on the table.

Norah backs up to the low settee with unsteady steps. She positions her feet with exaggerated care. She sticks her backside out behind and her arms out in front in precarious counter-balance. She hovers briefly before overbalancing backwards with a loud squeal. Sidney watches the replay of the horror movie in mute terror. He sees her flying size sevens lam into the table and he follows the flight of the glasses, rainbow spectrums sparking out from magnificent cut glass swirls. At last he gathers his wits and lunges to catch them as they zoom back down, but all he succeeds in doing is knocking one into the other, exploding them into fragments that tinkle down onto the pile.

A demented banshee wail, terrifying in its emotional power, rents the air, and Cynthia hoves into view, long-lensed camera clutched in her hands. 'How *could* you,' she sobs. She casts not a glance at Norah but stares with horror-struck eyes at the devastation. She kneels, risking cut knees from scattered shards, and aims her lens at the sparkling mound. The shutter clicks. The sharp sound stirs a memory in Sidney, but it doesn't register.

Norah, who had been stuffing her breast away, was now fumbling with the buttons on her blouse. The top one had connected with the second button hole, but she had given up and was struggling to her feet. She stands swaying, dishevelled, bleary eyed and blotchy faced.

'I'm shorry Mishus Shlocumb. All I did wash shit down.'

'Shit down!' Cynthia screams. 'Shit down, shit up, you're a shit, a brazen unpleasant shithole.'

Sidney is astounded. Was that his docile wife talking like that!

Cynthia whirls round on him. 'And you're a shit too you two-timing bumptious bugger.'

Suddenly he needs to go to the loo!

'No, you stay here,' she shrieks, seeing him turn. 'I *loved* those glasses.'

'I know you did petal. I'll buy you some more.'

She ignores his offer. Her voice lowers. 'I'll get my revenge on you if it's the last thing I do. You scumbag!'

And now he is shit scared because he knows she could get an Honours Degree in Revenge! He looks round for Norah but she isn't there.

He hears the front door slam and wishes he could join her in the wifeless freedom outside.

Hours later, he slinks out into the night and rings Norah from a public phone box.

'Is it all clear to speak?'

'Yes, Jeremy's in London,' she whispers, 'but my head is excruciating so don't shout.'

'Cynthia said she knew of our assignation but she won't divulge who told her, but I think it must by that dopey teacher at your school, she's a friend of Cynthia's at the art club.'

'Freda Field,' Norah snarls. 'Yes, she's been acting out of character lately.' There is silence.

'Are you still there?'

'I am thinking. What happens if Freda tells Jeremy ... my husband ... he mustn't know.' She groans as if in agony. 'And your wife ... she might cite me as corespondent in a divorce and, even though we didn't ... you know ... and Jeremy would think we did.'

'Nay, you can forget Cynthia. She says she did want divorce but she's change her mind. Now all she seeks is revenge. She says revenge wouldn't disrupt her life so much and it'd be more fun. He recalls the loathing in his wife's dung brown eyes as she lashed him with her tongue. Strangely he'd felt physically attracted to her, for the first time in years.

'Her revenge on me could be divulging our affair to Jeremy,' Norah cries.

'Nay, nay. It's only me she wants to get her revenge on. She says she's nowt but pity for thee.'

He had squirmed at those insulting words and pledged to himself that, if ever he got his wife back into the marital bed again, he'd go in for a bit of foreplay and even ensure she were satisfied. He couldn't have a wife of his pitying a woman he were nearly unfaithful with.

'So it's just Freda Field I have to fear. You must pay her off,' Norah Harker-Balls cries dramatically. 'She hasn't two pennies to rub together so tell her you'll give her money if she doesn't tell!'

'Nay, you just can't offer a respectable school teacher brass for doing nowt but keep her gob shut. It smacks too much of yankie movies.'

'Pay her off,' she commands. 'It's the only way. She needs money - I've heard her talk about her leaking roof. Everyone has their price.'

She can't be serious, Sidney thinks, but the mad woman gabbles on.

'If the parents of the thick-heads at my school ever find out about us, it would absolutely ruin my authority. They can't take their precious offspring elsewhere because there aren't other schools in the vicinity, but one would find it awfully hard to maintain one's image.'

Butter her up and the demented woman might simmer down. 'Aye, that school means a lot to thee sweetpea. You rule it all powerful like the Queen.'

'And I want to continue to do so,' she screeches. 'Think about it Sidney. The Queen is respected by her subjects because she's the only one of the Royals who's apparently not had an affair. I need that kind of respect too. Freda Field has to be silenced.'

Sidney reflects that he hasn't had his end away for months and now both women are out of bounds.

'I know!' Norah bursts out.

She's going to suggest I contact the Mafia and have Freda's pig's head sawn off and placed in her bed. There's hysteria in that voice.

'Freda does portraits. Commission her to paint you in your mayoral regalia and pay her handsomely for it - on condition she keeps her mouth shut.'

'Aye. I remember Cynthia telling me that Freda were good at portraits. How much do you think we could get away with paying?'

'Five hundred pounds,' she shoots back.

He gasps. He'd been thinking fifty quid would be a lot. But then he imagines an oil painting of himself all togged up in his finery, hanging in the Wood Hill village hall to remind future generations of Great Piddlehurst and District's most illustrious mayor. ''Tis a champion idea lass. It's a lot of brass, but it'll be worth it to keep your pure name unsullied.'

She wasn't to know that already he was planning to purloin the money from the Great Piddlehurst Council funds.

Thirteen

I still can't believe it. The early Sunday morning phone call leading to the clandestine meeting at the school. Mayor Sidney Slocumb offering me five hundred pounds to paint his portrait and keep my trap shut, and Norah Harker-Balls, all pathetic, beseeching me to accept the bribe. I'd have told them both where to shove their tainted money if another batch of tiles hadn't come crashing down early this morning. The imprint of the dark crater in the front roof is stamped into my brain like a black hole in outer space sucking everything in.

'You both wait here in the school office and I'll ring you with my decision within the hour,' I had boldly instructed. And then I'd raced round to Cynthia's to find out what happened yesterday and what she wanted me to do. After all, it was her husband who'd done the dirty on her.

I couldn't believe what she told me: how she'd pretended to set off to her sister's then looped back and hidden in the garden shed until Norah, 'the floozie', was ensconced in the house. Then crept indoors and up to the bedroom where she knew the action would take place because her slithy husband had already drawn the curtains in readiness.

The things she said our illustrious brazen Head and that bumptious little twit had got up to were unbelievable. But Cynthia didn't seem to care. The only time she sounded upset was when she said some special wine glasses had been broken.

I told her of their offer and she chuckled and said I was to take their filthy money. 'Make a name for yourself, you're brilliant at portraits,' she extolled.

Maybe she was right. Perhaps it was the impetus I needed to catapult me off the cliff-top to soar high into the clear blue yonder, mistress of my destiny, rich beyond my craziest dreams. I thought of our Tuesdays down at the art club, the sitters whose likenesses I'd captured. Perhaps I could pull it off. And if the mayor's picture turned out well, people would clamour to be painted by me. Famous people. Even Royalty. But, supposing I was commissioned to paint the Queen and she turned out like Mavis from Coronation Street (which she does a bit) and the corgis all came out like rats.

Cynthia's impatient sigh jolted me out of my chaotic thoughts. 'But if I do take it on,' I wavered, 'Norah will be getting away with it completely. Don't you want that despicable woman to suffer even a bit?'

'That despicable woman has suffered enough at the hands of my despicable husband, as I knew she would, but if ever I do need to make her suffer more, I have the means to.'

She didn't explain any further and I was anxious to go. I sped home and rang the devious duo, still waiting at the school. Sydney answered. 'I'll do it,' I told him. 'I'll paint your portrait for five hundred pounds and I won't breathe a word about your sordid affair.' I felt as if I were a character in a novel. Freda Field, part-time school teacher, artist and undercover agent paid to keep schtum. I warmed to the part. 'You can trust me,' I said softly. 'My word is my bond. The only person I shall ever tell is my husband, for we have no secrets in our marriage ... unlike some.' I added the last bit with slow meaningful deliberation, in full command.

Silence seeped out of the telephone into my ear. Why didn't he say something? Had I gone too far? Would they retract their offer? In my mind the five hundred pounds had already been handed over and the gaping hole in our roof repaired. Their muffled, distant discussion filtered through the ear piece.

Norah's voice became more distinct. 'You know. Bernard Field, the driving instructor,' she was saying, enunciating every word ultra precisely. 'Yes, the white car with the sign on top. You must have been nearly mown down by one of his learner drivers at some time or other, it's hard to av...' The words faded out of phone-shot, but soon Sydney's voice addressed me.

'Right Mrs Field - or should I now call you Freda - I agree. Your husband moost be trustworthy if he's a driving instructor, it stands to reason, so I'll come round to your house wearing me full regalia next Monday, ten o'clock, and you can get on with the job.'

My pulse revved up, thumping out fast staccato rhythms at every pressure point. Suddenly this wasn't a fiction story any more, it was real life.

'When it's finished,' he continued, 'I'll get it handsomely framed and it'll hang in place of honour in village hall. We'll have a grand unveiling ceremony, show the folks round here what we're made of.'

I replaced the receiver and dashed out to find Bernard. As I ran towards the mobile home where he was attending to the pig, my mind raced too. What had I let myself in for? Cynthia had said I was brilliant but what did she know? Down at the art club she always says she can't even draw a straight line, but when I watch her using a ruler to draw arms and necks I know that isn't true. She's extremely good at drawing straight lines. It's knowing when it's appropriate to use them that's her problem.

I slowed down then stopped, doubts returning. I wouldn't tell Bernard. I'd cancel the whole thing. How could I paint a portrait good enough to hang in public? An amateur like me. But I looked across the valley and thought: *be fearless and bold Freda. This could be the breakthrough. This could be the momentous start. This could be me taking off, soaring high. This could be the start of the Big money of my dreams*. With regained resolve I hurried across the yard and up the ramp where I gabbled out the incredible happenings of this morning to Bernie.

Pungent straw hung draped from the pitchfork as he stared at me. 'When I looked at you asleep beside me this morning,' he said, 'your titian curls spread out like a wondrous halo about your beautiful chubby face, I was filled with desire and disbelief that you were my wife.' He scraped the curved tines clean on the side of the wheel barrow. 'Now you're telling me you're accepting a monkey for your silence!'

'A monkey?'

'Gangster talk for five hundred pounds.'

Hermione came up and sniffed at my hand. 'We're going to be rich pigs,' I hooted, and my intelligent girl skipped up and down, tail whirling round in circles as if I'd said 'chocolate'.

Indoors, I re-read the dreams and hopes I'd set out on New Years Eve. There was nothing about aspiring to be a gangster's accomplice, or becoming a famous painter. But what the hell.

Rosita is packing to go home tomorrow and I feel very sad. Hermione seems to sense her impending exit from our lives. Her piggy eyes are doleful and this evening, for the first time, she tried to creep up and sit on Rosita's lap. She was shoved off, Rosita no doubt keen to travel back to Spain without crutches.

'We all change to be thinner and healthier thanks to you Freda,' Rosita said. 'Especially you change. Your new Jesus hair looks jolly good.'

'What do you mean, my Jesus hair?'

Her eyes twinkled. 'It come back from the dead just like Him!'

'That's a *jolly good* joke,' I laughed.

She eyed Bernard with affection. 'And thanks to you I now speak jolly good English.'

'You must be glad to be going back to your husband and son,' I ventured, puzzled by her reluctance to ever talk about her family.

She shook her head. 'Things were not good when I left. My husband, he has no respect for me and I was tired of him and his nasty remarks. But now I am refreshed and fitter and my English have, has, improved. When I return I get a courier job, taking British tourists around Barcelona. I will earn my own money and regain my pride. Maybe we become happy again but, if not, too bloody bad!'

'And your son?' I prompted.

'Ferdy is eighteen. I love him of course, that is why I had spoiled him. I receive his letter last week. He says he miss me. Soon I will see if it is me or my housekeeping services he miss.'

I tried to imagine having a son of eighteen who you doubted really missed you, but couldn't. I hoped Ferdy would prove he truly did.

Rosita insisted on ordering a taxi to take her to Heathrow. 'I want to practise the first thing you taught me Bernard. You remember: Do not rip me off you bastard.'

'I think the bastard bit was your idea,' he laughed.

She brought out a bottle of Highland Park malt whiskey, hidden behind a chair. When I go, you two enjoy this together.

'But that's full of calories,' I exclaimed.

'But a little, how you say, tipple, at night-time, make you happy. You go to bed and get together. When I no longer sleeping in the next room, you are able to make as much noise as you like.' She put a hand up to her mouth and giggled at her sauciness.

I caught Bernard's eye and he raised an eyebrow. 'Sounds like a jolly good idea to me,' he agreed.

It was eleven-thirty when we waved her goodbye. I was still sniffling at midday when I served up our Ryvitas. 'I miss her so much already,' I said, wiping my eyes.

'Yes, but as she says, we can make as much noise as we like now she's not here ... tonight ... in bed.'

What kind of noise were they banging on about? He only ever grunted and I hardly ever made a sound.

Next morning Bernard, grinning happily, complained of a headache brought on by me. I know he's only kidding, but now in the whiskeyless light of sober day I feel awful. I've never been so vocal in my life. I blame Rosita for planting the idea that connected my voice box to my Beatrice.

Later he reminded me of the bottle of scotch my parents had given him for Christmas. 'We can have a tot every night for months,' he said, giving a wink that was like the quick flash of sapphire and made my knees go weak.

I drove to school after lunch wondering how floozy Harker-Balls would react to me, but she kept out of sight, shut away with her part-time secretary in her office. When the bell went at the end of the afternoon, she emerged as always to stand on the step oozing charm and respectability all over the unsuspecting mothers as they collected their children. I caught her eye once and she turned away. You may well feel shame, I thought, and if it keeps you out of my hair, long may it last.

My hair, as it happened, had been the subject most under discussion at school. Children and grown-ups all said how very very much better I looked, which made me wonder how very very bad they thought I'd looked before.

At home I scrutinised myself in the mirror. A mass of flaming wood-shaving curls tumbled down, ending in a thick clubbed edge just above my shoulders. Short tendrils spiralled over my forehead. I felt pretty for the first time in years and, suddenly, I yearned for my mother to see.

She'll be seventy tomorrow, the same day that Hermione will be five. Father would be bound to take her out on the day, but I could ask them down to celebrate with us at the weekend. I'd already bought the pig a small Magic Roundabout cake. I could make a special birthday gateau for mother. Eagerly I picked up the phone. There was no reply. I tried all evening but no-one answered. I couldn't believe how disappointed I felt.

I did manage to get through next morning before setting off for school. I rushed through 'Happy birthday,' then asked what she and father were doing to celebrate.

'I'm not doing *anything* with your father,' she said in a tone that sounded amazed that I should think that she would do so.

'But you must celebrate your seventieth!' I cried, astounded because my mother has always made whoopee on the slightest pretext. 'Or is it because you're feeling dejected at reaching that age?' I added with a sudden intuitive rush of compassionate insight.

'Don't be bloody daft Freda. Once I'd got over the shock of being thirty the other zeros have been a doddle. Of course I'm celebrating. You're only seventy once in your life. But not with your father. My girl friends have hired a room above the 'Pig and Whistle' and laid on surprise entertainment for females only at eight. Probably a Tarzan stripper-gram if I know them. Don't suppose you've organised anything exciting for Hermione, like a well-hung boar!'

I waited for her childish sniggers to stop then invited them down to Wisteria Cottage for the weekend, but she turned me down, even though I said I'd make a cake for her. *Very* exciting, she had murmured, but there was a football match on Tooting Bec Common that she just couldn't miss. She must think I'm daft if I fall for that. But then I remembered. She did. Think I was daft. Daft and dull. And I needed to show her that I had changed.

'Why don't you come and join us at the 'Pig and Whistle',' she suggested without enthusiasm.'

'Thanks but I have school tomorrow and I need to be fresh,' I replied. And suddenly it hit me that I'd become the prissy school marm that she'd predicted all those years back.

I drove to school in a muddled state of mind. Should I make the effort to go to Tooting this evening? It would mean leaving Hermione on her birthday but, after all, the pig didn't know she was five. By home time I'd made the decision. I would go there.

The M25 was littered with cones and warnings of 'road works'. Not a sign about 'men works' so no lies being told there. Miles and miles of slow squashed-up traffic with the unattainable central lane coned off, delectable and bare. As I crawled along the hard shoulder, I worked out it must be a fiendish plot by the Government to prevent the fast lane surface being worn out, so saving money to dish out just before the next election.

When I eventually arrived at Tooting I couldn't find the pub. It was nine o'clock by the time I spotted it, and five past by the time I'd parked. I pushed open the door of 'The Pig and Whistle' and went out of the frosty air into the fug.

'If you want the Salmon party it's upstairs,' a bald-headed man behind the bar shouted over. He jerked his head toward a narrow staircase at the side, adding, 'You're late but you might just catch the fun.'

As I turned the bend at the top of the flight, the sound of music and the cackling of laughter hit me. I opened the door ahead and walked in to the full decibel din. Through the smoky haze I could see elderly women seated in a circle. And, in the centre, was my tiny mother, arms extended high and, for some reason I couldn't fathom, dressed in cowgirl clothes. A tall muscle-bound black man danced with her. He wore nothing at all, except a green sequinned pouch that just covered his knobbly bits. His oiled muscles rippled, flexed and twitched as he cavorted around.

I stayed hidden in the shadows. The women cheered and stamped their feet in rhythm as the dance grew frenzied and wild. Mother stamped her high-heeled boots, clicking her heels, clapping her hands, sending her fringes swirling. I watched fascinated and appalled. The music changed, the pace slowed and a singer, male and sexy sang strange words: 'You wanna hot dog in your roll ... you wannit hot 'cos you don't wannit cold ...' Then the women joined in with gusto, somehow knowing all the words, and the giant black man flashed the whites of his eyes and the white of his teeth at my mother, adding his strong deep voice to the rest: '... you wanna big one, is that what you said? Well I've got a dog that's gonna fill your bread!' He clasped both hands behind his head and jerked his pelvis in suggestive thrusts towards her. The women shrieked encouragement. My mother changed from Spanish dancer cowgirl to sensuous Arabian, rotating her hips and twisting her arms up high, like two snakes vying with each other for air space. Then, to my horror, she snatched at the sequinned pouch and hoisted it forward, peering inside. Howls came from the mob lusting for the ultimate exposure.

'Mother. You can't!' I screamed, dashing forward into the pool of light. I grabbed her arm which still clung onto its prize.

'Freda? Is that you? Your hair ... you look nice ...'

'Get her off' a woman cried.

'Get *it* off,' another yelled.

All this time the music continued blaring, the hunk continued gyrating, and my mother continued pulling forward on the glittery green pouch. She shook me off then whipped out the gun from the fancy holster dangling round her hips and aimed it at the contents of the bag. There was a sharp crack, a small puff of smoke and a loud bellow as she let the elastic go. A pair of strong hands grabbed me pulling me out of the way and the rest of the wild women mobbed the grinning Goliath, grabbing at his sweaty body, rumpling up his hair.

I sat down and mother slumped down beside me. 'What a spoil-sport you are. You always have been. It was only a toy gun with a cap that went bang you know, not a real bullet. I'd never shoot a man in the balls.'

' Happy Birthday mother,' I groaned.

The bald-headed man from downstairs suddenly came barging through the door. 'Okay girls. Time's up. Let 'im go. Colossus here's needed by some really wild women out east in Bethnal Green.' The big fellow pulled himself away from the mob and followed baldie out of the room.

The women stampeded over to us. 'This is my daughter Freda,' mother shouted over the babble of voices and hysterical laughter.

'But she looks nice,' someone said, quickly followed by several 'shushes'.

'Have a drink,' said a jolly white-haired woman, picking up a half-empty bottle of champagne.

And I did. Suddenly I wanted to be one of the girls. I wanted mother to be proud of me. And I was thirsty.

Two hours later it was agreed that I'd have to stay the night. I remember a blurred taxi drive, a vague conversation on the phone with Bernard who said he'd ring Norah Harker-Balls and tell her I was sick. Which was quite true of course. So what the heck, your mother's only seventy once in your life!

As I drove home Friday afternoon I realised how much I'd enjoyed staying with my parents. Mother had fussed over me when I woke up, making me take aspirins and a cup of tea. Amazingly, all that champagne and excitement hadn't affected her one bit. She said she *adored* my new hair-do and I kept catching her staring at me with narrowed eyes. When I asked her what she was thinking she said she was trying to imagine me thin! 'I *am* half a stone lighter,' I protested, but it made me resolve to carry on the battle of the flab even though my Spanish tum-mate has left.

I felt sorry for father. He seemed to have lost all his aggressive energy. He couldn't believe that she hadn't wanted him to share her special birthday with him. I hoped he'd never find out what she did.

As I turned right onto the Great Piddlehurst by-pass, I wondered how Norah had managed at school. She'd have to have given up her paper work to take our shared class. I worried about my sacrificing the poor children for the sake of my drunkenness. But then I reckoned the re-awakening of warmth between my mother and myself justified the selfish act.

As I took the fork that led to Wood Hill the realisation that Mayor Sidney Slocumb was coming on Monday hit me and panic grabbed me by the throat and half throttled me. Where was I going to sit him? How should he be positioned? What size canvas should I buy? How was I going to stop his bulbous nose looking like a fat strawberry, because that's just how it did look. I couldn't do it. I knew I couldn't.

On Saturday I bought a canvas, three foot by two, plus a tube of titanium white. It cost a fortune and I'm beginning to think it is money down the drain. I've lost all confidence.

Sunday, we shared the Magic Roundabout cake with Hermione, then I accompanied her to her quarters and tucked her up for the night. I stared down at my virgin girl snuggled into the fresh straw and wished we could afford to mate her with a worthy boar. I pictured the sweet pink piglets of the union and a lump came into my throat. But we couldn't afford it. Not yet. Piglets would need even more spent on electricity to keep them warm than she did. And then there was the extra food and vet's bills. No, my poor Hermione was fated to be childless, just like me. Unless I made my fortune painting portraits. I stroked her big head and she opened one eye and smiled. Maybe my babe, you *will* experience the joy of motherhood and I can share it with you. I was suddenly, and inexplicably, full of heady optimism. I rushed back to my man.

He was relaxing in front of a crackling fire made from twigs and branches collected from around the perimeter of the garden. The flames cast flickering shadows inside the inglenook and the dark oak bressummer glowed. I slid down beside him. 'If we had oodles of money is there something special you'd like to do?' I asked. 'Something you couldn't afford now?'

And, without a second's hesitation, he replied, 'That's easy. I've always wanted to have a go at driving a racing car.'

I was struck mute with amazement because for years that has been my secret dream too. One of my resolutions had been to do a daring activity. I hadn't spelt it out, but it was to speed round a track in a racing car, just once in my life, that had been my ambition.

I took his hand. 'One day, when we're loaded, I'll book us both in for a training session at Brands Hatch.'

Little did I know when I uttered those promising words just what pain and anguish they would lead to.

He gave me a pitying look as if I'd said I'd book for us both to travel round the world on Concorde. 'Thanks for the thought Freed,' he said. 'If you make our fortune, I'll keep you to it.'

He snuggled close and I felt his warm breath on my cheek. Then I thought of tomorrow's portrait and terror struck me. 'It's no use. I can't do it,' I moaned.

He shot back, hurt disappointment in his eyes.

'Not *it!* The portrait, I know it'll be a failure and I'll be a laughing stock.'

Bernard turned my face to his and tenderly kissed me. Mentally, I mixed the colours for the mayor's robust nose. Suddenly it struck me that the portrait was doomed from the outset because of the very nature of the sitter's face. Lips still latched to Bernard's, I groaned.

'I like it when you make noises,' he whispered, shifting his hand.

I remembered mother's boldness with the black man and shifted my hand too. And, for a while, the strawberry nose vanished from my head.

But, half an hour later, sated with love, I remembered that tomorrow had to come too!

Fourteen

Thank God he was going! I watched from the front door as he strutted to the gate. Just three hours since he'd arrived and he was disappointed the portrait wasn't finished! What did he think you did - wave a magic wand. I felt like saying: *Excuse me, this is an original work of art you know, not painting by numbers.*

Back in the sitting room I studied the canvas. My heart rose. He was already there. Only blocked in, but those thin flat colours had captured him in a flattering way. The tilt of his head showed pride without exposing his smugness. The background of books made him appear learned. 'I believe the general pooblic think 'ighly of a man sitting in front of books,' he had pronounced as he re-positioned the chair. And he was right. It was truly a masterly con trick.

As I waggled the brushes in the jar of turps I planned the next session. Sidney was impatient so I'd have to work fast, but that gave a picture life. Excitement flooded over me. He was due again tomorrow. My artistic reputation was all-but assured.

By bed time I was terrified at the thought of putting one more stroke of paint down on that canvas. I knew for absolute certain I would ruin it.

I waved him goodbye with a hand that was as heavy as my leaden heart. It was even worse than I'd feared. The thick paint had been shovelled on with a palette knife. It was the way I liked to paint. It was quick. It was bold. But this time it was hideous.

Bernard came in from a lesson. 'What do you think?' I asked, warily.

He stood, hands on hips surveying the mess. Seconds passed. His strong nose twitched. He stroked his jaw. He breathed in deeply then slowly released the captive air.

Come on! Spit it out. Let's hear the truth.

It was when he scratched his head, disorganising his meticulously executed side parting, that I knew the verdict.

'Well, what do you think?' I snapped, my nerves at breaking point.

'It's ... it's jolly good. There's no mistaking it's him. Yes, yes, it's him all right.'

His words were carefully selected to be kind.

'You don't like it,' I wailed. 'I can tell.'

'I *do* like it', he said aggressively.

'Come on tell me. What's wrong with it?' I dared.

His gaze sharpened. He stood back, holding up his hands to form an open box. He looked through it. He gave a shrug. 'If you really want to know ...'

'Yes! Yes I do.'

'I think you've plonked too much paint on.' The truth rushed out and he tottered back as if recoiling from shooting a gun.

'Plonked? *Plonked* too much paint on,' I screamed, knowing he was right. 'What d'you know about painting, the only thing you've ever painted is the front door.'

He looked hurt.

'And even that's got runs. What you call plonking paint on is termed impasto to those who understand.'

He looked even more hurt and sloped off leaving me with the smell of turpentine and oil paint and failure and guilt.

I had decided I wouldn't look at it for three whole days. Then I'd see it with new eyes and be objective but, next day, after school, I was drawn to the lurid canvas like a fly to a pile of shit.

Sidney's face leered at me, teeth bared exposing their falsity, bulbous red nose seeded like a strawberry, florid complexion accurate to the point of cruelty. Long strands of grey hair trailed over the dome of his shiny head, unequivocal in their absurdity. Everything too realistic, too brutally brash. His steel-grey moustache so wiry you could scour a saucepan clean with it. Heavy jowls hung over his white frilled jabot. The chain of office glinted with the brassiest of gold and the scarlet robes vibrated with the most hideous of reds. The colours screamed out and hurt my eyes.

My painting was about as subtle as a full-blown fart at a fucking funeral. (I don't know how many times I've used that word now, and I don't give a bloody damn.)

Thursday afternoon I paired the children off then instructed them to paint pictures of each other. Every single portrait was better than mine drying off at home. How *could* I take five hundred pounds for such a mess, even from him?

Friday at school was awful, with Norah Harker-Balls snapping and snarling at everything that moved. Going back home to my picture almost seemed pleasurable by comparison.

Tentatively I touched the scarlet robe. It was as thickly wet as the day it was painted. I'd never be able to paint on top of that gunge when Sidney came next Monday for what he firmly stated was his final sitting. *By gum Freda*, he'd said, *I can't waste 'alf me life sitting here when there's work piling up at Town 'all.*

When Bernard asked me what was up, this evening, I admitted I was in despair. But instead of being sympathetic he had to make one of his so-called jokes. He thinks it cheers me up I know, but it drives me round the twist. This one was worse than usual and I was not in the mood:-

'When you've got your five hundred pounds,' he said, 'you can pay to turn *despair* room back to a studio.' And then he wondered why I marched out howling.

I spent the whole weekend worrying about the picture, then came Monday, the unlucky thirteenth that lived fully up to its reputation when the two swine I love most in the world dashed my dreams to smithereens.

Pig One, Bernard, let Pig Two, Hermione, into the sitting room where my painting was set up, despite my express request to Pig One that he should keep Pig Two locked away outside. She blundered in, all skittish joy and honking clumsiness, barged straight into the easel and shot the canvas onto the floor, face up. And then, before I could reach it, she sat on it! I hauled and pushed and kicked and swore at her, but she sat firm, eyes glinting with angry reproach at the rough handling and harsh words. Finally I grabbed her ears and tugged and she rose up to her trotters with sharp squeals.

Huffily she turned her back, and there, straddling the two half moons of her backside, the face of Mayor Slocumb smiled proudly up at me. Jutting from the centre of his forehead was the three dimensional quiff of my girl's tail.

Bernard rushed in, at last aware of the rumpus.

'You left the door open!' I cried, 'and now the painting is ruined. It's taken me hours and was the best commission I've ever had.'

'The only,' he muttered pedantically.

'Well, thanks for reminding me,' I sobbed. I lifted the canvas and waggled it under his nose. 'That was going to make my name that was. Other commissions would have followed because of it.' My eyes weren't on the canvas original but riveted on the ghastly contact print displayed across the pig's bum. As she walked away the mayor's face distorted hideously and his pink curly quiff wagged.

'How do you get oil paint off?' Bernard asked. 'It makes her look ridiculous.'

'In this case with an extremely sharp knife across her throat,' I screeched, at that moment meaning every murderous word.

It was at this juncture that I heard the distinctive rattle of Sidney Slocumb's Mini as it pulled up outside. Suddenly I remembered that the front door was on the latch and I'd told him to come straight in for his final sitting. Desperately, I hauled my girl's body round to align her head with the sitting room door. Footfalls sounded in the hall. The pig pulled away snorting, eyes malevolent. I shoved and prodded, but wilfully she turned half-circle so that the vile picture was set full square to greet the mayor. The door opened. I froze. Then the wonderful velvet brown eyes of Cynthia peered in.

'Just wanted to record the progress of your masterpiece,' she said, holding up her camera. She stepped forward. She stopped dead. She peered down at the portrait of her husband leering up from the obscene buttocks of the pig. 'Nice one Freda,' she chuckled, aiming the lens. There was a flash and Hermione bolted into the hallway, honking with fear.

'Aye oop! What's going on in here?' asked Sidney as, fully robed, he entered the cottage.

Then dear Bernard saved the day by hastily booting the pig into the kitchen and slamming the door shut. Cynthia, at the same time, forcefully manoeuvred her husband round and ushered him back outside.

'Freda's not feeling well,' she explained. 'She's not up to painting today.'

The door banged shut and his disappointed voice could be heard as they retreated up the path. 'But I've put me robe and chain on special ... ' The crunch of their feet and his whining bleat faded.

I *wasn't* feeling well. My glorious dream had just been annihilated by my blundering swines.

'What a bummer,' Bernard giggled, peering round the kitchen door like a silly schoolboy.

'It's not a joke, it's a catastrophe!' I sobbed.

'More like a *pig*astrophe!' he flashed back, quickly ducking inside.

I ran upstairs and locked myself in the bathroom. It was all so unfair. If it hadn't been for my defunct fallopian tubes we'd have had sweet careful children instead of a clumsy pig. I sat on the loo and wept.

It is Valentine's Day but romance is not in the air. Hermione stinks of turpentine and her bum is streaked with garish colours where Bernard has done his best to clean her. I herded her into her compound and closed the gate. It's the first time she's ever been shut in and she reared up on her hind legs and tried to climb over the top. It was a futile attempt and she looked distraught. I hardened my heart to her plaintive honks and walked away.

Bernard had set the canvas back on the easel, but facing the wall. I am too dispirited to look at it, let alone try to carry on.

'You've done nothing but go on about it Freed,' Bernard complained. 'Why not forget the whole piggin' incident and start again.'

'Thank you,' I retorted, 'thank you very much for your support and kindness, thanks a bunch.'

'Listen. I was sympathetic Monday and Tuesday, but it's Wednesday now and you're still keeping on about it all the time. Why don't you work on what's left on the canvas - paint on top of what's there.'

He went out on a lesson and, with stomach turning trepidation, I turned the canvas around. I stood rooted to the carpet, unable to believe my eyes. It was magic. The paint remaining on the canvas had been dragged down, blending colours, creating mystique. The mayor's skin was toned down and his splodgy hooter was now subtly blurred. It just needed touching up, clarifying here and there and it was finished.

Eagerly I began unscrewing tubes of paint. At the end of an hour it was finished and I signed it with pride.

Bernard walked in and gasped. 'It's *brilliant* Freed. How did you do it? It's so much better than before. More impressionistic ... not so heavy handed ... no great dollops of paint.'

I bristled. 'Those great dollops of paint were intended. I told you, it was impasto.'

'Impasto, in pasta, the pre-pig portrait was ordinary. The post-pig portrait is sheer delight. You wait and see, everyone will love it. It's unique. And also very flattering to our conceited clot of a mayor. He'll love it.' He put his arms round me. 'You'll see,' he whispered, 'when the public see it at the unveiling ceremony you'll be inundated with requests. You'll get commissions galore, so you'd better not carry out your threat to exterminate the pig, you'll need her backside, it's vital to your technique. You could say the pig has saved your bacon!' He snorted at yet another bacon joke, then added, 'In fairness to Hermione, you should have signed it *The Pig and I*.'

And I knew he was right.

As I drove to school after lunch, I pondered: Could I really get Hermione to sit on subsequent portraits, giving a weird new meaning to 'a final sitting?

After school next day, I rang Sidney and told him the portrait was finished and ready to view. He's coming round tomorrow. I feel quite sick with apprehension. Was the effect too mystical for a John Blunt such as he?

'It's a miracle,' Cynthia gasped. 'How have you done it! You've made him look proud yet modest, a man of the people yet wise.'

Sidney's face glowed with pleasure. 'Aye, Freda, it's champion. You've captured me all right.'

A burst of ironic laughter erupted from his wife. 'Give her the money now,' she rapped and, with obvious reluctance, he withdrew his wallet from inside his jacket. Slowly he thumbed through a thin wad of notes.

'There's your brass,' he said handing me ten beautiful fifty pound notes. He took out a small diary and riffled through it. 'Saturday eighteenth March - that'll be the date for unveiling ceremony. I'll get all me influential friends from Council to attend. It'll be a grand affair and you and I will be the stars.' He seemed about to spring in the air.

'But ... but,' I stuttered, suddenly afraid.

'But nothing. I can see paint's nearly dry enough to get it framed now you've blotted so mooch off. Think on Freda, by the end of that day your name will be on everyone's lips. You'll be known as the famous portrait painter of Wood Hill. And it'll be all down to me.'

You and the pig's arse, I thought as I waved them goodbye.

I flicked through the sheaf of notes. Now all I had to do was ring the roofer. Or was it?

Fifteen

I tapped out three digits of the roofing contractor's number then stopped. Once that precious five hundred pounds had been spent that was it. Gone for ever. Just like the home tutoring money. People say you must speculate to accumulate, but what could I speculate on? I knew nothing about antiques or property. I started to dial again.

Then I remembered a man on TV last week saying how he'd made a fortune trading shares. If someone as dopey looking as he could do it, why couldn't I? I left the phone and searched out The Times, scanning the cramped columns of share prices for inspiration. And, suddenly, one name leapt out like a 3D magic eye picture. LUPIN PORK PIES ... O.19. Only nineteen pee! With my five hundred pounds I could buy thousands. And, with the pig/pork connection, maybe it was meant. I blanked my mind to the deadness of the pig in a pork pie and wondered how to set about buying shares. Then I remembered a notice in the village bank informing customers that they had started a share dealing service. Could I dare?

But, supposing it rained before the shares went up. Water would cascade through the neglected roof and we'd be back emptying buckets again. It was no use. I stabbed out six digits of the roofer's number this time before putting the phone back down. Supposing it *didn't* rain. Supposing we were in for a dry period. I turned to the forecast in the paper: *It will remain dry in England and Wales for the next five days*. It was the sign I sought. An omen saying, Freda Field, you go on out there and buy those Lupin Pork Pie shares because your attic will stay dry.

I spent all the next day worrying about whether I should buy the Lupin's. Bernard said I looked pensive and, for reasons I can't fathom, I didn't tell him why.

Finally I decided that if the TV weather man backed up the newspaper forecast that it wouldn't rain I'd go for it.

'The south of England will remain cold but dry until the end of the month,' Michael Fish stated.

That was it. My fate had been sealed in the cloudless sky. Quickly I worked out that I could buy a massive twenty-five thousand shares and still have some over for costs.

(At this point I hadn't noticed my error involving a decimal point and had also forgotten that Michael Fish had been the forecaster who in 1987 categorically denied there'd be a hurricane just before one hit the south of England, flattening it.)

I shut my eyes to the pile of dirty washing and sped down to the bank. Twenty minutes later the deed was done.

'Right Mrs Field, that's twenty-five thousand Lupin Pork Pie Shares at nineteen pence each,' the young man had stated, tapping at computer keys, then writing the details down on a form which he thrust at me, instructing me to sign. Then he tore the back copy off and handed it over. With shaking hands I folded the paper and placed it carefully in my bag. (*Failing to see the extra nought on the sum owed!*) It had been easy. Perhaps too easy? I had proffered the envelope which held the ten fifty pound notes, but he waved it away.

'Your account won't be debited for ten working days from now,' he said. 'Pay that in to your Higher Rate Deposit Account and earn some interest.'

Next morning, I tore open the City pages before Bernie came down and what I saw made my heart plummet. Weakly, I sat down and re-read the horror story:-

LUPINS CUT DOWN TO SIZE: Chairman, Percy Prune, stated that he regretted that talks had broken down and the proposed take-over of his company Lupin Pork Pies by Samuel Slaughter PLC would not now take place. He wished to reassure shareholders that his firm was run by an excellent management team and that the Pork Pies were in safe hands and would never be crushed.

My innards jolted into action as I stared down at the price:
Lupin Pork Pies 0.12 (-7)

Bernard entered. 'What's the matter?' he asked, 'you look green.'

'Nothing,' I lied, then dashed upstairs to the attic, stomach churning up bile.

What should I do? Sell immediately? Cut my losses. Confess to Bernie? Would the price keep bombing or might it rally round? What had I done! Anyone could be bold and daring if they were a penny short of a pound. Or, in my case, seven pennies short of nineteen. My teeth chattered with cold and anguish and I hurried back down.

Bernard was just going out to attend to the pig. As soon as the door was shut I rang the bank share dealing service. But, when the man answered, the words that had formed in my head refused to come out. Slowly I replaced the phone. Perhaps something would happen. But, with my luck, the only thing likely would be a month long deluge of sheeting rain with the whole of the Winchester area flooded, but only our cottage flooding from the top downwards. The only good thing about this week is that it's half term and I don't have to go to that hell-hole of a school. I almost wish I did to take my mind off the hell-hole of my mind.

The bold headline screamed out: *LUPINS ARE COMING UP ROSES!* Hope crept into my emptiness and I read swiftly on: *It is rumoured that Samuel Slaughter PLC will make a substantial bid for Percy Prune's Lupin Pork Pie Company today.*

My eyes skidded down the lists of shares, slowed down at the Food Manufacturers column and stopped at Lupin: I blinked. I read. I blinked again. It hadn't been a mirage: *Lupin Pork Pies 0.40 (+28)* I was saved. I would sell immediately. But even as the bank's number rang I changed my mind. Hadn't my ambition been to make BIG money. Dare I risk just one more day? Could I live that long with every nerve like a violin string tuned too tightly. Just one more turn of the screw and every one would snap. I was more on edge than I'd ever been before. Excited. Afraid. But this was living!

I sped pots and pans away, sorted cutlery, rushed and dashed at everything, jumping at every sound. Bernard kept casting anxious looks my way and when the pig unexpectedly barged in and I screamed out, dashing a cup to the floor, he took me in his arms and softly said, 'Calm down, sweetheart, you're getting uptight about the unveiling ceremony aren't you, but you'll be all right.' He held me out at arms' length and his wonderful eyes, brimming with tender concern, stared into mine. 'Enjoy it,' he urged, 'you've earned your success.'

I kicked at the broken china at my feet and burbled about clearing up the pieces. His eyes kept staring but I turned away unable to hold his gaze. I'd gambled with the money without telling him and I couldn't make out why. Perhaps it was because I was always so predictable that I needed to show him I had changed. Or maybe it was simply that I wanted to give him a wonderful surprise. I hoped that's what it would turn out to be. Wonderful. Not a disaster.

I crept down at five thirty hoping the paper boy might be early. Five mugs of coffee and two hours later the paper flopped onto the mat.

I spread it out on the kitchen table and ran my shaking finger down the list. *Lupin Pork Pies 0.59 (+19)* I almost fainted with relief. At eight, Bernard came into the kitchen, but still I didn't tell him.

'Are you sickening for something?' he asked, 'you tossed and turned all night and got up very early.'

'It's just my oh be joyful giving me stomach ache' I replied. At any rate that was half true. The curse had started bang on time again. That was a change of life over which I had no control.

I sped to the village, parked on a yellow line and ran into the bank.

'That was five thousand pounds well invested,' remarked the young man as he completed the selling order.

My legs turned to jelly. Five *thousand* pounds! Abruptly I sat down. 'Five thousand pounds,' I whispered, clutching at his desk.

'Yes, and now you have fourteen thousand, seven hundred and fifty pounds, less costs, so you've made a very handsome profit indeed.'

Better than you'll ever know, I thought. Better than you'll ever ever know!

'Over fourteen thousand pounds!' Bernard repeated for the third time, eyes out on stems. 'Come on, you're kidding me!'

'No, it's true.'

'Over fourteen thousand pounds,' he repeated again, clearly stunned. Suddenly he leapt up, yipping and yowling, pulling me up to my feet and dragging me round the room in a crazy polka. Hermione, eyes bright, flopped off the sofa and joined in, bucking and leaping in a frenzy of copypig joy.

'We're rich,' Bernard shrieked at her and, as if the words were picked up in her pig-brain as 'We're taking you to the abattoir,' she bolted, squealing with fright.

We crashed down together on the pig-warm sofa. 'I'll ring the roofer when I've got my breath back,' I panted, 'and ask for a price to re-tile the whole lot.'

'God but you amaze me these days,' he whispered, staring at me with admiration struck eyes.

You wait Bernard Field, I thought joyfully, *you ain't seen nothing yet*.

I rang Brands Hatch Race Track early the next day.

'We can fit you in this Monday. Seventy-nine pounds each for the Nigel Mansell Initial Trial,' the woman said.

I checked Bernard's schedule to see if he had any tests or lessons booked but, as expected, his day was free. 'Fine,' I replied, 'I'll take two places for Bernard and Freda Field.'

Later I asked Bernard to keep Monday clear. He was so absorbed in reading an article on *Unusual Uses for Pig Manure* he didn't even ask why.

Last night I dreamt I was half a bonnet ahead of Jacques Villeneuve blasting straight as an arrow towards the finishing line. Damon Hill and Michael Schumacher were lagging behind us. My foot was on the floor, the engine screaming. I knew I would beat him. Then I saw Norah Harker-Balls lying at the side of the track. I turned the wheel and with deadly accuracy ran over her. The black and white chequered flag was waved at Villeneuve as I regained control and closely followed him across the line. As we stood together on the dais, a mound covered by a sheet was carried on a stretcher directly in front of us. I shook the magnum thrust into my hand and sprayed champagne all over it.

Little did I know then that the dream would become a nightmare and the mound would be my Bernie.

At breakfast I broke the news that I'd booked us both in for a training session at Brands Hatch on Monday and he fell on me, bombarding my face with a sortie of Marmite pecks.

On Sunday I realised that it was easy having dreams of daring expoloits when they're at some unspecified time in the future. It must be like planned euthanasia. Easy when your number is going to be up another year, or even another month. But this is tomorrow!

Sixteen

Not counting when I missed the motorway exit and went round the whole M25 again, this is the longest, saddest journey of my life. I follow the wailing ambulance that contains my darling man, knowing the disaster was because of me. Bold, reckless, kamikaze me.

Bernard and I had arrived at Brands Hatch Race Track for the one day Initial Trial with hope in our hearts. Excitement had bubbled in my innards like laxative champagne. After the video briefing and the talk about braking, racing lines, the theory of high-speed driving, cornering techniques, and safety, we met the drivers who were to be our personal instructors for the day. Mine was Ray, a wiry, sandy-haired man with a narrow face and matching nose. Bernard had chubby Charlie who clutched his head groaning, 'Why do I always get the driving instructors!' Bernard had looked down on the five foot high man from his six foot high eyes and given his polite smile. I hoped Charlie wasn't going to spoil Bernie's special day. I didn't know then that it was I, his loving wife, who was going to be the one to spoil his special day by probably killing him.

Ray led me to a white car. 'This is what you'll drive around the track first,' he explained. 'It's a souped up sports saloon and it'll give you a chance to put the theory into practice.'

I wriggled into the driver's seat feeling strangely wonderful. I, the once frumpy Freda Field, now successfully de-frumped, was about to launch forth and drive round the famous Brands Hatch.

Ray crowned my head with a helmet and I secured it under my chin. He sat beside me.

'Okay, let's go,' he rapped.

Gingerly, I let out the clutch and steered the powerful machine out of the pit lane and onto the circuit.

'Don't be so timid,' he chivvied.

So, boldly, I pressed my foot down, speeding along the straight towards the distant bend.

'Give it more gas Freda, you're only doing twenty-five,' Ray grumbled.

I crushed my foot down harder. Faster and faster we bombed along until the side of the track was just a fast-moving blur. A yellow saloon car cruised up beside us and a hand waved as it passed by.

'That was your husband,' Ray said. 'Trust a driving instructor to take you on the wrong side!'

Poor Bernie. It was hard enough for me to remember to overtake on the left, but he'd spent years teaching learners to pass on the right.

'Concentrate!' Ray barked as the bend shot towards us.

I braked, changed down, changed down again, held the curve, accelerated, moving up the gears as we careered out the other side.

'Well done,' he muttered, 'you took the bend too fast but you remembered to cross your arms with both hands gripped to the wheel.'

Yes, I had remembered, and I glowed with the acknowledged success.

'I bet your husband was incapable of that,' he added with a sniff, and I worried again that Bernie would not enjoy this dream day.

Three glorious laps later and Ray instructed me to return to the pits. I drew up alongside Bernard. This was the de-briefing session where our performance and mistakes were analysed. Would he be demoralised by being on the receiving end instead of dishing out advice? But he was listening intently to Charlie with no sign of distress.

'Wasn't it great!' he called over, his eyes sparkling like an excited young boy's.

Pictures of us were taken by one of the mechanics who'd volunteered to take photos on our camera throughout the day.

'You did okay Freda. You took account of nearly everything you learnt in the classroom,' Ray was saying, 'now all you have to do is slow down on the bends and speed up on the straight. I'll show you - it's my turn to drive you round now.'

I changed to the passenger side, slipped into the safety harness, the engine roared and we were off. My God, the speed! The track streamed away under us like rushing water. He slowed down, swept into the bend then accelerated out and hurtled towards the next one while I sat stuck to the back of my seat with the crushing G force. All the time he was giving a running commentary and I wished he would stop yacking and concentrate on driving. But, even as we screeched round the next bend, Ray long-tongue prattled on: 'See how I pass that car on the left ... Notice the flag being waved as we lap ... Watch how I brake before the bend then accelerate through ... Notice the line I take to round the corners ...' I was awash with information, terrified, but at the same time deliriously happy. If only my fellow teachers could see me now, or some of my pupils, or their parents, or my own parents. They all thought I was such a fuddy-duddy. *If they could see me now* my inner voice sang. Suddenly I lurched forward against my safety strapping and we were braking into the pits. The excitement was over. I undid the harness and climbed out on wobbly legs.

'That was *wonderful*' I gasped, clinging on to the door.

'Okay, it's cup of tea time, then the loo, then you're out in a single-seater racer on your own.'

If we'd have left then, everything would have been all right. But of course we didn't.

The wheels thrust out from the fiery red car's low slung body and I stepped over the side, heart flacking around my rib cage like a dove caught in a trap. I eased myself down, wedging tightly into the cockpit, thankful I'd shed half a stone.

He handed me an all-engulfing crash helmet and, with a flutter of claustrophobic fear, I forced it over my head.

'Okay, you're ready to go now,' he said, 'and remember, you must keep an eye on the rev counter. If it goes over four thousand you could spin off and that'll be the end of your run. But I don't think we need really worry about that. Not with you.'

Rebellion stirred in my breast.

'Just you and your husband will be on the track now, the rest of today's intake will go on afterwards. We feel you're both pretty safe. Even your husband seems to have got the hang of it.'

Patronising bastard! All my grateful and kind notions about him had been instantly sucked away like fine toilet paper flushed down the loo. We'll show him we're not the green Fields he thinks we are. I could see Bernard squeezing himself into an identical car to mine. He donned his crash helmet then turned and waved at me.

'Just one more thing,' Ray said. 'That's the fire extinguisher in front of you there, in case you should crash and burst into flames.' He sniggered at the supposed impossibility of it. I tried reaching for the life-saving cylinder, but with the seat reclining and my still rotund tum, I couldn't even touch it.

'Look round and say Cheese for the camera,' the mechanic called and stupidly I smiled inside my armoured hat.

Bernard slowly drove past. He sat up from his reclined position and waved at me again. I didn't know it then, but that was the last communication we were to have, perhaps for ever.

'It'll look great for their photo album,' Ray shouted to the mechanic, 'but if they drive on public highways the way they drive on the track, neither of 'em would ever be had up for speeding!' Then they both laughed like stupid jackasses.

I'll show the insensitive know-alls, I vowed.

The engine was running. I put my foot down and Wheee Whaa! I was away, engine roaring into life as I sped onto the track.

I changed down, decelerating into the bend then, thrusting the gear into top, raced out into the straight. I knew I'd taken the perfect racing line and hoped that Ray had seen it. I lay back, nerves taut, every cell in my body alive. This was the ultimate experience and there were nearly four laps to go. Ahead I saw the tail-end of Bernard's car. I accelerated, snatched a glance at the rev counter, saw it nearing four thousand. Gravity seemed to double as I flew along in my magnificent precision machine.

Two laps later I'd caught up with him and we were racing neck and neck, hurtling towards the next bend that curved away to the left. Suddenly I wasn't Freda Field, housewife and part-time teacher, I was a pro taking on Nigel Mansell. As I pushed the car to its limits, the engine whined like mosquitoes provoked into rage. But to my right I could still see Bernard staying level. I pushed my foot down even harder, but suddenly it was all wrong, the bend was racing at me and I was running out of track. I screamed, jammed on the brakes and hauled on the tiny steering wheel battling to follow the curve. From the corner of my eye I saw Bernard's car, with no space to turn into, rocket straight ahead then veer sideways. I pumped at the brakes and the car spun half round, its engine roaring wildly before abruptly cutting out. There was a second's deathly silence before the muffled far-away crash. Across the other side of the circuit the blood red car was buried nose first in a still tumbling wall of tyres. White smoke began to pour out the back.

Bernard, oh my darling Bernard! I had to unclip the fire extinguisher and save him, but I couldn't reach it. I grappled with my safety harness and then an angel dressed as a steward ran up and deftly released me. A siren struck up warning bells and a small fire appliance raced into view. I wrenched off my helmet, snatched up the extinguisher and started to run. A low ambulance appeared, its urgent warble joining the siren in a clashing duet. I kept running across the no-man's land in the centre of the circuit, spurred on by terrible fear. As I pounded nearer, Bernard's helmeted head became visible through the clouds of belching smoke. It lay at a peculiar angle. It did not move. The steward puffed up alongside and grabbed my arm.

'Steady,' he panted, holding me back, 'the whole lot could explode.'

'But he's my husband, I must get to him,' I screamed, jerking my arm free. I sprinted forward, tears searing hot paths down my cheeks. *Bernard, oh Bernard, I love you. Don't be dead. And especially don't be dead because of me.*

The fire engine slewed to a stop and a man carrying an extinguisher leapt out and ran towards the car. Now terror took me by the throat and throttled me. My Bernie. Was he about to be cremated before he was dead! A rushing noise, like a water fall, filled my head. I faltered and the steward caught up with me and held me back again.

'No nearer Mrs Field, it could be dangerous and you'll get in the way.'

I struggled, but this time he hung on tightly. The ambulance raced up and two men in white coats jumped out. One carried a first aid box, the other an oxygen cylinder and mask.

The fireman leant over Bernard and the belching smoke abruptly stopped. He shouted to the medics that the engine was switched off and it was now safe to approach.

I struggled with my captor. I had to go to him too. But his grip tightened and I gave up, knowing in my heart that I'd be a hinderance.

The two men were bent over Bernie, their backs blocking my view. *God, make him be alive, make him be whole*, I prayed to a spirit I didn't believe in. At last Bernard's limp body was hauled from the cockpit and carefully laid out on a stretcher. He looked so beautiful, his thick sweeping lashes coal black against his dead white face. I howled. Loud sobs of terror. That phantom God had ignored me. My husband was dead. The man I loved and adored, even more than my pig. And it was I who had killed him.

The steward released me and I tore stumbling to Bernard's side. I knelt and gently kissed his lips. Their coldness chilled my soul.

'You'll have to leave him now,' the medic ordered, firmly pushing me aside. I went to follow the stretcher as it was lifted into the back of the low ambulance van, but was refused entry. 'You can see how cramped it is,' he said tersely. 'We need space to work on him while we get him to hospital. Meet us there.' He slammed the ambulance doors and they were off.

Suddenly, Ray drew up beside me in the souped-up white saloon. 'Hop in,' he commanded, 'we'll follow them.'

Seventeen

The flashing and wailing abruptly ceased as we drew up outside the hospital behind the ambulance.

'I'll drop you off,' Ray said, sounding gruff with emotion, 'then go back and organise someone to bring your Cortina to that car park over there. You can drive your husband back home in it provided he isn't ...'

I blundered out, the unspoken word bouncing around my skull as if it had been shouted: *DEAD DEAD DEAD. You can drive your husband back home in it provided he isn't dead.* Oh don't be dead my darling, don't be!

In a daze I watched Ray's car disappear and the ambulance doors swing open. I heard directions rapped out by a doctor. Then my Bernie, still sleeping, still ghostly white, but now connected by a thin tube to a bottle, was lifted out.

Please, *please*, I beseeched him, please sit up and give another wave. But he just lay on the stretcher, as still as a corpse. Mutely I followed inside where the doctor and two nurses transferred him to a trolley and, feet clacking with terrifying urgency, sped him away.

'I'm his wife,' I cried, keeping up with the flying entourage, my hands stretched out into the air he'd just passed through, as if sleep running.

A vigilant woman overheard my words and caught up, trotting down the shiny corridor alongside me.

'You must come to Reception. We need to fill in the details on his form,' she panted. I stopped. 'And we need your permission in case we need to operate ... or consent to donate his organs.'

I wasn't sure if I'd imagined the last words. They might have just lurked in my head.

He'd been X-rayed, examined inside and out and, at last, I was allowed to go to him. As I arrived at his bedside he opened his eyes, flickering and concussed, but proof that what the doctor had told me was true. My husband lived.

'Bernie, my darling,' I whispered, gently touching the warm living flesh of his face.

His features crumbled. 'Bloody hell it's agony,' he groaned, shoving my hand away.

'But they said you'd got off lightly with no broken bones.'

'As far as I know there aren't any bones in your dick,' he whimpered pitifully.

And that was it. Apart from the bump and graze on his forehead, his only injury was a bruised penis and tender balls!

'We'll have to keep him in for observation,' a pretty young nurse smirked. 'But rest assured, we won't have to Bobbit him!'

As I drove my lonely journey back to my hungry pig. I bawled my eyes out. We'd started out this morning with such wondrous high hopes.

Early next day, a harassed-sounding woman rang saying I must collect Bernard immediately because they needed his bed. With joy in my soul, I drove back to Kent in a manner that would have impressed Ray, but obviously did not impress numerous bad-tempered lorry drivers. Seventy is the speed limit and fast enough for anyone I thought grimly as, with menacing closeness, they tried to force me off the middle lane.

'He may be slightly concussed,' the nurse explained, 'so he should stay quiet for a few days. No more racing around Brands Hatch.' She paused, then added, 'I hear you're the one who forced him off the track.'

I glared across to the tell-tale-tit sitting fully dressed perched on the edge of the bed. I suppose he'd told *everyone*.

'You don't look like a racing driver Mrs Field,' she continued, 'I wish I had the nerve.'

I caught the look of respect in her eyes and felt myself blush. This young woman was admiring *me*. The new unstodgy me. Perhaps it didn't matter that people knew I was to blame for his crash. I stepped forward to kiss Bernard, but he reeled back, hands cupped over his crotch.

'He might strike out if you get within a mile of it,' the nurse warned, a smile twitching dangerously at her lips.

Bernard pushed himself up. He stood knock-kneed, bottom out, as if about to sit back down again. He took hold of my arm and together we began the long walk down the ward, his size elevens shuffling in fairy footsteps, our progress monitored by two bed-lines of eyes.

When we reached the corridor, a porter, pushing a sleeping man on a trolley, called out, 'Tell him to wear a cricketer's box next time.' His guffaw exploded out so loudly that the recumbent man on the trolley's eyes sprang open for an instant before clamping back shut tight.

'*Everybody* knows,' Bernard complained as we reached the exit. 'I'm the laughing stock of the whole hospital, thanks to you.'

I knew the hurt wasn't just physical. He'd badly wanted to take me on that bend and bomb across the finishing line like a champion.

'I'm sorry Bernie, I really am.' And I really was. Never again would I do anything so foolhardy.

Unappeased, he snatched his hand from my arm and headed unsupported towards the car park. John Cleese himself could not have concocted a funnier walk. Hands clasped over his injury, knees gripped tightly together, each foot in turn rose up and slapped down in a bizarre circular motion. It was very hard not to laugh.

He eased himself into the passenger seat and I tugged his safety belt out and leant across to connect it. But he made strange little animal noises and his hands fluttered up from his flies to grab and secure the metal tag before swooping back down like homing pigeons returning to their coop.

'Careful how you take this bend,' he screeched as slowly I inched the car forward out of the parking space.

At the exit I turned left onto the empty narrow road and, cautiously, we glided along. But, at even the slightest curve, Bernie became agitated, his voice rising in warbling semitones like a Muezzin calling the faithful to prayer. Once we passed a dark Islamic-looking man and, in the rear mirror, I saw him stop, scratch his head and look around as if seeking a minaret behind the hedgerow.

With relief I turned onto the M25. At last we were free from wiggly bends and Bernie's parallel accompaniment. But after ten minutes of yodel-free travel, we became stationary in a traffic jam. When I asked jokingly if my speed was safe enough now, he snarled, 'Don't be sarcastic Freda, it doesn't suit you.'

I decided to give up on trying to cheer him up, he was obviously not in the mood and, after five more minutes of stationary silence, the traffic began to move. As the revving cars and lorries gathered speed Bernard performed new warbling variations, impressive in their range. It would have been quite funny in other circumstances.

Back home, the first thing Bernie did was bolt the pig flap shut. 'Can't risk her barging into me, she's banned from the house,' he snapped. By the way he glared and eyed my body I guessed that I'd be banned too if I got within a foot of him.

When I innocently muttered, 'Poor Hermione,' his face contorted and he dragged one hand away from its protective intertwining and yelled, 'You don't know what the agony is like down there.' As he spoke he jabbed his index finger vigorously in the air at a safe distance from his damaged equipment.

But, by now, I'd lost all patience. 'Well, I've had to put up with the pain of periods for years and you don't know what the agony is like down *there*!' I retaliated, jabbing my finger vigorously towards my Beatrice.

He said nothing. Just mooched off into the sitting room where I heard the TV switch on. I crashed around tidying the kitchen, and suddenly realised that the relief of his being alive had put me into a strangely angry mood. I knew it was psychological but couldn't help it.

I've tried to be extra kind to Bernard. I've apologised about the accident till I'm blue in the face but he goes around muttering about my unbelievable stupidity and his pain. Finally I said to him, 'Bernard, if I could grow a penis I would, then I'd give you a cricket bat and you could whack it with it and we'd be quits.' But it didn't satisfy him, or even make him smile. Wisteria Cottage is full of gloom since the accident. And outside in the mobile home it is even gloomier. Poor Hermione, barred from the house and bored out of her tiny mind just lies on her bed looking glum. And all this is because I dared to have ambition.

The roof contractors began work at seven. Bernard winced at every single bang. Before I set off for school he invited me to inspect his swollen appendages. It was the first time he'd allowed me to view and I must admit I was astounded by the vibrant hues, they were such an inspiration in daring colour combinations. I mentioned this to him but, from the tirade that that evoked, it was obvious he didn't appreciate my artistic observations. As I went down the stairs I called back, 'I am a painter you know, and painters notice such things.'

There was no response until I was out in the front garden where his riposte reached me faintly through the bedroom window.

'You're the only painter I know who uses a pig's arse instead of a brush!' The harsh sound that followed just might have been a laugh.

Why were we being so nasty to each other I wondered. I guessed it was guilt with me. Perhaps it was disappointment with him. His life-long dream of being a racing driver painfully knocked on his head.

Mother rang up to enquire about 'His Nibs'. 'Or should I say 'His Knobs' she chortled. She's really quite a card at times.

I went out to feed the exiled pig before breakfast. She golloped it down then flopped back on her bed, sad piggy eyes clearly pleading with me to know what she'd done wrong.

'It's not your fault babe,' I whispered, clasping her plump shoulders in my arms. Then a sudden brilliant flash of light made us both jump. I turned to see Bernard, camera held up to his eye with one hand.

'I wanted to use up the film' he explained, 'so I can see the pictures the mechanic took of us at Brands Hatch.'

At least he had dared remove one protective mitt from the danger zone I thought, heartily thankful that at last his manhood must be on the mend.

As I drove to school I thought about the money situation. Even after the roof job and Brands Hatch, there was still about nine thousand pounds left, more than I'd ever dreamt of before, but still not enough to retire on. I wondered if I dare risk another gamble on the stock market.

Saturday, I scoured the jumbo paper for another likely share. I knew I'd never make such a killing as with Lupin Pork Pies because I'd be sure to buy the right amount next time, but perhaps I could make a profit of some kind. A name attracted my eye: *Magnetic Field Enterprises*. Wasn't I a Field? Wasn't I enterprising! But at ninety pence they were a different kettle of oysters from the Lupins. Hastily, I closed the paper as Bernard walked in.

'You're looking thoughtful Mrs Field,' he remarked. 'What are you dreaming up now?'

That was it. The sign. He'd said Mrs Field instead of Freda! I decided to buy them on Monday, first thing. 'Just wondering what to wear for the unveiling ceremony,' I fibbed.

Bernard was always clean shaven at breakfast. It wasn't until afternoon that the navy blue shadow appeared. But this morning there was a definite smattering of dark stubble above his upper lip. As I watched, he began stroking the faint line of bristles with gentle upward movements of his index finger.

'I've decided to grow a moustache,' he proclaimed, catching my quizzical eye. 'A full one, just like Nigel Mansell's.'

Poor Bernie. He couldn't become a racing driver, so he'd live out his fantasy by trying to look like one.

'You're dark like Damon Hill and he's clean shaven, and so is Michael Schumacher,' I observed, trying to put him off the 'tash idea because I didn't fancy my tender skin being scratched and gouged each time we kissed.

'Also,' he continued, as if I hadn't spoken, 'one day I'd like to go for the Super Trial day at Brands Hatch. Would you want to have a go too?'

I was astounded. 'I'll never go on that track again for the whole of the rest of my life.' I gasped, amazed at such a foolhardy suggestion. 'And I find it incredible that you'd want to after what happened. Wouldn't you be scared?'

'Not now you've said you won't be going!' he retorted, face lighting up with a grin. 'Honestly piglet, despite what happened it was the most exciting day of my life.'

When I thought about it later, I realised it was all bravado. He'd never risk crashing again.

Daring, that had been my aim, but as I signed the buying order I felt a rush of fear. The figures swam and I had to blink hard to re-focus. Carefully, I scrutinised the page, re-reading every word before handing it back to the man. The deed was done. I staggered out of the bank into the freezing air and, with icy certainty, I knew I'd gone too far. Eight thousand pounds blown on unknown shares, leaving just a few hundred left in the account. Greediness. That's what it was. Why couldn't I have been content with what we had. But later I consoled myself. It wasn't like the National Lottery. You didn't lose your entire stake. There was always something to sell off at the end. But how much, I asked myself. How much would those shares be worth at the end? And when was the end? How could one tell?

I stared at the pristine newspaper lying on the kitchen table, too fearful to open it up. But at last I forced myself, heart pounding like a sledge hammer smashing through concrete ribs. I spread out the city pages and read the headline. I rubbed my eyes, looked away then back again: *MAGNETIC FIELD ATTRACTS BIG MONEY*. Well I knew eight thousand pounds was a lot, but I thought they dealt in millions in the City. My finger skimmed down the columns, then stopped: *Magnetic Field Enterprises 120 (+30)!!!!!!* I dashed up to Bernard and blurted out what I'd done.

Next morning we pored over the paper together.
    'Look!' he gasped. 'Flipping heck Freda, you're a genius.'
    I read where his finger pointed: *Magnetic Field Enterprises 155 (+25)*
    'Let's sell as soon as the bank opens,' he sang, his fledgeling moustache spiking quills at my skin as he kissed my cheek.
    I pulled away. 'No,' I firmly stated, 'we'll wait to sell until tomorrow.'
    He didn't demur. Just stared at me. Never before had I received a look so intense. Never before had I held such power.

'Look out Freed, don't barge me off the track again.' He fell against the wall, laughing, as I beat him to the paper on the mat.

'I wish we had Teletext on our TV,' I said as we spread the paper out. 'Then we could see the price changes throughout the day, not just the day after.'

We peered down, heads touching.

'Sweet piglet,' he whispered, 'you can buy two new TVs if you want to now!'

Magnetic Field Enterprises: 180 (+25)

The investment had doubled in less than four days.

'Okay we'll get out now,' I rapped, heading for the phone.

Friday play-time I watched Norah Harker-Balls haul little Annabel Aspry from the playground into the school. She held the sobbing girl up by her collar so that her twinkling toes barely touched the ground as she was rushed along. 'SHUT UP YOU SNIVELLING LITTLE NON-ENTITY,' she ranted. 'BAD GIRLS LIKE YOU DON'T DESERVE TO BE LET OUT TO PLAY.' Then her laugh juddered through the air like a thunderclap, silencing all the children within earshot with terror.

I knew then that I would have to act quickly to release the children from this woman. But how? She had inherited the school building - a bungalow that had been converted - and she owned everything in it, lock stock and desk. She had absolute control. I knew I must wrest it from her. And soon.

At Sidney's request, I accompanied him to a frame maker's shop in Great Piddlehurst, even though the town is always crowded out on Saturdays. He said he wanted my advice. However he ignored it completely and, after nearly an hour of humming and hawing, selected a broad ornate gilt frame suitable for a Rembrandt. The young man who served us said my painting was the best portrait he'd ever seen in his life. He only looked about sixteen but nevertheless I felt proud.

Bernie has had the Brands Hatch photos developed and sits endlessly flicking through them, an expression of rapture on his face. He keeps pointing out how good we both look - how professional. He wagged a photo in front of my nose for the umpteenth time and I regarded myself packed tightly into the cockpit of the racing car, spirals of flaming hair flickering out from under my helmet. But the memory of what happened killed any pleasure or conceit.

At last he tired of looking at them and sat deep in thought, face radiant, mind obviously blanked out to the pain of the disaster. I watched him. He was even more handsome now than when we first met. The jet-black hair, silvered at the temples, plus the thickening moustache, looked so distinguished. He caught my admiring look, flushed, and ran his fingertips down his side parting, tidying non-existent wayward hairs.

'Why don't you get a crew cut,' I suggested.

'Good idea,' he replied.

He went out next day and came back with his hair cropped short all over. Not a parting in sight. He looked wonderful. I realised that life had seldom been better and wondered how long it could last. Then Bernard dropped his bombshell and I knew the answer was, *not long*, because he's sneakily booked to go on the Super Trial Session at Brands Hatch on Monday. And I am scared witless.

Eighteen

'Don't worry piglet, I'll drive carefully,' he assured me.

As I waved him off I regretted making the money and rued the unspoken pact that all of it went into a common pot. Not so long ago he couldn't have afforded this second attempt at death.

I spent the day in a frenzy of spring cleaning: scrubbing bathroom tiles, polishing wood, vacuuming carpets. As I laboured at getting the heavy chintz curtains down to wash, I saw a ghastly vision. It was crystal clear. Carelessly, Bernard was taking both hands off the steering wheel as he blasted across the finishing line. Then, turning his head, he waved to the skeletal man who had flacked the chequered flag. I stayed balanced on the step ladder, hand poised on a giraffe neck hook as the horror movie played on the retina screens of my eyes. Time changed down into first gear as his car veered sideways, straightened, then smashed head-on into the brick wall. The cavernous orbs in the skeletal man's skull swivelled towards the wreckage and the silhouette of his flag transmuted to the ghastly shape of a scythe. I closed my eyes to shut out the horror, but the film continued relentlessly in the darkness behind my lids. Bernard's body was being dragged out and laid on the tarmac. In sharp focus I could see his face, as white as virgin snow, eyes staring vacantly upwards to the glowering sky. How I yearned to reach out and touch him but, instead, I reached out and removed a long hook from a pencil pleat.

By lunch time I'd convinced myself that what I'd witnessed was a terrible premonition of what was to come. How else could I have seen the detail so clearly. I wept as I took the curtains in off the line. I wept as I fed the pig. By three o'clock I was exhausted with grief. By four o'clock new worries had surfaced. Should I buy a black dress for the funeral or something more colourful. Should I stay alive and Bernardless to grow sadly old or should I commit suicide and join Bernard in eternity? And, if I did the latter, who would take care of my pig? I couldn't slaughter her as well as me because I didn't trust my parents not to chop her up into joints of pork and store her in their freezer. As I ironed the curtains practical worries surfaced too, for, besides the tragedy of losing the only man I had ever loved, where would I find a gardener to mow our vast back lawn?

At six o'clock the door slowly creaked open and the apparition appeared. My husband stood unaided and obviously quite alive. The pent-up tension that had reorganised my innards into griping tangles suddenly released, unravelling my gut in one furious rush. 'What're you doing here?' I snapped.

'Why, I live here,' he smiled. 'Remember?' And he dangled his house keys as proof.

'Oh Bernard,' I cried, throwing myself into his arms, 'don't you ever get killed like that again.'

Like what?' he asked, perplexed.

As I tried to study the share prices Bernie regaled me with his adventures of yesterday. He was quite over the top poetic: the racing car throbbing under his control, an extension of him, his fearless foot an integral lever, a direct line of transmission to the pistons that hammered ever faster, pounding their rhythmic dance to his daring command. But the best bit seems to have been that there wasn't a female on the track.

'When are you going again?' I asked, my inner voice screaming *Never! Never!* inside my sound-proof skull.

He prevaricated, going off into raptures again: the engine whining, the quick throttle back, tyres screaming, taking the bend, accelerating out, the G force crushing his body, the chequered flag splicing the air.

'But when are you going again?' I persisted, dreading the answer.

But again he ducked the question with all the artfulness of a politician. 'It's dangerous for sure,' he expounded, eyes dreamy, 'but marginally less life threatening than teaching learner drivers.' He gave a wry smile.

'But when are you going again?' I shouted, exasperated. '*Answer* me!'

There was a long pause, then: 'I'm not,' he said flatly. 'At fifty-one I'm too old to be a racing driver.'

'Thank God,' I cried, 'I couldn't go through a day like that again.' I was over the moon ecstatic, but when I saw the look on his face, I hoped that whoever had advised him he was too old had been tactful with their words.

He shrugged as if unloading a weight from his shoulders. 'I've decided to take up snooker instead. Would you like to play too?'

'I would. I would,' I cried joyously, 'because no-one gets hurt at that game!'

'You've never seen anyone rip the baize with their cue,' he retorted ominously.

Why did I leave it so late. It's the unveiling ceremony on Saturday and I've nothing to wear. Mother's derogatory remarks about my best blue pleated dress had made me give it to a charity shop and there was nothing else remotely suitable. I drove into Great Piddlehurst, in a tearing rush because I was teaching at one o'clock.

'I want something modern,' I gabbled to a young girl serving in the first dress shop I came to in the High Street.

She rummaged around then pulled a garment off the rail. 'This would look good with your rich auburn hair,' she said, holding up an emerald green moire jacket. 'And you could team it with this.'

The second 'this' was a navy-blue dress with a minuscule straight skirt. Quite unsuitable, but she had nothing else to offer so I went into a cubicle and threw the garments on. When I saw myself in the mirror I could hardly believe it. I looked so glamorous, even chic. 'Don't you think this skirt's too short for me ... at my age?' I asked doubtfully.

'If I had long legs like yours I'd always wear a mini,' she replied. And in a flash I'd whipped out my credit card and bought the ensemble.

Norah Harker-Balls has organised a school choir to sing 'God Save the Queen' at the unveiling ceremony on Saturday! No-one had asked her to but she said it would be good publicity for the school. When I asked Cynthia if she minded the Evil One, as we call her, being present, she replied that, on the contrary, she would be very pleased. Sometimes I find my friend very hard to fathom.

I asked Mrs Harker-Balls if her husband Jeremy would be in attendance tomorrow.

'In a Village Hall!' she exclaimed. 'Don't be stupid. You must remember he is an awfully important man at the Palace of Westminster!'

I wondered if he really was as snobby as that or if it was just her.

I'm getting terrified of being in the limelight tomorrow but am hopeful that it will be the start of a lucrative artistic career.

We walked past the duck pond towards the entrance of the flint and brick village hall. It was half past two. The unveiling was scheduled for three.

'Remember sweetheart, this is your very special day. You're responsible for nothing except being there, so just enjoy the experience.' Bernard held the door open. 'Relax darling,' he said, 'you look terrific and there's nothing that can go wrong.'

If only I'd known what was to come, I'd have turned round and fled straight back home.

Nineteen
Intrusion 4

Sidney sits on a throne-like chair on a specially constructed dais positioned against the long wall of the hall. His portrait hangs hidden behind short blue velvet curtains behind him. Freda Field sits on his right and on his left is an empty chair. He eyes the clock. It is twenty to three. He eyes the empty chair with apprehension. 'Appen it had been a last minute invitation to Robert Bambridge to do the unveiling, but you'd think he'd turn up in good time. He dreads the important man won't show.

Sidney reflects on his disappointments. All of the town hall dignitaries were too busy to unveil the masterpiece, or so they said, *and* the local MP. He'd contemplated asking Maggie Thatcher, whose cause he'd backed over the years, but quickly had decided that, whilst it might help boost her flagging image, it'd do nowt for his own. When Robert Bambridge, Wood Hill's richest and most influential man, had agreed he could scarcely believe his luck.

He sees, at the far end, a regiment of Norah Harker-Ball's pupils lining up on the stage. Norah takes her seat on an orange plastic chair set down beside them. Glinting diamond earrings dangle from her mean pink lobes and narrow gold bracelets festoon fat wrists. Spasmodically she swishes the baton into the palm of her hand, provoking harsh warnings from rattle snake bangles. The children stand mute and erect. Not one fidgets.

He glances round at Freda and is arrested by the sight of her long legs, twisted around each other. His eyes meander up over her knees, along the thighs, across a narrow band of navy skirt, over brilliant green, to the tumble of auburn curls that frame her chubby freckled face. She tugs at the hem of her skirt then fiddles with her hair and he realises this must be the biggest event in her dull life. But he looks again and revises this opinion. If he didn't know it weren't so, he could be muddling her with a younger sister of the frumpish school teacher who'd put on the Nativity play, and the insecure artist who'd done his portrait just six weeks ago. He marvels at the change.

Voices are getting louder and louder in their effort to be heard and Sidney watches anxiously as yet more people swarm in to the already jam-packed hall. The three rows of chairs that face him, reserved for his special guests, look in danger of being swamped by the crowd that jostles behind them. He catches the eye of Cynthia in the front row. She pats the camera resting on her lap and her buck teeth ease out into an enigmatic smile. She's taken to photography lately he muses, eyeing her automatic SLR Canon which looks a baby beside the zoom lens Pentax of Peter Poop who sits beside her. Sidney inclines his head at the rangy young local reporter, known locally as Poop the Scoop.

He waves at his cronies who take up rows two and three, winking at Bill Boggins and Jake Glazier his builder buddy. He remembers the brush-offs from some of the Great Piddlehurst Councillors: the ones who always looked down their righteous noses at him. The tossers! They'd wish they had attended when they read about the glory of this unveiling.

He reflects moodily that, although he's lived in this picturesque village for nearly a year now, he still doesn't feel at home. Some of the villagers still shun him because of the housing development he'd thrust on them. But he recognises some of them are here, grouped at the far end, close to the stage, videos and cameras in hand. Only in attendance because of their kids' performance, but soon they'd be re-directing their cameras at his portrait and at him. His pudgy fingers tidy sparse long hairs, guiding them over the high dome of his head inside which he is picturing the magnificence of the portrait soon to be revealed. She'd made a good job of it, caught the proud gleam of his steely grey eyes. Managed to blur his protuberant nose with sensitivity. Made him look quite handsome. Still, for five hundred quid you'd expect it.

'Shall I sit here old chap?' Robert Bambridge's tall figure looms in front of him.

Sidney leaps up and pumps the distinguished man's hand. An elegant blonde stands with him and is introduced as Poppy, his wife. She wears a sage green, fine leather jacket and long narrow black skirt with side slit that shows a slim leg. A faint expensive perfume hovers round her. He beams, delighted with the added touch of class she brings to the gathering.

'Sit down there, Poppy me love, in the space next to me wife,' he gushes, suddenly relieved Cynthia bought the expensive all wool speckled brown suit she wears. He shuts out the memory of his ranting at its price.

Freda has left the dais and is talking to a tall man sporting a full black moustache who sits the other side of the gap. Must be her 'usband. Couldn't be better. All three of their spouses together looking on with pride. Freda steps back up on the dais and sits down.

Robert Bambridge leans across him to speak to her. 'You put on the school nativity play didn't you,' he says, grinning. 'It was brilliant ... so funny.'

Her white face changes to pink.

Sidney sees it is three o'clock. He rises from his chair. He clears his throat and adjusts his scarlet robe with a swirl. He assumes a posturing pose. No-one seems to notice he has shifted. He tugs at his white frilly jabot, pulling it crooked.

'SILENCE FOR THE MAYOR OF GREAT PIDDLEHURST AND DISTRICT,' Robert Bambridge's rich voice commands.

A hush settles and Sidney raises one hand, a gesture emulating the divine magnanimity of the Pope. More masculine, he has recently concluded, than his previous fluttery movement modelled on that of the Queen.

Sit down,' Robert Bambridge hisses at him.

Sidney plonks down, and Bambridge stands. 'It is my privi...'

Suddenly the choir bursts into song. Sidney looks at the stage bewildered. The bun on the back of Norah's small head wobbles in time to her thrashing baton. 'God save our gracious Queen ...' the children sing. The three rows of VIPs noisily rise to their feet. 'Long live our noble Queen ...' Gradually everyone joins in. 'God save our Queen ... Send her victorious, happy and glorious, long to-o-o reign over us, Go-ud saaaave ooooour Queeeeeeeeen!'

Cheers and clapping erupt and Norah turns and bows several times. 'This is the choir of my school,' she enunciates with the sharp clarity of a laser strobe. 'The Harker-Balls Establishment, an independent school of which I am frightfully proud.'

Sidney rises, obligated to thank her, but he goes unheard due to the clattering of chairs as the VIPs sit back down.

Robert Bambridge's handsome face hardens. He holds up an arm and silence quickly falls.

'It is my privilege,' Bambridge begins again, 'to unveil this portrait of our mayor: the most worshipful mayor of Great Piddlehurst and District.' His head swivels from side to side as he speaks, swirling his long fair hair in a smooth flowing rhythmic dance. He is in total public-school-followed-by-Oxbridge command. 'As you know, our charming village is on the outer boundary of the Great Piddlehurst District and it is therefore an honour that our mayor and his wife have chosen to live here among us.' Loud clapping comes from Bill Boggins and he grins at Sidney, thrusting up a thumb. 'He has served on the Council for many years, representing Lower Loo, one of the central Great Piddlehurst wards.'

Sidney feels as if the top of his head could explode off like Vesuvius, engulfing the audience in his bursting hot molten pride. He catches Cynthia's eye again and she smiles sweetly. By gum, he thinks, that woman must feel right proud!

Robert Bambridge continues. 'Sidney Slocumb's reward for all those years of dedicated service was to be elected as mayor and it is only fitting that his portrait should hang here, in the village that is now his home.' He turns to Sidney and half-bows. 'We are honoured Mr Mayor ...' Sidney inclines his head graciously in acknowledgement, dislodging a strand of hair. His heart is full, his emotions indescribable. This is the proudest moment of his entire life. '... and it gives me great pleasure to pull the cord to ...' Poop the Scoop aims his lens. Cynthia lifts her Canon. '... unveil this portrait of our illustrious mayor, SIDNEY (his voice crescendos as if introducing a music hall act) SLOCUMB!' He grips the golden tassel and yanks the cord. The curtains part.

There is a stunned silence, then uproar breaks out. Hysterical laughter wells up and loud clapping erupts. Feet stamp. 'Bravo,' somebody calls, 'serve the conceited bugger right.' Children squeal and giggle, cameras and videos click and whirr. Inside the ornate gold frame, exposed for all to see, is a three foot by two foot photograph of his face beaming out from the gross backside of a pig.

Wild-eyed he turns to his wife. Stone cold eyes glint back. And then he understands. This was the Revenge she had promised. Far more dreadful than anything he had feared.

He hears Robert Bambridge hooting with laughter. He hears the loud sobbing of Freda Field as she rushes and tugs the curtains back across the vile humiliation.

Twenty

Six days since the portrait humiliation. My soul is crying in despair. The memory of the unveiling debacle eats into my very being, consuming me like a ghastly flesh eating disease. Except that my flesh is not diminishing, it increases daily. Depressed people turn to gorging for comfort. Well, I am deeply depressed and all my slimming progress has been wiped out with that one fell pull of the cord.

I thought Cynthia was my friend, a person I could trust, but she betrayed me. The 'Ho-ho-let's-all-have-a-laugh-at-Freda-Field-and-the-Mayor story' was splashed across the front page of the local, illustrated by a disgusting colour photo in sharp focus, headlined: THE MAYOR'S MAGNIFICENT *PORK*-TRAIT! I am the laughing stock of Wood Hill.

At school the children have been insufferable, sniggering behind their hands and making bottom jokes. It suits their taste in humour of course. Even Norah Harker-Balls looked gleeful. I've kept well clear of her and the rest of the staff and have hidden in the stock room at home-times until everyone has gone. Bernard says see the funny side, but he would wouldn't he. It wasn't his ambition that was dashed to shreds.

On top of the unveiling humiliation and everything else, there was a letter from Rosita saying she had left her husband and that her son was a greater swine than Hermione. Everything is gloom and doom. Even my oh be joyful has arrived. I'd give anything for a good hot flush. I just hope that one day when I am very old and very miserable and very close to death, I can look back and remember that things had once been much worse.

Cynthia has rung every day. Even when I gave vent to my feelings and shouted at her she didn't sound sorry that she'd treated me so shamefully. She declared that the Revenge (with a capital R, she gaily stipulated) on her husband had been worth upsetting a chum. (The chum being Muggins of course.)

I don't know why I talk to her when she rings, except that I don't have another good friend. Yesterday she sounded perplexed. She said that Sidney was slobbering all over her, telling her he admired a woman with spirit. He'd even presented her with a bunch of daffodils. 'That's all I need,' she'd said, 'the nauseating little toad trying to be nice to me. He's pawing me all the time.'

I tried to picture her being pawed. From what she's told me, she's always either knitting or making jam tarts. Did she continue these activities while he mauled her? Even with my vivid imagination a picture refused to conjure in my mind.

'I said to him,' she had continued, 'you go back to your fat floozy if you want some of *that*.'

It's still hard for me to think of the grande dame of our school in terms like that.

Today Cynthia told me that Poop the Scoop had been back to the Village Hall and taken photos of my 'masterpiece' which she personally had re-hung in the Village Hall the day after the event. So now Revenge is an Event I thought bitterly, wondering about, then discarding, the idea of trying out an Event on her.

A photo of the painting is plastered all over the front page of the Daily Echo. But this time the original oil, not a cheap contact print. I have read and re-read the accompanying article, becoming dizzier with joy each time. It transpired that Poop the Scoop had taken his friend Calypso Tinker with him to view the picture. Calypso Tinker! The famous art critic who writes for The Times. And she was so impressed she agreed to write about it in our local! I devoured the column again:-

It is a work of great subtlety, equal to any portrait I have ever seen. Never did I expect to see a painting of such superb quality in an out-of-town Village Hall. Freda Field has rare talent of which the people of Wood Hill must be proud.

I *had* to go and see it hanging in its rightful place. I told Bernard. He said he wanted to see it too. We sped there in the Cortina. A notice outside the Hall announced that the Women's Institute was holding a sale of home-made jams and cakes inside. We hurried up the path, but at the threshold of the open doors I faltered. I couldn't face it. Supposing ...

'Come *on*' said Bernard, tugging me across the flat hurdle into the milling crowd.

I didn't look at the long wall for fear anyone watching me would think I was full of conceit. Instead, I pushed my way along the side of a trestle table running parallel.

'Would you like to buy a chocolate sponge?' rosy-cheeked Mrs Norris asked, leaning forward, thrusting a dark brown cake under my nose. I could resist the temptation no longer. My eyes slid past the offering, past the smiling woman, to the centre of the wall behind her. Mayor Sidney Slocumb smiled back from the confines of the ornate gold frame. His teeth flashed with false naturalness. His blurred nose had a certain dignity not normal in a protuberance of that size. His expression gave no indication of his pomposity. It was truly a masterpiece of flattering misrepresentation.

Mr Radford called over, 'That's a brilliant picture Freda, I didn't know you could paint.'

'But why did you paint the other one on your pig's bum?' asked the woman from Rugged Farm, peering at me suspiciously, as if suspecting I was going to run off a limited edition of prints.

'It put that stupid arsehole in his rightful place!' Mrs Norris declared loudly and everybody laughed.

I opened my mouth and guffawed with the merry crowd. I didn't care about the pig-bum portrait any more. Fame and fortune were beckoning, closer than they'd ever beckoned before. A finger hooked forcefully into my sleeve and I screamed.

'I only wondered if you might want to buy a pot of rhubarb jam,' a surprised little lady gasped.

It is Wednesday, the twenty-ninth of March, and congratulations have been pouring in. Parents of my pupils, my colleagues, Cynthia, people I hardly know. But at the end of the day there had not been one request for me to paint another portrait.

I picked up the ringing phone. 'Is that Freda Field the artist?' a woman asked.

Trying to sound duly modest, I agreed that indeed it was she.

'I'm Mrs Smith, 'I want you to paint me, and I wannit done quick.'

She sounded like a gangster in a film!

The only Mrs Smith I knew was the old lady from The Bungalow on the corner of Bramble Lane, the one I sometimes waved to as I passed.

'I'm old' she continued, 'but I want a portrait that will expose my character as well as the wrinkles on my face.'

If it *was* her I hoped her character had changed, because she had the reputation of being the most bad-tempered person around.

'According to the local rag you've got talent,' she went on, 'but you can't believe a blind word they say. I'll only fork out if I like it, otherwise you've wasted your time, so it's up to you. D'you want the job or not?'

The truthful answer was that I'd rather take in ironing or hang suspended by my wrists in a damp cell for a week than paint this old woman, but I couldn't refuse her. Another successful portrait would boost my artistic career. 'All right Mrs Smith,' I forced myself, 'I'll do it.'

'Good. When you've done I'll send it to my niece in New York to let her see ...' she trailed off. 'To let her see I'm still alive. You'll have to do it straight away, here, where I live. I can't get out.'

'Is that The Bungalow on the corner of Bramble Lane and Primrose Hill?' I queried to make sure.

'Of course,' she snapped, 'I've bloody well lived here since it was built in 1930. I thought everybody knew that.'

I drove to The Bungalow after school. I didn't take my painting equipment because I needed to store up an image of her face animated by conversation, not drained with the boredom of sitting. A bent old lady opened the door and peered up at me with piercing dark eyes.

'You look different from what I remember, with all that ginger fuzz,' she sniffed, turning to lead the way in.

And you look different from what I remember, I thought, horrified by her deterioration. I followed her into the wide hall and into the musty smell of old cooking tinged faintly with acrid urine. She shuffled to a room to the right just ahead, and I followed, trying not to breathe in.

'Welcome to my humble abode,' she said, throwing out a hand to the large sitting room that must once have been superb. A welcome drift of lavender scent briefly wafted from her wrist.

'Sit down where you bloody well like.' Her strong voice conflicted strangely with her weak body.

Two winged, high-backed armchairs covered in worn chintz, and a sofa in matching material, were grouped around a tiled fireplace. I walked across to one and sat down.

'Not there!' she snapped, 'that's mine.'

I was beginning to doubt that it would be possible to depict her character without the aid of Hermione's softening backside. I removed myself to the other chair and she took my previous place. But, no sooner had she sat down than she was struggling up to her feet again, saying, 'I'll go and make some tea, I'm bloody thirsty.'

'I'll help,' I offered, jumping up.

'NO! SIT DOWN. I'll soddin' do it while I'm able ... it won't be much longer now.' She rushed in a barely controlled headlong lunge and disappeared through the doorway.

I glanced around. An old piano with hinged brass candle holders stood in a wide arched alcove in the wall behind me, and a dark wood glass-fronted cabinet displaying china took up part of the side wall. Flaky french windows gave a view of the large back garden where straggly rose beds dotted an overgrown lawn. Shelves crammed with books were built into the space between the chimney breast and the side wall. I walked over a worn Persian rug to examine them. The top shelf was assigned to gardening, the rest were mainly a variety of paperbacks, including Len Deighton and Ken Follett. I was surprised.

As I studied the room, something niggled. I was somehow familiar with it, but knew that I couldn't be because I'd never been inside before.

Pictures in dark frames hung crookedly on faded wallpaper, their mounts dappled with foxing like the brown spots on their owner's hands. One hanging in the shadow of the alcove suddenly arrested my eyes. Through the grime of the covering glass, two familiar piggy eyes were peering out at me. I went over, stretching over the piano to get a better look. A plump pink pig was rearing up, front trotters hanging loosely over the top bar of a gate. The ears were pricked, the snout looked damp. It was a wonderful old water colour and it was my girl to a Tee!

A crash followed by Mrs Smith's sharp scream suddenly rent the air. I raced out to the hall and towards an open doorway across the other side.

'Shit, bugger, fuck!' the old woman cussed. She stood looking down at broken shards of china and pools of tea. A silver tray wobbled in her hands. I grabbed it before the remaining cup and saucer shot off to join the mess.

'That's what happens when you're old,' she blazed, glaring at me as if it were somehow my fault. She snatched up the full cup off the tray, saying, 'You'll have to do without.' Then she tottered back to the sitting room, tea sloshing everywhere as she went.

I dallied, searching for a dustpan and brush or a cloth amongst the clutter that covered every surface. Like ours, her kitchen doubled as a dining room, but hers was far larger. A chunky table surrounded by six matching chairs stood at the far end. Next to the greasy electric stove was a closed door. Somehow I'd known it would be there. Somehow I knew too what lay behind it. I took a step towards it.

'Where *are* you?' her sharp voice shrilled.

I turned and hastened back to my permitted seat.

'Why haven't you brought your painting stuff?' she grumbled. 'I told you I haven't much time.'

Forget the mess on the kitchen floor, I thought, just concentrate on memorising her. A sickly pallor tinged the dry wrinkled skin. Her steel grey hair was secured with kirby grips behind large fleshy ears. Her strong nose curved over like an eagle's beak. Sparse dark hairs, that would have passed for a skimpy moustache on a man, sprouted amongst a welter of fine crisscross lines above scarcely visible lips. Her dark eyes stabbed into mine.

'Well, have you had a good decko!' she said nastily.

I felt myself flush. 'Just planning ...'

'Well don't! Just get on with it. It isn't much to ask.' Noisily she slurped her tea. The sound made me realise how thirsty I was. I looked round.

'What do you want?' she barked.

'A cup of tea would be nice ... I'll make it,' I stammered.

'No time for that stupid, if you're not painting you'll have to go. But first, how much lolly d'you want for doing it?'

If she hadn't been so ghastly I'd have said seventy pounds. Instead I blurted: 'Seven hundred!'

'Agreed. That's as long you finish it before I'm dead because you'll receive nothing from my estate.' Her frown deepened.

'And also providing I like it. And I warn you, I'm not the type to say I like something when I don't.'

She levered herself up, gnarled knuckles pushing down on the arms of the chair. In the same barely controlled dash as before she headed across the room and out to the front door. I followed in barely controlled anger.

'I'll expect you tomorrow at ten. Come prepared,' she commanded, almost pushing me out to the front garden.

I hurried down the path, past the magnificent oak tree, towards the gate. I didn't want to come back. I couldn't do it. I didn't want to do it. She wouldn't like it. I would ring her and tell her it was off. As I went out the gate I looked back.

She stood in the open doorway like a tiny frightened bird. She didn't look at me. Her eyes roved her untidy garden. They held a look of infinite sadness and defeat.

I knew I would have to return.

Twenty-one

As I made up my girl's bed with fresh straw I pondered on whether I could really portray Mrs Smith's character without being callously unkind. I felt muddled and unsure how I should start. By my side Hermione drank noisily from the trough and I wished my brain were as clear as that flowing crystal water diverted from the spring.

When the sweet smelling straw was fully strewn over the palliasse Hermione strew herself down on it and I trundled the barrow of pungent used straw away, down the ramp, across the yard and over the bumpy pig-rooted grass where I heaved it into the trench at the end. The time was nine o'clock. She had summoned me to be there at ten. Birds twittered and sang but the worry of the portrait distracted me from the glories of a perfect spring morning. I puffed back up to the house, wending between the rivulets of clear spring water that meandered down to the distant valley stream. Should I paint Mrs Smith full length like the picture of Whistler's mother, I agonised, or just head and shoulders like the famous Rembrandt self-portrait? Both worked well. A cuckoo sang out its distinctive call as if mocking the effrontery of such pretentious thoughts.

Bernard blocked my way. He smiled. His eyes twinkled. 'Your mother rang while you were outside.'

'Tell me later, I must wash and get changed ...'

'She's leaving Tooting right now to come and see you.'

'But you know she can't!' I exploded. 'You should have put her off. You know I'm painting Mrs Smith this morning.'

'April Fool!' he chortled, slapping his knees, killing himself with laughter.

'Ha *HA*' I shouted, shoving him out of the way. I'd forgotten it was April the first, but I might have guessed there was a catch in it when he'd looked so pleased at the prospect of mother coming.

She had agreed that I move her chair near the tall front window to include the oak tree in the picture, then she had sat in silence for nearly two hours, her face wreathed in its natural scowl. The air filled with the smell of oil paint and turps, masking less savoury odours. The canvas filled with thin colours that could still be easily changed. I stood back from the easel and my hopes surged. Faintly beady eyes peered out from under eyebrows that would finally be touched in with straggly hairs. The aquiline nose was there in the making and, already, I had modified the grim expression to a vaguely serious look. The frailty of the figure was emphasized dramatically by the strength of the mighty oak tree in the background. It was coming on fine.

'All finished for today,' I announced, waggling the brushes in white spirit. 'I'll be back tomorrow.'

'But I might not have a tomorrow,' she protested, straightening slumped shoulders, shaking out a stiff spindly leg. She half rose and I took hold of her arm to help her up but she pulled herself away. 'Come the same time as today,' she ordered, at last up on her feet. She took a tentative step forward, sliding one foot along the carpet, swaying, arms out, as if balancing on a tight rope. Then suddenly she fell into her usual headlong dash making for the front door. As she opened it she sighed and said 'I suppose there's a chance I'll still be here.' Then, voice flaring, 'So you can earn your seven hundred quid.'

I stepped back from the sun-faded blue door, panic rising. It was ten o'clock and I had rung the bell three times. She was slow moving but she knew I was expected. Yesterday she'd been watching from the kitchen window and had let me in with only a short delay.

I went to the window and cupped my hands to my eyes, peering in at the untidy kitchen, but nothing moved. I walked back past the front door, past tulips nearly out, through long grass to the sitting room window. I peered in, dreading what I might see. Then the dread became reality. She was lying on the floor, her back towards me. She didn't move. Frantically, I rapped on the window but her body remained deathly still.

I tore out onto Bramble Lane, ran past a small field to the house of Mr Sharpe, half hidden amongst some trees. I *had* to get to a phone. I rammed open the gate and panted up the long path. Please be in I implored as I banged the knocker wildly. He opened the door slowly, his face suspicious. I knew him because he had once come to school to talk to the children about his comic writing. He'd steered clear of including the sex. 'I must use your phone,' I gabbled, pushing past him, barging rudely into his spacious hall.

He went to a black lacquered table and lifted a wilting plastic penis with two rigid testicles attached. 'This is it,' he said apologetically.

I took it from him, holding it fastidiously between my middle finger and thumb. With the digit finger of the other hand I jabbed out Nine Nine Nine. A woman asked what service I required. 'Send an ambulance to The Bungalow in Bramble Lane,' I shrieked into one of the balls.

This afternoon I visited Mrs Smith. She had been admitted into the geriatric ward of the Great Piddlehurst General Hospital. It was like entering the bowels of hell. The shrill voice of the wizened woman opposite never stopped: 'Harry. Harry. Harry. Harry,' she called and I guessed she cried out for her husband, who was dead.

'Hurry. Hurry. Hurry. Bloody well hurry,' Mrs Smith parodied, and I was in no doubt she cried out for death.

'How are you feeling?' I asked inadequately, not knowing what else to say.

'How would you feel being incarcerated in here with this load of lunies,' she blazed.

'How's your leg?' I asked, mentally ducking from the onslaught to come.

'It's agony you blithering idiot, bones generally are when they're broken!' She wiped the back of her hand across her eyes.

I'd had enough. Even my father didn't speak to me like that. I rose to go.

'Come tomorrow won't you?' Her anxious eyes stared up at me.

'Goodbye Mrs Smith, I'll come some time ... when I'm not busy.'

'Please,' she whispered. 'There's nobody else.'

I didn't have the heart to go to the Art Club. Poor horrible Mrs Smith imprisoned in that ward, how could I concentrate. My thoughts were gloomy. Each and every one of us was doomed to finish up like that unless we were struck down by lightening or some other such merciful disaster. I reflected that being dashed to pieces on a rock by a freak wave, or having a cricket ball smash into one's head when passing the village green, might be preferable to an old people's ward. My thoughts turned to my parents. They were the next in line. On a sudden compassionate impulse I decided to give them a ring.

'How are you?' I asked mother who answered.

'I'm well,' she said warily and I felt guilty that she should feel suspicious because I'd called.

'And how's father?' I enquired.

'Silly devil's gone mad. He's cleaned the car, cut the grass and mangled the front hedge with blunt shears.'

'Why silly devil?'

'Because he's dashed off now all hot and bothered and late.'

'Late for what?'

An appointment at the surgery to have his blood pressure checked! And he'll wonder why the quack will prescribe stronger pills.'

I didn't join in her laughter. My father was forging ahead on the path to eternal oblivion. I often didn't like him much but I've always loved him and I'd miss him in a way. 'Goodbye mother,' I said, gulping at the finality of the word, wishing I'd said Cheerio. 'Tell him I enquired after him.'

'Good God. D'you want him to have a heart attack!' she replied.

I replaced the phone feeling worse. Bernard came in from the garden, poured himself a glass of milk and knocked it back, then cut a chunk of cheese. 'All that cholesterol' I chastised. 'Don't blame me if you finish up dead.'

He fell about saying everyone did that: finished up dead, even the Queen and the Pope. But I couldn't laugh. Somehow Mrs Smith's impending demise haunts me and makes me dwell on our mortality. If she were a dog or a horse she'd be put down quickly, but she's a frail old human being, so has to endure all that pain. I took out my blocked in picture and she peered out at me with an expression of unveiled animosity.

When I told Bernard about how depressed I was over Mrs Smith and all the people suffering in the geriatric ward, and the fact that my father was going to die, and my mother, and him and me, he said: *Don't forget the pig*. Dear old Bernie, always so understanding. Always the soddin' clown.

I visited Mrs Smith later. She grimaced and shut her eyes tightly as I took the seat beside her bed. She didn't speak but slowly her gnarled hand slithered over the sheet towards me.

'Hold my hand,' she said. And I took it in mine. She opened her eyes then quickly shut them.

I was overwhelmed with pity for her. 'Mrs Smith,' I began.

'Call me Gertrude,' she interrupted gruffly, then, voice hardening. 'But don't you ever take advantage and call me Gert!'

Norah Harker-Balls swept into my classroom this afternoon and marched over to Jason, one of the timidest of our shared boys. He slid down in his seat as she bore down on him, terror contorting his face. A fearful hush filled the room as she hauled him up to his feet and dragged him over to me.

'Tell Mrs Field what you got up to this morning you vile creature,' she snarled.

He was struck dumb with fear and she shouted at him again. 'GO ON, DUNDERHEAD, TELL HER!'

A tear rolled down his cheek as he looked at the floor. 'I only did one sum,' he snivelled.

'Did you hear that Mrs Field. The lazy tyke only did one sum. I want you to make him do three full exercises NOW.' She twirled round and strode out, slamming the door behind her.

'I couldn't do it,' Jason sobbed, 'and I couldn't ask her how because she ...' He juddered. '...she makes fun of me.'

As I drove to the Great Piddlehurst General Hospital I vowed to myself that before very long I would humiliate our hateful Head as she humiliated those poor children. But I had made those inward pledges before, I seemed to remember, and still couldn't for the life of me work out how. I wondered how two such obnoxious women as Norah H-B and Gertrude Smith had intruded so largely into my life.

But when I got to her bedside Gertrude had miraculously become pleasant. She told me about her husband, Freddie, killed at the beginning of the war. She said the shock of losing the only man she'd ever loved had induced a miscarriage, but added that she hadn't minded that too much because it was he who wanted kids, not her. Although, she conceded, maybe it was different when they were your own. She lifted her head.

'You're a school teacher aren't you. How do you stand all those little brats?'

'Every child is special,' I said carefully, 'but you're right, it must be different when a child is your own.' The old familiar ache invaded my soul again. 'I have a pet pig as a substitute. One like the beautiful picture over your piano. She's very dear to my heart.'

Her head fell back, the grey hair spreading like a soft dark cloud against the starched white pillow slip. 'There's only been one child dear to me and that's my niece Dora, my late sister's girl. I was special to her too until she married that damned Quicknicky and buggered off to live in New York.' There was a faraway look in her eyes. 'She used to be so attentive ... she was the only one who cared.'

'How old is she?' I asked.

The lines in her brow deepened in thought. Then, with a look of amazement, she exclaimed, 'She'll be sixty this coming June!'

It is the seventh of April, the last day of term thank God. I couldn't stand another second in the same building as *her*.

'I'm going to die so you can kiss your seven hundred quid goodbye,' Gertrude snapped. She was sitting propped up looking more like her old bad-tempered self. I preferred the soft vulnerable one to this. That one had humility. This one was just plain rude.

'I'll visit you again in a week,' I said, hurriedly rising, dying to get away.

'Come tomorrow,' she replied. 'Please.'

And I knew I had to.

An angry nurse accosted me saying that Gertrude had rudely turned down the chance to be wheeled to the Sunday service. Apparently she had sworn like a trooper, stating that she wasn't prepared to talk to a God who could inflict such agony. The nurse seemed to hold me to blame. I entered the ward dreading the mood Gertrude would be in, but her erstwhile pleasantness had returned. She chatted like a normal person telling me about when she and Freddie had first moved to Wood Hill, explaining that it had been a toss up between two newly-built bungalows, both exactly the same except that one had the young oak tree in its front garden.

It was then that the penny landed. Our school further along Bramble Lane was the twin of The Bungalow. It had extras added: the hall, toilets and wash basins. Fireplaces had been blocked off and blackboards attached to chimney breasts, but the room dimensions and details were the same. That was why it had seemed so familiar in her sitting room. The windows, the arched alcove. It was my classroom!

'Dora Quicknicky will inherit the lot,' Gertrude suddenly stated and, inside my head, I silently begged her to change her mind and leave it to the children of Wood Hill. They needed that sanctuary far more than a far-flung uncaring niece.

I had studied myself in the mirror before getting dressed. Despite the healthy diet there was still chubbiness under my chin and flabby folds over my ribs. I decided to join the newly opened health club in the Old Mill Hotel near Orlford. This afternoon I drove there and paid the five hundred pounds annual fee. I felt like a millionaire, being able to splash out money like that. Then I did ten laps in the luxury pool and could almost feel the fat flowing off me.

Next day, when I suggested to Bernard that he come to the Health Club as my guest, he said there was too much to do in the garden. I laughed to myself as I sped along. I'd been forced out of my routine by the scorn of mother and Rosita and him, and there was he, still in his! I admit to feeling quite smug.

Bernie sounded harassed. He says he needs to decorate the cottage but there's the gardening to be done. I realise my new freedom is just a postponement of jobs to fit in at convenient times, not total abandonment. And he has too much to do. I took stock of the money situation. There was seventeen thousand pounds in the Higher Rate Deposit Account. I rang a firm of decorators and asked for an estimate to do the lot. Bernie was overjoyed and I'd never quite realised before how immensely pleasurable it was having money. Although it still couldn't buy the thing that mattered most: the elimination of nasty Norah Harker-Balls!

Twenty-two

The last three weeks have passed in the re-vitalisation of the cottage and the de-vitalisation of Gertrude. We have lived in a muddle of wallpaper, paint and workmen who terrified the pig. Gertrude has lived in a muddle of pain, indignity and doctors who terrify her life.

She was making a good recovery until she fell out of bed, snapping her left collar bone and fracturing her arm. She denied she was lashing out at a retreating nurse when she over-balanced, but eyewitnesses say differently. I often think it would have been kinder if she'd died when she first fell in The Bungalow. Certainly kinder on the nurses who labour to keep her alive. No doubt God, in His infinite wisdom, is keeping her on hold in a last ditch effort to hang on to His heavenly peace. But, strangely, I feel I have come closer to her in the last few weeks. At any rate, as close as you can get to a pain-ridden rotweiler.

The Queen, Princess Margaret and the Queen Mother were shown on TV at some big function, cheerfully dressed: Q in red, P.M. in yellow and Q.M. in blue. The colours reminded Bernard that he should go to Orlford and join the snooker club there. An hour later he came back mightily pleased that he was now a fully paid up member. Apparently I can go as his guest - providing I'm careful! It's his birthday tomorrow so I drove to Great Piddlehurst in the afternoon and bought his presents. I can't wait to see his face when he sees what I've got.

Bernie slowly opened up his cards. My two packages, one long and thin, one bulky, glinted silver on the table in a shaft of sunlight. One of the cards, designed like an L plate, was from my parents, five of them displaying a variety of car driver jokes were from his pupils and the last showed a picture of high cliffs and sea. That was from Rosita. She wrote: *I wish you a happy fifty-two birthday on ten of May and much jolly good fun. I miss you both.*

Finally he pulled over the bulky package and pressed and poked it all over, staring at me with sparkling eyes. 'I wonder what it is?' he said.

'Why don't you open it,' I urged, even more impatient for him to undo this gift than I'd been for my mother to open hers at Christmas.

At long last he tore at the paper. He gasped. His face shone with radiant joy. He drew out the sheepskin jacket and stroked it lovingly, then held it up high. 'Oh Freda!' he whispered, 'I've always wanted one.' He thrust his long arms in and shrugged it on, then took me in his arms and hugged me closely, and the warmth made me glow inside.

Then I pushed over the long thin package that he seemed to have forgotten and he ripped off the metallic foil, drawing out the long black leather case inside. He looked mystified as he pulled at its zip then grinned with recognition, drawing out two rods which he carefully screwed together.

'Oh Freda,' he whispered again, 'my very own cue.'

My darling man. Fifty-two today and still I ached with love for him. Where had all the years gone? We'd shared our lives together, just we two, until he'd bought our beautiful girl to share it with us. At that moment the beautiful girl in question barged in squealing excitedly. On the end of her snout was pink icing sugar, and chocolate-flecked spit bedecked each side of her mouth.

'You PIG!' I screamed, chasing after her into the kitchen where all that remained of Bernard's birthday cake was a few crumbs scattered on the floor.

Later, when we sat on the sofa sipping champagne, Bernard said it was better that the pig got fat than us. He patted my almost flat stomach and that's when the fun began.

I've watched pages of share prices scroll round and round on the screen of our new Teletext TV for days, but have lost confidence in deciding which ones to buy. So, early this morning I spread out the newspaper, closed my eyes and stuck a pin in, three separate times. Consequently I have just bought Smith and Niece Healthcare, The Warthog Merchant Bank and Brownbread Breweries. Three thousand pounds gambled on each. After all our free spending lately, it's all the money that's left. Now I have to wait and hope for my usual good luck. I feel quietly confident.

All three shares have gone shooting up. I imagine the news being whispered from City whiz kid to City whiz kid, flashing around the super highway of the Internet, clogging up Modems sending computer systems crashing: *Freda Field is investing: BUY BUY BUY!*

I thought I'd take a drive to Great Piddlehurst to visit Gertrude and tell her of my good fortune, but when I rang the hospital to see the best time, I was told she was heavily sedated and so wouldn't know I was there. It triggered off my obsessive doom and gloom thought trail again. I saw clearly that no matter how much success you have, no matter how you live your life, it always ends in a long drawn out death or a short sharp chop, so what does it really matter that I'm trying to transform myself. So what if I become thin. It just means a narrower coffin at the end. And even then my revamped hair would be hidden under the lid. What is the point, I wonder. What really is the point?

Bernard came in singing *Life is just a bowl of cherries* and my spirits rose, until I reflected that after you'd taken your fill of them, all that was left were dead pips. When I confided in Bernie, he pointed out that cherry pips were far from dead, they were the seeds that held the miracle of new cherry tree lives. Then I understood what was bugging me. My depressions always boiled down to my miraculous seeds that refused to take root and grow new lives that would continue when we were dead and gone. My hopes of an extended family now definitely lay with my pig. But I needed to sell the shares to afford a boar's service and the upkeep of grand-piglets.

It is the twenty-fourth of May and Gertrude is still comatose and kept alive by machines. I have come to the conclusion that you have to make the most of each and every day while you can, so I went out and sat in the sunshine reading the paper. The sports' page headline is: *Nigel Mansell's Career Flagged to a Halt.*

Bernard didn't comment on the article but he shaved off his moustache this afternoon. He's obviously abandoned all ambitions to be a racing driver. I expect his main hope now is to improve his snooker and achieve a break greater than nine.

Norah Harker-Balls frightened one of the five year old boys so much that trickles of wee ran down his spindly legs soaking into his socks. She has got me so tense, at any moment I will snap. I accompanied Bernie to the snooker club for the first time. A picture of Harker-Balls cold malicious eyes sprang into my head just as I pulled back the cue and I hit the white ball so hard it careered off the table and struck the club's cat.

'I've potted the wrong black,' I cried. 'Look, I've killed him!'

Bernard bent over its prone body stretched out on the floor. 'It's okay,' he said. 'See, he's breathing, he's only asleep.'

I was pretty certain that before I hit the ball the moggie had been wide awake sitting up on the arm of the chair!

I'm in despair at my lack of power to do anything about the mental cruelty going on at school. I can't even give in my notice because at least my being there protects the children in our shared class for half the week. I couldn't just abandon them. Besides, I couldn't retire on the paltry dividends from my shares.

I have worked out how much my portfolio of shares is worth and it's fifteen thousand pounds. When I told Bernard, he growled, 'Only if you sell them.'

Stupid man, I thought irritably, my shares always rise.

It is Monday twenty-ninth of May and all my shares have plummeted. Not the others. Just mine. I feel like an expanded balloon: just one more puff of air, and I will explode.

'Told you so,' said Bernard. And that's when I went off bang!

My shares are down again. Especially the Warthogs. The three thousand that had quickly become five thousand has now equally quickly become one thousand two hundred. I am in a dither of indecision about whether or not to sell. Bernard has spent the day gardening and refuses to comment. My nerves are still jangled after yesterday's big row.

Cynthia came round this afternoon, which took my mind off things. She confided that her slimy toad of a husband was still pursuing her with chocolates and promises of undying love. I wondered if she didn't rather enjoy playing her role of the unforgiving cheated wife.

She told me again of her first marriage. 'I loved Graham so much Freda, and when he died I wanted to die too, but I had two young sons who needed me and, besides, I adored them as well. Then dear Sidney Slocumb appeared. He'd come down from the North to Southampton, joined the Conservative Party and came to Great Piddlehurst on a Tory rally. I met him there. He was lonely and I was lonely too, so things developed, but now I'm sure he only feigned love because I owned a house. It was only a small two up two down in a run-down part of the town, but it was fully paid for by Graham's life assurance. Sidney was an antique dealer so any income came in fits and starts, so a home already paid for gave him security.'

She looked sad and I touched her hand. 'You've done well though,' I consoled. 'That new house you've bought, built in old Radford's garden, that must have cost a lot.'

Her face flushed and she looked uncomfortable. 'My boys couldn't stand him of course,' she said, changing the subject, 'they went off to live in New Zealand and I haven't seen them for years.'

I wondered if it were worse to have children but not be part of their lives, or not to have children at all. If you had never held them in your arms, never shared their jokes, never loved them with all your heart, there was nothing to miss, except the dream of what might have been.

'I have three grandchildren too,' she cut into my thoughts. 'Two girls and a boy, but I've never met them. They don't know me and I only know their glossy photo smiles.'

But you do have some, I thought. It was strange how my overwhelming yearning for children had changed to overwhelming yearning for grandchildren, even if they were to be in the form of little pigs!

As I waved her goodbye I wondered again how they'd managed to buy their new house. I wouldn't give tuppence for it, squashed in with the other identical four in the new Eldorado Close, but anything in Wood Hill costs a bomb now. She was holding something back about Sidney, of that I was sure.

Bernard asked me why I was looking so fed up.

'Because I have no-one to leave my worldly possessions to.'

'Hermione will be an orphan, so leave the money to set up a Pig Sanctuary ... you could call it Save Our Bacon, or SOB.'

I gave a sob as I dashed up the stairs. How did I ever think that being sexy, daring, slim and all those other vain ambitions, makes up for being childless and powerless against the likes of Norah Harker-Balls.

Suddenly the phone rang. It was Poppy Bambridge. She's just seen the real mayoral portrait in the Village Hall, as opposed to the pig-bum photo that her husband unveiled. She was raving about it and has asked me to paint her husband's portrait as a surprise for his forty-eighth birthday. 'If you agree, Robert will arrive at your place on the day, but he won't know why. I want it painted on the same size canvas as the mayor's and I want you to paint it in the same inimitable style.'

My heart sank. Inimitable was the word!

'How much will it cost?' she asked, and, taking a deep breath, I replied, 'Nine hundred pounds.'

'Is that all!' she exclaimed, 'For work of that quality I'm amazed at how reasonable you are. You'll probably get more requests from his business friends when they see it.'

With pulse racing I agreed to undertake it.

'Good. His birthday's not for over two months ...'

I sighed with relief.

'... August the fifth to be precise, but I wanted to book you specifically for that day. I'll get him to arrive at your house at ten o'clock.'

I put the phone down and grinned to myself. I had plenty of time to practise paint dragging techniques to perfect that mystical blending of paint that was my so-called 'inimitable style'. And, if I couldn't do it, there was always my pig's backside to fall back on!

Twenty-three

Two months since my shares all took a dive but, incredibly, they've gradually risen and this Friday I sold the Warthogs for a profit of almost two thousand pounds. And I am going to blow some of it on mother tomorrow, spoiling her for once in my life, for I find I yearn to get back to the closeness we had when I was young. Maybe it's because she's now seventy and I am haunted by the plight of Gertrude Smith and realise my mother's also on the final run.

We had arranged to meet at midday in Fortnum and Mason's in Piccadilly. I entered the Food Hall at five to twelve and spotted her ahead. She held a jar at arm's length, head cocked to one side. Her hair was swept up, casually secured with fancy red combs, blonde wisps trailing to her shoulders. Her scarlet and white sun dress hung loosely, ideal for the sweltering heat, and her white stack shoes were held in place by crisscrossing ties. She looked incredibly young.

Arm still outstretched, she turned and saw me. 'You look glam,' she called, grinning and waggling the jar at me.

I knew I was looking good for, yesterday, I'd been to Raymond's for my regular colour touch-up and trim, and today I wore an emerald cotton dress that showed off my new slim shape. I hastened to her.

'Look, oysters, if they weren't so dear I'd buy them to get your father go ...'

Quickly I planted a silencing kiss full square on her indiscreet mouth.

'The smell of all this food's making me hungry,' she said. 'Let's get out of here and have a chat over a hamburger.' She took my arm and began pulling me towards the exit.

'Hang on! I've booked a table here at the St James' Restaurant on the fourth floor,' I laughed.

But, instead of looking pleased, she looked alarmed. 'I can't afford that,' she whispered, still tugging at my arm.

'You don't have to. It's my treat,' I explained, rewarded by her sharp look of surprise.

'You've changed,' she observed, taking a long sip of wine, then gobbling down a stuffed mushroom. 'And it's about time. It was only after you left me you got so boring.'

I bridled, angrily reflecting that the person I turned into when I left home had probably been reaction to having lived with her so long. I prodded at succulent smoked salmon and we finished the first course in silence.

But soon conversation began flowing, along with the wine, and as we tucked into the lamb cutlets, new potatoes, asparagus, baby sweet corn and mangetout, mother revealed that she and father were hard up because he'd retired early on a low pension.

'When your father had his plastic hip ten years ago he'd jumped at the chance to leave the bank,' she said with unintended humour. 'He hated that job so much he'd have had anything surgically removed to get out of it.' She took another long slurp, then added, 'I often wish it had been his tongue.'

I remembered once going into the small branch office where he'd finished up as manager. It was dark dingy and airless. No wonder his fiery spirit had turned morose. It was so sad. But this was my mother's day, not his. I raised my glass. 'Here's to us,' I said, and we clinked and took more gulps.

As we ate strawberry gateau piled high with cream, (by then I'd abandoned all thoughts of diet) her true feelings tumbled out. I'd never fully realised that her bright exterior has hidden such deep discontent for years.

'It's Sockeye, your father,' she said (and that was no surprise). 'He always puts me down.' Her wine-sodden eyes turned maudlin. 'In just one way I've always envied you and Bernard. You're so secure in each other's love.' Her smile was sentimental and she reached out to stroke my cheek. 'Your banter is good humoured, but your father's words are always intended to wound.'

'You must tell him,' I instructed. 'Be like me. Resolve to say what you think.' I blotted out my failure to stand up to dame Harker-Balls.

'Yes, I will,' she affirmed, dabbing her napkin at wet eyes. 'I'll try and be more like you.'

Never had I thought I'd ever hear her utter those incredible words.

As we finished the meal with cheese and biscuits, she disclosed that she had nothing to wear for a wedding at the end of the month.

'Whose wedding?' I asked.

'My brother Harry's clottish granddaughter. I haven't seen her since she was fourteen and she looked quite intelligent then. But to get hitched these days when even the church says it's not sinful to live in sin! She must be crazy.'

'I'll buy you a wedding outfit,' I volunteered, the words tumbling out in a stream of new-found-love-for-my-mother recklessness. I signed the credit slip to pay for the meal and handed it over to the girl at the till, blanking my mind to the extravagant amount.

'Tha'sh my daughter,' I heard mother say with pride.

And that was my costly reward.

Down on the first floor we entered the magic kingdom of clothes and mother immediately began snatching up bright garments off the racks. Then I sat outside the changing cubicle while she wafted in and out like a model on a catwalk, displaying each one with flamboyant verve.

'That's the one,' I declared the fourth time she appeared. She looked a million dollars in a tight-fitting, scooped neck dress made of turquoise silk, patterned with swirls of black. My brain, still veiled in a mist of fine wine, omitted to check the price on the dangling label before committing itself.

I placed another flimsy credit slip into my purse and mother took up the carrier bag containing the dress. Her eyes were shining, but I was beginning to wonder if the high gloss was worth nearly four hundred pounds.

'Thank you so much Freda,' she said with passion, squeezing my arm.

'It's to make up for the Christmas present you obviously hated,' I replied, unable to resist the topic that till now had been taboo.

As, red faced, she began to mumble a sort of apology, an image of the pig's haughty expression looking down her snout at us, the chiffon scarf slung carelessly round her shoulders, flashed into my mind. And suddenly I was hysterical. 'Hermione looked terrific,' I screeched, tears streaming. And she joined in, dubiously at first, then howling uncontrollably in relieved laughter. Slowly, we snorted our way back to self composure.

'Let's get out of here and go over the road to the Royal Academy?' I giggled, wiping my eyes. I knew the annual Summer Show was on, but there was also a smaller exhibition, 'Monet to Gaugin', and I desperately wanted to pick up impressionist ideas, because I was no nearer mastering mystical colour blending techniques now than I was almost two months ago when Poppy Bambridge had commissioned the portrait. The portrait that was due to be started terrifyingly soon.

But, 'You and your boring pictures,' mother replied. 'Let's do something more exciting. How about a gamble at a casino? There's one just up the road.' Her face glowed with eager anticipation. 'You're meant to give a day's notice to become a member and be allowed in, it's the law, but you just leave it to me.' She tapped her nose and winked conspiratorially.

I sighed. It was her day. Let her have her choice. We walked to Piccadilly Circus, turned into Shaftesbury Avenue and above a nearby building I spotted the benign-looking sign: *The Golden Nugget Club*. Little did I know then what was to come!

'Just keep your trap shut,' she whispered, pushing at the door and walking straight up to a big man behind a counter where boldly she proclaimed she was a member.

'Name?' he asked, staring with sharp suspicious eyes.

'Mrs Blenkenthrop,' she answered, darting a sideways warning at me. 'I've forgotten my card.'

'Address?'

'My life! You don't remember!' She spread her hands upwards and raised her shoulders, then gave her so-called abode.

I gazed at her thin straight non-Jewish snitch and couldn't believe he'd be taken in. But he went to a cabinet, then said, 'Okay, you're number 80027. Sign your guest in here.' He pointed to an open book. She signed and a few seconds later we were shooting upwards in a small mirrored lift.

'Mrs Blenkenthrop is my friend at the bridge club,' she explained. 'I came here with her once and she won two hundred pounds. She's better at roulette than playing bridge, I can tell you!' She led the way into a vast gaming room. Under subdued lights groups crowded around roulette tables. Her pace quickened as the sharp click of bouncing balls excited the atmosphere.

'I must find a lucky table,' she said sniffing the smoky air. Eagerly, she circled tables, like a finicky dog straining at the leash to decide the best spot to relieve itself. And, like a dutiful owner, I followed hotly on her trail. 'That's for craps' she informed me, slowing down to point to a long counter. But before I could investigate she was off on her quest again.

'This is the one,' she suddenly asserted, stopping dead. 'It's lucky. I feel it in my water.'

And I half expected her to cock up her leg and pee against it. A despondent looking man vacated a stool and, immediately, she elbowed her way to it and perched on its edge. I pushed in to stand alongside her.

'Fourteen's my lucky number. It could come up next. Buy a colour quickly' she hissed.

As she spoke, thrusting hands were scattering coloured discs all over the table. The dark, long-haired, croupier in the slinky red dress, tidied the piles with deft hands, then clasped the silver knob of the wheel. Two men in formal dress suits stood beside her, following every movement with serious probing eyes.

'My daughter wants to buy a colour,' mother suddenly yelled.

Caught up in the urgent excitement and confidence in my mother's power to win, I took out a twenty pound note and swapped it for ten yellow plastic chips. The beautiful girl's hand went back to the knob and with a jerk she spun it.

'No more bets,' she intoned, casting the small white ball in the opposite direction of the well oiled wheel.

'Quick, put one on the line covering fourteen,' mother urged, snatching one from the pile and doing it herself.

'No more bets,' the young lady frowned.

Mesmerised, I watched the ball bounce from number to number. Then, abruptly, it stopped, wedged in the narrow walled space labelled fourteen. We'd done it! But the wheel was still turning and suddenly the ball shot out and hurtled into thirty-five. The croupier raked in my yellow two pound chip with all the colourful rest, leaving just two turquoise chips on the winning number.

'Black thirty-five,' she confirmed, and the man who sat beside mother received three piles of turquoise chips and he didn't even smile.

'Next time!' whispered mother, her face alight with hope.

Fifteen minutes and one hundred and twenty-five pounds later we stumbled out to the explosion of bright sunlight and noise outside.

'Look,' she whooped triumphantly, 'there's a number fourteen bus.'

I groaned to myself. If only we'd gone for a ride on it instead of going in there where fucking fourteen was as rare as a virgin in a labour ward! The reckless waste of money had left me shattered. We trudged down the steps to Piccadilly Underground to go our separate ways.

'That was the best day of my life,' she enthused, Fortnum and Mason bag clutched in her hands, cupboard love glinting in her eyes. She hugged me close to her thin body then turned and disappeared into the crowd.

As I stood on the escalator I reflected that it had been the most expensive day of my life. But maybe it was the price I'd had to pay to make up for all my drab years that had so disappointed her.

Mother rang early to thank me for yesterday. She told me she was going to be more assertive like me. It isn't true but I was flattered all the same.

I've been practising dragging dollops of flesh coloured oil paint over various blues and greens but all I produce is a mess. Mounting hysteria at the forthcoming portrait ferments like a lethal cocktail inside me, irritating my bowel and my mind. Months I've had to prepare and I'm still no nearer the magic formula. And yet, when I paint a picture unpressurised down the club, it always turns out well. But different from my so-called 'inimitable style'. More straightforward. No smudged and blended colours. It seems the magic that Poppy desires can only be created by my pig. I felt sick. Only the day after tomorrow and Robert Bambridge would be standing on my doorstep. How would I cope?

Mother phoned and the impending portrait session was temporarily blasted from my mind.

'I've left him,' she stated without emotion. 'I gave him due warning. I said, You call me a silly bitch once more and I go.'

I listened to my mother's voice but it was as if someone else were speaking. Surely they'd been together far too long to part like this?

'I told him that all through our married life I've felt like a spring bubbling with life, forcing my way up through the earth, but wherever I emerge there he is like a heavy stone to crush me down. You stupid bitch, he replied. That's it, I am leaving, I stated and he said, Silly bitch, where could you go! You've called me bitch once too often, I shouted. You never show me respect. Silly bitch he said yet again. So I packed my bags and left. You'll be back he shouted as I marched out the front door.'

'Where are you staying?' I asked, my brain somehow turning out a proper sentence.

'I'm at my friend Dolly Potter's. D'you remember her? She's got a squint and a finger missing, but she's very nice all the same. Her husband died last year and she's lonely. She welcomed me with open arms. She said it would save buying a dog.'

This was all my fault, I knew. She'd been determined to be assertive as she thought I was. And now my poor father was abandoned, all alone. Then the worry hit me that he might expect to come and live with me!

'D'you want my new number' she was saying, and like an automaton I wrote the digits down.

All this on top of the Bambridge portrait to be started tomorrow. It was all too much.

Twenty-four

Robert Bambridge stood on the doorstep waggling a flowery birthday card at me. 'You must know something about this,' he said,smiling. 'And it's not hard for me to guess what it's about.' He read from the centre page: 'Go to Wisteria Cottage in Nuthatch Lane at ten o'clock today, fifth of August. Wear something colourful and be prepared to sit with Freda Field for two hours. Surprise. Surprise. Happy birthday, All my love, Poppy.'

Half an hour later I was making tentative marks with charcoal on the expensive linen canvas, my easel set up on the paving stones outside the french windows. He sat in a wicker chair, our beautiful view shimmering in a heat haze behind him. 'I'm a country man born and bred,' he had explained. 'So a background of sky and countryside is right for me.'

As I sketched in the outline, he suddenly asked what it was like to have a clumsy swine as a pet, obviously his way of getting onto the subject of the humiliating pig-bum portrait he'd had the misfortune to unveil.

'I don't think of Hermione as a pet,' I replied defensively, 'she's more like the daughter I was unable to conceive.'

He gave me a funny look then shrugged and proceeded to tell me about his daughter, a real one he needlessly defined. 'She had everything,' he said wistfully. 'Brains, beauty, our money behind her ... and the careless child became pregnant at nineteen.'

I thought of my mother, in the same cart at the same age, with my cells multiplying inside her. She'd once told me that it had broken her father's heart. He'd had faith in her, had ambitions for her, but when she became pregnant he was powerless. There was nothing a working class man could do to help a beloved daughter in those days - and probably nowadays as well.

Robert Bambridge swept his fingers through his silky blond hair. 'She sent the young blighter packing of course but, thanks to him, Poppy and I have a grandson whom we adore - and from tomorrow he and our daughter will be living in the cottage on our land.' His handsome face lit up with pleasure.

I remembered being puzzled why he and his wife were sitting at the back of the school hall during the nativity play. So that was why they were there: he and Poppy were checking the school over for their grandson. As I squeezed out tubes of colour I remembered my mother's description of her tiny flat in Kensal Rise, a million miles away from the picturesque flint and brick cottage in the grounds of The Manor House. Lucky daughter, I thought, suddenly overcome by an unexpected surge of sympathy for my young mother.

'She's been living in our pied a terre in London, but it's not suitable for the young lad and now the cottage has been done up and she's agreed to take it,' he continued.

How magnanimous of her, I mused, loading thick juicy paint onto a stiff hog-hair brush. Then, for the next ninety minutes, I thought of nothing but the painting.

'I enjoyed relaxing in your garden and getting to know you,' he remarked as he left. 'Look forward to seeing you next Friday.'

It had gone well. The blocks of thin colour were in pleasing proportions to the whole, and the figure was in harmony with the surroundings and already recognisable. I too, surprisingly, looked forward to the second sitting.

I rang father. He sounded pathetically upset. 'I miss her you know Freed,' he said with a catch in his voice. And my heart ached for him.

Father rang me late in the evening. 'See if you can get her to come back,' he beseeched, 'I miss her so much.'

How could mother leave that poor lonely old man I wondered, very nearly feeling sorry enough to suggest he came to us.

I jabbed out mother's new phone number.

'Mrs Potter here,' a nasal voice answered.

'I should like to speak to Mrs Salmon,' I said stiffly to the woman with the squint and the missing finger.

In the background I could hear the conversation. '*Mrs* Salmon,' my mother's voice exclaimed. 'It must be Freda being awkward, all my friends would ask for Maeve.' I heard the phone being lifted.

'Freda is that you. Listen, from now on I'm reverting to my maiden name. I am Maeve Edwards. For the first time in fifty years I'm M. E. and that spells ME! So if you want to go all formal it's Miss Edwards, or Mzzzzz Edwards, but not Mrs Anything. Especially Salmon.'

'Mother, father wants you to go back home.'

'I'm sure he does!' she said, voice triumphant, 'but you just ask him why.'

I felt depressed. If we'd had children I wonder if we'd have given them so much grief and stress.

I rang father. 'Why do you want mother back?' I asked.

'I told you why,' he replied. 'It's because I miss her.'

'But why do you miss her?' I persisted.

And he replied: 'Because there's no one to cook and clean for me.'

I bashed the phone down. Mother was right. Let the old devil stew!

I thought I couldn't feel more depressed than I did at that moment and then my oh be joyful arrived. *Oh please let me start the menopause so that I can live free from the ridiculous notion that a miracle might occur and make me pregnant,* I pleaded to God who I didn't believe in anyway because if He really existed He'd have responded to my monthly outcry years ago, even if only to get me off His back. *Anyway God, forget it,* I continued in the inner sanctum of my mind, *my plea was automatic but I've recently realised that I don't want babies any more. I'm too old.*

I took a bet on with myself that now I've expressly told Him that I don't want to conceive, He'll straight away enrol me in the pudding club.

I rummaged in the bureau top drawer and found my old Pig Lovers Diary. I re-read the New Year Resolutions on the last page:-

1. I will lose weight. (*Just a couple of pounds to go and that will be enough.*)

2. I will speak my mind. (*I am more forthright, even just occasionally with Norah H-B.*)

3. I will make money, hopefully BIG. (*I have made a lot but not what you'd call big. I must invest in more shares and make a good job of the Bambridge portrait to get more commissions and charge more.*)

4. I will be more sexy and try to surprise Bernie in bed. (*The book I found in the library called 'The Self-help Guide for the Sensual Female,' proved useless. Every woman knows that to touch a man's equipment gets him going. It's being able to reach it while he's performing that's the difficult part. I'll see if I can hire a video that gives more enlightenment.*)

5. I will do a daring activity. (*Brands Hatch was as daring as I am prepared to go. One activity that would be daring for me is to dive head-first into the Health Club pool, but I cannot do it. I resolve to keep trying.*)

6. I will save the pupils from their tyrannical Head. (*The most important aim, I've realised, and the one I'm failing at.*)

7. If I make enough to afford it, I'll get my girl mated, and rear a family of grandchildren piglets. (*My dear porker is getting old and will soon be past it, so I must make more money - and quick.*)

The sun still shines so Robert Bambridge was able to sit outdoors again for his second sitting. He exuded happiness as he told me that his daughter and his grandson were now residing in the cottage - and they *liked* it.

Bully for them, thought I.

As I mixed cobalt blue and white for the sky, he asked about the Harker-Balls School. 'Zak will need a good education of course,' he said, 'but my daughter feels strongly the school must be local. She thinks that being an only child, he needs friends close by.'

How much should I reveal to him I agonised. For years I'd always remained loyally secretive, hoping I could change the way our ghastly Head treated the pupils, but I knew now that she would never change.

Tentatively I began, meaning to just hint at the problem, but once the frustrated anger had begun to trickle out, the full pent-up pressure exploded into a roaring torrent. I sloshed the blue on with careless strokes. 'Norah Harker-Balls owns the school and she is a monster. A mean vicious woman who delights in humiliating little children with her razor tongue.' Furiously I mixed up grass colour. 'She has fooled the parents. They're impressed with her imperious manner ...' I skimmed the slippery green oil across the canvas into the purple of his shirt. '... and her queenly diction...' My palette knife flashed. '... and her simpering smile. They are fooled by her lies.' The venom rose up in me as I struck wildly with implement and tongue.

'Where is the next nearest school?' he asked, eyes shocked, expression appalled.

I forced myself to calm down. Took a deep breath. Slowly dragged the paint down in a vain attempt at misty magic. 'There's a State School in Orlford, but they're not obliged to take children from here and it's always full. The schools in Great Piddlehurst have places, but twenty miles is too far for the little ones to travel every day.' I tried to scrape off some of the Cadmium Lemon trowelled on for his hair.

'What happens if Wood Hill parents can't afford the fees?' he asked.

I jabbed at the remaining harsh yellow with the pad of my thumb, swirling it around, mushing it in. 'Most of them can afford to pay. Wealthy people have moved into the village. It's not like when we first came.' I scraped at the canvas with a rag. 'The ones that can't afford it make sacrifices. They go without holidays. Mothers get full-time jobs.' I tried not to capture the worried frown on his face, but, the way the picture was going, there was no way I was capturing anything about him. It was a total disaster. As I laboured to recapture the promising picture it had once been, I told him about The Bungalow, and of my dream that one day it might become a community school. 'But there's no way we could afford to buy it and, besides, poor Gertrude Smith isn't dead yet.'

Shame at the last words I uttered created a tight feeling deep inside my chest. I pictured her on my last visit. Her sunken face still scowling, her body limp. 'I'm coming home next Tuesday, they can't keep me here,' she had moaned.

I stared at the vibrant jumble of colours on my canvas and suddenly realised that Bernard's psychedelic penis had been tame compared with this.

'Session over,' I said briskly, whipping the damming evidence off the easel and rushing it indoors so he couldn't see it.

'Can't I look?' he called as I hurried it away.

'No,' I called back, 'it's going to be a surprise.' I ducked into the inglenook and placed the vile picture, face to the wall, in the dark depths. As I ducked back out I wished those words weren't so true. It was most likely going to be the biggest and most horrible surprise of his entire life!

Next day, I took the canvas out and studied it. Tears welled. How could I take nine hundred pounds for that hash? I'd let Poppy down. And what about my dream of fame and fortune? I pushed back tendrils of hair, feeling wretched and distraught. I imagined forcing Hermione's backside down onto the picture, but knew I couldn't. A deliberate act like that would be a different kettle of pilchards from the genuine accident that had happened before.

I decided to go to the Health Club to swim. Then I would come back refreshed and make something of it. I had to. For my sake. For Poppy's sake. For Robert's sake. For nine hundred pounds' sake - and for the sake of commissions to come.

I stood back from the pool feeling even more of a failure here than I did at home. I'd just spent at least five minutes teetering on the edge, willing myself to make the headlong plunge into the water. But I didn't have the nerve. Dejected, I leaned against the wall, idly watching two young women and a child standing by the deep end. As the young women conversed I saw the boy suddenly dart away, a look of mischief on his angel face. He ran then slipped on the wet surface and, without crying out, he fell in, cutting the water cleanly with hardly a splash.

I screamed to the women as I ran forward, seeing the dark shape of the child disappear in the shadowy depths. I wavered on the edge then, casting aside my fear, raised my arms and hurled myself in a headlong dive into the water. Heart beating wildly, I surfaced then powered to where he had disappeared. I screamed up at the women but they were engrossed in their conversation and my voice was only one of many hollow echoing cries. Fear turned my wildly beating heart into a sledge hammer. I squeezed shut my eyes and dived down through the water, down and down, until I was dying for air. My flailing hands touched something and I opened my eyes to stare straight into the wide blue orbs of the child. They didn't blink. They didn't see. I grabbed him by his tiny shoulders and kicked up to the surface, breaking through from the lonely silence to a sudden boom of noise. I sucked in great lungfuls of air, kicking my legs to stay afloat, his limp body trailing in my arms.

I kicked my legs more frantically, propelling myself to the side. Suddenly the little body was snatched from me by clawing red-nailed fingers. I looked up into a paper-white face stricken with fear, then the boy was gone from me and I hung onto the side and wept.

There was a bright flash and I saw that a man had taken a photo of me, and was now aiming his camera at the boy. A plump woman in a shocking pink costume was kneeling beside the tiny form giving the kiss of life. The beautiful blonde stood shaking uncontrollably, her red talons digging cruelly into her paper-white face, her eyes never leaving the perfect body lying in a puddle on the tiles.

Weakly, I pulled myself along the edge, hand over hand, until reaching the steps, where I hauled myself up the narrow rungs on rubbery legs. Gentle hands helped pull me up and a towel was thrown around my shoulders. A thin young man stood away from the cluster of people, a video camera held up to one eye. People were saying *Well done*. There was another flash of a camera, then a man asked my name. I heard the warble of a siren outside as I told him, then he asked for my address. Shivering, I gave the information, longing to get away.

Two people in uniform rushed past us. They carried a stretcher and a cylinder joined by a tube to a mask. They took over the attempt at resuscitation. I couldn't look at the motionless body again. I tottered to the changing room, threw clothes onto my damp body, then hurried away. My teeth chattered as I drove home and I fell into Bernard's arms howling uncontrollably with the shock.

By early evening, men with cameras had gathered outside the gate. I peeped round the curtain, watching their numbers increase. I hated each and every one of them. How could they relish such a tragic drowning. Then one walked down the path and knocked on the door. Bernard opened it.

'Will Freda Field come out and tell us how she saved the boy's life,' he said.

I rushed out to the hall. 'Saved his life! Is he alive?'

'Yes, and you're a heroine. We'll all go away if you'll oblige us with the story and a photo shot.'

I watched the ten o'clock news on BBC One in disbelief. There I was, hanging on the side of the pool in tears, then climbing out. A man's voice was telling the story of the brave rescue. The camera panned to the boy's inert body and his quivering mother. Then came my interview in our front garden.

Bernard put his arm round me. 'Just look at the gravel path, it needs weeding,' he teased.

Then another scene emerged on the screen: the beautiful blonde from the pool stood in front of a border full of flowers. 'I should like to thank Freda Field,' she said, 'for saving my darling son Zak.'

The name dinged a bell, but still I was unprepared for the shock to come. Suddenly Robert and Poppy Bambridge were standing beside her!

Robert said, 'My grandson's precious life has been saved by Freda, a very talented artist whom I happen to know.' His eyes pierced into mine. 'So, if you are watching Freda, thank you from the bottom of our hearts. We've been at the hospital until now and he's doing fine.'

Poppy's wet eyes filled the screen then faded.

The excitement of being a national heroine was momentarily over-shadowed by his worrying description of me being a very talented artist. Little did he know. But then Bernard suggested we open a bottle of champagne and that worry gradually fizzled out. As the bubbles reached our inner depths we turned into giggling teenagers petting on the sofa in front of the empty hearth.

Then the phone went and it was mother.

'I saw you on the box,' she said, sounding amazed. 'Well done, but how come you have so many adventures these days?'

Did I imagine the tinge of jealousy in her voice?

'You race at Brands Hatch, you make loads'a money on the stock exchange and now this!'

Yes. She was obviously proud yet definitely miffed!

'When you live life to the full, adventures come to you,' I answered, feeling deliciously smug.

'I knew my genes would dominate in the end,' she riposted, thereby succeeding in taking full credit.

I went back to Bernie-baby waiting on the sofa. As the air became charged with passion, as the sparkling champagne bubbles reached parts that lemonade bubbles missed, I remembered mother's insinuations about Mars bars, and her sex maniac gibes. But then I remembered that, with our diet, there wasn't a single bar of chocolate in the house. I abandoned myself to our predictable timetable of lust. At least we were always pretty certain of a satisfactory result. But some day soon I planned to get more adventurous. A frisson of excitement shot through me in sensual anticipation, and Bernard gasped.

'I like it when you quiver,' he whispered.

Just you wait, I thought, but then realised I hadn't a clue what the wait would be for.

Bernard went out early and bought six Sunday papers. He said his back was aching with the weight of them all. My picture and the rescue story were on the front pages of each one. The phone didn't stop ringing all day. Parents, people from the Art Club, my Uncle Harry who extended a belated invitation to me to attend his granddaughter's wedding, all three of my colleagues: Sylvie Shepherd, Brenda Wilson and Elizabeth Blessing. Even Norah Harker-Balls who pronounced: 'One is so tremendously proud when a member orv one's staff does something so courageous, it encourages parents to send their children to my school.'

So that's it, I thought sadly. You do your best and save one child's life and thereby condemn countless others to hell.

Robert Bambridge rang. He said he'd tried to get through before but the phone was always engaged. His thanks were overwhelming. He said he and Poppy could never repay me. You just wait till you see your ghastly portrait, I thought, you can repay me by pretending you like it!

He's coming tomorrow for another sitting and I am consumed with fear.

Twenty-five

I regarded the childish picture. Two stick people lay flat on a crooked rectangle of splodgy blue water. The big one held on to the little one. Grown-up letters spelt out: THANK YOU. Underneath, spidery letters spelt out: ZAK. I re-read the letter from Pippa, Robert and Poppy's beautiful daughter whose son I had saved. The thanks were effusive, written from the heart. I would keep it for ever. But somehow it made the failure of her father's portrait even worse.

I forced myself to look at the canvas I'd just worked on for over an hour. My heart sank. Zak's effort had more charm. His was direct, painted with verve and vigour, then left. Confident. Engaging. Mine was an overworked mess. Today's desperate efforts had made it even more horrendous than when I started. The paint was piled on thicker than the marmalade on Bernie's toast. There was no doubting that the figure relaxing in the chair was Robert Bambridge. I could always get a likeness. Maybe it would be kinder to him if I couldn't.

I sank down on the sofa. Forget the picture. Think of his exciting words. Just a short time ago as he had sat and I had daubed, he'd said that he wanted to reward me with more than just the gifts he'd brought. (In front of me, the mass of long-stemmed red roses filled a tall vase. In the fridge, two bottles of 1982 Bollinger Champagne chilled.) He stated that he wanted to buy suitable premises for a Wood Hill Community School. And when that was done set up a trust fund to pay for its running costs.

'It's as much for me as for you,' he had said. 'I want Zak to be happy. And my daughter wants him educated in the village.' He smiled. 'And you want to save the children from the tyrant Head.' As he left he had kissed my cheek. 'Don't forget, The Bungalow might never come onto the market, Mrs Smith's niece may not want to sell, so keep a look out for somewhere else that would be suitable.'

I fervently hoped that Dora Quicknicky didn't intend to return to England to live in The Bungalow when it became hers. It was the ideal building for our school. Surely she would sell it? I'd planned to visit Gertrude later but my emotions were in turmoil. How could I look her in the eye when I was already planning what to do with her home? Bernard came in from a lesson and I told him of my nagging feelings of guilt.

'Let's go round to her garden and work on it,' he suggested. 'You told me she wanted to come home and, just in case she's ever strong enough to do so, let's make it tidy for her. She'll probably never see it, but it'll help clear your conscience as well as the weeds.'

Dear Bernard. That was such a kind idea. Before we set off I rang the hospital.

'She's getting stronger,' a rather grim voice stated.

'Strong enough to be let out and visit her home?'

'Maybe we could let her out for a short while, but she couldn't possibly stay. We'd like you to come in as soon as you can because Dr Simpson wants to talk to you about her future.'

I agreed to go in tomorrow. It seemed that she had become my responsibility. I wondered if Dora Quicknicky would ever appear and start earning her inheritance by showing some concern.

We drove to The Bungalow, the Bernard Field School of Motoring sign on the top, the lawn mower and garden spade in the opened-up hatch. In my large canvas bag were trowels, garden gloves and a kneeling pad.

Bernard began mowing the overgrown lawn and I knelt at the front border and started weeding. As I dug into the soil, I thought of how pleased she would be if she could see us tending the garden she loved. I tried to imagine her sour face transformed to a look of delight. But, as I worked along the line, the picture of Gertrude's face was replaced by the image of happy children laughing and playing on dark grey tarmac where now there was lawn, a netball pitch marked out in white lines on it. I straightened my aching body, feeling even more guilty than yesterday. Poor Gertrude. Poor, poor Gertrude.

Dr Simpson explained that she was far too weak to be taken home yet, even just for a short visit, but she had a strong constitution for a woman of ninety-four and her bones were mending. 'But, we can't keep her here,' he had continued. 'She must go into a nursing home. We'll let Dora Quicknicky know. She's registered as her next of kin, so she must organise the finance.' He frowned. 'It slows the procedure down with her being in New York. But we've faxed her office and now await her reply.'

I felt another rush of pity for Gertrude. Her once proud independent life had now been completely taken over by others.

I hurried into the Florence Nightingale Ward, aching to see her. She sat propped up against snow white pillows. Her sharp eyes followed my progress as I headed towards her bed.

'About time,' she muttered angrily as I pecked her dry cheek.

Since selling the Warthogs, I've bought and sold others and my luck still holds. And the realisation has wondrously hit me that, at last, we can afford to have Hermione mated. A stream of squealing sugar-pink piglets flowed through the floodgate of my imagination and I was overwhelmed by their beauty. I would tend them, stroke them, nurse them through piglet ills. I would watch them grow, share the miracle of their existence with Hermione, as mother and daughter should. If we left it any longer she'd land up middle-aged and childless, just like me. I rang the Pig Farm where Bernard had bought her and where we always bought her feed.

Alfred answered and, when I requested a mate for my girl, he said, 'We've several stud boars. Why not come over and take your pick.'

I grinned to myself. At last I had the advantage over real mothers and could choose my son-in-law.

I looked over the bar of the gate at the long back of the boar. The swine turned and stared up with malevolent eyes. Green spittle foamed at the sides of its mouth. It yawned displaying dangerous yellowed teeth.

'He's a handsome chap,' Alfred observed. 'Sometimes he turns nasty but he's fertile all right.'

Not him! Even if I did think him 'a handsome chap', which I certainly didn't, I knew it wasn't the looks that counted when selecting a mate. It was choosing one with a kindly disposition, like my Bernard. And, kindly, this swine was not!

Alfred led me to another pen across the yard where an enormous boar stood on its hind legs, front trotters draped over the bar, his male paraphernalia blatantly exposed as if advertising his wares. But I didn't give him the pleasure of dwelling on the exposure. Instead, I studied his face. Would his eyes be kind and friendly? Would he be the one? But he gazed back through long white lashes with a look of utter contempt, and then he snorted disdainfully, disengaged his legs and turning his back on me. No way could I entertain this unfriendly arrogant swine.

I hurried along to a sleepy boar lying spread out on the concrete floor of his small pen. He opened a gentle eye and I was just wondering if he would do, despite the small concertina snout and matching penis, when I glanced round and saw him.

Two pens along, friendly inquisitive eyes twinkled at us from a smiling pink face. He squealed and wagged his curly tail as our eyes met and I knew that this was my boy. I pointed him out to Alfred, and was overcome with feelings of deep emotion as I rushed to the amiable swine. This was the boar who would have the honour of impregnating my virgin daughter. For a while I was so overcome that I couldn't speak. Finally I burst out, 'This pig will have the privilege of being the father.' Then, rather belatedly, I peered underneath and was stunned. His portions were somewhat larger than the usual meat and two veg! How would my innocent lamb cope? She'd never met another pig in her life, let alone one hung like this!

'Arr. That's a good choice Mrs Field. Percy's got a way with females and your Hermione will be a challenge. Five years old and still a gilt. Arr, she'll be a challenge all right.'

The line of adorable pink piglets ran across my vision again. As each passed, it turned its head, and every little face was wreathed with the smile of Percy. I turned away, once again overcome with joyous emotion and too choked to speak.

'Are you sure you don't want artificial insemination instead?' Alfred asked, doubtless assuming my mute state was brought on by the shock of seeing what was in store for my girl.

'Positive,' I replied, knowing for certain that I wanted her to experience the real thing, even though the real thing was so alarming. I hoped that, after the event, if she could speak, she would thank me, although, remembering my honeymoon experience, I wasn't so sure.

'When a sow is kept on her own, it's hard to know when she's on heat,' Alfred was saying. 'And it only lasts about twenty-four to thirty-six hours anyway, so we've got to get the timing right.'

My poor Hermione. *We've* got to get it right. She's like poor old Gertrude: out of control of her life.

As we walked through the smelly yard Alfred said, 'The nearness of the boar always intensifies the signs of heat.' He spoke as if reciting from a Pig Manual. 'So we need to get her in the pen next to Percy and keep her there for several days: it might be more than a week.' (The words, delivered in his slow comforting farmer's way, shook me rigid. More than a week without my pig scampering around my feet!) 'They can touch each other through the bars' he continued, 'and the sight, sound and smell of him will get her going.'

Get my poor innocent pet going! I was askance. 'How will you know the signs that she's on heat?' I asked, feeling a little faint, glad that the onset of my oh be joyful wasn't intensified by Bernard's sight and smell.

'She'll probably squeal more and she might even go off her food. But the main way of telling is that she'll stand very firmly and be unwilling to move when you lean on her back. Then you know she's ready to take on the male. It's called the 'standing position.''

As we entered his wooden lean-to office I thought of the times when Hermione had refused to budge. I'd put it down to sheer stubbornness, but perhaps she'd been waiting for her Prince Charming to trot into the kitchen and take her from behind. Alfred looked down at a book. 'She'll have to be serviced three times to make sure, and Percy's booked up for tomorrow.' (How *dare* he! I thought.) 'So we'll collect Hermione next Friday and keep her until, hopefully, we achieve success. It's not guaranteed. Especially at her age.'

Don't I know it, I mournfully reflected, thinking of myself, serviced on average every ten days for twenty-nine long years. I drove back home in a tizzy. How would Hermione cope with Percy? How would she cope with being away? How would I cope with her absence? But the balls were rolling, I had signed the papers and Hermione was about to find out that eating, sleeping and rolling in mud weren't the only pleasures in life.

I brought out the canvas. It was glistening with thick wet colourful goo. I recognised the same brash awfulness as the pre-pig Sidney Slocumb portrait. At that moment she barged in, snuffling and snorting for food. Nervously I stared at her backside. It worked before. Dare I? I was desperate. The Bambridges, who were now my friends, were coming on Monday evening to view it. No way could I show them this. Nervously, I placed the canvas face up on the kitchen floor, then lured Hermione to it with a biscuit. Suspiciously she approached but, no matter how hard I shoved and pushed down on her, she stood immobile, refusing to oblige. I wondered if she was being obdurate or was on heat and taking on the standing position. Finally, I gave up and took the disaster up to the attic out of sight.

Bernard went out at ten to give a lesson. He was due back at eleven. I had just one hour to perform a plan born of desperation that had formed in my mind. I hurried up to the attic studio and grabbed up a box of man-size tissues, a bottle of turps and the gooey canvas. I tottered down the narrow stairs and into the bathroom. The picture, I laid out on the cork tiles, and the tissues and turps on the bath edge. The scene for the last-ditch attempt to save my picture was set. I shot the bolt on the door then looked all around, ridiculously fearing the long lens of a reporter's camera at the window to make me a laughing stock. I yanked the blind down to be sure, turned on the light and hurriedly undressed.

I stood naked, ears sharply listening, eyes darting, There was no sound. Nothing moved. I placed each foot carefully astride the picture. I stretched my arms forward and began the slow squat down. My bottom neared the thick oil paint but I paused in my descent. This was ridiculous. Foolhardy. I wouldn't carry on with it.

The sudden piercing ring of the doorbell made me scream and over-balance, falling backwards, grabbing the sides of the bath and the wash basin as I went. My backside skidded across the canvas then I pulled myself up to my feet. I stood stock still. Shaking. There was silence. Had whoever it was gone away?

Suddenly the shrill sound rent the air in short sharp stabs and my heart careered around my chest like a squash ball rebounding off walls. Time passed. Silence settled. I stared at the bolt on the door, half expecting it to slide back so someone could enter and witness me stark naked with the colourful arse of a baboon. Minutes passed. I was terrified the air would again vibrate with the strident sound of the bell. But the atmosphere settled into mute stillness.

At last I dared move. I lifted one foot up onto the wash basin and the hand mirror up off the shelf. I bent forward, thrusting the mirror through the fork of my legs. Awkwardly, I positioned it to view the disaster area. It was even worse than I'd imagined. Winsor and Newton paint clogged up my bum cleavage and the blurry image of Robert Bambridge lounged across my buttocks in a smudged background of lurid green and blue. It was disgusting. I groaned. At least the mayor's portrait had only straddled the bum of a pig, not a person, and not a person who was me!

Manically I attacked my shamed flesh with tissues soaked in turps. As each gungy wadge was dumped in the flip-top bin, a new lot was grabbed from the box. Pitiful primeval moaning now accompanied each fevered foray. I sweated in the hot confines of the bathroom, bent over double, body contorted, blood rushing to my head.

After what seemed like hours, and what must have been the hundredth time, I thrust the mirror through to inspect my tingling bum. And, at last, it was clear. I straightened my aching back, feeling dizzy. Now I had to rid myself of the stink of turps. My hand was on the tap, about to turn it, when a hammering on the door right beside me made me cry out, then freeze. Bernard was back already!

He banged again. 'Open up I'm dying to go,' he bawled.

'Who is it?' I stupidly called out, playing for time, grabbing up my knickers from the corner of the floor.

'It's me,' Bernard answered. 'Who did you think! Buck up in there, I'm dying for a pee.'

I jabbed each foot in and hauled the white lace up over my rear, covering the raw smelly evidence. 'Hang on a minute,' I called back, leaning forward, angling my breasts into my bra. 'You're not the only one needing the loo.' I hooked the bra together then threw on the rest of my clothes. I was flummoxed and my heart was now madly bouncing around my chest as if trampolining on my diaphram.

'Come *on*' he called.

I took a deep breath, lifted the canvas and, with studied nonchalance, sauntered out.

'You look flushed,' he remarked, barging past me. Then he stopped short. 'You've done it again Freda!' He sounded incredulous. His eyes lingered on the canvas, before diving in and slamming the door. 'It's brilliant,' he called from within.

I held the canvas out and surveyed it. He was right! The way the paint had been blotted off and dragged down gave the magical effect I'd been after. 'Thank you, thank you oh painter's spirit,' I breathed softly as I carried the masterpiece up to the safety of the attic.

I bounded downstairs and soon Bernard joined me. 'Congratulations piglet,' he enthused, pulling me into his arms. 'You're a wonderful artist ...' Then, quickly he thrust me away. '...but you don't half pong!'

I felt myself blush. He must never discover precisely the source of the stench!

'You look funny,' he observed. 'You must have been working at it too hard. How about you soaking in a nice hot bath and I'll bring up a glass of the Bambridge champagne. You've earned it.' He tapped my offending bottom as I hurried away.

If only you knew the truth, I mused, as alcoholic bubbles fizzed down my throat and fragrant bubbles cosseted my body. But this was a shameful secret that I'd never divulge to anyone, not even him.

The bell rang. I opened the door. It was that woman from Rugged Farm. She handed me a bag of rotten apples for Hermione. 'I came round yesterday but there was no reply. I expect you were round the back at the bottom.'

I agreed that indeed that was so. Though not quite round the back at the bottom that she had in mind!

'I *love* it!' exclaimed Poppy, clapping her hands.

Robert stood back, grinning. 'It is good,' he agreed. 'How did you do it. I can admit now that when I glimpsed it from time to time after the various sittings I didn't like it at all.'

'I ... I like to keep the finishing technique a surprise,' I stuttered. 'The making of the picture often comes after the final sitting, up in my studio.' I did not explain that, in this case, the making of the picture came after the final sitting up in the bathroom.

Next day I went up to my studio intending to practise paint-dragging techniques by more traditional methods, i.e. using brushes and palette knives instead of tender flesh. I knew I had to master it to cope with future portrait requests, although I was beginning to doubt that I could stand the strain of another commission. But I realised that this might be the only way to make the big money of my dreams.

I began by thickly painting the front of The Bungalow from memory, the oak tree in the garden spreading darkly across the sky. Then I scraped at the paint with my long triangular knife, shunting the malleable paint in all directions. I heard Bernard moving about in our bedroom below.

'Will you come up and tell me what you think of this,' I called down.

He appeared. He cocked his head, then scratched at his crew cut. 'Is it an abstract?' he asked.

'An abstract depicting what?' I asked warily.

'Maybe a portrayal of death?' he hazarded, also warily.

He went back down leaving me stunned. Is that what I had wanted? Had my subconscious dictated the picture. Was I hoping for Gertrude's quick demise so I could get my hands on her home. I felt shaken and appalled.

Early next day I set off to visit her at the Twilight Nursing Home in Orlford where she'd just been transferred. As I sped along the lanes I wondered if my picture had been a melancholy portent. Supposing I had influence: supernatural powers that could kill Gertrude off at will. My imagination was in top gear like my car. I parked, tore up the drive to the rambling Victorian building impelled by the terrible guilt. A woman showed me her room. I entered then halted in surprise. Gertrude was slumped in a chair beside her bed and an elderly man stood beside her. She'd never had another visitor before and I wondered who he could be. She looked across and saw me. She beckoned me in. As I drew closer, her lips drew back into a hitherto unseen broad smile. I stared, amazed at the transformation and the neat completeness of the set of ivory teeth. She held out shaking arms and the warmth of the greeting made me feel even guiltier than before. She clasped my hands in hers and it felt as if I was gripped by fragile ice.

'I do appreciate you coming,' she said, not letting go. 'This is my solicitor, Felix Gray. I have just given him instructions to alter my will.' Her smile was secretive, even roguish. 'There will be something to your advantage because you have been so kind. You've been thoughtful ... unlike, unlike ... others ... but she is a long way away ...' She trailed off, looking wistful.

Felix Gray cast me a knowing look and I felt quite dizzy with glorious hope. I collapsed down on the bed and sat perched on the edge, not quite believing what I had heard. She was going to leave The Bungalow to me. She'd said it, in so many words. My mind raced ahead. Robert would pay for the conversion and upkeep. The Community School would be born. The pupils would transfer to the new school, which would be non-fee paying. And Norah Harker-Balls would be redundant.

'I wish I could be there to see your face,' Gertrude said, solemnly, 'but of course I won't be.'

Alfred drove Hermione up the ramp, another man guided her with a wooden pig-board. Oh Hermione, my poor baby. She turned and threw me a reproachful look, then the back of the trailer was noisily slammed up and bolted. And they were off. I wept as I tried to imagine Percy's great body straddling her back as she took up the 'standing position'. I hoped it would be more enjoyable than my first experience in the missionary position. I blew my nose. Now all I could do was wait in hope that we should eventually be blessed with the pitter-patter of tiny trotters. It was such a beautiful thought that I burst into tears again.

The phone rang. It was mother. 'I know you said that because you were only invited as an afterthought you weren't going to go to the wedding tomorrow, but you bought me the dress so I thought you might like to see me wearing it,' she stated. But I could tell she really wanted me to be an escort because she didn't have father.

'I'll meet you at Bournemouth Station and drive you there,' I sniffled, still emotional about my pig.

'Weddings always upset me too,' she replied. 'Brides always think they'll live happily ever after. They look so trustful, so expectant. It's so sodding sad.'

I was grateful for the distraction. At least going off to a family wedding in Dorset would concentrate my mind on something other than Percy's mammoth willy ramming into my precious babe.

And guilt-ridden dreams of Gertrude dying so that I could get my hands on her beloved Bungalow.

Twenty-six
Intrusion 5

Maeve sits on the London bound train reflecting on her new Hector-less life. Hector-less and hectorless she muses, seeing the apt connection for the first time. At the beginning it had been exciting. The brave new adventure. Independence. Girls' talk. Sharing a house with a chatty friend. But quickly she had realised that Dolly's verbal onslaught never ceased. Every waking hour, jabber, jabber, jabber, with seemingly no pause to draw in breath. Sixteen long days of not getting a word in edgeways. Two weeks and two days of listening to widow Potter yack. And here she was on a train racing back to the rabbiting hell.

Maeve thinks of Dolly's deceased husband Stan. He'd endured fifty years of ear-ache before escaping to death. She wonders if, as he'd taken his last breath, he had welcomed the prospect of heavenly quiet and was now flitting around soaking up peace and dreading the time when his wife would zoom up on a long-winded outflow of trivia to join him. Maeve notices the eyes of the man opposite. They flicker up and down as if connected to the foot of her crossed leg which, just like Hector's habit, was jerking up and down. Was his a nervous reflex action brought on by the aggravation of her? she ponders. Could it be possible that she stressed Hector as much as Dolly stressed her? It was an idea that had never crossed her mind before and it confuses her.

She sits vacantly staring through the carriage window, deep in thought. Dolly's dull monologues drone inside her head: the blow by blow accounts of how she cleans the house, the fascinating outbreak of blackheads on the face of her neighbour's son; the hourly details of her chronic constipation. Why does she think I give a shit about it, Maeve rails, faintly roused from her drowsiness by the wit of her inner thoughts.

As the train races towards London where Dolly waits, she concludes that she'd had a more scintillating conversation with her grandmother on her death bed than she'd ever had with her friend.

She thinks of life with Hector. He might have been like a rock constantly crushing her down. He might have shown her scant respect by calling her bitch all the time. And he might have stunk the toilet out every morning. But at least he didn't have verbal diarrhoea. Reluctantly, it dawns on her that she misses him in bed too: his heavy arm draped over her, his squidgy bits pressing in.

She stares down at her turquoise silk lap, tracing the black swirly patterns with her eyes. Forget Dolly Potter. Forget Hector Salmon. Think of the wedding she'd just been to and all the events of the day.

When Freda had met her at Bournemouth Station at midday she had looked ravishing. Like the colourful butterfly she used to be, save for some laughter lines. As they had driven to Ridgy-Didge village, she had told her daughter about her gabby friend. So you'll go back to father, Freda had said, all full of eagerness. Not while he calls me a silly bitch, she'd replied. And even as she had said it she was wishing she could pocket her pride. Wasn't 'silly bitch' really his term of endearment? she reasoned. And, even if not, the silent spells that punctuated every day, more than made up for the insult.

As they drew up outside the church she'd spotted her brother gazing at a headstone beside the path. 'Hello Walter, are you choosing your plot?' she had quipped, but he didn't laugh. Ignoring his grumpiness, she'd called over, 'Nice to see you, you haven't changed a bit.'

'You've always said daft things Maeve, ever since we were kids,' he exploded, nearly falling off his walking stick. 'It's been six years since we last met and in that time I've had me seventy-fifth birthday, gone bald and had another false hip, so don't you go telling me I haven't changed.'

Then his wife Winnie had sailed up in a red and white striped dress like a billowing spinnaker, her red wide-brimmed crooked hat awesome in its perfect co-ordination with her red wide-mouthed crooked smile. Inexplicably, a dog's lead trailed in her hand. Maeve had greeted her sister-in-law with a kiss and, tactfully ignoring the missing dog, had pleasantly remarked on what a good day it was for the wedding.

'Are we at a wedding?' Winnie had beamed. 'That's nice. Who's getting married?'

'YOUR GRANDDAUGHTER,' Walter had roared, tottering sideways with the exertion.

'That's nice,' she said again, turning and heading off towards the man who stood nervously by the church entrance clutching a grey top hat. 'And who are you?' she said brightly to her son, the father of the bride.

'That'll be me in a few years if I stay with Dolly, completely doolally,' Maeve had muttered to Freda as they entered the shady church where Winnie's loud hoots of laughter were shattering the calm.

'Oh look, my bag has escaped!' she shrieked, waving the dog lead for everyone to see.

'At least she's happy in her senility,' Freda remarked. Meaning, Maeve conjectured morosely, that she's better off than me.

Freda led into a back pew and Maeve sat down by the edge. She was glad to have a clear view of the aisle and altar. She was glad to have her daughter by her side. She put her hand in her handbag to find a hanky but there wasn't one. Suddenly she missed Hector again. He knew how weddings upset her and always carried a spare for her to snivel into. With a jolt of belated awareness, she realised that she'd always taken his thoughtfulness at weddings for granted. She felt sad. He wasn't all bad. But, as she idly watched the people as they took their seats, she tried to remember another instance of her husband's kindness, but nothing came into mind.

All wedding guests seemed to look and act the same she mused as she looked at the bridegroom's side of the church, picking out aunts, uncles and cousins without even knowing them. But then Winnie demolished the assumption that all wedding guests acted the same by suddenly flinging her large-brimmed hat towards the altar. An instant hush descended on the whispering congregation as if conducted by a choir master. All eyes were on the spinning red frisby as it headed straight for a magnificent display of flowers, precariously balanced on a slender column. Time changed to slow motion as the missile homed in on its target. The roses, lilies and carnations stood in glorious immobile profusion in the hat's path, but then, caught by a sudden draught of wind, the twirling missile veered sideways and the scything brim merely clipped a single long-stemmed rose which flew high in the air before landing head first in front of the altar. The hat slowly descended to the floor where it rested like a circular pool of blood.

'It's a ruddy miracle,' a shrill voice piped up. 'I prayed to God that the flowers wouldn't be harmed and the hat bleedin' well changed course!'

There was a collective gasp and Maeve hadn't been clear whether it was because of the wondrous miracle or because of the language the woman had used. The quivering blooms slowly regained their static equilibrium and Winnie turned to the stunned audience and bobbed a curtsy, crookedly grinning with delight. Polite clapping came from one or two unsure people, like sporty cricket fans acknowledging the opposition's well hit boundary.

A handsome dark-haired lad hurried down the aisle to take up his bridegroomal position. Maeve looked at her watch and saw that he had cut it fine. She noticed too that he winked at a pretty girl who winked back at him.

In the meantime, Rose, the bride's mother, had sunk to her knees, and everyone in the tiny church could hear her loudly whispered prayer: 'God,' she had said, 'I expect you've forgotten I exist because I haven't talked to you since I asked you to help me with my spelling test at school, but, as I haven't been a nuisance to you like those who bother you all the time, will you please grant me one wish. Please make my little girl happy with her new husband so she won't come running back home to me.'

Then the organ burst into the joyful, jubilant, thank-God-she's-arrived, 'Here comes the bride,' and everybody stood. But instead of the bride appearing, a broad-shouldered crouching man scuttled down the aisle, a bulky camera clutched in his hands.

The winking girl had turned to look as the bride appeared and Maeve saw that their eyes had briefly locked. She caught the smile of triumph under the veil. She also caught the look of a pregnant belly under the shiny white satin frock. So, she wasn't completely stupid after all. There was a good reason she was getting wed. Maeve saw that the winking girl was dabbing her eyes and in a flash realised the devious intelligence of her great niece.

The bridegroom had stepped out and the vicar began his chat, but Maeve couldn't see a thing because of the lank-haired man with the camera who blocked the view. As the young voices pledged their troth, tears slid down Maeve's cheek. Although her wedding fifty years ago had been in a registry office, not a sumptuous affair in a church, it still brought it all back. The promises. The chaining together of two young lives. She asked Freda for a hanky, and a disintegrating tissue appeared.

When the vicar had come to the bit about anyone having just cause or impediment as to why these two should not be united in holy wedlock, she'd felt like shouting: Me! I have just cause. I am here as a witness and that bloody photographer is blocking my view!

Maeve smiles as she thinks of the reception held in the church. The food displayed on a long table had been snatched up and hogged down before the bride and groom had even appeared. The best man couldn't read and spent what seemed like hours sounding out the letters on the greetings telegrams and cards. And a toast for the happy pair had been called by the bride's father before a drop of champagne had been poured. She pictures the raised empty glasses and her mouth twitches.

She looks up and sees the man opposite giving her a funny look. Her heart sinks. She'd almost forgotten she was on a train speeding inexorably back to Dolly Potter. She knows that at Waterloo she could easily take the underground to Tooting Broadway and her husband, instead of alighting early at Clapham Common to go to her gabby friend. She wants to. So much she wants to. But she won't. She cannot give in.

She wonders if, over the years, she has grown to love Hector. Her Sockeye Salmon. But she shrugs the idea away. That's how Dolly Potter gets you, she thinks angrily: daft in the head!

Twenty-seven

I drove mother to her brother's granddaughter's wedding at
Ridgy-Didge village and on the way there she poured out her
heart to me. She isn't happy living with that Dolly Potter. She
said: The one good thing I can say about your father is that he
doesn't yack all day. That was the first complimentary thing I'd
ever heard her say about him and I'm hopeful that a reunion
will soon be on the cards. The wedding turned out to be an
expensive shambles which I predict will end in tears.

On Sunday I rang father. 'Why did she go?' he asked forlornly.
   'Because you crush her spirit and call her a silly bitch.'
   'But she *is* a silly bitch,' he replied, completely bewildered.

On Monday I rang mother. She sounded lost, her voice lifeless.
I suggested she returned to father and she whispered that she
might be forced to. I could hear Dolly Potter prattling in the
background even as we spoke.
   Father rang. Voice quavering, he told me that after fifty years
of marriage he now realises he must love the silly bitch.
   I felt too choked with heartfelt emotion to speak. They were
the words that made my existence blameless. They were the
words I'd always dreamt of hearing, but never believed I should.

It is Tuesday, the twenty-ninth of August, four long days since
Hermione went off to the farm. I wonder if my parents miss
each other as much as I miss my babe. Bernard doesn't say
much about our girl's absence, but he's painted the walls of
her bedroom powder blue and touched up the PIG STY sign
on the mobile home door. It's his way of showing he cares.

I rang father with trepidation, but instead of the usual
mournfulness, he sounded very pleased with himself.

'Has mother returned?' I asked, holding my breath, hardly bearing to wait for the answer.

'No, better than that. I've taken on a housekeeper,' he replied jubilantly.

His words tore at my heart. This was the narrow end of the wedge that could split them asunder for good.

'I can afford it on what I save on your mother's grub,' he explained, ramming the wedge home. 'She'll come in for an hour every day.' The wedge eased back. At least the dangerous woman wasn't living in. 'She started yesterday,' he stated with smug satisfaction.

'What's she like?' The steadiness of my voice surprised me for it gave no indication of the turmoil inside my head.

'Very different from your mother. She's sensible and acts her age.' He let out a sharp excited buzz.

'How old is she?'

'About fifty!'

That was my age. How were you expected to act? Who laid down the rules? Did this woman think to herself each morning when she woke up: I am fifty so I will deliberately quell any forty year old ways. Anyway, he was only guessing. Maybe she was forty and acting older, or maybe she was sixty or seventy and not acting her age at all. How was my clever-dick father to know?

It is the last day of August and I now understand how doting mothers feel when their children leave home. It's called the empty nest syndrome I think. Although, in my case, the empty pigsty sydrome is more apt. All the bustle and activity and fun has gone. Bernie and I practically tip-toe around the cottage, it is so quiet. Each day I have walked up the ramp and gazed at her vacant bed, trying to visualise my bloated girl in labour. I wonder what kind of mid-wife I shall be. Bernard and I are both reading books about farrowing. He pores over them, muttering about things he must remember and things he must make.

I swam twenty lengths at the health club then drove to Orlford and visited Gertrude in the Twilight Nursing Home. All the anger and fire that was her personality has died, leaving her shell of flesh and bone to gradually follow. I stayed a while, holding her hand, futiley wishing her eyes would blaze and her tongue would lash out once more.

Alfred rang from the PDQ Pig Farm. He said Hermione had been a natural. (Did he mean my girl was a minx?) He said Percy had served her well and she had taken him without flinching every time. He said that he, personally, had checked that the boar had been fully inserted. A mental picture of two bulbous space craft docking together guided by a God-like spirit called Alfred popped into my mind. He said that they were bringing her home TOMORROW! Tomorrow! My sweet child. I rang mother to pass on the good news that Hermione was returning and could be in-pig, farm shorthand for pregnant, but she showed no interest whatsoever. On impulse I asked her if she would come down and look after Hermione while we went away for a short break before the onset of school next week, because we hadn't had a holiday in years.

'I will if you ask your father to join me.' she whispered.

And my spirits soared.

I rang father. A woman's soft voice answered. 'I want to speak to Hector Salmon,' I snapped.

When I told him what mother had said there was a long silence, then: 'Tell her I'll pick her up from Dolly Potter's tomorrow at four. We'll get down to you before six.' He sounded close to tears. I was ecstatic. The soft-voiced siren was clearly no match for my ma.

The PDQ Piggery truck arrived outside at ten. Hermione was shunted into our front garden by two men with pig boards then the gate was shut. Our girl was home! I ran to her. Her eyes darted wildly around and sharp grunts peppered the air. A frown plunged her forehead into deep pink pleats. I flung my arms around her but she squealed and trotted away. I felt wounded, as if a knife had been stuck into my heart, then twisted. Bernard bounded to her and managed to pat her head, but she shook his hand away and ran, honking, round the back to her quarters. Tears welled.

'I'd expected her to want to be indoors with us,' I sniffled.

'Leave her,' Bernie advised. 'She's probably traumatised.'

Or missing her husband I thought, visualising the smiling face of her lover and wondering if she could possibly have fallen in love with her swain. Her swine swain. Her swain swine. I mulled over the glorious words that spelled out Percy as I mooched indoors. Maybe the experience had changed our girl for ever. Maybe she wasn't ours any more. Maybe she was Percy's.

But, at lunch-time, she came barging through the pig flap just like she used to. She stared up at me and within those piggy eyes I swear I saw a new worldly look. She had been there. Fulfilled her purpose on earth. Had it off with her lover. Yes my girl was a fully-fledged female now, no longer an innocent abroad. I stroked her flank and was filled with wonder. Right now, under my hand, cells might be splitting and compounding, growing tiny grandchildren for us to deliver and rear. Unless, of course, she had defunct tubes like me.

My parents arrived. They acted like strangers to each other. I kept catching father eyeing her when she wasn't looking. She spoke about the traffic on the motorway and he didn't tell her she was wrong. She spoke of the weather and he didn't interrupt. I could hardly bear it. This formally polite couple wasn't them. It was spooky. Hermione relaxed and sprawled herself out on the sofa. I felt uneasy. Just as she was beginning to settle down we were going to abandon her again. I regretted my impulsive decision to go away tomorrow, but, if it succeeded in getting mother and father together I supposed it would be worth it. I regarded the mute pair and rather doubted it would be the case.

They stood close together in the mobile home, her shoulder almost resting against his broad chest. A night in a double bed seemed to have done wonders for my parents.

I explained the procedure with Hermione's food. 'Fill her trough with the feed from the opened bag and add any fruit or vegetables you can find plus some milk.'

Father nodded but I wasn't sure he'd taken in a word because all the time I was speaking he'd been staring down at mother's hair, a rapturous smile on his face. She caught my eye and jerked her thumb towards the exit. She took my arm and guided me out leaving him in charge of ladling out feed for the eager pig. I looked back. Was she acting hungrier? Was she eating for who knows how many?

Mother dragged me down the ramp and through the yard to the lawn. 'I just wanted you to know that I was kidding last Christmas,' she said, nudging me in the ribs and looking saucy.

I didn't know what she was on about.

'You know. Your father. The Mars bar. He didn't really, you know ... like that Rolling Stone ... he never would. I was teasing everybody to get some action.' She looked at me sideways. 'You know ... Christmas was boring then, like you were. I had to tell you before you go off on this second honeymoon. I didn't want to be responsible for any damage. You know ...' The smile on her face was more enigmatic than the Mona Lisa's.

'No, I don't know,' I said, feigning deliberate innocence.

She grinned sheepishly and whispered, 'Your Beatrice!' then added, 'and Bernard's dodgy back.'

This was the mother I loved and now appreciated. Outrageous. OTT. We linked arms and sauntered back. I hadn't thought of our mini-holiday as a second honeymoon, but I suppose it could be. I hoped that the same would go for them, alone here, away from the housekeeper with the soft voice and Dolly Potter with the verbal squitters. Already I was dying to get back to see how they'd got on and we hadn't even left!

We were shown to our room on the top floor of the hotel by a friendly porter. It was huge. In the corner was a television set, in front of that a table which held a large bowl of fruit. Beside it, a small sofa. Raised on a carpeted platform at the back, was a king-size bed with flowery duvet and frilly pillows.

'This is the best room in the whole place for views of Lyme Bay,' he announced, throwing out one arm towards the vast window.

Vague outlines faintly showed through the veils of misty rain that swept across the wide vista. The faint sound of a distant foghorn sounded and the sudden shrill scream of a gull.

'It's perfect. We'll have dinner up here,' Bernard instructed, 'and bring up a bottle of Moet champagne.'

I turned in amazement and caught my breath at the blaze of intensity that shone at me from his wonderful black fringed eyes.

I woke next morning feeling that I wanted to stay with my incredible lover in our eyrie for ever. Twenty-nine years together but never before had it been like this. When Bernie had first pulled me onto the bed, champagne bubbles had buoyed my senses casting me naked and free on the wild sea of lust, and we came together in a writhing climax, more explosive than the storm that raged outside.

We dozed, entwined together, then he had whispered, 'Do you have a secret perversion? Do you have a special request?'

Now was the time for the new bedtime activities of my New Year resolutions. Champagne still fizzed, releasing inhibitions, creating daring. I thought of mother's Mars bar insinuations, but, on permanent diet, no wicked chocolate bar was ever bought, so none could pass my lips! I remembered the bowl of fruit on the other side of the room.

'Roll a fruit all over me,' I suggested, not knowing from where the weird idea came.

Slowly, he began to roll the tangerine in the path of a figure eight, outlining each breast. With closed eyes I followed its unhurried sensuous route. It climbed up to the tip of my nipple then dived down into the broad valley, rearing up to the opposite peak. My nipples tingled with desire and tangerine zest. It zigzagged down over my ribs and naval to the furrow between my legs where, at a snail's pace, it crept up and down, dividing the flesh with its weight. I was aware of nothing but the movement of that fruit. Harder it pressed inwards. I groaned, arched my spine, threw my arms back, in a frenzy of animal lust. I needed that object inside me: press harder I silently implored. My shameless thoughts imagined leering reporters videoing the scene. I opened my legs to their lenses and cried out, lunging at the soft fruit as if to devour it. Then suddenly, it was over in a climax of earth-shattering quakes.

Limply, I lay spread-eagled, aware of the tangerine resting against my inner thigh. Never had I been that intimate with anything or anyone before, other than my Bernie. I thrilled to the sense of daring, and the desire to do it again. I shamed to the sensation of embarrassment, and the exposure of kinky desire. I opened my eyes. I lifted my head. Bernard still knelt before me, sniffing at me like a dog.

'You smell like marmalade,' he said, licking his lips. Then he crawled over me and again I abandoned myself to the passion of my man. In the early hours when his caressing hand awoke me, the bubbles had cleared and, as he stroked, my thoughts drifted to mother and father. I hoped they were delighting in each other's bodies too, but not with this intensity, it would kill them!

When Bernard tenderly cajoled me to kneel up on all fours, I thought of Hermione in her standing position. I imagined the voyeuristic spirit God Alfred checking on Bernard's entry and collapsed in stifled giggles onto the bed.

'I shouldn't have expected you to hold that position, you must be exhausted,' Bernie apologised.

I tried to contain the laughter, but it burst out, and he joined in, not knowing why. For him it seemed to be an outburst of sheer joy.

We showered and dressed then went down to the dining room for a late breakfast. I watched Bernard eat his marmalade toast greedily. Between bites he stared at it. Did I imagine the lascivious looks? Would everybody notice and realise? I blushed and looked round at the couple at the nearest table, but they just stared into space, not even seeing we existed. I glanced further afield but the few people left seemed only to be interested in eating.

We donned waterproofs and went outside, finding a shelter on the sea front to sit in. Enclosed by a gossamer curtain of softly falling drizzle, we were in a secret world of our own. We talked of our dreams and hopes as we'd rarely talked before. We decided we were two incredibly lucky people, but if Bernard could find a safer occupation than teaching learner drivers, and if I could start up a new school, and if Hermione had conceived, and if my parents would get back together and live in harmony, our happiness would be complete.

'Pigs might fly,' Bernard quipped drily.

'You never know,' I responded, the notion of a Hermione with wings galloping full pelt down a runway flashing into my mind.

I pushed open our cottage front door. Their voices came from the kitchen. We stood quietly for a few seconds, hoping to hear loving words.

'*Why* did you take notice of which way you were going to Ridgy-Didge Village,' he was asking, sounding exasperated.

'What do you mean, why?' she replied.

'What I say! When Freda drove you to the wedding, why did you specially take notice of the way there? You weren't going there again. So, what was the reason?!'

'Because I wanted to know.'

'But *why* you silly bitch. Who is going to go there?'

My heart sank.

'*We* were going there - Freda and me.' She laughed, ignoring the fateful female dog word.

'Cooee,' I called, and Bernie and I entered the apparent war zone. But I was in for a surprise. They both greeted us with enthusiasm. They both smiled. I detected a look of affection that darted between them. Was their spat just good humoured banter, with an especially sharp cutting edge? It would be asking too much to expect them to change completely. Mother reached out and touched his hand, and then I knew.

Just then Hermione struggled through the pig flap and ran over to greet her.

'She's getting fat,' Bernard observed.

'So she should be,' mother said. 'A man called Alfred came round yesterday and took her off for a special scan. He said he was too impatient to wait for the normal tests.'

'AND?!' I shouted, legs going weak.

'And she's pregnant!'

I sank to my knees and hid my face in her side. Rough hairs pricked at my face and hot tears pricked at my eyes.

'Congratulations,' said father, helping me up. 'You're going to be a grandmother.'

'Stupid dog!' said mother, doubling up with laughter.

'She can't seem to cotton on to the fact that 'silly bitch' is my term of affection' he grumbled. 'So now she's countering with that stupid 'stupid dog' tag.' His following buzz was benign.

'Quite right, stupid dog!' she reaffirmed, splitting her sides once again.

He rolled his eyes, held his hands up in submission and smiled. There was definitely humour in their bickering now, I hadn't imagined it, and an undercurrent of caring that might even be love. I caught Bernard's eye and he winked. Father started talking to him about football and mother edged me into the sitting room.

'I'm returning to the stone,' she announced. 'He's easier to live with than dopey Dolly. But then so would anyone be, unless you were fortunate enough to be stone deaf … and completely dumb.'

'Is that the only reason?' I asked. 'Are you only returning to him because he's easier to live with than your impossible friend?'

'Well, I did miss him,' she admitted.

'And love him?' I pursued.

'Yes. That too I suppose.' Her eyes looked shocked as if it was a revelation to herself as well as me. 'But it's taken over fifty years of purgatory to get to it,' she flared, 'so it had better be worth the wait.'

That was my mother. Back on form.

As we walked with them to their car parked outside, they were still arguing.

'Okay, I promise I'll eat less so we can afford to keep the cleaning woman.'

'No need to have her now you're coming home.'

'So that's all I am is it, a char!'

But she had given him a twinkling look that clearly said that wasn't all she intended to be.

As we waved them goodbye I was euphoric. I had parents who loved each other, a husband I adored and a pig who was pregnant. Then I remembered that school had started and I was due in tomorrow to begin my two and a half day stint. The vision of Norah Harker-Balls loomed, contaminating my mind with its presence as the real being contaminated the pupils' lives. Patience, I consoled myself. Just a little longer before The Bungalow is mine. Even as I thought it, the familiar guilt engulfed me. The salvation of the children could only commence when poor Gertrude died. I hoped it would be quick for all our sakes. And especially hers.

Assembly was the most miserable, unjoyous occasion I have ever attended. Norah wiped the floor with Toby because his tie was crooked. She berated a new five year old girl because her cardigan was light blue instead of the uniform royal. She accused Gregory, an overgrown puppy dog of a boy, of pushing over little Emily Green who everyone, including Emily herself, said had accidentally slipped. I have never known her more unfair and more foul than today.

She stood in the hall doorway, arms crossed, glowering at the children as they began to file out. I stepped forward and, in a low voice that others couldn't hear, told her she had been too harsh.

Loudly she bawled, 'Mrs Field. We must have discipline in my establishment. If one doesn't like it, one can leave. There are plenty of excellent teachers who would jump at the chance to teach here.'

She had me. There were no other jobs. Besides, the children needed me as an ally and protector. I watched the cowed children and the three other teachers as they silently passed through the doorway. The bright shiny faces of a new academic year had quickly become tarnished like neglected silver.

Just a short time in her presence and I was tense and dejected.

I yearned for the day when the pupils could transfer to The Bungalow to be educated in an atmosphere of care and love. It was now up to Gertrude and her Maker, or, more aptly, her Annihilator. I couldn't quell my wicked thoughts, but consoled myself that Gertrude yearned to be released from life as well.

Twenty-eight

As I said to Bernard: You can't tell me pigs don't have a fifth sense - just as the voice on the phone began to tell me that Gertrude had died, Hermione rolled over onto her back and closed her eyes. It was as if she knew.

'Sixth sense,' Bernard corrected. 'We have five senses. It's the sixth one that is intuition.' And then to emphasise the point he counted them off on his fingers. 'One sight, two hearing, three touch, four taste, five smell.'

'Female pigs don't smell,' I retaliated, 'so it was Hermione's fifth sense.' I knew, as I spoke, I was being ridiculous, but it delayed taking in the sad news.

'Anyway, she's always lying on her back and closing her eyes,' he reasoned. 'It's not psychic pig power, it's the desire to be tickled on the tum.' He gazed at me, perturbed. 'You must feel upset that Gertrude's finally gone. You'd got close to her, hadn't you.'

It was then that it hit me and I broke down, howling my eyes out for my poor friend. She was better off out of her living hell, I knew that, but never again would I be able to visit her and take her hand in mine. Never again would I be able to look down on her frail spent body and wish that her eyes would open up and blaze with angry life. I cried and cried for her, and for the terrible finality of death.

But later, when I had recovered, excitement gripped me. I remembered the impish look, that was almost loving, when she informed me she'd changed her will to my advantage. And the solicitor's knowing smile when he confirmed it. She'd been let down by the niece who had once adored her, but who had shown no interest in the past few months, maybe even the last few years.

My mind raced out of control, down the lane of hope that led to The Bungalow. Again I went over the plan. Robert

Bambridge's money would pay to convert the building and his trust fund would finance running the school. The education of all Wood Hill children would be free, in every sense of the word. A plaque would be on the wall in Gertrude's memory. My thoughts were off on a runaway flight, but caution eventually intervened and grounded the fantasy. Perhaps she *had* left The Bungalow to Dora Quicknicky as she'd always intended. It was possible. Gertrude hadn't spelt out my inheritance in unequivocal words. Suddenly, and quite stupidly, I found I was praying to her, 'Please, Gertrude,' I whispered, 'if it isn't mine, please perform a miracle and send your ghost down to alter your will before anyone sees it.'

I grabbed up the phone. 'Is that Freda Field?' a man asked.

'Yes.'

'This is Felix Gray, we met at The Twilight Nursing Home.

I felt weak. This was it! 'Yes, I remember,' I said.

'Mrs Smith indicated to you that you were a beneficiary in her will.'

'Yes.' Suddenly I was trembling all over and had to sit down.

'It gives me pleasure to inform you that she has left you something she told me means a lot to you.'

I couldn't speak.

'I am happy to inform you that the Victorian water colour picture of the pig that hangs over Mrs Smith's piano is now yours.'

Time ticked by as the message slowly sank home. And then I laughed.

'She told me you would be delighted,' he said. 'I'll bring it round later today.'

'Now we'll have to wait and see if Dora Quicknicky wants to sell or keep it,' Robert Bambridge responded when I rang and told him the news.

I put the phone down, but hovered near it. I had her New York number. Would it be too indelicate to ring and ask if she intended to sell it before her aunt was hardly cold? I decided to wait. Probably she'd fly over for the funeral on Friday anyway, and I could talk to her then. I pictured a younger version of Gertrude Smith, the scowl framed in blue rinsed hair.

At seven I opened the door to Felix Gray who handed over the picture with the happy smile and magnanimity of a jolly Santa Claus. I asked him in but he said he had to go. My fazed mind half thought he'd said Ho Ho Ho.

I held it out, scrutinised it. It was beautiful. A faded version of my porcine girl. *Thank you Gertrude* I silently prayed. *It is lovely. I didn't mean to be ungrateful. It was very kind of you to bequeath me the picture that I had so admired.* A vision of her face appeared with a gleeful look in the eyes, and the serious doubt crept in that she knew of my yearning to own her home and this was her merry revenge.

I hung the picture over the fire place and it looked perfect there. *Thank you* I reiterated, deciding to give her the benefit of the doubt.

The tapering oak coffin rested on rollers in front of plain green curtains. My wreath of pink rose buds lay in pride of place on top. The meagre scattering of mourners had stood and sat and prayed and sung. The priest had spoken shallow words about Gertrude Smith's long life. 'In an English Country Garden' was being played as the final farewell.

I remembered my last visit to her when the priest had appeared, supposedly to utter words of solace. But he'd tactlessly asked if she had any special requests for her funeral service and she had reared up from her pillow and blasted him into hasty retreat, shrieking after him that she didn't give a sod 'cos she wouldn't be there. I wonder now if it was that final incredible surge of energy that finished her off.

'In an English Country Garden' continued and a vision came to me of her flying over the straggly rose beds of *her* English country garden. She landed, pirouetting on her unkempt lawn. Then a throng of angelic infants skipped into the dream scene. They joined hands in a circle around her and sang 'Farmers in his Den.' The flashing eyes of the ghostly Gertrude transmuted into the flat fish eyes of Norah Harker-Balls. The scene became translucent. Through the now-silent dancing children I saw curtains open and watched the pink rose buds slowly glide away on their expensive chariot. I tried to block my imagination as she headed into the incinerator, bunioned feet first. But it wouldn't block and I saw Gertrude's wasted body cooking in the fiery furnace, and felt hot prolific tears roll down my cheeks.

But I knew I was not crying just for the fate of my friend. I was crying for myself. For the dreadful knowledge that one day I, like all mortal souls, would be laid out in a coffin with fearsome flames consuming me. I could almost smell the charred meat of a barbecue, could almost see bones melting down into glue.

Shakily I stood and tottered out with the nine or ten others into the weak autumn sunlight. Four sprays of flowers and a large wreath of white lilies were set out on stone flagging beside a rectangular pond. I bent, weaving between them, reading their messages. They were tactful, from kind neighbours, giving no hint of her surly ways. I read the last card attached to the wreath: *I thought the world of my aunt when I was young and thank her for everything. Dora.* I wondered if she had stopped thinking the world of her aunt when she was an adult and if the thanks were for the rich inheritance she knew was to come.

I cast my eyes over the other people. They were all men and women I knew from the village, except one. I approached the big woman with the tired face and introduced myself, expecting an American twang in reply. But the twang was only a Hampshire accent and it turned out that she was a carer from the Twilight Nursing Home who'd come on behalf of the staff.

'I didn't really know her,' she said, 'not the real Mrs Smith, just the disintegrating body and mind.'

'Count yourself lucky,' a voice muttered behind us.

I walked away, too sad to joke and too annoyed at the missing Quicknicky to converse.

It was a beautiful sunny day but that only made me more depressed. It was all there. The clear blue sky. The autumn leaves. The fresh air. The birds singing. But dead people like Gertrude and my grandmother couldn't experience it. They had departed from the grand jamboree planet Earth party, but it all still carried on. The horror of being dead clung to me like a leach sucking out blood.

Bernard tried to cheer me up by pointing out that before I was born I'd been missing it all too but that that didn't seem to bother me.

'But before you are born you don't know there is anything to miss,' I cried, amazed that he couldn't see it.

'Think about it,' he said, holding his palms up, 'it's no different missing it all before you were born to missing it all after you are dead.' He nodded his head reassuringly and smiled. But his words did not impress.

'Life is meaningless,' I cried. 'All of this: the cottage, my pig, saving the children, getting thin, you. It's all meaningless.'

'Listen,' he said, still patient. 'You didn't exist when your grandmother was dancing the charleston and that didn't worry you. And you didn't exist when your father was singing treble in the choir and that didn't worry you. So, after you're dead it will be like that. People will be dancing and singing but you won't be here. So cheer up. It's nothing to worry about.'

The black wispy cloud that had hung over me at the start of his philosophical reasoning became an enveloping cloud of choking smog. Dear Bernard, he had meant so well but failed so fucking dismally.

I changed into a track suit and trainers to go out for brisk walk to help rid myself of death blues. I left the cottage, strode out along the lane and turned right into Church Road. In the distance the slim stiletto spire stabbed into the pale sky in its vain attempt to probe heaven. At the lych-gate I turned my back on the church with its grim reminder head stones and hurried along the short High Street, passing the Corner Shop and the Bank. I shunned eye contact with other people and even crossed the road to avoid Mrs Trugshawe. As the bitter aroma of beer from the Black Sheep Pub greeted me, I hoped she hadn't seen my hasty side track. I watched her disappear into the newsagent then crossed back again, passing the passage that led to The Old Bakery Art Club. At the junction I turned left and, at the end of Cross Street, turned left again, heading back for home along Bramble Lane.

But, as I turned the corner, the shock of what met my eyes, stopped me dead in my tracks. Erected in The Bungalow garden further along at the junction with Primrose Lane, was a FOR SALE sign. Coming out of the front doorway was Sidney Slocumb and Bill Boggins. They looked furtive and Bill Boggins hurried towards his car. Toby Mole's father came out behind them, closing and locking the door.

With mounting horror, I studied the board. In bold red letters the sign proclaimed: FOR SALE by Mole Estate Agents. An Orlford phone number screamed out its digits beneath. I don't know if they saw me as I began to run. I didn't care. I had to get home to the telephone. My mind was in turmoil. Surely this devious pair weren't going to buy it before we got a chance. They couldn't dash all our hopes and dreams to the wall.

I staggered into the cottage and dialled the Mole Office. Gasping for breath, I panted out my question.

'The asking price is two hundred thousand pounds,' she replied. 'That price reflects the fact that the building and the garden have been neglected, but there is already an interested party, so, if you're serious, I advise you to view it soon.'

I rang Robert Bambridge and imparted the shocking news.

'I'll be round tomorrow early,' he tersely replied.

He went over his plan: straight away he would offer the full asking price but make it subject to planning consent being granted for change of use to a school. If the executors accepted that and if planning consent were finally granted, he would pay for the conversion and set up a Charitable Trust to run it. He must have noticed my concern at the large amount of money involved.

'Don't worry about the finances,' he said, flicking his silky hair off his face. 'I'm lucky. I inherited the Estate and my business is thriving.'

I could just catch what he was saying through the thumping of my pulse bombarding my ears. We were on the way, at last.

'Your job is to let everyone who will be affected know,' he continued. 'Maybe the rest of the staff and the parents will be against the plan. Maybe they're satisfied with things as they are. We must check before we get in too deeply.'

'No, no! Not the teachers. They're not satisfied. They'd do anything to get the children away from the Harker-Balls' influence. And they all need to keep their jobs, so they'll be with us.'

'Good. But what about the parents?'

'The parents don't know what goes on. They don't believe their children when they complain and so the youngsters eventually stop complaining, knowing it's no use. The parents are duped by her lying words. They are impressed by her queenly articulation. They are foxed by the academic results, which she explains are excellent for the ability of their child. But, in truth, most of the pupils are so screwed up, I'm convinced they could do better.'

'You'd think the doting mums and dads would see it,' Robert mused. He looked puzzled, as if doubting my words.

'I'm not exaggerating. The parents are blinded to the unhappiness of their children and the warping of their personalities by the grand presence of their Head. They are sure that if anyone is telling lies it must be their sons or daughters, not her. She is articulate. They are under the misapprehension that she is respectable and good. Only the Moles seem to have an inkling of what she's really like.'

'So how will you set about it?' Robert asked.

'First, I'll have a meeting of my colleagues here.' A plan formed as I spoke. 'Then, if they agree, we'll organise a secret meeting of the parents and I'll tell them the truth. We'll hold it in The Bungalow if Mr Mole will agree.'

'What happens if we don't get The Bungalow after all that?' he asked. 'What will you and the teachers do, having exposed the shortcomings of the Head Mistress to the parents?'

My mind went blank. I could think of nothing. 'We *will* get it. We must,' I stated. Hadn't I vowed to be strong. Hadn't I made resolutions to succeed.

'Fairy stories always have happy endings, but real-life tales often don't,' he warned. 'Do you still want to go through with it? You're risking your job.'

'More than ever,' I affirmed.

I rang Sylvie Shepherd, Brenda Wilson and Elizabeth Blessing late the next afternoon when I guessed they'd be home from school.

Elizabeth was incensed by Norah's behaviour today. She said, 'She's always bad on Mondays but today she even locked Toby Mole in the stock cupboard, then denied it was deliberate. The poor kid was shaking and crying buckets when he was finally released. And the trouble was there was no proof that it was done purposely. She's so crafty she gets away with murder.'

I agreed. We all knew she was adept at covering up. And maybe it *had* been an accident, but we both knew that it was more likely that it was not. 'Come to the meeting here tomorrow, we may have a way of helping Toby and all the other pupils,' I told her. 'Come on your way home from school, and, apart from the other teachers, no-one must know.'

I replaced the phone. I'd like to ask Cynthia Slocumb to come too. I knew she'd jump at helping in a fight against The Evil One. But, she was the wife of the man who could scupper our plans. I decided to trust her. After all, to have a spy in the opposition camp could be an advantage. And, if it was a fight between me and her husband, I was sure she'd be on my side.

Next day, they came, eyes blazing on all fronts like ack-ack guns. Norah Harker-Balls had apparently been worse than ever. When they heard the plan the blazing transformed to sparkle and the tight lips relaxed to smiles. Yes, yes, they agreed with the plan and it couldn't be put into action too soon for any one of them. They agreed to let Mr Mole in on the conspiracy. His son was the most unfairly treated and, besides, he had commission to earn on the sale. He would surely unlock The Bungalow door for the meeting, knowing that, by the time the parents left, they'd be desperate for Robert Bambridge to buy it.

Cynthia said she would prepare letters to hand deliver to the parents. 'I will spell out that children are not allowed to be present and that it is imperative that a mother or father from each family should attend, preferably both. And, above all, that Norah Harker-Balls mustn't know. They'll assume we're planning a special surprise for her.' She grinned. 'Which of course we are!'

The date was set for Sunday the twenty-ninth of October, the last day of the week long half-term holiday, when any families who'd gone away should be back ready for school the next day. We were sure that Mr Mole would stave off accepting an offer from Slocumb and Boggins when he learnt of the scheme.

Elizabeth Blessing rapturously announced that this wonderful happening was all down to God because she had prayed so hard for His intervention. I felt miffed at her notion that Robert Bambridge and I were being directed from above. No credit for his generosity and my bold initiative. I felt like saying that it was a shame that her benevolent God hadn't intervened sooner for, if He'd welcomed the poor suffering Gertrude into His house earlier, the innocents might already be safely ensconced in their new happy school.

'If you want to help,' I snapped back at her, 'set your God onto Bill Boggins. He's bound to be after The Bungalow for another of his moneymaking distasteful developments that will ruin Wood Hill.'

She answered meekly that she would try.

I shut the door behind them. Now twelve whole days to wait. But, in the meantime, Robert Bambridge's architect was drawing up plans.

The phone went. It was Robert. 'Do you want the good news first or the bad?' he asked.

'The bad first.' I replied, filled with dread.

'The Squeezamin Property Development Company's offer has already been accepted, subject to planning permission to demolish it and erect flats.'

Oh no! How could that be. We were so close.

'The good news is that our offer has been accepted too, subject to planning permission being granted for the school. Dora Quicknicky is the executor as well as main beneficiary of her aunt's will. She sent a fax saying that whoever completes first gets it. She isn't a woman who cares.'

I was tempted to ring Elizabeth Blessing to ask for her prayers!

Mother rang with the hot news that father has bought a CD ROM computer.

'He has!' I exclaimed, amazed.

'Not only that, he's paying to join the Internet.'

I was struck dumb. My father, catching up with technology!

She continued, 'I'm glad because he says you can surf on it and I've always wanted to have a go at that.'

Before I could say anything, she went on, 'He spent hours in front of the screen yesterday. He said he was experimenting with his mouse.' She laughed suggestively. 'In my young days, pocket billiards was what that activity was called!'

I smiled as I replaced the receiver. Good old mother. These days she always cheered me up.

But the smile soon disappeared when I sat down to work out what I was going to say to the parents. However I put it, they were going to be shocked and disbelieving.

Twenty-nine
Intrusion 6

Sidney Slocumb sits in Bill Boggins' flash red Porsche parked in the shade of a tree at the side of a quiet lane. His weasely friend sits in the driving seat beside him.

'Blimey, if the Council'd wear it, we could make a bleedin' bomb out of developin' that gardin,' Bill Boggins says. He turns and raises an enquiring eyebrow at Sidney.

Sidney knows what he means. He smirks as he remembers the way they'd pulled if off last time. The old feller with the garden that were too big for him. The offer to buy his land. The opposition from the villagers: a development of five houses too dense for such a small plot and the modern architecture out of keeping with the rustic charm of stuffy Wood Hill. But he had greased the palms of his cronies on the council and got planning consent, despite the objections. Aye, and he'd gained his rich reward. The exchange of his humble dwelling in Great Piddlehurst for the pick of those five luxury homes.

'There'd be a lot'a dosh in it fer you like last time if you could fix it,' Bill states.

But then, Sidney reflects, he was on the Planning Committee. Now he was the worshipful mayor, so barred from being on any committee at all. Now it would be a sight harder to fix than last time.

'We can chop dahn that friggin' great oak tree and there'd be room for two blocks.' Bill practically drools.

Sidney's brain is racing. Happen he could not only make a lot of brass from his wily mate here but, like before, make extra from Jake Glazier if the building work were given to him. He wonders if he can pull off another scam though. Already some were suspicious of him at Great Piddlehurst Town Hall. That's why they mustn't be seen together. Just one more load'a brass and he could afford to fade quietly out of public life and retire with his posh house and his Jag. He quivers with excitement and rubs his podgy hands.

Bill suddenly shoots forward, peering anxiously through the windscreen. From Sidney's view, his partner in crime's long nose acts as a pointer, marking the faroff woman walking their way. He imagines the nose as a projectile launcher to be activated if the unsuspecting lass got within range. Sidney's gaze sharpens. She looks like his Cynthia, but she musn't see him in Boggins' car, she'd know they were up to no good. He leans forward. *Was* it his wife? Her with the puritanical conscience? Her who'd been furious with him last time, even though it meant moving to a sought-after residence in up-market Wood Hill. But the figure turns into a gateway and disappears and he whistles his relief. The missile launcher wheels round and aims close range at himself.

'Well, what about it then?' Rodent teeth emerge and the thin moustache lengthens sideways like a strip of black liquorice over the enticing smile.

He decides to take the plunge. 'Aye. You give the building contract to Jake Glazier, and enough brass to satisfy me and the rest of me friends at Town Hall, and planning permission is as good as granted.' Sidney closes one eye in a long wink and repeatedly taps the side of his bulbous nose which squidges disconcerting warning flashes of red into the vision of his open eye. He wishes he were as confident as he sounded.

The sharp point of Bill Boggins' nose seems about to spear him, but suddenly it pulls back. 'Great!' says its owner, 'I've already offered the estate agent git Mole the full asking price subject to planning permission, and 'e's waiting fer a bell or a fax from Fastnicky in New York. I fink we c'd say it's in the bag!' He slaps Sidney's rheumaticky knee sending judders of agony along the short length of his leg. Sidney makes a mental note to hold their next clandestine meeting somewhere where there'd be more space to escape that enthusiastic hand. Somewhere like a glade in The New Forest, or the waterside at Southampton Docks.

They say their goodbyes and Sidney hauls himself out of the low seat and starts the long walk back home.

'Hello, you look like a lame duck,' Cynthia says brightly as, splay footed, he limps down the path.

He might look like one, he thinks, but lame ducks are failures and his whole being resonates with the delirious happiness of success. In his mind's eye he is already gliding into the village in his gleaming dark green Jag.

Thirty

It is Sunday the twenty-ninth of October, the day of revelation. The french doors leading to the back garden are open wide and the over-spill of parents are bunched together outside. I stared around the room that, until a few months ago, had been Gertrude's cherished home. The fern patterned wallpaper was faded, but over the piano was a rectangle of fresh bright green where my picture had so recently hung. Poor Gertrude.

I glanced over at my colleagues standing together by the door. Sylvie Shepherd was staring intently at me and gave an encouraging smile. Elizabeth Blessing held her hands together as if in permanent prayer. Behind her, tall Brenda Wilson nodded and pointed down to her watch. It was time! I cleared my throat and raised my hand. I asked for silence.

The hubbub subsided, but a woman's penetrating whisper was heard saying, 'Now we'll know why we've all been summoned here. It's probably nothing more important than collecting money for a surprise present for Mrs Harker-Balls.' A low wave of speculative chatter surged, then slowly ebbed away.

When there was absolute silence, I began. Hesitantly at first, I told them that their children spoke the truth when they complained of their Head's fearsome ways. Gathering strength, I told how she humiliated them and ridiculed them and terrorised them too. Emphatically, I told them that this was no way for their precious children to be educated, As I spoke I quaked inside. Was this really the right thing to do?

'I don't believe it,' Mrs Jones said hotly. 'Mrs Harker-Balls is always very nice to me.'

There were other mutinous mutterings of agreement, then Mrs Trugshawe's doubtful voice spoke out. 'Once when I crept into the school with Daisy's P.E. kit, because she'd forgotten it, I heard Mrs Harker-Balls.' She cast a worried look at me. 'The classroom door was shut but I could hear her screaming at the kids inside. Suddenly the door flew open and a little girl came flying out - it was as if she'd been brutally pushed. Then I heard our Head Mistress say ...' Mrs Trugshawe lowered her voice as if ashamed of what was to come. 'You stay outside you nasty snivelling little turd.'

'You're exaggerating,' the father of a girl in my shared Class Two called out. 'We all know children do things that are wrong and need chastising. It's called discipline. Anyway, you probably misheard.' He almost sneered.

'But it was your daughter she was abusing,' Mrs Trugshawe proclaimed. 'I didn't want to upset you so I didn't name her.'

His face became suffused with puce fury. He opened his mouth to speak then changed his mind. I scanned the concerned faces and assured them that Mrs Trugshawe and I spoke the truth.

'I still don't believe it,' shouted Mrs Jones. 'She's always been very pleasant to me. She always seems to care. She told me that kids always make up stories about school.'

Then Sylvie Shepherd came forward and told them of the names their respected Head called the tender children in her charge. She had clenched her fist and banged it into her open hand as she spat out each word: DOLT! BLOCKHEAD! IDIOT! FOOL! CRETIN! MORON! SIMPLETON! DIMWIT! Gasps of horror punctuated each insult as it seared the air. 'I could go on and shock you even more but I can assure you that the only time she is civil to your children ...' She jabbed her finger at individuals in the front row. '... is when she knows any one of you is in the school.'

I saw the look of dawning comprehension and horror in their eyes. At last they were believing us.

Then Mr Mole pushed himself forward. In a voice charged with emotion, he said, 'My son Toby has changed since starting in her *establishment*.' His face contorted as he parodied her word. 'My boy has been in that school for just over one year and she has delighted in making him a laughing stock. When he started he was a carefree lovable lad ...' He gulped '... but now is so full of pent-up rage and frustration that he's changed to a hostile rebel.'

'They often do change at that age,' Mr Smith laughed. 'Yours has grown stroppy, mine has grown big.'

I remembered Gregory, his overgrown son, reduced to tears by her when she falsely accused him of knocking down little Emily Green.

Mr Smith continued, still smiling, 'My son is always telling us that things aren't fair, but kids always say that, don't they.'

'You may not believe your boy,' Mr Mole hissed through clenched teeth, 'but I do believe mine. He tells us things she has said to him and, no matter how bad he has been, they are words that shouldn't be uttered, even to a dog.' He turned to me. 'We were about to take him away and, if the school in Orlford was still full, my wife was going to educate him at home.'

I could just see Mrs Mole's head in the crowd. I was amazed. She was always so nervous but was prepared to take matters into her own hands.

Mrs Parcel, a top class mother, put up her hand to speak. In a soft voice she said, 'I once broached the subject of electing school governors, but Mrs Harker-Balls rejected the idea out of hand. She said that she didn't want jumped-up parents prowling around her establishment. When I questioned whether it was unlawful not to, she curtly told me that The Children's Act of 1989 made it clear that she wasn't obliged to. It was as if she was scared to open up the school to a Governing Body because she had something to hide,' Mrs Parcel wiped her hand across her brow, then added, 'But she did eventually smile sweetly and thank me for my interest.'

Pale blonde Mrs Monroe called out from the squashed group just outside the french doors. 'I wandered into the school once and saw children cowering away from her, literally cowering. She was lambasting a girl who was sobbing her heart out but, as soon as she spotted me, she patted the child on the head and sent her back to her desk. It made me anxious about the school so I made excuses and looked in on the other three classrooms. But there the little mites looked happy and well-occupied. I thought at the time that maybe Mrs Harker-Balls was having an off day.'

'We could complain to the Education Secretary of State if we had proof,' cut in Mr Jones, who I knew was a Civil Servant of some kind. 'But it's possible she'd fool him just as she must have fooled the Local Inspectors who have to call in regularly to observe.'

I could see by the horrified looks on their faces that the revelations about the woman they'd always looked up to were now totally believed. It was the equivalent of telling them that our gentle Queen Mother was really a mass murderer. They stood in troubled silence staring at me.

'So what are we to do?' Mr Jones asked. 'We can't take our kids away, there's nowhere for them to go.'

Now was the time to tell them of Robert Bambridge's plans for The Bungalow ... and of Bill Boggins' interest too.

The meeting went on and on but at the end of it every single person voted for the setting up of the new community school. Every single person agreed to keep it secret from their children in case they gave the game away, and in case we couldn't pull it off.

'We'll get it I'm sure,' cried Elizabeth Blessing, her radiant face aimed at the crazed ceiling, above which she no doubt thought God was hovering, with nothing better to do than hang on her every word.

'Yes,' Mrs Monroe agreed, 'the Council won't give that spiv Boggins' permission for flats, it's obvious they'd prefer a school.'

'But they gave permission for those houses squashed into the ghastly new Eldorado Close,' they were reminded by Mr Mole.

'I'm sure we'll win,' I said, 'And, when we do, we must have prepared a method of walking away from her with quiet dignity. No angry words to upset the children. No big scene. We shall give her no notice. We will walk out of the Harker-Balls Establishment to this, our haven. We deserve a glorious revenge. Obviously, she must have no inkling, for, if we lose, we're stuck with her until another suitable property comes along.'

I watched their faces relax, heard them whisper words of comfort and optimism to each other. Then Mr Smith announced that he would set up a pyramid of parents' names and telephone numbers so that information could cascade down. And several mothers volunteered to give coffee mornings to pool ideas for the controlled walk-out, already code-named Operation Salvation.

The meeting ended. As they drifted out, I wondered if Elizabeth could be persuaded to ask God to arrange for Boggins' financial downfall. I drew the line at requesting God to snuff him out!

One full week has passed. I have been too busy with school duties and meetings with Robert and the architect even to pay much attention to Hermione. But, the plans for the conversion have been completed and the requisite six copies have been sent to the Great Piddlehurst Planning Office with the fee of one hundred and sixty pounds. Now we have to wait to learn if our application will be heard at the next Planning Committee Meeting. They're held on the third Monday of each month. Two long weeks and one long day to go.

In the meantime, we know that it is Council procedure to send out letters immediately to neighbours who could be affected by The Bungalow's change of use. I am terrified that one will be sent to the Harker-Balls' school. But Sylvie Shepherd is getting in extra early each day to look through the post to see if she can spot the envelope and purloin it.

Sylvie came into my classroom as I chalked up some work on the board. The children still waited outside in the playground. Furtively she showed me two narrow buff envelopes, each marked: Great Piddlehurst Council. She handed one to me and we ripped them open.

I read the notice held in my shaking hand. It stated that an application had been received to convert the nearby dwelling, known as The Bungalow, into a school. It asked for any objection to be put in writing and sent to the Town Hall to arrive by the seventeenth November. Sylvie thrust her letter under my nose. The wording was the same except that it referred to the application for two blocks of flats to be built in The Bungalow gardens.

'We must destroy them both,' I rapped, hearing the clang of the bell outside. The realisation had suddenly hit me that our Head would welcome blocks of flats that might bring in more children to her highly profitable school. As we began tearing the notices into tiny pieces, I could hear her voice booming out insults as she marshalled the silent children inside. Sylvie hurriedly tipped the confetti letter into the side compartment of my open handbag, then hurried away. My fragments followed and I zipped the damning evidence away. As the children entered

I thought of Bernard's words last night: *Harker-Balls has no mortgage. She pays low salaries. She charges high fees. She must be making a bomb*! Hopefully that bomb was soon about to explode, demolishing her lucrative business and blowing her to smithereens.

Robert Bambridge rang me. He had heard from the Council that our application wouldn't be considered until the meeting of the eighteenth of December, because the November meeting was already full.

In panic, I rang Cynthia to find out if she knew when the Boggins' application was to be heard. She didn't know, but rang back soon after with the information that it was the same date as ours. I sighed with relief. At least the race was still on an even field. We still had the best chance to win.

Bernard has been unusually morose lately. When I asked him if he was unhappy, he grumbled that I was devoting all my time to fussing about Hermione's possible morning sickness and to meetings with Robert Bambridge and various parents regarding the school, and that he had been utterly ignored. 'You've even been too tired in bed,' he complained, mooching off.

It was true I realised. Ever since our passionate stay at Lyme Regis, sex had been far from my mind. And, even on that second honeymoon, now I thought of it, it had been he who'd been pleasuring me. But though I was nearly fifty-one, I still didn't really know what turned a man on, except for the obvious. I decided to find out. I would excite him. I would surprise him. If only I could discover how.

Bernard went up to bed looking doleful because I didn't go up with him, but I stayed downstairs to set up the video to tape some likely sounding late-night films!

Bernie went out early to do four lessons on the trot. He looked fed-up and weary. As soon as he was gone I pressed the rewind button of the video machine, pen in hand to make notes. I was about to learn some new tricks to make Bernard happy and I could hardly wait. But, when I played it back I was disappointed. 'Behind the Bedroom Door' turned out to be an old black and white romance, so I knew that any sex in that would be fully clothed with one foot on the floor. And when I fast forwarded to 'The Orgy', it was so full of blood and gore that I had to turn it off. It was disgusting. In a fit of desperate daring, I drove to Great Piddlehurst to find a video shop.

Furtively, I scoured the shelves for a likely title. A spotty youth loomed out from the shadows and asked if he could help. When I said that a friend of mine was looking for a sex manual he cheekily eyed me up and down and I wished I hadn't worn my short skirt. I felt myself hotly blush. Casting amused glances my way, he fingered through a row of boxes, eventually pulling one out. Then he went behind the counter, filled it with a video tape, and dropped it into a vibrant yellow Video Shop bag. I grabbed it, paid the money, and hurried out. Outside, I felt that everyone on the crowded pavement knew of the erotic smut that I carried in the blaring bag.

I sped home. Bernard was in the kitchen. I scurried into the sitting room and hid the box containing the tape on the top shelf between Shakespeare's Full Works and Acol Bridge for Beginners. Its title, *The Climax: Seventh heaven and beyond*, deliberately hidden.

Bernie had two lessons this morning. As soon as he was gone, I took down the video and put it on. It was shocking. So blatant. I just could not believe my eyes. No way could I attempt any of that stuff! Hermione barged in and I felt envious. No distasteful deviations for porkers, just a good clean doggy-fashion fuck. I decided to try out a few variations on the video antics tonight. But with modifications that made allowance for my age, my squeemishness and my dodgy back.

Next morning, Bernard brought me up a cup of tea and three aspirins. He smiled down at me tenderly and told me to lie flat while he was out. As if I was capable of doing anything else! 'If it's as bad when I get back, I'll call in the doctor,' he said, stroking my hair then gently kissing my forehead.

'But what will we tell him?' I wailed, knowing I wouldn't be able to look Dr Aegen in the eye and tell him the truth.

'You could tell him what happened.' His eyes held a faraway look and his lips a stupid grin. 'Your back went out while you were bending over in bed. And that is the truth!'

I remembered him hauling me back off the floor when I slipped over the edge in my first effort. Then, encouraging me in the quest to find his G-spot. From his groans and noisy cries of ecstasy, I deduce that he enjoyed my finger's inadvertent probing of his A-spot (which I hoped was clean) and then his squidgy B-spots, which produced bellows of joy as loud as when the G-spot was finally located. If I ever try it again, God forbid, I'll know to follow the fine seam that runs neatly down the back of his D-shaft leading to the spot in question, rather as the pointers of The Plough lead lost sailors to the N-star.

From the volcanic eruption that followed when my finger arrived there, I wondered why on earth it wasn't called the F spot and be done with it. The video didn't explain what the G stood for but I guess it's Grateful, at least in Bernie's case. There was him spread out groaning in paroxysms of delighted delirium and me groaning in suffocating agony under a feather duvet, stuck on all fours, with my lumbar disc out. It took forty minutes to get me straightened (once the duvet was removed I could see the bedside clock) and a further half an hour to get me onto my back with my head the right end of the bed.

Bernard is pathetically appreciative, but if he thinks it's the start of something that'll be a habit he's got another think coming. I'll never try that out again. I came. I saw. I conquered. Except that it was he who came, not me! It didn't do a thing for me poking around in the dark fug, and I have no desire to conquer again. G stand for Gone as far as I'm concerned.

I hobbled into the shop and handed the video back. The three aspirins I'd taken before I left had helped dull the pain.

'You've tried it then,' the twerp said, giving an offensive leer.

It was humiliating and I thanked my lucky stars that, although his pimply face looked somehow familiar, our paths had never crossed before.

'Didn't you once teach me?' he shouted after me as I limped out the door.

I didn't need any pain killers today so my disc must have slipped back fully into its slot again. Poor Bernard looks bright eyed and full of expectation. You'd think he'd realise, in view of what happened, that the other night was a one-off, but he obviously doesn't.

Today is my fifty-first birthday. A whole year since I vowed to transform. Well, I reckon I've practically succeeded in all my ambitions, plus extras like becoming close once again to my fun-loving mother, and more understanding of my 'stupid-dog' dad. And more important than my change in looks is the impending pitter-patter of grandchildren piglets. But, by far the most important is to rid the school of its Head. And that's just a matter of waiting a short time.

I sit in front of the dressing table mirror, naked under my new black satin dressing gown, basking in birthday contentment and the deep satisfaction of success.

'What are you looking so happy about?' Bernie asks, our eyes meeting in the mirror as he comes up behind, cupping my breasts in his warm hands.

'I've succeeded,' I crowed. 'I've de-frumped myself, made money, transformed.'

But, as I dressed, buttoning up my long jade silk shirt, I realised again that trivialities such as slimming, with-it clothes and re-vamped hair, were nothing compared with the big aim. I would only truly have succeeded when the pupils were sitting at new desks in the safety of their new school.

I twiddled nervously with a strand of hair. Just three days before the Planning Committee meeting: the final hurdle. Surely we couldn't fail now. But then I remembered the corrupt pair we were up against and doubt fluttered inside my chest like a captured moth. I reassured myself that the Council must prefer a community school to blocks of flats. But, might not the devious duo somehow swing the Planning Committee vote? The feeling of wings beating inside my chest rose up to my throat, and I found it hard to breathe.

Thirty-one
Intrusion 7

Bernard runs a comb lightly through his short cropped hair. What a difference a year makes, he muses. Last time he'd accompanied Freda to the annual Christmas dance at the school as a duty. He'd even stipulated that he'd only go if she drove, so that he could drink. He remembers her look of disappointment and his churlish response: It's either that or we walk. It had been sheeting down with rain and she had been wearing a flapping full-length skirt. He feels retrospective remorse.

As he knots his tie she enters the bedroom. She wears a simple black ankle-length dress, its narrow skirt slit up one side, its pouched top held up by dainty glittering straps. A choker of large shiny pearls encircles her neck. She looks stunning. He marvels at the rebirth of his wife.

'I'm worried about Hermione' she says, tugging down nervously at a spiral of hair. 'She's just been stuck in the pig flap for ages, she's so fat, and I'm worried that our babies could get hurt.' She lets go the tress of hair and it bounces back to a corkscrew curl. 'I've locked her out for tonight, but I'm scared that all the pushing and shoving to get her free might bring her on early.

'That woman from Rugged Farm, although peculiar, is reliable when it comes to four legged creatures,' he reassures her. 'And she's promised to look in on her every half hour while we're out and come and let us know if there are signs.'

'But she's only used to expectant donkeys, not expectant pigs who've been stuck panicking in pig flaps.'

He is touched by the earnest worry shining from her cat green eyes, and tries to reassure her again. 'I expect the procedure is much the same with pigs as it is with donkeys.'

'I'll go out and see if she's bearing down and braying then,' she responds, giggling anxiously as she goes out.

He's read everything there is to read about farrowing and wants to be in the heat of the labour ward with Hermione as much as his tenderhearted wife, but he's sure the pig's not ready yet. He's kept a keen look-out for the signs.

He scrutinises himself in the mirror. Tall, broad shouldered, flat stomach, smart charcoal grey suit, tie of vivid blue that he suddenly notices exactly matches his eyes. He smiles at himself, reassured that he wouldn't let her down. He hears the hoot of the taxi she has ordered outside.

They sit at the long table reserved for the staff. He has greeted Sylvie Shepherd, Elizabeth Blessing, Brenda Wilson and their various partners. Norah Harker-Balls faces him, minus her husband whom, she has explained, is too fraightfully busy to attend a school hop. She is dressed in floating purple chiffon which looks quite hideous. Freda sits biting her nails beside him. He knows she is terrified that a teacher or a parent will let the cat out of the bag about the new school and Operation Salvation that they've all been planning in minutest detail.

The four piece band starts up a quickstep and Sidney Slocumb, bedecked with his mayoral chain, sidles up to Freda and asks her to dance. Bernard notes the look of thunder on Norah's face as they pass her by to get onto the floor. He knows that the hoity-toity Head Mistress had invited the mayor 'to impress the parents', despite the embarrassment of their past sordid affair. He'd learnt from Freda, that Cynthia had agreed to accompany her husband provided they didn't sit anywhere near his erstwhile 'bit on the side.' So they were at a table at the far end.

Norah Harker-Balls casts an expectant simpering smile in Bernard's direction, but he ducks the obligation to dance with her and hurries over to Cynthia. He likes this little lady with the buck teeth and twinkly brown eyes. As they glide round with ease, he wonders why she ever tied the knot with the bumptious clot. He sees the bumptious clot twirling Freda round, his domed pate bare of its long strands of grey hair that drift absurdly in his wake. The music finishes with a trumpet screech and he ushers Cynthia back to her seat, then hurries across to

Freda abandoned by her poxy partner at the side of the dance floor.

She looks flushed. She whispers that Sidney has found out about Robert Bambridge's application to change The Bungalow to a school. He has put two and two together and is threatening to tell Norah about the intention to hijack her pupils, unless they give up the idea. Her eyes flash like brittle emeralds. 'I said no of course,' she said, 'but what if he does tell Norah and then permission to convert to a school isn't granted?' He puts his arm round her waist to guide her back and feels that she is shaking.

They take their seats and the band starts a romantic waltz. Sidney Slocumb appears at their table again but, this time, holds out his podgy hands to Norah. Her eyes light up like clear light bulbs and she lumbers up to her feet, her lips parting in a shocking pink smile of gratitude. The bun on the back of her head wobbles joyously as the arm of the mayor cups round her waist. Bernard strains his ears to hear what they are saying as they glide off.

'Oh Sidders,' she gushes, 'I've been wanting contact with you ever since ...'

But they twirl into the jostle of dancers and he catches no more. He watches intently, sees Norah talking, notices Sidney's excited expression gradually darken to miserable gloom. Every time he glimpses them through the melee it is her mouth that is moving, never the mayor's. Freda takes his hand and grips it so tightly it hurts. He knows that this apparently innocent waltz is the most crucial dance ever to be stepped out in Wood Hill. The future of the village children depended on Sidney Slocumb not blowing the gaff.

The music finishes and dancers chatter and clatter their way back to their tables. He studies Norah's face as she approaches alone. There is no sign of shock or fury in her transparent eyes, no frown on her perspiring forehead. She casts him a jubilant smile as she sits down, as if to say: see, someone wanted to dance with me. It was quite obvious she didn't yet know of the plans for the rival school. He wonders why Sidney held back from his threat.

'How Deep is the Ocean' starts up and quickly he grabs Freda's hand before anyone else can. As he leads her out he sees the mayor heading towards the bar. He's noticed that

Sidney's already knocked back several whiskeys between dances. He wonders how much he can hold. Freda nestles in to his shoulder as they glide and swirl. He catches the admiring looks and hears snippets of conversation as they pass by: She saved the child in the summer ... her portrait of the mayor is incredibly good ... they didn't have teachers like that when I was at school. He doesn't hear one whisper of The Bungalow or the community school, but he feels the tension in the air, a suppressed excitement that is just waiting to explode. They finish with a twirl then regain their seats under Norah H-B's watchful eye.

The guitarist announces that the next dance will be rock and roll, and a plump woman in a short slinky red dress walks out and takes up the mike. Her rich voice begins to belt out the words of Rock Around the Clock. Sidney totters over to their table, a glass still clutched in his hand. He bangs it down then takes Freda's elbow, forcing her to her feet. 'Mishus Field. Freda. 'Appen you'd like the *h*on -ner of jiving wi' the mayor and listening to what he has to say.'

Ignoring her protests, he pulls her onto the floor. Cynthia slips into the empty seat beside him and holds him back. 'Leave the silly sod,' she instructs. 'Freda can cope and if he's dancing with her he's out of harm's way.' Her eyes slide meaningfully to the glowering face opposite.

He watches his wife being shoved around in circles by the sweating ponce. It aggravates him and he fervently wishes the stupid clot would drop down dead. No sooner has the fervent wish passed through his head than Sidney's feet shoot up and he crashes down backwards onto the hard parquet floor. The rotund little man doesn't move. His eyes are shut. And he looks remarkably dead.

Bernard, galvanised into action by the horror that the body lying prone on the floor is his doing, pushes his way through the gathering crowd and out of the hall. He flies along the passage-way to the office, where he dials Nine Nine Nine.

What a night! At last they are back home and the events of the evening are overtaken by concern for their girl. They race round the back of the garage, across the yard and up the ramp and through the swing door. There she lies, snoring peacefully in the heat of her room, her babies still securely locked away inside her. They smile broad grins of relief at each other and tiptoe out into the cold dark night.

'That was a dreadful fall Sidney had,' Freda remarks as, hand in hand, they hurry back to the cottage.

And, though he is sure that the timing of his wicked death wish was just coincidental with the event, he is thankful that the darkness of the starless night hides the guilt that must show on his face.

Up in the bedroom, as they undress, she affirms how terrified she'd been that Sidney would really divulge The Bungalow plans to Norah. 'She would have ripped me to shreds with her tongue and sacked me on the spot if he had,' she says, adding, 'It was lucky he had the fall because, as we jived, he had panted that he was definitely going to tell Norah as soon as we stopped, unless I promised to back off and leave The Bungalow to Boggins and his terrible blocks of flats.'

Bernard keeps his anxious thoughts to himself as he slips into bed. But, sleep doesn't come for hours, and then only fitfully, through the illogical fear that he might really have been responsible for the scything down of the mayor.

The phone rings. Bernard fumbles for it, half asleep. He sees the time is eight o'clock. Could it be news of the mayor? He wants it to be, and yet he dreads it too. 'Yes?' he whispers, afraid.

'It's bad news,' the sad voice of Cynthia whispers back.

Terror stabs shooting pains into his brain. *Oh God, You Idiot!* he silently blasphemes. *Couldn't You tell it wasn't a serious wish. Can't You recognise a joke?* 'What is the bad news?' he weakly asks.

'The bad news is that the silly bugger's alive and well!' Cynthia whoops. 'He's just got a headache that's all. Can I speak to Freda.'

Mutely he hands the phone over. *Thank you God* he thinks meekly, hoping He hasn't stored his sacrilegious outburst on His celestial CD ROM with its infinite megabyte memory.

He hears Freda say 'You think he remained unconscious because of the drink.' Then, 'I didn't think he could have told her.'

When she eventually gets off the phone she tells him that Cynthia said Sidney had fully intended to tell Norah during their first dance, but she hadn't stopped talking and had been totally overbearing, so he postponed it. Now he'd agreed to keep the knowledge to himself, saying she'd find out soon enough if the school conversion were approved by the Council Planning Committee.

As they watch TV in front of the blazing log fire they sip wine. 'Here's to your success tomorrow at the Council meeting,' he says, raising his glass. And, as she responds, he sees the excitement and fear in her eyes. 'You'll be all right,' he assures her, finding out for the first time how difficult it is to hold the stem of a glass with crossed fingers.

Thirty-two

I crouched beside my baby and stroked her trotter. She lay over on one side, her enormous belly spilling out over the fresh bedding. A drop of white milk oozed from a swollen teat. She gave a deep sigh and stared at me with a look that clearly said: *Don't leave me. I'm afraid. There are things wiggling about inside me and I don't know what I should do. I am so heavy that when I stand my legs wobble. I have lost my skittish joy for life and want to stay here in my powder blue bedroom with you. Please do not leave me.*

If Percy's sperm had hit the bulls eye on the virgin entry, it was possible she could go into labour today. Three months, three weeks and three days. The exact time it takes to grow a piglet from scratch.

Bernard came in, set up a deck chair beside her and sat down for his pig watch, the Farrowing Handbook clutched in his hands. Desperately I wanted to stay with them, but there were some things even bigger than this. And maybe the Town Hall meeting wouldn't take too long. I murmured my apologies to Hermione and kissed Bernard goodbye.

'Good luck,' he called after me.

'And good luck to you too,' I called back, hurrying out to Robert Bambridge who waited in his Bentley outside.

We sat on chairs set out in a semicircle for visitors at the rear of the oak-panelled room. Several yards in front of us, Planning Committee councillors were positioned each side of a long table, seven seated each side. The Chairman at its head faced our way. Fifteen in all. Fifteen responsible men and women who held the fate of present and future generations of Wood Hill children in their hands.

Six other proposals had to be discussed and voted upon before the two Bungalow applications, the Squeezamin Property scheduled immediately before ours. In the background of my innards my defunct nervous bowel syndrome cranked into life again.

Sidney Slocumb was sitting at the other end of our curved row. I tried to catch his eye but he refused to look my way. He was up to no good, I was sure. But what could he do here now? Large notices dotted around stated that observers would be ejected if they interfered in any way. It was clear there were no exceptions, even for mayors.

The table that the councillors sat round was a piece of furniture in keeping with the grandeur of the chamber: green leather top, expensively embossed with gold. These men and women were used to good taste and tradition, they weren't the kind of people to grant permission for ugly blocks of flats to ruin a lovely old village like Wood Hill. Then I remembered that they'd sanctioned the tasteless Boggins' Eldorado Close development and my confidence waned.

'Planning permission not granted,' the Chairman said tersely, turning down a plan for a granny flat extension with garage to house a hearse.

At last it was time for the The Bungalow conversions. I shivered and just held back from clutching at Robert's arm. The Chairman lifted a fat file off the diminishing pile. I snatched a glance at Sidney and intercepted a cunning look passing between him and a weedy looking man at the table. Two others whispered together then softly laughed. Suspicion stirred.

'Next we have ...' He coughed then stretched over to take up a decanter. He pulled out the stopper and leisurely poured water into his glass. He took a lingering sip, then, slowly replaced the top. *Get on with it. Get on with it!* my inner voice screamed.

'Next we have ... the application sent in by Mr William Boggins, proprietor of the Squeezamin Property Development Company. He requests permission to demolish The Bungalow in Bramble Lane, Wood Hill, and erect two three-storey blocks of flats on the plot. May I remind you that there is another application to follow for change of use to a school. If this Squeezamin application is passed, then the school project must be rejected. You have all had the opportunity of studying them both. They may both be rejected. However, if one application succeeds, the other is entitled to appeal. May we hear the Planning Officer's report.'

Robert Bambridge shot forward in his seat. I sat stiff-backed, afraid to move, afraid to breathe, almost afraid to listen.

Thirty-three
Intrusion 8

Stop blathering. Get on with voting! Sidney listens as the fool of a Planning Officer grinds out his report. What a pedantic twit! 'Ee couldn't give a toss about builders needing work or the making of brass. Nay, aesthetics and the environment was all that bothered him. The dopey bugger.

He remembers Cynthia's angry words just before he left: Do the right thing for once in your life you bastard. We can live without such corrupt money, and the children need that new school more than you need a new car. He hadn't mentioned a word, but she seemed to smell out his fiddles like a sniffer dog seeking out drugs.

He steals a look at Freda and the rich toff, Bambridge. That lucky sod can afford to chuck his brass around. Anyone could be magnanimous if their millionaire parents had, with kindly consideration, pegged out at an early age, like his had. It was so bloody easy for the likes of him to go straight. But, when this scam was over, he too would have made his pile. He would retire and give generously to buskers in Great Piddlehurst precinct and even buy The Big Issue from nose-ringed young women and men. A jab of excitement hits his body like a harpoon piercing a whale.

The droning voice of the Planning Officer halts at last. Now get on to the show of hands Sidney mutely urges. This was the biggest and the last trick. In two days his year would be up and there'd be a new mayor and he would quietly fade away from Town Hall life into the sunset.

The Chairman was announcing that there was one letter and one petition objecting to the proposal to demolish The Bungalow and erect flats: The petition was signed by thirty villagers. It stated that they objected to the charm of Wood Hill being spoiled by such an eyesore. The letter was from The Bungalow's closest neighbour, Mr Sharpe: *A block of flats would be a blot on the landscape*, it succinctly said!

A woman councillor, whom Sidney has never liked, jumps to her feet. She slaps her hands on the table and leans forward, writhing from side to side like a menacing snake. She hisses that the development would be a di-sssaster and that she would be voting NO. Sit down you blewdy windbag, Sidney rails.

At last she coils back down and the Chairman announces that it is time for a show of hands. Sidney grins, sure in the knowledge that Bill Boggins' proposal is about to be passed, for seven of the fourteen councillors were in the palm of his greasy hand. And, even if all the remaining seven were against it, the Chairman would make the final decision.

'Hands up all those in favour of the Squeezamin Development Company's application.'

Seven hands shoot up.

'Hands up those against.'

'Seven other hands punch the air.'

'Seven for, seven against, therefore, according to the rules, I have the casting vote.'

Sidney knows the Chairman will look for confirmation from him that the thousand quid he'd demanded on the phone earlier would be forthcoming from Bill Boggins. The spuriously thoughtful eyes start to wander over the semicircle of observers, starting the opposite end.

Greedy excitement grips Sidney. When those crafty eyes meet his, he will nod, and then his wily mate will know that his brass is assured. And with that nod, Sidney knows that his own financial future will be assured too, for the deal is a double whammy. If the flats get passed, he not only gets loadsa brass from his mate Bill, but also even more from bent contractors. He waits impatiently for the slyly meandering eyes to reach him.

The picture of Norah Harker-Balls scaring a tiny child so much that wee trickled down his spindly legs flashes into his mind. Cynthia's saintly words replay themselves in his head: *Do the right thing for once in your life you bastard. We can live without such corrupt money ...*

He wavers. Turn this down, and the school proposal stands an excellent chance. But, that's nowt to do with thee lad, he berates himself.

Norah Harker-Ball's voice seeps into his conscience: DISCIPLINE? SURE, THAT'S EASY, THE LITTLE THICKOES ARE WIDDLE-SCARED IF I SO MUCH AS LOOK AT THEM.

Poxy women. How could saintly Cyn and nasty Norah shake his intention so.

The Chairman's eyes divert from the centre of the row, flick high to the ornate cornice, but, as Sidney knows they will, quickly zoom back down to skim along the line of spectators and rest on him.

Nod and be damned he tells himself. He imagines the disgust in Cynthia's honest brown eyes. Her honest shit brown eyes. Bugger 'er sanctimonious crappy goodness.

The Chairman's gimlet eyes bore into his and, with heavy regret, Sidney slowly shakes his head.

Surprise flares, then the baffled orbs snap back to the fourteen members waiting expectantly round the table. Sidney wants to catch his eye again. He wants to shout out it was a mistake. But it is too late. The car of his dreams silently glides out of his life for ever.

'I vote against William Boggins' application,' the Chairman raps, slamming the file shut and casting it away. 'The next submission relates to the same property.' He lifts the next bulky file up, dragging out a wadge of plans and notes. 'Robert Bambridge has applied for change of use of The Bungalow from private dwelling to community school.' His voice is strangulated and he suddenly rubs his fists into his eyes, like a small child trying not to cry.

Sidney curses his moment of weakness. He sees Bambridge and Freda whispering together. He sees the hope shining on her lovely face, polished with the duster of his wife's purity.

The Planning Officer begins to read his report.

'You! You acted on your conscience,' Cynthia exclaims. He lets his shoulders droop and she throws her arms around him.

'No. I acted on your conscience,' he replies.

'I'm beginning to like you,' she unexpectedly proclaims, kissing the top of his head.

And then the idea came to him. It was as if her lips had fertilized his brain cells, as a gentle bee brushing against a flower. It's a good job she can't see inside me 'ead, he smirks as the picture of the FOR SALE sign outside the vacant Harker-Balls School billows into his mind.

Thirty-four

'I can't take another night out there on pig duty,' Bernard said, yawning sleepily, 'so I'm going out to buy one of those baby listening devices to rig up between the mobile home and our bedroom.'

When he was gone, I steeled myself to ring Bill Boggins.

'Changed yer mind abaht selling off yer gardin?' he asked eagerly when I announced who I was.

'No.' Then, trying to sound nonchalant, I asked, 'Do you intend to appeal against last night's decision?' I held my breath. If he did, the process could take months.

'Wiv my infloonce darlin'' he replied, 'I'd hoped ta git the preservation order on that ugly great tree lifted, but I've just this minute 'eard that the Green ponces wouldn't play ball and, wiv all them whackin' great roots an' branches, there ain't enough room fer two blocks, so it's all yours sweet'eart.'

It was ours. The Bungalow was ours now, for sure. He had just said so. Quickly, I said goodbye, then skipped outside punching the freezing air. 'We've won. We've won!' I whooped.

I headed into the compound, just in time to see my naked shivering girl barging back through the swing door into the mobile home. On the concrete by the gully fresh droppings steamed. Nowadays, that was all she ever dragged herself out for. I hurried in after her in time to see her flop down on her bed.

The recurring dream image of myself, young and heavy with child, came and went in a heart beat, leaving no residual pain. I knelt beside my porky girl. Her long white lashes blinked at me and her eyes held a baleful glare. 'We've done it,' I told her. 'Boggins isn't going to appeal. The Bungalow is as good as ours.'

She rolled her eyes like Bernard when he couldn't give a damn, but I gabbled on, the news spilling out in a torrent of joy. 'If Robert can get everything signed, sealed and paid for by the time the nativity play starts tomorrow, we can go ahead with the mass walk-out and humiliation of Norah Harker-Balls.'

Her gaze narrowed and the silence was only broken by her irritable sigh.

'Maybe it's a pregnant pause!' sniggered Bernard who'd quietly crept up behind me.

As I recounted the fantastic news, Hermione emitted streams of grunts like a small motor bike that wouldn't quite start.

'She's really brassed off with the subject,' Bernard laughed, eyeing the honking pig fondly as he manoeuvred me out to the ramp. 'What did Robert say when you told him Boggins wasn't going to appeal?'

I stopped dead. 'I haven't told him yet!' I exclaimed, appalled.

'You might find he's slightly more interested than the pig,' he shouted as I dashed off to get to the phone.

'The play starts at two thirty so we must have the keys of The Bungalow by then,' I reeled off to Robert. 'If the innkeeper wears a green turban, the audience knows that Operation Salvation is on. If he wears red, they'll know it's off and the full-length nativity will be performed.'

'It should be all systems go,' he said cautiously. 'My solicitor, Cecil Rampant, of Droop, Droop and Rampant, and Gertrude Smith's solicitor, Felix Gray, have drawn up the contracts ready to exchange and complete at the same time. All I have to do is instruct my bank in Jersey to transfer the funds. But, remember, it's not ours for sure until the purchase is legally finalised.'

'Oh, I won't count my piglets till they're hatched,' I agreed, knowing full well that I had already done so. Nothing could go wrong now. Mr Mole would hand over the keys and our victorious army would march down Bramble Lane to our new quarters leaving Norah Harker-Balls bewildered and alone.

As I replaced the receiver mother and father arrived for their Christmas sojourn. I told them of tomorrow's plan. 'Less than twenty-four hours to go!' I burbled, heady with excitement and success.

I made a pot of tea and we sat down. Mother's eyes sparkled. 'It's more interesting out in the country than one would at first think,' she murmured. 'I was even looking forw....'

The phone shrilled. It was Robert. 'I thought you should know that the Jersey blighters won't accept my instruction to transfer the money at such short notice, by phone or fax. They needed written notice. But don't worry, it should be all right.'

'*Should* be!'

'The Bank Manager of my local branch must formally identify me. Then the Jersey pedants will deign to transmit the funds by telegraphic transfer direct to Droop, Droop and Rampant's office.'

Warning bells clanged in my head. Not now. Not after we'd gone through so much. All our plans couldn't be scuppered now.

'I'm off to Great Piddlehurst straight away. The Bank Manager knows me of course, but I have to go in so he can see I'm not an impostor.' He gave a brittle laugh. 'I'll ring you as soon as I get back home.'

Two long hours later he rang back. 'The Manager has sent a fax to Jersey formally identifying me,' he said cheerfully, 'so the transfer of money will go through.'

I lay in bed listening to the snuffles of Bernard's cold coming from the pillow one side, and the spasmodic grunts of Hermione coming through the loudspeaker on the other. I put my arm over Bernie.

'Nod tonighd thank you,' he said.

Wednesday, the twentieth of December. End of term. The end of Norah Harker-Ball's cruel reign too. There was nothing now that could stop us. Or so I thought.

The door bell screamed its early warning. Robert barged in. Grim-faced, he told me that his Jersey bank was refusing to transfer the money until four o'clock. 'They're sticking rigidly to the rule that they must have twenty-four hours notice,' he fumed.

'But that's too late,' I wailed. 'Can't we have the keys before then?'

'I know. I know. I've talked to Felix Gray, but he says the only way he'll authorise the handing over of keys before the sale is legally complete, is if Dora Quicknicky gives her consent.' Robert paced the floor. His eyes blazed. '*I've* had keys handed over a week before a deal like this has gone through. I mean you're not exactly going to wreck the property you're intending to buy are you!'

'But surely Dora Quicknicky will give her permission if she knows how urgent it is?' Even as I spoke I wondered if a woman who didn't even bother to attend her benefactor's funeral would take notice of our plea.

'Apparently she's never divulged her home number,' Robert said, 'just her office telephone and fax in Manhattan, but Gray assures me she's always at her desk by nine.'

'So ring her now from here,' I urged, seeing by my watch that it was already five past.

'You've forgotten the time difference. They're five hours behind. Felix Gray has already sent a fax, look here's a copy.' He thrust a sheet of paper at me. 'Even if she gets in promptly, she still won't read it until two o'clock our time.'

'But that's cutting it so fine. We have to known before the performance starts at two thirty' I thought of the disappointment of the parents who'd planned the operation and trained their children with such care. It hadn't been spelled out to the youngsters what it was all about, but they instinctively knew that if they played their part it would lead to something good. Toby Mole, the innkeeper, was the only child fully informed.

'Poppy and I have worked out a plan,' Robert said. 'She'll wait in Mole's Estate Agent's Office in Orlford and I'll stay in Felix Gray's office in Great Piddlehurst where, hopefully, the reply fax will come through from New York. If Quicknicky gives her authority to hand over the keys, I'll ring Mole and he'll give them to Poppy who will speed over to you at the school. Then Gray and I will go across the road to my solicitors, Droop Droop and Rampant, to be ready to exchange contracts and complete the sale when the money comes through at four.'

My heart sank. It was all so complicated.

'You must stand in full view at the side of the stage so Poppy can see you as soon as she enters the hall. She'll leave Mole's Office at two twenty, even if she hasn't heard from me, that way she'll just get to you before the stage curtains are drawn back. If she hasn't heard, or if the answer's no, she'll give you the thumbs down. But, if Quicknicky has faxed her permission, she'll be dangling the keys.'

I leant weakly against the wall. 'But it's leaving it so late.'

'It's the best we can do,' he snapped, turning for the front door. 'But, however it goes, remember, The Bungalow is ours.

It's just that you'll all have to forego the pleasure of your mass walk-out.'

I felt ashamed. He'd been so kind and generous and I wasn't satisfied because the timing was a little wrong. But deep inside I knew that the grand exit did matter. It was psychological: a spiritual cleansing of the suffering the children and the rest of us had endured. The parents, the pupils and the staff all needed to see the look on her face. We needed to see her comeuppance. We needed our triumphal revenge.

At the front gate he turned and waved and I called my thanks. Now it was down to an unknown woman in a far-off land. Would she co-operate and allow us into her inheritance early? Why should she? She couldn't possibly understand what was at stake. I read the copy of the fax still held in my hand:-

Your permission is urgently sought by Robert Bambridge to authorise the Estate Agent, Mr E Mole, to hand over the keys of The Bungalow to allow access two hours before the sale has been completed. It would mean a great deal to the children of Wood Hill and their parents. There is no foreseeable danger that the sale will not go through. I should be grateful if you would fax your reply to me immediately. Felix Gray.

Mother rushed in from the back garden. 'I checked on the pig while you and Bambridge were talking and she's kicking up her straw and honking non-stop,' she said, face flushed.

Oh God, don't let her start the production just now. I had to go to school soon to help organise an equally important one. And I needed to be present at both performances. I ran out to the powder blue delivery room to see what my girl was up to.

Hermione lay mute and motionless on one side, but her belly was alive with tiny movements thrusting out from inside. As mother puffed up behind me, our mother-to-be darted her a malevolent look then heaved herself up to her feet. Her great bulk teetered for a moment on fragile trotters, then her legs buckled and she clumped back down on her other side. The long back that now faced us juddered as she breathed a long impatient sigh.

'When I came in before, as soon as I got close to her she set up a racket and wouldn't stop,' mother complained. 'Now she's deliberately turned away from me. She's never liked me.'

'It's not personal, she's just in a funny mood,' I ventured.

Mother's offended expression changed to annoyance. 'Pigs can get away with funny moods,' she grumbled, 'I couldn't when I was expecting you.'

Do the memories of such crucial life events ever fade from your mind? I wondered. If I had had a baby would I talk about the pregnancy fifty years hence. I guessed that maybe I would. Why should I be any different from any other mum.

As I drove along the lane to school, I speculated as to whether a wondrous crucial event that no-one would ever forget was about to take place this afternoon in the hall. Or whether the excitement that had charged the Wood Hill air was about to evaporate in an atmosphere of dull legal conveyancing, too late for triumphal revenge. Would it be the red turban on Toby Mole's head, or the longed for green one?

Thirty-five

Quaking inside with excited hope and dreadful fear, I stood, as planned, at the side of the stage, eyes fixed on the far left corner of the hall where everyone entered. Please come soon Poppy. Please bring us the keys so we can march to our place of safety down the lane.

Norah Harker-Balls was greeting parents as they entered the back of the hall. Her large smooth forehead shone like a polished pebble. Her small white teeth glinted in her saccharine smile. Her hair, black save for the central slash of stark white, was scraped back into the usual unflattering bun. Dangly ruby earrings raked the air with crimson spikes.

'Fraightfully pleased you could come,' she gushed to someone and my heart missed a beat for I saw it was Mrs Mole she addressed. Would the estate agent's wife, the innkeeper's mother, the woman with the nervous disposition, the woman who had sussed our Head out, be able to calmly respond? The whites of her flicking eyes flashed out a semaphore call for help in my direction, and, even from where I stood, I could hear the squeak of the terrified mouse. But our dear Head, as ever insensitive to signs of distress, was already sailing on, podgy hand extended to Mrs Trugshawe.

'Fraightfully pleased to see you,' she repeated and Mrs Trugshawe managed to contort her mouth into an almost convincing smile.

The atmosphere building up in the hall was eerie, like the stillness before a storm. I willed the audience to chatter as normal, but knew each person was scared to speak for fear of being the one to give the game away. Even my mother was sitting next to father in silence, her lips unnaturally still. Her eyes sparkled and her forefinger and thumb pulled at her nose as if determined to elongate it. Clearly this drama beat even the heady excitement of Tooting high life.

I studied my father's jug ears, remembering the flare up of fiery red last year: the portent of disaster that came true. But they jutted out into the atmosphere, pale pink and benign. Poppy *would* come in time. I hugged myself, trying to calm my shivering body.

I tried to picture her speeding to the school in her smart red sports car, the keys lying securely in her lap. Come on Poppy, I urged her, it's getting horrendously late. My eyes scoured the in-coming faces. I could hear faint shuffles of feet, the murmur of polite replies to Norah's greetings, an occasional cough, the clearing of a throat, once a truncated giggle, but no hubbub of conversation. It was unreal.

The hall was almost full now, each person sitting stiffly to attention, following the last minute instruction not to look round. Eyes swivelled in immobile heads as if an outbreak of stiff necks had hit the district. Someone explosively sneezed and it was like witnessing the sudden tremor of an earthquake as, in unison, the whole assembly jumped. I dreaded that even Norah would pick up the charged emotions building up in this hall.

My gaze didn't waver from the entrance. Please Poppy come. Don't spoil it. I willed her to appear. But only a tardy father darted in and then there was no-one else. Everybody was now in place. The scene was set. The full length nativity performance would soon begin. We were robbed of the triumphal exit we had prepared for. My heart ached with disappointment and disbelief.

Beside me, but out of sight of the audience behind the curtain, stood Toby Mole clutching two strips of material in his hands. Which one was I to bind around his head? The red or the green? The stop or the go? The cruel verdict that there was to be no public humiliation of Harker-Balls, or the glorious revenge of the oppressed?

Suddenly, a dark figure sidled in at the back. It must be Poppy. We were saved. But, further in, I recognised it was Cynthia. I watched her ease her way along the back row to a free seat, remembering that last year she'd sat in the front row with Sidney, the then newly elected mayor.

Elizabeth Blessing gave me a despairing look from the floor and began pulling the curtains across the side windows, shutting out the cold winter light. It was twenty-seven minutes past two.

Twenty-seven minutes past nine in the morning in New York. Hadn't Felix Gray stressed the urgency to Dora Quicknicky? Was she being bloody-minded or could she have taken the day off work? Whatever it was, it was too late. We'd been cheated.

Norah Harker-Balls minced down the aisle and took her place in the centre of the front row. She looked satisfied, successful. A woman completely in control. Maybe it would be a relief to abandon the walk-out. Maybe she hadn't been that bad. She looked up expectantly at the stage, caught my eye and jabbed at her watch, a thunderous frown convoluting her brow. Mr Jones, sitting beside her, turned his face to hers, and, with practised ease, her forehead sprang back to flatness and her mouth leapt into a smile.

With heavy heart I took the red cloth from Toby's hands, coiled it round his head and secured it with a brooch. Thirty seconds to go. I peered out into the dim hall and suddenly there she was. No mistaking the silhouette as she strode in, but she stopped, hung back, lost in the darkness.

I strained my eyes. Did she hold the keys? I couldn't see. Come on. Come *on*! Hold up your hand. The pale disc of her face looked my way. Her arm raised. My blood ran cold. Her thumb was pointing downward. She stepped forward into a chink of light and waggled her hand at me. And then I saw that it wasn't a thumb but shiny silvery keys. She waggled them again and the precious metal glinted with shimmering guiding light.

'We're on our way!' I whispered to Toby.

'Oh miss!' was all he replied.

Quickly I unwound the red turban and changed it for the green.

The curtains drew back to display the usual scenery, and Mary and Joseph plodding their weary way across the stage. This year, though, there was no real-live donkey to act up and ruin the performance. Norah Harker-Ball's unsuspecting face gazed up, smiling proudly. Little did she suspect what was to come. But should we do it? Was it too cruel? Don't weaken. You know it is right, I told myself, unsure and afraid.

Joseph knocked at the imaginary door of the Inn and Toby appeared. A gust of whispers blew through the hall as the colour of his headdress was seen. Norah Harker-Balls' head jerked round. She issued a loud 'SHHH' then folded her arms across her chest and turned her attention back to the stage.

This year, there was no doubt that rebel Toby would co-operate, for this drama would release him from the person he loathed and feared most in the world.

'Why don't you come in,' he beamed, as rehearsed, and Mary and Joseph followed him into the Bethlehem Inn. Other children appeared on stage. None of them spoke. All that could be heard was the clumping of their feet on the wooden boards. More joined them. The trickle became a stream. They walked in silent procession across the stage, through the imaginary doorway and out of view. Wise men, shepherds, angels, backstage helpers, every single one of the seventy-two pupils in the Harker-Balls' School was exiting with glowing faces and eager feet. A tiny angel rushed back and bent to pick up the tinsel that had fallen from her golden hair. She stood facing the audience, twisting her skirt up, knock-kneed, unsure.

'WHAT'S GOING ON?' Norah shrieked out, and the poor child squealed with fright then fled. 'HALT. TELL ME WHAT IS HAPPENING?' Norah boomed at the queue of her pupils traversing the stage.

Not one child answered, but their footsteps quickened as they made their dignified escape. I watched the children with pride. These eager youngsters were to be the rich kernel of our brand new school. As the last child disappeared, the whole audience rose and, with a shuffle of feet and a scraping of chairs, person by person, row by row, they filed up onto the stage and across to the Bethlehem Inn where they disappeared through the imaginary doorway that led to their children's salvation. Elizabeth Blessing stood by my side and the two of us exchanged nods and smiles with the people as they passed us.

'WILL SOMEBODY TELL ME WHAT IS HAPPENING!' bawled Mrs Harker-Balls, wild eyed, alone.

But the tribe kept walking. They were on their way to the promised land. No-one spoke. My mother came up the steps and winked at me as she passed. Father paused and I saw incredulity and admiration in his gaze. 'Well done Freda,' he whispered and my heart rose. His respect was the confirmation I needed to be absolutely sure that I had truly truly changed.

I knew that Sylvie Shepherd and Brenda Wilson were helping the children don outdoor clothes and that parents were leading the long file of children safely along the lane. Slowly I walked down the steps to Norah where she stood as if super-glued to the spot, hands clenched into dumpling fists.

'WHAT IS THE MEANING OF THIS MRS FIELD,' she shrieked, 'IS THIS SOME KIND OF A JOKE!'

I took a deep breath. 'You have abused your power Head Mistress,' I hissed. 'You have no right to be in charge of little children.' I looked deep into her transparent eyes and saw the fear. Don't feel sorry for her, don't give in. Remember all the unforgivable things she has said and done.

'YOU IDIOT!' she exploded, 'WHAT DO YOU MEAN I HAVE NO RIGHT. THIS IS MY SCHOOL. WHATEVER IS HAPPENING NOW, THEY WILL ALL BE BACK NEXT TERM. THERE ISN'T ANOTHER PRIVATE SCHOOL FOR MILES AND THE STATE ONES ARE ALL FULL.'

'Do you want to bet they'll be back,' I retorted, holding her outraged gaze.

'YOU USED TO BE SUCH A WIMP. I ALMOST LIKED YOU. BUT LOOK AT YOU NOW. YOU THINK YOU'RE SO BIG, STRUTTING AROUND SHOUTING YOUR MOUTH OFF. WHAT HAPPENED?'

'I got wise Norah and if you were wise you'd keep away from children. You damage their minds.'

'HOW DARE YOU' she screamed. She lifted her fists like a boxer about to spar.

'If we were men we might fight,' I said trying to resist the temptation to sock her one. 'But, as we are not, it's just plain Goodbye.'

As I ran out to follow the others, I marvelled at what I had said. One year ago I hardly dared speak to the terrifying woman. Now I'd unflinchingly said my piece and was on my way to our new school.

Slocumb's Mini was parked outside The Bungalow and, as I drew level, Sidney hauled himself out.

'Congratulations Freda,' he said, 'I want you to know that I did the right thing and helped you get that.' He jerked his head at The Bungalow, then looked sadly at his car. 'Cyn said I were to park this 'ere because she might need it later,' he added, patting the short bonnet.

I left him locking the car doors and briefly wondered why Cynthia would need it. For shopping I supposed. But all such thoughts vanished from my head as I stepped into the garden. I wanted to skip and dance and whoop like a kid as I went down the path towards our haven. We'd done it. We'd really done it. Or so I thought.

Half way, I stopped to read the shiny new plaque roughly tacked to the thick trunk of the oak tree: *THE ACORN SCHOOL where each child will be gently nurtured to grow into a strong oak tree.*

At the partly open front door I halted, expecting to hear a hubbub of noisy excitement from inside, but there was silence. Mystified, I pushed the door open and walked straight into the sound of muffled laughter and a hallway full of people jostling for a view.

'Three cheers for Freda Field,' Mrs Trugshaw shouted, 'Hip hip ...' and a roar came back, 'HOORAY.' The cheers rang out twice more and I hid my face to cover my embarrassment and pride.

When the final hooray had died away, I dropped my hands. Mothers and fathers were crowding up to me, their voices rising in thanks. I spied Elizabeth Blessing in the doorway of Gertrude's erstwhile bedroom, flacking her praying hands obviously jubilant that God had at last delivered the goods.

Bright eyed children began darting from doorway to doorway, calling their parents to see the bare faded rooms that hopefully, by next term, would be proper classrooms. I pushed my way further in. My back was patted and words of praise boosted my rocketing ego into the stratosphere. I snivelled uncontrollably with laughter and tears. This was truly the proudest day of my entire life.

Then mother's penetrating voice piped up from the kitchen. 'Hoo-bloody-ray for the woman who is setting me up to be great-grandmother to a litter of piddling pigs!'

Shrieks and squeals of laughter floated like bubbles in the air.

'HALT!' a voice called out behind me. Then, 'STOP!' the same voice cried. 'THERE'S BEEN A MISTAKE. YOU'VE JUMPED THE GUN.'

And the fragile bubbles popped with the vibrations of the harsh voice.

A spectral man, all in black, stood tall and thin in the doorway. 'Where's Mrs Field?' he shouted, eyes darting wildly.

With leaden feet, I walked forward.

He grabbed hold of my arm and shook it. 'You shouldn't be here. Get everybody out.'

I pulled my arm free. 'What do you mean? Who are you?'

'Droop Senior, of Droop, Droop and Rampant, solicitors to the Bambridge family.'

'You received permission from Dora Quicknicky for the keys to be handed over early didn't you?' I asked, bewildered.

'Yes. Yes. Yes.' He screamed. 'But we jumped the gun. It was Rampant's fault, it always is. He's too old. He should retire. At least get his cataracts done.'

My heart seemed to stop. 'What do you mean, we've jumped the gun?' I whispered.

A child began to sob and others picked up the knowledge that something was terribly wrong and whimperings and sobbings revved up all around.

'Mrs Quicknicky faxed her permission to let you have the keys early because Rampant assured Felix Gray that the exchange of contracts and completion was assured.' His dry solicitor's words fell from thick wet lips.

'Well he was right wasn't he. The completion was assured - must have already happened.' I checked my watch, it was twenty past four. 'The money was transferred at four and the exchange and completion must now have taken place.'

'No he was wrong. Rampant should have gone through the Deeds beforehand.' Droop gave a despairing sob. 'But he didn't. Or else he did and he missed it because he's as blind as a bat. Or else he *thought* he'd gone through them but hadn't because he's losing his mind. But whatever happened he missed it and it wasn't until the point of exchanging contracts that Mr Bambridge witnessed the Deeds and saw the restrictive covenant.'

The deathly hush that had descended scared me.

'What restrictive covenant?'

'Gertrude Smith's special covenant that she had added when she and her husband bought the newly-built bungalow in 1930.' His old voice was hitting highs and lows like a teenage boy on the turn. He dabbed at rheumy eyes. 'It means that this bungalow must be kept as a place of residence and is specifically, I say specifically, not allowed to be converted to a school. Therefore, the sale HAS NOT GONE THROUGH! Bambridge has returned home and is attempting to sort it out by taking outside legal advice, but, as I've told him, it's impossible to revoke such a covenant.'

The swell of chatter that suddenly erupted hurt my ears.

'Now our poor wee mites have no school at all,' a woman shouted.

What had I done? The foolish parents had trusted me. Now there was nowhere to go - except the unthinkable return to the establishment down the lane. The noise grew louder, then:-

'QUIET!' a familiar voice rang out.

I looked across the tops of heads in the sitting room. That was Cynthia. Then her small figure emerged from the throng and she came beside me.

'QUIET!' she commanded again, and the racket slowly died down. 'There is a chance that I can fix it,' she explained. She took hold of my arm. 'Just give Freda and me half an hour - maybe a bit more - organise yourself into carol singing groups, or go through the full nativity play. Whatever you do don't panic, keep the children calm. And remember, all is not lost.'

She began to manoeuvre me towards the open door through which Droop was already departing. I stared at her in amazement. It was as if I'd never seen her before. I'd never heard her raise her voice and I never thought she had it in her to take command like that. She grinned up at me as if savouring the surprise, then forcefully shoved me outside, tugging me along to the Mini at the kerbside where quickly she unlocked the doors.

'Get in,' she ordered, 'we're going back to nasty Norah.' She revved the engine into life and I sat rigid as a corpse as she scorched along the short stretch of lane to the Harker-Balls School. I closed my eyes as the familiar high brick wall appeared. The car veered into the driveway and came to a clattering halt outside the prison that, barely one hour before, we had escaped from.

'Come on,' she urged, leaping out. 'She may not have gone yet. We may just be in time.'

Norah Harker-Balls stared across at us with startled frogspawn eyes. 'How dare you show your face back here,' she croaked. Scattered around her were crumpled and torn sheets of paper. Suddenly she slapped her hands down on our shared desk and reared up like a vast Brunnhilde. 'You've ruined me,' she snarled.

'Sit down Mrs Harker-Balls,' Cynthia commanded. 'I think you may want to hear what I have to say.'

She dragged two small chairs over and sat on one. 'Why don't you join me in the negotiations Freda,' she said, patting the other one for me to sit on. I squatted down on the low chair and she delved into her capacious handbag searching for something.

'There is nothing you can negotiate with me,' sneered Norah. 'I suppose you've gone too far and now have to bring my pupils back. Well I knew it. There isn't another school for them to go to.' She glared at me. 'But you'll never get your job back. You'll never get a job anywhere, ever, with the report I'll write out on you.'

I averted my eyes from the hatred in her stare. What a tragic disaster. How could an idea that had seemed so right go so tragically wrong.

Cynthia had taken out a largish slim envelope and was holding it tightly as if it contained something of value that might be snatched away. 'Your husband,' she said, 'I understand he is related to royalty.'

Norah gave a supercilious smile. 'Yes, of course. He is a cousin three times removed from the Queen. He is fraightfully proud orv the connection.'

She was back to her upper class drawl.

'And he is a senior civil servant, working for an important cabinet minister I believe,' Cynthia purred, tapping at her prey with a soft paw.

'Certainly. He is awfully important. In fact people say the government could collapse without his guidance.'

'You wouldn't want him to see this then,' Cynthia stated, drawing out a photograph with unfurled needle claws.

I craned my neck but couldn't see from the height of my child-sized chair. I looked up at Norah. Her face was contorting like a grotesque Spitting Image latex mask. Her hands flew up to flaming cheeks. They pulled downwards, hideously distorting her nose and eyes. Then she clutched at her fleshy throat and gave a ghostly groan.

I stared, mesmerised by the dramatic performance that even an opera Diva would find difficult to surpass.

She let go her throat and made a grab at the photo, but Cynthia was too quick for her.

'This is blackmail!' Brunnhilde screamed.

And dear Cynthia serenely smiled as she gave an affirmative nod. 'It sure is Mrs Harker-Balls,' she confirmed, turning to me, thrusting the photo under my nose. 'What do you think MR Harker-related-to-the-queen-Balls would think of that then Freda?' she asked.

I took the glossy picture quite unprepared for what I was about to see. I stared, bug-eyed, in disbelief. It couldn't be! I'd never been so shocked in all my life. Could the squiffy trollop really be the hoity toity sanctimonious Headmistress of the Harker-Balls Private School? She was sitting on the edge of a bed, fat knees spread apart, a great breast lolling out of her open blouse. Beside her sat Sidney, his arm draped round her shoulders, his hand resting on the mammoth tit.

'What do you want?' Norah moaned, and I had the strange feeling I was living in a bad movie.

'Sell Bambridge this building,' Cynthia shot back 'and everything in it.'

I gasped, astounded by her brilliance.

'It's no good to you,' she continued. 'You have no pupils, no *establishment*.'

A cunning look had crept into Norah's eyes. I knew her. She had spotted a way out. She could sell the school for more than it was worth. She could make up a retirement story for her husband. She could save her stupid face. But I'd go along with that. If we could get this building it would be better than The Bungalow: No alterations, no buying of desks and equipment, no disruption. No restrictive covenant.

Cynthia's rosy cheeks billowed out into a sunny smile. 'We'll give you two hundred thousand pounds, the same price as The Bungalow,' she said. 'I expect you know that it was built at the same time as this building and they were both exactly the same.'

'But you're forgetting,' Norah exclaimed, casting a triumphant leer. 'This has expensive additions - extra toilets, the hard playground and the expensive assembly hall.'

'No I haven't forgotten,' Cynthia sweetly replied. 'And it also has desks and chairs and blackboards, shelves and books, games and art equipment and all the rest of the stuff needed to run a school. So, we'll be fair. We'll add on one hundred pounds to cover the whole lot!'

'BUT THAT IS PREPOSTEROUS!' Norah exploded.

And I felt inclined to agree.

'It is,' Cynthia grinned, nodding sagely, 'but you see I have the negative of this.' She turned to me. 'Isn't the Government trying to clamp down on sleaze, Freda?'

I couldn't believe it. Cynthia. My docile friend! But it was I who had resolved to be courageous and bold, and all I was doing was sitting listening and watching like a dummy. I took a deep breath, then launched forth. 'And, if you don't do as Cynthia says ...' I stopped because I hadn't a clue what to say next.

Cynthia's velvet eyes stared at me expectantly.

'If you don't do as Cynthia says, we'll tie you up and bring the parents back to hack you to bits.'

'YOU PILLOCK!' Norah roared.

And for once I knew she was right.

Cynthia drew up by the public phone box at the side of the lane. 'Quick, tell me Bambridge's number' she rapped.

I held the door open with my foot, listening to her explaining what had happened to Robert.

'Good. So you agree. Get a Droop, but definitely not Rampant, and go to Harker-Balls' house straight away. She'll be waiting for you there ready to sign. Don't ask me how I did it. Just get there. Don't give her time to change her mind. Don't let her stitch you up, I've got enough dirt on her to make her *give* the school to you.'

Again I marvelled at the daring of my friend. Again I felt as if I was in a 'B' movie. We got back in the car and sped to The Bungalow. The strains of 'Once in Royal David's City' came from inside. I flung open the door and the voices halted. Tired fearful eyes stared at us.

'We're going back to the Harker-Balls Establishment,' I panted.

'How *could* you!' Sylvie Shepherd muttered savagely.

I tried again. 'We're going back ...'

'What Freda is trying to tell you,' Cynthia cut in, 'is that Freda and I have just arranged that your old school will be bought by Robert Bambridge and will become your new community school: The Acorn School. The same as we planned, but not here - there! And without the present Head.'

A joyous commotion broke out. A few people cheered.

'But there isn't an oak tree,' laughed Mrs Jones.

'Well we'll pretend there is,' called out Mrs Trugshawe, 'because I forked out the money and had the brass plaque made.'

'Come on, follow me,' I said, at last taking control. 'Let's have the same orderly return as we had withdrawal.'

As we left The Bungalow for ever, I tore the brass plaque off the tree. Whoever subsequently bought Mrs Smith's home from Mr Mole would not need that. We marched along Bramble Lane, wheeling left into the old familiar drive. 'Halt, two, three,' I shrieked, half way up, and the tired army obeyed. I held the plaque up to a tree that grew at the side of the path and thrust the jutting nails into the soft bark of the narrow trunk.

In the gathering dusk it was just possible to read: *THE ACORN SCHOOL, where each child will be gently nurtured to grow into a strong oak tree.*

'But it's a crab apple tree!' Mrs Jones cried with mock horror and I, quick as a flash riposted, 'INITIATIVES, THAT'S WHAT THIS SCHOOL WILL TEACH YOUR CHILDREN!' I hoped to have a better future than the originator of those words.

My mind raced as I drove, with my parents, back to Bernard. Dora Quicknicky was going to be upset at having lost the sale. I thought of the unfinished portrait of her grumpy aunt and decided to send it to her. I smiled to myself, unsure whether I was giving the painting as generous compensation, or vindictive revenge.

I dashed into the cottage, mother and father close on my heels. We all wanted to be the one to tell him the dramatic news. 'Bernard! Bernard! Where are you?' The door from the hall to the kitchen was open - he wasn't in there. I ran into the sitting room. The silence was only broken by the slow ticking of the clock, and spasmodic murmurs of barely flickering flames behind the fire guard.

Hermione! He must be with her. Perhaps she had started.

'Where is he?' mother asked, head cocked on one side like a bird listening for worms.

Father had limped up the stairs, calling his name. He puffed back down. 'Never here when you want him, he growled.

'I must go to my pig,' I rapped, barging past them, 'Bernie must be with her.'

Thirty-six

A beam of light shone out like a beacon from the dark bulk of the mobile home. Even from outside the walled yard I could hear the sound of snuffling from within. Then Bernard's tall dark figure loomed at the doorway. He blew his nose, then sneezed. 'Is thad you Freda?' he asked thickly, peering into the darkness.

'Has she? Let me ...' I pounded up the ramp.

He stood aside. Her bloated body was stretched out, intact, on the straw. She gazed at me without pleasure, jaw gyrating purposefully as she chewed on a hank of straw. Her morose stare sharpened. The look seemed to say: *You're responsible for this and you call yourself a caring mother*.

I imagined the discomfort of the piglets squashed up like sardines inside.

Bernard sneezed and blew his nose again. 'I think she's coddoned on to the baby alarm,' he snuffled. 'I reckon that whenever she feels lonely she squeals extra loudly knowing I'll cumb running out.'

'What an intelligent girl,' I murmured, stroking her snout, but she shook my hand off and ground her teeth harder at the mouthful of straw.

A shallow wooden box lined with soft towelling had been placed on the floor. I squeezed his arm. 'Thanks for making it. I can picture the piglets laid out in there, head to tail, like sardines in a can.'

'I hobe nod! Id's only an emergency ward for problem piglets. They should pop out and make their own way round, unaided, to the milk bar.'

I studied the lines of swollen teats oozing droplets of milk. Definitely not long now. 'How about if we both go indoors and have a drink with mother and father, and then I come back and stay with her. I can call you on the baby alarm if anything happens.'

'Good idea,' he said, and I wasn't sure if his streaming eyes were caused by deep emotion or stinking cold. Maybe a little of each.

As we jogged back to the cottage he remembered to ask about the school. 'I suppose you're safely incorporated in The Bungalow now,' he puffed.

'No we're not!' I puffed back.

Inside he listened as the three of us poured out the momentous events of the day. 'Thad's truly amazing,' he said, when he'd untangled the gist.

But later, as we drank steaming cocoa round the table, it was my girl's confinement that filled my mind. A plaintive grunt sounded from the baby alarm speaker in the kitchen and I knew it was her way of asking me to go over and be with her.

She was scrabbling up mounds of straw all around her. She saw me and collapsed down panting, looking like a great plucked bird in a huge untidy nest. I knelt and took her trotter in my hand. My poor Hermione. How I wished her body could spring open and disgorge its heavy load, leaving her free to frolic around the garden as she used to.

Suddenly she levered her body up onto ballerina points, dislodging me, and chassé'd to the trough where she drank noisily and long. I sank down into the deck chair. She sank down into a tutu of golden straw. She closed her eyes. I closed mine. It was sweltering hot. I could hear water lapping. I half-opened my weary eyes. I was at the seaside. A sardine can was thrown down at my feet by a glinting wave. I picked it up, turned it round and round in my hand, but could find no way in. I yearned to see the little creatures packed tightly in their amniotic oil, but they remained hidden and inaccessible. The sudden cry of a seagull made me scream.

'Good God Freda! You gave me a hard attack!' Bernard stood looking down at me, red nosed, sleepy eyed, plaid dressing gown flapping over blue striped pyjamas. 'The loudspeaker was ride by my ear - I thoughd you were being murdered.'

'Oh, pardon me for still living,' I retaliated, feeling stupid, averting my eyes. And then I saw it. Under Hermione's wagging tail, the second exit down, a teeny weeny snout was showing. I clutched Bernie's arm trying to speak, but no words came.

'Id's starded!' he exclaimed and a rush of annoyance surged over me that he'd been the one to say it first.

Hermione grunted and strained and slowly the piglet emerged. 'Look! Look! It's got ears!' I exclaimed in wonder, now mercifully unstruck dumb. Suddenly, its whole tiny body shot out in a slithering rush and it lay inert on the straw, eyes closed, connected to our girl by its fine umbilical cord.

'It's dead!' I cried, but even as I spoke it rose shakily to its perfectly formed little feet.

'Our firsd grandson,' Bernard said gruffly. 'We'd better call him Jesus ... you know, rising up from the dead like that. He gave an affectionate grin.

As Jesus tottered round the pantechnicon body of his mother, the cord stretched tightly, then snapped. I clung to Bernard, overcome with the emotion of this miracle. That baby was so small and perfect. That incy wincy curly tail. Those ears. Its ickle pink body. The piglet turned and faced us and, dear Jesus, on his sublime face was the glorious smile of Percy. I was overcome with love. He turned back to his mother, stretched open his minuscule mouth and latched on to a teat.

'Number one safely docked,' Bernard announced. 'I wonder how meddy more to cumb.'

'No matter how many,' I said softly, 'sweet Jesus will be the most precious one for me.'

Ten minutes passed, then Hermione's body tensed again and another snout emerged.

'Holy Mary!' Bernard whispered.

'Only if it's a girl,' I quipped, feeling almost delirious with happiness.

The second miracle shot out onto the straw. And it *was* a girl. 'Now we have our pigeon pair,' Bernard said softly, squeezing my hand. I stared at our second born. She was immaculate.

Bernard set up another deck chair and we sat close together watching our labouring girl. About every quarter of an hour a new life emerged like a sausage from a machine. It was the most awesome night of my life.

It was after the tenth and last piglet was born that the disaster occurred. Hermione began rapid grunting, tapping out sharp dots and dashes of snorts like an SOS being urgently transmitted in Pig Code. A small sac that was the afterbirth slithered out and suddenly she lumbered up to her feet. I watched a swirl of pink bodies dash to the ground. Then she crashed down heavily on top of them.

I screamed, clumsily tried to pull myself up, but fell back down again.

Bernard was already up, manoeuvring himself into the narrow space behind her. He pressed his back into the lovingly painted blue wall and strained to roll her up off them. I joined him and, groaning, we struggled to lever our careless girl up to her feet.

'Get *up*!' I cried, but she squealed hysterically at our interference and stubbornly pressed back down. Five piglets had miraculously remained clinging to life-giving teats. The other five were gone. I howled for those fragile cherubs that had so recently been packed safety away inside their mum and were now so hideously crushed underneath. One of my streaming teardrops hit the closed eyelid of a suckling pig, shooting it open with the unexpected shock. But immediately the lid clamped shut, its tiny owner preoccupied with guzzling its mother's warm milk, unfazed by the sudden disappearance of its sisters and brothers.

'One, do, three, go,' Bernard instructed, and we heaved with all our might until at last he could insert his hand beneath her. I pushed back into the wall trembling with the effort as I tried to keep a hold on her enormous weight. Bernard was kneeling, part of our girl's bulk held up by his shoulder. He stretched and, a second later, pulled an inert piglet into view. He left it and frantically delved under again.

As I strained to hold her, my eyes became riveted to the rescued piglet. Jesus. Was it my precious Jesus lying so still? I looked for the Percy-like smile on its miniature face, but, if it had been there once it wasn't there now. I guessed that even such a convivial hog as Percy would have had the smile wiped off if a ten ton porker had suddenly dropped on him.

Soon Bernard was yanking another crumpled body out. Hermione honked and grunted her disapproval. She turned her head glaring at me, squealing baleful outrage at our rough handling. Bernard bent lower, stretched out his arm, all the time shouldering Hermione up as he groped blindly for more. My grunts outdid the pig's as I strove to hold up the pink steam roller that had just bulldozed our dreams. Drips of my sweat and tears settled in her coarse white hair forming little glistening pools of sadness.

When all five were retrieved I let the dead weight go and leant, shaking, against the wall, tears still streaming.

Bernard prodded each Play-Doh baby as if trying to poke it back into shape, then, with gentle care, he lifted each one into the towel-lined box. He took up the first one in trembling hands. Was it Jesus? Was it? He placed it to his mouth and began his futile attempt at resuscitation. I gazed in wonder as rhythmically he blew his cold germs into the tiny snout. His wonderful eyes held an expression that said: *I've missed out on having children of my own and I'm sure as hell not letting these grandpiglets go.* He placed the crumpled body back at the head of the neat line, then tenderly took up the next. I loved him more at that moment than in the whole of the rest of my life.

Hermione was still honking and squealing and her front legs were doing a frantic entrechat, trotters criss-crossing like a prima ballerina doing her stuff. My girl was panicking and I had to calm her. I remembered countless old films where the perspiring brows of labouring mothers were cooled with wet cloths. So I dipped my hanky in the trough of freezing water and began mopping her forehead. But that made her squeal even more hysterically and she shook my hand away and tried to bite it. I stared down at my almost injured hand feeling terribly hurt, and, in that fleeting second, she reared up onto all four trotters. I looked up to see the five unsquashed suckling piglets dangling then falling with a volley of thuds to the ground.

'Christ! Be careful Freda,' Bernard bawled, pausing between sucking and blowing at a non-breathing snout.

Be careful! What did he think I was doing. Couldn't he see I was trying my best.

Hermione's legs suddenly buckled and I could see she was about to slam down on two squealing piglets that wavered in her landing spot. Spurred on by the blame implicit in Bernard's thoughtless words, I dived forward, sweeping the bodies to safety as the crashing body of their mother missed me by a hair's width. I scooped up the two crying babies with my mercifully unbroken arms and reconnected them to rubbery teats in the completely vacated array. Like homing missiles the other three zoomed back and latched on to spares. I sighed, relieved that the babies in my care were still in perfect shape.

Four tiny bodies lay in neat formation inside Bernard's emergency box. I gazed at the first, staring hard at its toy-size chest. Was it moving? Was it breathing? Was the dear little creature alive? What I saw made my heart lurch with the unforeseen shock. I slid my eyes along the row and burst into tears again. I couldn't believe it. Despite Bernie's clumsy endeavours, every miniature rib cage fluttered with life. I stared in wonder, unable to take my eyes off the tiny miracles. But what about the fifth one? I turned to see my darling man holding it up to his mouth, looking for all the world as if he were about to bite the head off a pink sugar pig from a Christmas stocking. The piglets in the box were beginning to stir so, gingerly, I lifted one out. Its body was warm and smooth and three-dimensional. Its eyes were closed. And on its face was that smile. Carefully I placed it at the juiciest dug of the milk bar, then quickly attached the others to those that were left. Automatically the diminutive mouths gaped open and began sucking. I turned to see if Bernard had performed the same miracle on the fifth.

Our eyes locked and I saw the panic in the brilliant blue depths. The piglet, held so tenderly in his strong hands, remained lifeless. Harder and harder he blew until it seemed the poor creature must surely explode. Abruptly he stopped. And I shall never ever, in the whole of my life, forget the look of misery on his face as the piglet slowly deflated like a wizened lopsided balloon. Reverently, he placed it back in the Emergency Ward which now doubled up as a morgue.

'We'll leave the disposal of the body till afder we've beed to bed,' he said, taking my hand. It was three thirty in the morning. I turned to wave goodbye to Hermione but her eyes were closed. At her belly swarmed the nine tiny new lives that were now our family. Bernard led me from the fug into the cold December night air, but it failed to liven me up. I felt dead. Dead as the poor wee assymmetric baby left on the slab.

I heard the bumble of my parents' voices below. I looked at the clock. It was gone eleven. Bernie stood beside me.

'Led's creep out and bury our baby,' he said. 'Id's rained so the ground should be soft enough to dig under the abble tree.'

I shall always be haunted by the reproachful expression permanently pressed into the two-dimensional face of the dead piglet. Bernard lifted him from the mortuary and we processed down the garden to perform the last rites. He held the convoluted body in his hands, like a concertina. I half expected him to squeeze both ends and sing a mournful dirge.

Under the tree, I held the cold body in my arms as Bernard dug the hole. We wrapped him in a teacloth shroud and, together, we lowered him down.

'Ashes to ashes,' I murmured, wondering if we should have cremated him. But Bernie had decreed that he should be buried, stating that, tempted by the aroma of roast suckling pig, my parents would have no compunction about eating him.

'Flesh of my child's flesh,' I intoned, as Bernard threw sods of earth over our baby. I wiped my eyes. He'd had such a pitifully short, painful life.

'What're you doing?' mother called, approaching fast.

Hurriedly I offered up a prayer on the off-chance that there was a Pig God and a porker after life.

Mother bore down on us. 'What're you doing?' she asked again.

'Burying the piglet.'

'A good place too. Instant apple sauce!'

But before I had time to react to her insensitivity, she'd plonked a kiss on my cheek and squeezed me tightly, so I knew that she cared.

'Come and see the family,' I quavered. 'They're beautiful.'

We walked across the grass, united in the bond of our new-born family. We entered the tropical heat of our girl's room. She gazed at our naked squirming family for several long minutes, then she clasped her hands to her chest and gushed, 'Congratulations daughter, they're a credit to you.'

And I'll never be sure to my dying day if she meant it, or was, as usual, taking the piss!

Sylvie Shepherd called round early to report that she'd heard that Norah Harker-Balls was to move to London with her husband, to be near his work. Apparently she'd been heard to say that it would be 'fraightfully convenient and so much smarter than living out in the sticks.'

'Good riddance,' I retorted, 'I've never ever heard such fraightfully good news!'

And we both cracked up, snorting louder than the cacophony of pig sounds coming through the speaker into the room.

As Sylvie left, Bernard came in from tending the family. His eyes shone. He leapt high, clicking his heels in the air. Clearly he was high on the adrenalin of grandparenthood. 'There are no neighbours to kick up a stink aboud the pong, so how aboud us sedding up a proper pig farm ad the end of the garden?'

I was amazed because that was just what I'd been thinking myself.

'We can afford a proper pig unid, and you could help me run id if you wanted, and still carry on part-time teaching,' he rushed. 'Don'd you think it would be jolly good?'

'Jolly jolly good,' I affirmed. 'And considerably safer for you than teaching driving.'

'Don't forget, you'll have to take the little piggies to market,' father said softly from the end of the room. Then, as if to make up for his sobering caution, he added, 'If you like I'll put a notice of their births on the Internet bulletin board. We can inform the whole world of the joyous news on the information superhighway.'

I stared at him suspiciously. Was he 'doing a mother' and taking the rise? There was a rare twinkle under his hooded lids.

'Unless of course,' he said, with barely controlled mirth, 'you're announcing it in The Times.'

'That's exactly what I shall do,' I replied, scuppering his fun.

'Don't mention my name then,' said mother, who'd just entered. 'Think what a field day they'd have at the bridge club, with a grand master such as me being announced as great-grandmother to a litter of piglets!'

I climbed up to the attic to draft out an Announcement in secret, then crept back down to our bedroom and rang it through. She was always testing us with her wackiness, now she'd be the one on trial!

I grabbed up The Times, found the Personal Column headed BIRTHS: And there it was:

Field - on 21st December, to Large White Hermione and Percy Boar, nine surviving swine: four boys and five girls. Much wanted piglets. Adored great-granchildren of Maeve and Hector Salmon of Tooting. The first two hogs born have been named Jesus and

Mary. The rest are being named by great-grandmother Maeve Salmon after her friends at the Tooting Bec Bridge Club.

I left it open on the kitchen table and headed out to my babes.